A sudden [illegible] a car wreck at h [illegible] on collision. The ground beneath Emma's feet shook. She lost her balance and stumbled toward the door.

Outside, she expected to see a horrible motor vehicle accident and bodies strewn everywhere.

But there was no crash.

No cars.

No one.

Nothing else, except the house and…

She turned back to the garage. Her breath caught in her lungs. What had been the spotless three-car garage was now a two-story wood barn. A buckboard sat to the side. A tall windmill towered behind the wood structure; on the opposite side, a horse grazed in a paddock.

And one very tall and handsome man with piercing blue eyes that rivaled the Montana sky stood before her. His thick blond hair caressed his forehead. He wiped his hands on a rag, then tucked it into the side of his denim overalls. His rolled-up shirt sleeves exposed tanned muscular forearms. Where did he come from?

She glanced at the house, at him, then back again, and trembled involuntarily. The house had suddenly changed. It looked different—the roof had shingles. Smoke billowed out of the chimney, the smell filling her head.

"Ma'am?" The man's gaze swept over her from head to toe; a gentle smile touched his lips. Something akin to recognition flickered in his eyes. "Are you…lost?"

Who is this guy, why is he here, and how the hell did my life just get turned upside down?

Wrapped Around My Heart

by

Heather Alexander

Wrapped Around My Heart

Cover Art by *Rae Monet, Inc.*

The Wild Rose Press, Inc.
PO Box 708
Adams Basin, NY 14410-0708
Visit us at www.thewildrosepress.com

Publishing History
First Edition, 2022
Trade Paperback ISBN 978-1-5092-4209-2
Digital ISBN 978-1-5092-4210-8

Published in the United States of America

Dedication

For my mom.
I love you and miss you every minute of every day.
Thank you for being the wind beneath my wings.
And for Frank, Emma, and Rascal, my loves.

Chapter One

"What do you mean you're in Montana?" Her best friend's voice screeched from the rented SUV's Bluetooth. "I just saw you last night. In New York! You told me you weren't going. How the hell did some crazy attorney convince you of an inheritance when you have no relatives—dead or alive?"

"I only made up my mind to come out here this morning—"

"You're not the fly-by-the-seat-of-your-pants kind of girl. WTF, Em?"

"Sorry, you're breaking up. I gotta go. Call you later. Love you."

Emma Cole disconnected the call and pushed out a deep breath. Now was not the time to be lectured about her decision to accept the all-expense-paid trip to Whisper Creek. While she had given the matter plenty of thought over weeks of brief conversations with the attorney, she hadn't lied to her best friend. Only this morning did she decide to hop on the plane and get to the bottom of the mystery. Which, she had to concede to Amber, was totally unlike her. But there was something about the attorney's account that hadn't just piqued her curiosity; it had consumed it.

Following the GPS, she turned onto the long tree-lined driveway. The gravel pathway opened up a half mile later to a beautiful one-level ranch home surrounded by an overgrown garden of knee-high grass, shrubbery, and a variety of vibrant wildflowers. The house boasted a wrap-around porch reminiscent of homes back East, complete with two wood chairs, a bench, and two small tables.

She parked and sat behind the wheel for a moment before reaching for the large white envelope on the passenger seat. The attorney with whom she communicated refused to discuss any details over the phone, no matter how many questions she threw at him. Yet, something compelled her to make the trip. Curiosity? Or maybe because photos of the house shook her with a feeling of déjà vu.

Slowly she got out of the vehicle and stood behind the door as if it would protect her—from what, she didn't know. She scanned the surroundings and couldn't shake the feeling of something familiar about the place—the same feeling she'd had since the attorney contacted her. She tried to ignore it. Tried to chalk it up to an overactive imagination, but there she stood.

Up close, the sizeable log structure appeared inviting, though sad from a lack of upkeep. The grounds, she imagined, had once been perfectly manicured. While it didn't look abandoned, it certainly didn't look like anyone had lived there recently.

She wiped her sweaty palms on her jeans. Anxiety spurted through her. She drew in a deep breath. *Let's do this.* She removed the key from the envelope, climbed the steps, and slipped it into the lock. It turned. Her heart pounded. She pushed open the door and stepped into the foyer.

A faint smell of sawed wood and hearth permeated

the air. She closed her eyes briefly. And in that instant, she had a *vision* of the inside of this very home…in another *time*. No need to consult a floorplan to know the parlor would be to the right of the entrance, followed by the dining room, a study, and the kitchen out back with a large pantry. To the left, down the hall, sat three bedrooms. All rooms featured wood beams, stone fireplaces, and dark wood floors. Behind the house, there was a two-story barn that once sheltered horses and cows with a large fenced-off paddock.

How the hell could I know all that?

"I'm glad you decided to come."

Emma whirled around so quickly she nearly lost her balance. Strong arms reached out to steady her.

"I'm sorry," the man said, stepping back. "I didn't mean to frighten you. I should've told you I'd be waiting inside."

She nodded and caught her breath. "James Matheson, I presume?"

The handsome thirty-something attorney smiled. "In the flesh."

He gestured to the parlor with a sweep of his hand. She followed and took a chair by the hearth, pulled out a small water bottle from her purse, and took a sip.

"Again, I apologize," he said. "I didn't mean to startle you. Are you all right?"

She nodded. "Yes, thanks. It's not you." She glanced around the room, frowning at the sofa, then the chairs. They weren't right. They weren't hers. While the furniture didn't look like the ones in her mind, they were the same style and colors from what she remembered.

Remembered?

3

A shiver danced up her spine, tingling the hair at the base of her neck. "Just a weird feeling of…déjà vu."

"Then this all might make sense to you." James walked to the hearth and reached for the large envelope on the mantle with the name *Matheson & Kincaid* stamped on the top left, same as the one sent to her. He removed the contents; two documents and one smaller but very old envelope, judging by the looks of it. He placed them on the coffee table. "When we spoke on the phone, I explained this has to do with an inheritance."

"Yeah, see, that's where I'm a bit confused," she told him. "I don't have any relatives in Montana—or anywhere else, for that matter. My mom passed away last year, so this can't be related to her estate. I'm her sole heir: I should know."

He smiled, assessing her for a moment. "Ms. Cole, I realize what I'm about to share with you may…come as a shock." He opened his mouth to say more but instead turned his attention to the documents. He carefully unfolded them, placed each one neatly beside the other on the coffee table, then sat down on the sofa. "*This*," he said, handing a document to Emma, "is the deed to this house."

She looked at him pointedly. "*This* house? This very one we're sitting in right now?"

He nodded. "You'll notice it has your name on it. And *this*"—he handed her another document—"is the last will and testament that names you as beneficiary to said house and property, among other items."

Her brows furrowed. She stared at the documents, which needed to be handled with care. The paper was thick, yet the edges crumbled easily between her fingers. The printed type on the pages had faded over the years to a muted brown.

"Beneficiary?" She cast a wary glance at the attorney. There was something familiar about him. But she couldn't put a finger on what. He sat silent and gestured to the documents.

Turning her gaze back to the deed, she gasped. Her skin tingled in an eerie way, like someone just walked over her grave. She scanned the contents. *Blah, blah, blah, owns property at such and such location in Whisper Creek and...*

Her heart stopped.

Her name—*Emma Christine Cole*—appeared on the deed. *What?* The end of the signature was blurred by age, she assumed, and a typed portion of the document looked too faded to read. She recognized her first, middle, and last names; however, the second last name remained illegible. Not only that—it was dated *1882*.

"How...?" she stammered, confused. "I don't understand."

"I realize it's a lot to digest," he acknowledged in a thoughtful tone. "That's why I insisted you come to Whisper Creek. Something like this shouldn't be left to letters and emails."

Emma put the deed aside and focused on the second document. Carefully, she held the delicate paper in her trembling hands and read through the contents of the will. Something cold and clammy engulfed her. It was signed by...*her*. Not just someone else from the past with the same name. That was *her* signature on the document!

She met the attorney's gaze. "This is insane. I don't

have—I wasn't named after anyone else in the family. My parents weren't even from Montana. They—"

"There's more," James admitted, holding up a hand.

Seriously? How much more absurdity could she take?

"We found *this*"—the yellowed envelope—"with the deed and the will. They all came to our firm in 1927 when the First National Bank of Helena burned down. After the fire, all that remained was the safe. Inside the safe, these documents were found in a packet with your name and the year on it."

He handed her the yellowed envelope. Just seeing the writing on it made her heart hammer in her chest. In all caps, it read: *EMMA COLE. DO NOT OPEN UNTIL 2022.* The writing also included her current home address *and* cell phone number. How could anyone know her cell phone number in 1927? More importantly, how could it be in *her handwriting*?

Coldness crept into her veins. Her mouth went dry. She licked her lips. "This doesn't make any sense," she managed, unable to wrap her mind around the whole thing. "Are you sure these are legit? Anyone could make these look authentic."

James shook his head. "My firm has a team of experienced researchers at our disposal who have verified the authenticity of all the documents. These are quite legit, I assure you. I wouldn't have dragged you two thousand miles across the country were it otherwise."

Emma stared down at the letter. It was like being in a real-life episode of some zany sci-fi show about alternate realities and time travel. With her heart

6

hammering in her chest, she unfolded the letter and read it:

Emma,

I know this will all sound bat-shit crazy to you, but just know you are not going crazy. It's true. This letter is from you—the you/me from the past.

I'll make a long story short. Get your ass back here to 1882 before the fires start. The lives of your husband, children, and neighbors depend on it.

Hurry!
Emma
December 1, 1882, Whisper Creek

Husband? She wasn't married—didn't even have a boyfriend. And, now there's *children*? To use one of her best friend's favorite expressions, *WTF?*

Emma sat, stunned. *Everyone on the planet knows going back in time is impossible. So, what explains my handwriting?*

"Are you all right?" James asked, easing her away from her thoughts. At some point, he must've gotten up to pour her a scotch from the bar in the corner of the room. Because when she could focus, the rocks glass sat on the table in front of her. How did he know she liked scotch?

She shook her head. With a trembling hand, she picked up the glass and took a sip, then looked at him. Barely able to speak, she managed a raspy, "W-what the h-hell—?"

He nodded, as if this wasn't the first time he had to break news like this to someone. "Shocking, I know. May I?" He gestured toward the letter.

7

She inclined her head. He picked up the letter and read the contents. His facial expression gave nothing away. He leaned back in the chair, cocking his head to study her. She returned his gaze and sensed...she had met him—*known* him before from somewhere else. But where?

"I can imagine how overwhelming this must be for you," he said at last in a soothing voice. It irked her that he could be so calm. *Maybe he knows something I don't?*

Finally, able to speak, she shot out, "Overwhelming? Try nuts. Nuts! How is it even *possible* I could've written *that* letter?" She bolted out of her seat as if propelled by an unknown force and paced. "No one's ever been able to travel through time. No one. You would think if anyone could, it would have been Einstein!"

"True, but—"

She stopped. "Maybe this is just some kind of crazy scheme to get me all the way out here to hire you for something or buy a time share. Because if it is—"

James shook his head. "I can assure you this is all quite legitimate. I know it's a lot to digest. But like I said, my firm had these letters in our possession for almost a hundred years now. We ran forensic tests on each of the documents, and they are all authentic." He produced a document that looked very wordy with a seal and signatures at the bottom, indicating said documents had, indeed, been tested for authenticity. "And, no. I don't want you to hire me for anything. I just want you to consider what's in these documents, and we'll go from there."

She paced again, shaking her head. "I don't know."

Her mind reeled. It was *impossible* for this letter to be written by *her* in 1882. Right? Yet, her letter, the deed, and the will all said otherwise. Even though it all sounded like some crazy time travel movie—or she was just losing her mind—something inside her told her she would come face to face with her future in the past.

James crossed the room, his gaze on her. Why did he look familiar? Something about his...eyes. *Think, think, think.* She wracked her brain but came up empty.

"Why don't you look around the place? Get a feel for what's here." He stared at her for a moment, then checked his watch. "I'll run into town and grab us some lunch. I shouldn't be more than a half hour-ish." He took a step closer, then stopped as if debating on whether he wanted to say something more. "I'll be back," he said, then turned on his heel and walked out of the house.

Emma waited until she heard his car drive away before exploring the property, beginning with the parlor. The antique furniture seemed familiar, yet new pieces from this century had been added in—an eclectic mix of rustic, western, and traditional. Two large leather chairs toward the back of the room flanked the vibrant painting of a sunset overlooking snow-capped glaciers from a nearby Montana park. A floral vase adorned the mantel. The pattern of pinks and mauves reminded her of something. But she couldn't put a finger on what specifically.

The oversized dining room featured an antler-style chandelier, placed strategically above the center of a long wide mahogany table with seating for eight. On one wall stood a matching hutch and sideboard devoid of any dishes or adornments. The furniture appeared to be handcrafted—and familiar. *There's that word again. Why is this all so familiar?* She closed her eyes and ran her hand across the table's smooth surface. This table…she could see it in her mind. In a room like this, but in another time.

Her eyes flew open. She shivered. *Okay, now I'm just freaking myself out.* She rubbed her arms for warmth and continued her stroll through each room of the house, all teasing her with memories she once experienced but couldn't quite grasp.

When she returned to the main hallway, she stopped. The smells of the home—wood, cinnamon, and earth—wafted through her senses, playing upon her memories, bringing her back to another time. She closed her eyes. Through the open windows, the sound of children's laughter echoed around her. A smile touched her lips. She tried to picture two small children—a boy and a girl—running through the house. Then, the presence of someone with a smooth, velvety voice called her name in a familiar tone, blanketing her with warmth. It sounded like it was…

Right behind her!

She whirled around, expecting to see him— *someone.*

*Breathe. One one-thousand. Two one-thousand…*The voice sounded so real. *Three one-thousand. Four one-thousand…*She felt him brush by her…*Five one-thousand.*

After a few moments, she collected herself and wandered into the study with its floor-to-ceiling bookcases, a large, handcrafted mahogany desk, and matching chairs. A shiver swept through her veins. Her fingers tingled. The smell of the room pricked at her memory. She hugged herself, then moved around the room, admiring the perfect craftsmanship of the woodwork. She *knew* these bookcases, this desk…

A few newspaper clippings on the desk caught her eye. From the *Whisper Creek Gazette,* to be precise. Judging by their frail and timeworn appearance, they weren't from a recent printing. The one on top, dated December 13, 1882, featured the headline *BOYDS ARRESTED FOR STAGE ROBBERY OUTSIDE WHISPER CREEK*. Another clipping beneath it read in part *FIRES THOUGHT TO BE RELATED TO BOYDS AND…* She swallowed. Fires? 1882? As in the fires mentioned in *her* letter?

She shuddered and backed out of the room, trying not to trip over her own feet. Time to get some air.

Emma walked outside and came upon a small stone path. She followed it to where a barn *should've* stood back in the nineteenth century. *How did I know that*? Now, though, stood a tall and wide three-car garage with the exterior built to look like a barn matching the style of the main house.

Inside, two vehicles, a gray SUV and a black pick-up truck were parked side by side in what could only be described as the most immaculate garage she'd ever seen. The registration sticker on the license plates indicated they had expired by nearly two years. A floor-to-ceiling storage unit with countless shelves and containers occupied the rear wall. Whoever built this and the house happened to be very orderly, to say the least.

A sudden crash outside the garage drew her attention. The noise sounded like a car wreck at high speed or, more precisely, a head-on collision. The ground beneath her feet shook. An earthquake in Montana? She lost her balance and stumbled toward the door.

Just outside, she stopped abruptly, half expecting to see a horrible motor vehicle accident and bodies strewn everywhere.

But there was no crash.

No cars.

No one.

Nothing else, except the house and…

She turned back to the garage. Her breath caught in her lungs; her blood stopped pumping through her veins. What had just been the spotless three-car garage moments ago had been replaced with a two-story wood *barn*. A buckboard sat to the side. *What*? A tall windmill towered behind the wood structure; on the opposite side, a horse grazed in a paddock.

And one very tall and handsome man with piercing blue eyes that rivaled the Montana sky stood before her. His thick blond hair caressed his forehead when the wind blew. He wiped his hands on a rag, then tucked it into the side of his denim overalls. His rolled-up shirt sleeves exposed tanned muscular forearms. Where did *he* come from?

"May I help you?" He walked toward her. His voice reminded her of smooth velvet—the same voice calling her name earlier. Recognition tried to grasp hold in her mind. But nothing registered.

She glanced at the house, at him, then back again, and trembled involuntarily. The house had suddenly *changed*. It all looked different—the roof had shingles. Smoke billowed out of the chimney, the smell filling her head.

She turned to the handsome man who politely waited for her to say something.

"Ma'am?" The man's gaze swept over her from head to toe; then, a gentle smile touched the corner of his lips. Something akin to recognition flickered in his eyes. "Are you…lost?"

Momentary panic seized her mind. *Who is this guy, why is he here, and how the hell did my life just get turned upside down?*

"Who…?" She licked her lips. She had cottonmouth, like whenever she had a cold. Her head spun, pressure banging at her temples. "Where…where did you come from?"

He grinned, exhibiting perfect, straight white teeth. Then, in three long strides, he stood in front of her. "I live here," he stated simply, towering over her. "Where'd *you* come from?"

Emma remained rooted to the ground, blank, dazed, and very shaken. Maybe she hit her head when she fell—did she fall?—and he was a figment of her imagination. But then what would explain the faint smell of sweat and hay emanating from him, tickling her nose?

She bit her bottom lip and reached out to touch him. Oh, hell, he was *real* all right. Deliciously corded muscles flexed under her icy fingers. His skin was warm and smooth. The mere touch sent her heart slamming.

"I'm Wyatt," he offered, extending his hand. "And you are…?"

Considering the sudden shift in her surroundings—not to mention the sudden appearance of one very hot guy—either she had just lost her mind…or traveled through time.

"In shock," she whispered at last, before the blackness engulfed her.

Chapter Two

A clock ticked rhythmically in the distance. *Tick-tock, tick-tock, tick-tock.* With each *tick*, the mental fog dissipated. Emma sunk back into the softness beneath her, then sighed. She licked her lips. They were so dry, they almost burned when her tongue touched them. The soft rustle of curtains blowing through a nearby window elicited the sound of a whisper-soft kiss against the sill. The room smelled like cinnamon rolls and—she frowned—*hay*? That didn't make sense.

Her mind searched through the mist for memories. It took a moment for the fog to clear. She recalled a garage, then a loud noise. It sounded like a car crash. And…

Wyatt, did he say?

She forced her heavy eyelids open and blinked several times. Everything appeared hazy. It took several seconds for her vision to adjust. Her brows knitted together. What happened to the leather wing chairs by the hearth? And the painting hanging above the mantel?

"Here," said a masculine voice. "Drink this." A hand came up behind her head as a glass pressed to her lips. Water. She took a sip, then lay back.

"I've heard of women swooning before, but I've never actually seen it happen," Wyatt said. He placed the glass on the table, then sat in the chair, his gaze fixed on her.

"First time for everything," she managed in a croaky whisper. Her stomach churned like it would whip butter. Nothing could squelch the panic welling up inside her. *Where am I?*

"How do you feel?"

She eyed the handsome stranger, noting his sharp and assessing blue eyes. Her head ached as if she'd had too much to drink. Rubbing her forehead, she replied, "Like I got run over by a bus."

"Well, I can assure you weren't run over." His voice was calm, his gaze steady.

A swirly sensation in the pit of her belly turned up a notch. She had to take an extra breath, then two. "It feels like it," she muttered. Her chest tightened. She sucked in another breath, needing to remain calm.

"Now that you're awake, would you mind telling me what you're doing on my property?" While his voice remained low and gentle, it did have a firm inquisitiveness she couldn't ignore.

"Do you mind telling me *where* I am?" she countered, sensing blood rush to her head.

His brows furrowed together. "*Where*—hell, you must've hit your head hard when you fainted." He paused. "For starters, you're in Whisper Creek. Montana. I'm Wyatt Kincaid. And you are…?" He gestured for her to continue with a circling motion of his hand.

Kincaid—as in *Matheson & Kincaid*? The attorney who paid for her trip? Wait. Yep. Now, it made sense. This all had to be some kind of scam James and this Wyatt guy cooked up. *An 1882 letter from myself, my ass.*

"Leaving," she replied, swinging her feet onto the

floor. Her head spun like she just came off a tilt-a-whirl. She gripped the cushions to steady herself.

Wyatt sat on the sofa next to her. "I think it's best you stay here. At least, until you can walk. You're in no shape to be going anywhere."

"I'll be fine." She rubbed her temples. "I just need some air."

"That I can help you with." He stood up and, in spite of her protests, took her hands in his. Her skin sizzled from his touch. He had a few callouses, but overall, his hands were smooth, warm, and strong.

She stood up and swayed. He placed his arm firmly around her waist for support. Her legs still wobbled, so she didn't object. However, she was conscious of where his warm flesh touched her.

He led her down a hallway, then through a rear door. Outside he directed her to one of two chairs on each side of a wide wooden table. She sat down and closed her eyes.

"Slow, deep breaths." His hand remained on her shoulder for a moment, then he took a seat across the table. He stared down at his hands, flexing them, an indication they might have seen a hard day's work.

Emma watched him out of the corner of her eye. A tug of recognition stirred somewhere in her mind. His face, strong and angled, featured dark blond brows slashed neatly over deep blue eyes. *I know those eyes!* His tanned face, kissed just enough by the sun, made those pearly white teeth stand out. If his sinewy arms were any indication of the rest of him, she could imagine six-pack abs and rock-solid thighs beneath those ridiculous overalls.

"What's your name?" Wyatt asked, cutting into her

thoughts. He ran a hand through his hair. His square jaw set, waiting for her to answer.

She cleared her throat. "Emma. Emma Cole."

"Nice to meet you, Miss Cole." Her skin burned under his steady gaze. "Tell me, what brings you all the way out here?" He gestured with a sweeping motion of his arm toward the property stretching for acres and acres. "I didn't see you arrive on horse or by wagon. Though, in those clothes"—he tilted his chin toward her outfit—"I'd expect you to be in a saddle."

Why, there was nothing *wrong* with her clothes. Dark skinny jeans, a button-down designer shirt with a fancy pattern—a birthday present from Amber—tucked into the waistband, and a pair of blush-colored sneakers.

"Look, I don't know who *you* are or how *you* got here, but I was waiting for someone to come back with lunch." She glanced over her shoulder, wondering if James would actually show up so she could give him a piece of her mind.

He rubbed his jaw thoughtfully. "Well, if you're hungry, I've got some leftover stew and apple pie." His eyes raked over her again, then he stood up. "C'mon. I'll fix you some."

Fix me some? In my *house?* She wanted to yell at him but refrained.

Emma pursed her lips, then followed him into the kitchen. And froze. Just moments—or was it hours?—ago she had walked through that very same kitchen. Only, *this* kitchen didn't look the same. Yes, both the hearth and wood-burning stove sat in the same places. However, the flooring consisted of a darker shade of stained wood. The walls featured a bright flowery-style wallpaper, not paint. And an array of pots and pans hung from wooden pegs on the wall with an overhead iron rack above a table doubling as an island. Either someone had taken her to a different house when she passed out, or…

Fear skidded down her spine. Her heart raced, nearly exploding in her chest. *Either I'm losing my mind or…the impossible happened.* She'd traveled back in time to write the letter. But nothing in the world could make her wrap her mind around such an insane idea.

After all, time travel is impossible. Right?

But what else explains the changes in the house? The barn? Not to mention, this hottie?

No. Way. That's just too ridiculous for words.

She spun around to face Wyatt. A burst of courage coursed through her. "Look, pal, I don't know what scheme you and James have got going here, but this bizarre joke has gone on quite long enough. I can assure you, if you don't leave asap, I'm calling the cops."

She reached for the cell phone in her back pocket. Damn. She must've left it in her handbag.

Wyatt folded his arms across his chest and tilted his head. "The *cops*?"

She seared him with her gaze. "Seriously? You know, the heat. The boys in blue. The fuzz. The *cops*."

He gave her an odd look. "I think you hit your head harder than you think, Miss Cole."

She threw her hands up. "Why, because I want you out of here?"

His eyes narrowed. "Darlin', this is *my* house; therefore, *I* won't be going anywhere. But you are welcome to stay until you feel better." He stepped closer, towering over her. "In fact, I'll even take you into town to see the doctor. Just to make sure."

"I don't need a doctor!" She stomped a foot. "What I need is for you to either admit to this crazy scheme you and your buddy have cooked up—or get the hell out of *my* house."

His eyebrows shot up. "*Your* house?"

She clenched her fists at her sides, then marched back into the parlor to collect her handbag. As soon as she called James and gave him a piece of her mind, maybe this guy would get the hint. Unfortunately, she could find neither her handbag nor her phone. Did she drop it somewhere? She searched around the couch, chairs, and even in the foyer. And that's when the blood drained from her face.

A tall ornate grandfather clock stared back at her. The gold face within reflected a hint of light pouring in through a nearby window. The pendulum inside ticked away the seconds, reverberating in her mind. It hadn't been there that morning. She definitely would have remembered it. And considering its size, the enormous clock wasn't something she could've missed. Nor could it be something to magically appear in the time it took her to go outside, explore the garage-turned-barn, and come back inside.

Okay, Toto, we're definitely *not in Kansas anymore.*

Wyatt came up behind her and touched her shoulder. She whirled around to face him. No words came.

"Why don't you sit down?" he offered in a gentle tone, taking her by the hand. "You look like you're about to swoon again."

This time, she allowed him to lead her to the sofa. She closed her eyes and counted backward from twenty. Inside, she wanted to scream. *How could this be? There's no such thing as time travel!*

Twenty. Nineteen. Eighteen...

When she got to *one*, she opened her eyes. Wyatt leaned against the mantel adorned with unlit candles. She wanted to remain mad, but the sight of him triggered a memory she couldn't quite grasp, not to mention some sizzling action zipping through her system. Her breath quickened. So much for counting.

"Where's my handbag?" she demanded.

Puzzled, he frowned. "Your what?"

"My bag," she said, exasperated. "I had it with me when I arrived."

He shrugged. "I haven't seen a bag or anything else of yours."

"You know what I think?" she charged. "I think you stole it. You're keeping it from me, so I can't call the cops."

"You know what *I* think? I think you're a long way from home, and you're...lost. And, believe it or not, I'd like to help you," he added softly.

Some of her anger deflated at the gentle timbre of his voice. Her eyes narrowed. "Why would you want to do that?"

"Like I said, I think you're far from home. And I know how isolating that can be. At least, initially. Am I right?" When she didn't respond, he continued, "Anyway, I'm offering you a place to stay—for now."

Her chin went up a notch. "What's the catch?" she challenged.

He shook his head. "No catch." His gaze shifted to

her left hand, rubbing his jaw. "There's only one problem. I don't see a wedding ring on your finger. And an unattached man living with an unmarried woman under his roof in 1882 isn't considered proper."

Why did his voice have a hypnotic effect on her?

Wait. What?

"Did you just say *1882*? As in the *nineteenth* century?"

He nodded.

She jumped to her feet, tripping over herself in the process, bolted out the door, and ran to the garage—barn, whatever, then came to an abrupt stop inside the large doorway. Her heart slammed against her chest like a sledgehammer. How could the garage suddenly change into a barn? Was she suffering from a concussion? Or had she truly stepped back in time? Nothing else could explain this insanity. Well, that or she completely lost her mind.

Wyatt walked up behind her and laid a hand on her shoulder. "Are you all right?"

"I…I don't know." She inhaled, then pushed out a deep breath, trying to absorb the events of the last moments, the last hour. Everything around her *felt* real. Wyatt. The house. The barn. The property. *Maybe it is possible I traveled back in time. No, I can't go there. Just the thought of it.* She shook her head.

"What's today?" she asked, clenching her eyes shut. "The date, I mean."

"May fifteenth."

Okay, so the date remained the same, but that didn't mean anything. This could very well still be the twenty-first century.

Yeah, then what would explain the garage

morphing into a barn? Or the difference in the house? Or the horse, wagon, windmill, and chicken coop suddenly appearing?

All right, all right. Maybe I really did travel back in time.

Or it could just be some elaborate scheme to cheat her out of—what? Money? James hadn't asked her for any. In fact, he had paid for her entire trip. While they might be able to convince her it was 1882, they couldn't very well construct an entire town in an hour. If money is what they were after, they would be sorely disappointed when they found out she didn't have any.

Until she uncovered the truth, she thought it best to play along with this—craziness. "All right," she said at last. When Wyatt looked at her questioningly, she went on, "I'd like to take you up on your offer to stay. For the time being, that is," she said, bestowing on him her most dazzling smile.

His face broke in a wide smile. "That's great."

"But before I do, would it be possible to go into town?" *Just so I know you're not really conning me.*

"Sure, to see the doctor?"

"No, I need to—" Did they have telephones in 1882? Doubtful, at least, not in such a remote town. What about mail? Nah, too slow. She wished she had paid better attention to inventions in history classes back in school. "Send a wire," she said at last.

"A wire, huh?" An eyebrow shot up. "I'm happy to oblige, ma'am. Let me just hitch up the wagon." He walked away, bumping her in the process. He touched her arm in a gentle apology. "Sorry."

Her skin tingled under the soft brush of his fingers. She looked away and nodded.

"Haven't seen those 'round here before," he went on, indicating her footwear. "That's some fancy shoes you got on. Are they fashionable where you come from?"

She looked down at her sneakers. "Oh, um, I guess so."

"And just where would that be, by the way?"

Best to stick to the truth as much as possible. Then she wouldn't have to undo any lies later on. "New York."

"Figures," he mumbled.

Within minutes, Wyatt hitched a magnificent chestnut horse to the old-fashioned rickety wagon. He swiped his hat off the fence post, tugged it on, then slapped his hands on his pants before extending one sweaty hand.

"Allow me," he offered. She looked at the wagon, then him questioningly. "I'll help you up," he explained when she didn't move.

She squared her shoulders, then slipped her small hand into his large one, his grip tightening around her fingers. His hands were warm and slightly sweaty. Just the mere contact made her body fill with heat, burning her to the core. She rolled her eyes, chiding herself for responding like a lovesick teenager. Then again, how could she not be attracted to Wyatt? He was incredibly handsome—correction, *hot,* in an entirely delicious way—not to mention charming and chivalrous. But still, she had to consider him the enemy. At least, until she could figure everything out.

Once they arrived in town, she would know for certain whether she was the victim of a crazy scheme or had actually managed to break through the barriers of time and space and end up in the nineteenth century.

****

"You don't look so good," Wyatt told her. They stood smack-dab in the center of Whisper Creek's dirt-lined Main Street.

Buh-bye reality; hello, mental institution.

Gone was the town of the twenty-first century, filled with local businesses, souvenir shops, and a myriad of restaurants that Emma drove through hours earlier. Now, in its place stood a bustling metropolis reminiscent of the Old West mining towns she had seen on a cable history channel more than once. Horse dung dotted the dirt-covered road. Boarded sidewalks lined each side of the thoroughfare flanking various establishments, ranging from saloons and inns to the blacksmith and doctor's office. The bank and livery sat toward the far end of town, along with a water tower, tall windmill, and other buildings.

Men on horseback, many with revolvers holstered to their hips, tipped their dust-covered hats as they rode by. Wagon drivers, on the other hand, scowled as they were forced to navigate their large conveyances and horses around her and Wyatt.

Women garbed in colorful dresses and bustles gawked as if she wore the scarlet letter emblazoned on the front of her shirt, whispering to each other behind cupped hands as they hurried by. Apparently, they didn't take too kindly to her twenty-first-century attire.

Her fingers chilled into icicles. *Okay, an entire town can't be part of such an elaborate scheme, right? This has to be real! That or I've actually gone nuts. Insane. A few clowns short of a circus.*

"I think we could both use a drink," Wyatt

announced, reaching for her elbow. Within seconds, he led her off the street and into a nearby restaurant—or was it an inn?

The hostess took one look at Emma's apparel, sniffed with indignation, then led them to a table in the back. Wyatt ordered two whiskies as he pulled out her chair.

When the drinks arrived, she downed the liquid with one quick tilt. He shrugged, then followed her lead, drained his glass, and ordered another, along with something to eat.

"Like whiskey, do you?" he commented, settling back in the chair.

"I prefer scotch, actually, but this'll do," she replied absently. The liquor burned its way to her stomach. Her gaze traveled around the room, taking in every fascinating detail. Beautiful Victorian wallpaper enveloped the room in warm coziness. Lace curtains hung strategically over the front window, veiling the bustling activity of Main Street. She noted the men's fashionable trimmed mustaches and the women's feminine bonnets pinned perfectly to coiffed hair. Talk about surreal!

The food and a second round of whiskey arrived. Her meal consisted of some type of gravy-drenched meat, potatoes, and green vegetables. While a second shot of whiskey tempted her, she needed to stay calm and have her wits about her until she figured everything out. Already the amber liquid filled her head with a fuzzy warmth.

She picked up her fork, studying Wyatt as he dug into his meal. So far, he seemed to be the kind of guy who could take whatever came his way with a grain of salt. The calm and steady type, that is. Her showing up unexpectedly didn't faze him. *At all*. And, considering she accused him of scheming with James, it surprised her he treated her so well.

Still, she couldn't wrap her mind around the idea she had stepped through a time portal that transported her nearly a century and a half into the past. She had no idea how long she would be there for, nor how to return to her time. If only the stupid time portal thingy came with an operator's manual, she'd be all set.

"Penny for your thoughts," he said, tracing an invisible line on the tablecloth. He cocked his head, observing her every movement.

She held his gaze and smiled. "My mom used to say that."

His eyebrows lowered. "Used to?"

She nodded. "She passed away. Last year."

He reached across the table and squeezed her hand. "I'm so sorry." Something in his eyes said he understood that kind of grief, but she didn't ask.

"Thank you," she mumbled, her eyes stinging. The grief still felt raw. She didn't like to talk about her mom's passing, as it happened quite suddenly. She cleared her throat, then said, "Tell me about you. Do you have family here?"

Wyatt released her hand and stared down into the amber liquid, swirling it around before taking a sip. He nodded. "A brother. Josh. You'll meet him soon enough. He lives with me. And speaking of that," he said, leaning forward on the table. "I'm glad you accepted my offer."

She cleared her throat, fidgeting in the chair. "It'll just be for a few nights."

"It'll be more than that. I doubt you have anywhere else to go." When she gave him a sharp look, he explained, "I just mean, you seem far from home."

She nodded. "Got that right," she mumbled.

"You're from New York, huh?" he went on. "Well, Montana Territory is a lot different than New York. The people here are nice, but you'll need to be careful. Keep your own council but use good judgment when making friends. Word travels like wildfire in these parts, so be mindful who you trust and what you say."

She tilted her head, studying him. "What about you? Can I trust you?"

He placed a hand over his heart. "Yes, ma'am." When she didn't say anything further, he continued, "I want to assure you, to promise you, I'm a gentleman, and I won't make any demands on you. But you have to understand, we'll need to come up with an explanation for your sudden presence—and reason for living with me and Josh."

She played with the cloth napkin on her lap and shrugged, giving in to this crazy idea of living with a complete stranger. Make that *two* complete strangers.

"Housekeeper?" she suggested, hopeful.

He eyed her suspiciously. "Can you cook?" She took too long to respond, so Wyatt continued with a snap of his fingers, "I've got it! Mail-order bride."

Her eyes widened. *Mail order—what*? "Are you nuts? Look, I don't mind posing as your housekeeper, but—"

"Lower your voice," he said in a hushed but firm tone. He cocked his head toward their audience. Patrons at nearby tables turned in their direction, disapproval evident on their faces.

She stiffened, leaned over the table, and whispered, "As I was saying, I don't mind being your housekeeper in exchange for a place to stay—*temporarily*. And believe me, I do appreciate the help."

"Glad to hear it."

"However," she said, "I'm not going to be your *bride*. Hell, I don't even do online dating! How could you think I'd be a—"

"You don't do on the line what?"

Emma bit her lip. *This is the nineteenth century, girl, not the twenty-first. Of course, he has no clue what that is.*

"I mean, I'm happy to be your housekeeper, but anything else is out of the question," she said emphatically.

He leaned back in the chair, eyeing her over the rim of his glass. He finished the whiskey, placed the empty glass on the table. "All right, then, *Mrs.* Cole. You're hired."

She smiled. "Thank you."

"You're welcome." He grinned. "Now, the first thing we have to do is get you out of those clothes—"

"*What*?!" she cried; her heart thudded in her chest.

"—and into something more appropriate for your position," he added with a wink.

"Oh."

She pushed out a breath and fanned her flushed face. Living under Wyatt's roof would cause her many sleepless nights due to the delicious fantasies that would no doubt run through her mind.

****

Having landed in the nineteenth century with nothing but the clothes on her back and not even a cent

29

to her name, Emma's handsome new employer insisted they visit the dressmaker to have her fitted for a wardrobe suitable to her position. It was disconcerting not to be able to provide for herself. She had always been independent, even at an early age. It gave her a sense of financial responsibility. After she graduated college, she launched a side business making high-end fashion jewelry and accessories. Two years ago, thanks to the power of social media, her business took off, affording her the opportunity to hire a small staff to help execute her designs.

Now, she hoped Amber would be able to manage the business until she returned.

Wait. What if I don't return? What if I can't figure out a way to go back? She couldn't very well be a housekeeper for the rest of her life. There was nothing wrong with that profession, but it would stifle her creativity. She needed to draw, write, and create. Just the mere thought of the possibility shattered her.

The bell over the front door chimed when they entered the quaint one-room shop. The sound reminded her of the small handbell her kindergarten teacher would ring when she wanted everyone to "freeze" before directing the class to a new activity.

Wyatt closed the door, silencing the sound of Main Street. The rhythmic sound of a ticking clock filled Emma's senses. Her gaze traveled around the room, but she couldn't quite pinpoint its location. The smell of new fabric, mixed with an inviting aroma of jasmine and coffee, wafted through the air.

Within seconds, an attractive thirty-something brunette emerged from the portiere. Her snug-fitting blue dress accentuated her ample bosom, and the high bustle gave her a curvy allure. Her mahogany hair, neatly coiffed into a loose bun, highlighted her delicately sculpted face and expressive green eyes. No makeup needed on her flawless face. Talk about stunning, Emma thought. If she had to say one thing she liked about the nineteenth century so far, it definitely had to be the femininity of women's fashions.

"Good afternoon, sir, ma'am." The woman cast a quick glance over Emma's garb and smiled, then turned her attention to Wyatt. "I'm Mrs. Heughan. Will I be outfitting your lovely wife today, sir?"

A flush crept across Wyatt's cheeks. "Hello," he said, rocking on his heels. "And, yes. I mean, no. I mean, this lovely lady isn't my wife."

One perfectly shaped mahogany brow rose in question. Her gaze traveled from Wyatt to Emma then back again. "Oh?"

He shook his head. "She's my new housekeeper."

Mrs. Heughan extended her hand to Wyatt first, then Emma. "Lovely to make your acquaintance, Mister…?"

"Kincaid. Wyatt Kincaid. And this is *Mrs.* Emma Cole."

If the beautiful brunette didn't believe Emma was Wyatt's housekeeper, she certainly didn't let on. Her smile never wavered. "Delighted."

"Mrs. Cole will need several items," he told the dressmaker. "Actually, more than several, come to think of it," he added, scratching the back of his head.

"Why don't we have a look at some material for day dresses?" Mrs. Heughan suggested.

She led Emma to the counter covered with fabric swatches, from gingham and calico to muslin and linen, along with silks and taffetas. The seamstress separated bolts of fabric as she spoke about each one.

"You'll want cotton and gingham. It's more practical in these parts." Her gaze swept over Emma briefly, but not with judgement. "What you're currently wearing would be better suited for riding horses…privately," she added under breath.

Emma's clothing was considered anything but appropriate for a woman in 1882. Thankfully, she had the ability to think fast on her feet and came up with a story she hoped would be believable.

"In case you're wondering, there's a reason why I'm inappropriately dressed," Emma began, feeling self-conscious in her tight jeans and trendy shirt from a future century. "You see, I, um, was traveling from New York City. And after I got off the train—er, railroad, our stagecoach was…robbed. All my belongings, save what I'm wearing, were stolen when the…bandits left us for dead." She nodded for emphasis. *Please believe this ridiculous story. Please, please, please.*

Mrs. Heughan raised a hand to cover her gasp. "How dreadful! And what of your husband…?"

Think fast! "Oh, um, he…passed away in New York a few months ago. It's why I wanted to come out West. To, um, start over." *Sounded good. Right? Kinda, sorta true. Well, the part about traveling from New York. In a roundabout way.*

"You poor dear." Mrs. Heughan took Emma's hand and led her to a comfortable upholstered wing chair toward the rear of the shop. "Allow me to serve you both something more suitable for such news. I'll be just a moment." Then she disappeared through the curtains and into the back room.

Wyatt, having not moved since they entered the shop, wandered over, hands tucked into his overalls. He towered over her, rocking on his heels. "Is that really what happened?"

Her face burned. She hated to tell lies, but how else could she explain her sudden presence—and her clothes? She couldn't very well blurt out the truth: *I came here through some zany time portal from the twenty-first century. Yeah, that would go over like a lead balloon.*

"Of course," she replied, her eyes downcast. "How else would I end up here dressed like this?"

Mrs. Heughan returned with a tray of savories, pastries, and a full tea setting. She placed the tray on the table and handed teacups to both Emma and Wyatt.

"I thought, perhaps, tea or coffee might not be strong enough," Mrs. Heughan said, noting the half-filled cups of whiskey. She took the remaining cup and saucer off the tray and toasted. "To a new beginning."

Emma liked Mrs. Heughan. She seemed genuine and kind, yet at the same time, out of place in Whisper Creek. Her accent wasn't native to the territory. She sounded rather more British or Northeastern. And judging by her dress and the assortments of luxury fabrics in the shop, Mrs. Heughan was accustomed to designing clothing for women in more affluent settings.

"Since my housekeeper doesn't have any other belongings," Wyatt began, speaking directly to Mrs. Heughan, "I'd like for you to size her for a complete wardrobe. I'll leave you a deposit now and give you the rest when you're finished. She'll need a dress or two to begin with, though." He put the cup on the tray, stood up, and turned to Emma. "Mrs. Cole, I'll let you and Mrs. Heughan work out the details. I'll be back in two hours. That should give you enough time. Ladies." With that, he turned on his heel and left the shop.

Right away, Mrs. Heughan moved to sit in the opposite chair and leaned forward. "Your employer is *very* generous," she commented.

"Indeed, he is," Emma agreed, touching her warm cheeks.

Mrs. Heughan nodded. "It must've been horrible for you—the attack," she said quietly, squeezing Emma's hand. "I hope they didn't…that the bandits didn't force—"

Emma waved a hand. "No, of course not. A few kind gentlemen were there to…fend them off." *More lies.* She stood up and walked to the counter to examine the swatches. Time to change the subject. "Since I'm from New York, you'll have to tell me what's fashionable here, so that I don't stick out like a sore thumb." *Like I already do.*

Mrs. Heughan smiled. "I do like your vernacular, Mrs. Cole. Very refreshing. Of course, I'll be sure to dress you in the best that Whisper Creek has to offer. It's the least I can do, considering your employer is requesting a handmade wardrobe and not the ready-made dresses from the mercantile," she said, approaching the fabric table. "Tell me, dear, which station did you pick up the stage from?"

Oh crap.

****

Wyatt shoved a hand through his hair, then rubbed his neck. A cloud of cigar smoke enveloped him. He would reek of the vile odor later. The Copper Pan

Saloon happened to be Whisper Creek's finest watering hole. Hard to tell, though, considering the sawdust-strewn wood floors, the scruffy crowd quenching their thirst after a hard day, and the wet splotches of tobacco spittle inches from spittoons placed beside all the tables.

He took a long swig of the room-temperature beer, leaned back against the bar, then gazed through the haze of tobacco smoke. For midday, the place seemed empty. During the busiest hours, the piano near the front door usually had someone banging out bawdy tunes while saloon girls shook their bustles at male customers. Now, no one played. Only two tables happened to be occupied with a few men trying their luck at Faro and poker.

"Is your house done bein' built?"

Wyatt turned back to the bartender. "Just about."

The owner of the Copper Pan, a friendly old coot to boot, also happened to be the eyes and ears of Whisper Creek. The marshal could always count on Davis Cooney to report if he heard or saw anything suspicious. And by anything, he meant drifters, a gunfight, or some such nonsense.

"I've never seen such a fancy house get built that quickly 'fore," Davis commented. "You and your brother work mighty fast. And speakin' of your brother—" He nodded toward the swinging doors.

Josh Kincaid, a slightly older version of Wyatt except with green eyes, ambled into the saloon, arriving at the bar just as Davis poured a tall beer. Josh grabbed the mug, raised it in thanks, then gulped down the liquid within seconds.

"One more, Davis." Josh clapped Wyatt on the

back. "How are you, little brother?"

Wyatt tapped his fingers against the glass, then announced, "Got some news."

Davis served another round of beer, sliding two tall mugs in front of them. "On the house, boys."

The two brothers clinked glasses, then took long sips. Josh wiped his mouth with the back of his hand, studying Wyatt. He waited. "All right, let's hear it," he pressed.

Wyatt licked away his beer mustache. "Got us a housekeeper."

Josh frowned. "I thought we decided not to hire anyone?"

"It was all I could think of at the time." He leaned his elbow on the bar and lowered his voice. "This woman—Emma Cole—came out of nowhere on the ranch. *Nowhere*, do you hear me? And if you saw what she was wearing." He shook his head. "Shit, Josh. We can't let her stay here alone. It's too dangerous."

"Ah. I see." He nodded, elbowing Wyatt. "Gone sweet on some pretty little lady that—"

"Yeah, she's beautiful," he cut in. "But that's beside the point. I think she's...*lost*."

Josh was about to take another gulp but stopped. "Are you sure?"

Wyatt nodded. "You'll see when you meet her."

"And when, pray tell, will that be?"

He glanced at the clock on the opposite end of the bar. "In about ten minutes."

Chapter Three

Emma had a mini panic attack, mentally cursing Wyatt for leaving her alone with Mrs. Heughan. Only because the woman shot a barrage of questions at her in rapid-fire time. Thankfully, she dodged them and avoided stumbling over her lies about *how* she arrived in Whisper Creek. To her relief, once they started selecting fabrics, the conversation turned to fashion.

"You look lovely," Mrs. Heughan beamed. She smoothed out a wrinkle in Emma's dress, then stood back to admire her handiwork. "I'm so pleased—and surprised—this dress and the other two fit perfectly." A frown creased her features. "It's odd, though."

Emma met the dressmaker's gaze in the mirror. "What is?"

Mrs. Heughan pursed her lips as if debating something. "You might find this a bit, well, peculiar, to say the least. But a few months ago, something told me I had to make these dresses for someone." She cocked her head, studying Emma. "With your exact measurements."

Emma sucked in a breath. Shivers spread in all directions. *Just a coincidence?*

Mrs. Heughan waved a hand. "Don't mind my prattling, dear." She went to the roll-top desk and scribbled on some paper. "I'll see that the rest of your items are ready by the end of the week."

Emma had a hard time understanding how she could have written herself a letter from the nineteenth century. It made her wonder if she and Mrs. Heughan had some kind of connection. Did they know each other from...*before*? But did 'before' actually happen, even if she didn't remember being in the nineteenth century to begin with? How did all that work exactly?

She turned back to the oval mirror. Thanks to Mrs. Heughan's artistry with fabric and Wyatt's generosity in coin, she no longer resembled her twenty-first-century self. The blue muslin dress fit her like a glove, the result of the super tight corset Mrs. Heughan *insisted* she wear. Once Emma had to dress herself tomorrow, she would forgo the corset. Her bra would do just fine. Unfortunately, the soft-heeled shoes had zero support and fit too snug for her liking. She would have to come up with some old-fashioned footwear on her own.

The bell on the front door jangled. Mrs. Heughan backed out of the room. "Excuse me for a moment."

At the sound of Wyatt's hushed voice, Emma tingled all over. She sighed. Too bad she and Wyatt didn't meet in the twenty-first century. Maybe, just *maybe*, they would've dated—or even more than that. Well, one could only hope.

"Mrs. Cole?" Mrs. Heughan had returned. "Mr. Kincaid is here."

Emma pushed out a deep breath, took one last look at herself in the mirror, then stepped through the portiere separating the back room from the shop.

Wyatt was in mid-conversation with another man. When he saw her, he stopped talking. His gaze swept over her from head to toe. His smile widened in approval, which sent her pulse racing. Damn, why did he have to be so good looking?

The other man cuffed Wyatt on the arm and mumbled something she couldn't hear. He had butternut blond hair and piercing green eyes. She noted his banded-collar shirt tucked into tight brown breeches, worn leather hat, and dusted boots. Apparently, Whisper Creek had more than its fair share of attractive men.

"As I explained to Mrs. Cole," the dressmaker said, handing a parcel tied with string over to Wyatt, "her wardrobe will be ready by the end of the week." She gave him a slip of paper. "All the details are on here if you would care to review?"

Wyatt took the paper, but his eyes remained on Emma until the other man elbowed him. "Right," he mumbled, then glanced at the paper. "Thank you, Mrs. Heughan. Everything looks perfect." The man with Wyatt coughed. "Where are my manners? Ladies, this is my brother, Josh Kincaid. Josh, may I present Mrs. Emma Cole and Mrs. Heughan."

Emma did a mental facepalm. How could she have missed the resemblance? Both men towered over her at nearly the same height. They both had the same squared jaw and features, but Josh had eyes like green ice. Both brothers happened to be beyond handsome. Clearly, only one brother could get her blood racing.

"Delighted," Mrs. Heughan said, extending her hand in greeting.

Josh then turned to Emma and took her hand. "I'm glad my brother finally got around to hiring us a housekeeper. Thank you for accepting the job." He had a genuine smile that put her at ease. "Beautiful dress by the way," he told Mrs. Heughan.

Mrs. Heughan inclined her head, glancing at Emma. "Consider it a serendipitous undertaking."

A spark of recognition flickered in Emma's mind. She remembered Mrs. Heughan...from somewhere. *Probably from here. I mean, where else?*

Wyatt tucked the parcel under his arm, they said farewell, then Emma and the two good-looking Kincaid brothers left the shop. Had she been back in her own time and showed up *anywhere* with these two at her side, she would be the envy of all her single girlfriends—especially Amber.

Outside, the sun beat down from a cloudless blue sky. Unaccustomed to the heat in nineteenth-century attire, Emma grew uncomfortable and sticky with sweat, especially between her breasts, almost immediately. The tight corset and layered material of her dress didn't help. Not only that, she had to pee. *Where did people go to the bathroom in the nineteenth century?*

She stopped, which elicited a questioning look from Wyatt. "I need to use the bathroom," she explained, searching for the right word or phrase. "I mean, I need to use the toilet. No, that's not right. Water closet? Wait. Privy?" *What did they call it?*

He glanced down the street in each direction, then back at her. "You might want to wait until we get back to the ranch."

She bit her bottom lip. "I don't know if I can."

Wyatt exchanged a glance with his brother then said, "I'll take Mrs. Cole home and get her settled in. Will we see you for supper?"

Josh tipped his hat back and grinned. "You can

count on it, little brother. Unless you'd prefer, I seek sustenance elsewhere?" His left eyebrow had a devilish arch to it.

Emma's face burned. In the twenty-first century, she would definitely welcome Josh playing matchmaker. But *here*? How could *anything* develop between her and Wyatt when she didn't plan to stay long? *Then again, how long am I going to be here*? It all depended on the fire—and finding a way back through the mysterious time portal.

A short time later, when they arrived back at the ranch, Emma almost burst. She hadn't used the toilet since early that morning—in the twenty-first century. Without waiting for Wyatt, she hopped out the wagon, picked up her skirts, and headed toward the house, stumbling along the way. Damn those soft shoes.

"Mrs. Co—dammit. Emma!" Wyatt shouted after her." When she stopped and spun around, he asked, "Where are you going?"

Seriously? "I told you. I have to use the—" She made circling motions with her hand. "—the bathroom or toilet or whatever you call it."

"I know." He pointed behind the house. "It's over there."

She frowned. "What is?"

He rolled his eyes, amused. "The *privy*. It's outside. For now, anyway."

Her stomach sank. As a kid, she had once used an outhouse during a camping trip with Amber's family. Not fun. At all. She wrinkled her nose at the memory.

Wyatt reached her in a few long strides, crooked his finger, and said, "Follow me."

As they trod through the tall grass, she couldn't

help but admire his squared shoulders, nicely toned ass, and perfect posture. If only she were the type of woman to have a fling, she would be all over him right now. Instead, she'd have to fantasize about all the delicious sex they would never have. It would be better that way. Less entanglements, less attachments for when she had to leave.

Yes, just keep telling yourself that.

About fifty or so feet behind the house stood a small wooden structure painted white. It reminded her of the mini garden sheds they sold at a local home improvement store. A two-step staircase led to a door with a black iron handle.

She turned to Wyatt. "*This* is it?"

"What were you expecting?" Before she could answer, he prattled on, "I forgot. You're from New York. But this is how we do it out here on the ranch." He leaned closer and added, "Don't worry. It's hardly been used."

Her eyebrows shot up. "Really?"

He nodded. "It's a week old if that. I tore down the old one." He gestured to the heap of old lumber several yards away. "It's only temporary. As soon as Josh and I have all the piping figured out, none of us will have to trod out here anymore."

Good to know indoor plumbing was coming to the Old West, and just in time for her arrival. She shook her head. Until then, she'd have to deal with the outdoor shack.

He climbed up the steps and opened the door. She gave him the side-eye, then peeked inside. Wow. Not what she expected at all. White paint covered everything—the walls, the ceiling, and the floor.

Seafoam green curtains hung from the two open windows on each side. A stack of toilet paper sheets sat on the small shelf next to the makeshift toilet—or more specifically, the shelf with the hole in it. No odor of any kind, except for fresh paint. Maybe it wouldn't be as bad as she thought.

"There's a fresh bucket of water just around the side, or you can use the well behind the house to wash up when you're finished," he told her.

She waited until he reached the wagon to unhitch the horse before venturing inside. Unbelievable. Wagons, bustles, and outhouses.

What could possibly happen next?

****

That question got answered when she returned to the house, and Wyatt gave her the grand tour. Déjà vu filled every fiber of her being. Just that morning, she moved through the same rooms—in another century. So far, they all remained in the same order—the parlor to the right of the entrance, followed by the dining room, the study, and the kitchen in the rear.

Each room boasted beamed ceilings built in the same style as the rooms in the future house. Both the fieldstone fireplaces and wood flooring appeared nearly the same, except for the shade of floor stain. Some rooms needed either paint or wallpaper, not to mention a piece or two of furniture or accessories here and there. The home looked a bit sparse—or maybe just needed a woman's touch.

Wyatt entered the second to last room at the end of the hall, then turned just inside the doorway. "This'll be your room," he said.

Hell-o, gorgeous mahogany poster-bed. Memories

of her and Wyatt entwined in the sheets skipped through her mind. *Memories? Hell, yes. She remembered that*! She cleared her throat and gazed around the rest of the room, admiring the tall bureau, dressing table, and large oval mirror in the corner. Two small wing chairs flanked the stone fireplace on the opposite wall. Neatly folded bedding and the parcel from the dress shop sat on the bare mattress.

"My room's at the end of the hall." He pointed to the parcel. "You may want to change now. The dress you're wearing is, well, it looks great. But you might want to wear something a bit more casual. You know, first day on the job." He winked at her, then walked out.

She turned to the bed and sighed. It would be best to make the bed now, not five minutes before bedtime. Sooner or later, the trip through time would catch up with her, and she wanted to be able to be asleep before her head hit the pillow and not worry about making it first.

That done, she swapped her new dress for a cotton blouse and muslin skirt. She managed to remove the corset on her own, sweating up a storm in the process, then slipped her bra back on. Much better.

Not wanting to keep her new boss waiting, she searched the house for him. She stopped just inside the kitchen doorway. Wyatt leaned against the table with legs crossed at the ankles, hands on hips, and his mind apparently elsewhere. It gave her a moment to openly admire him. Her heart fluttered. With every passing moment, the pull grew stronger. Memories danced through her mind. She closed her eyes. She *knew* him. Inside and out. Knew what made him tick, his likes, and dislikes. *He loves whiskey and red wine, not to mention apple cinnamon pies. He loves woodworking and creating things. He has zero tolerance for maliciousness. And he…*

Like the waves on a shore, memories ebbed and flowed in her mind. She tried clinging to each of them, but—

"Are you all right?"

Emma's eyes popped open. Wyatt stared down at her, his brows furrowed. She hadn't heard him approach. She sucked in a breath and nodded. "Yeah, just…"

"Overwhelmed?"

Not in the way you think.

"Just getting acquainted with my new surroundings."

He nodded. "Speaking of surroundings," he said, retreating into the kitchen and spreading his arms wide. "What do you think?"

"I love it." She circled the room, noting the differences between this house and the one from her time. "Everything looks new. Did you build these—the island and cabinets?"

"Yep." The beginning of a smile tipped the corners of his mouth. "The entire house, too."

She met his gaze. "You're a carpenter."

His eyebrows arched; he nodded. "I have a shop in town, but I'm rarely there." He threw a hand in the direction of the barn. "I sectioned off a corner in the barn for my workshop. It allows me to get some chores done around here at the same time." His grin widened. "But now that *you're* here…" Wyatt cocked his head, folded his arms across his chest, and studied her. "I don't want to make assumptions, but is it safe to say you've never worked in a kitchen like this before?"

Her eyes surveyed everything, mentally comparing this kitchen to hers in the future. Hers, of course, had various modern appliances and gadgets to simplify cooking. She loved to cook, but she'd never had to make a meal in a nineteenth-century kitchen before. So, it wasn't a lie when she replied, "That would be correct."

"This should be interesting," he mumbled, shoving a hand through his hair. "There's a river just over the hill out back." He pointed somewhere beyond the kitchen window. "See if you can catch some trout for dinner." He then moved to the icebox. "There are leftover potatoes and vegetables in here. Make do with what you can. Tomorrow, we'll go back into town and stock up on some foodstuffs since it slipped my mind today…with everything going on."

Wait. What? "Um, did you say *catch* some trout?"

He grinned. "You have excellent hearing, Mrs. Cole. Indeed, I did. Ever go fishing before?"

Thanks to her ex-fiance who loved to fish, she learned not only how to fish, but also how to prepare and gut them. It probably wouldn't be a good idea to go into those details now, though. "Actually, yes."

"Good." He walked to a tall cabinet, pulled out a fishing pole, then handed it to her. "Then I don't need to show you how to bait a line."

Pole in hand, she headed out the door, following directions Wyatt shouted after her until she could no longer hear his voice. The trail to the river seemed endless, but it came into view as she ascended the hill.

Catch some trout for dinner. She would keep up this housekeeper charade for now. Tomorrow, when they go into town, she would excuse herself and research what she could about the fire.

But just how would she do that? After all, she couldn't very well go into the local library and look up Montana history on the internet. There would definitely be no internet and no library, for that matter. According to her letter, the fire didn't occur until December 1882. *Damn it. That's seven months away.*

Picking up her skirt, she trudged through the tall grass, shrubs, and colorful wildflowers, until she reached the river. It wasn't wide by any means, nor did it look all that deep. But to be on the safe side, she stayed on the bank, tucked up her skirt, and cast a line.

Further down the river, she spotted a young woman wading to her knees, skirts ruckled up to mid-thigh, also fishing. Not to startle the other woman, she sang out, "Hell-o!"

The blonde head turned toward her and smiled. "Hello!" she returned with a wave.

"Mind if I join you?" Emma waggled the fishing pole. "I'm hoping to catch some dinner."

"There's plenty to go 'round." The young woman smiled and spread her arms. "You may want to stand over there, though, so we don't tangle our lines." She indicated with a nod of her head. "By the by, I'm Cassandra Burns. Cassie."

She inclined her head. "Nice to meet you. Emma Cole."

Cassie eyed her up and down, but not in an off-putting way. "I haven't seen you around before."

She nodded. "I'm Wyatt—er, Mr. Kincaid's new housekeeper. He lives just over that hill—"

"Yes, I know the Kincaid brothers." Cassie's

eyebrows knitted together. "But—housekeeper?"

Emma nodded. "Yes. Why?"

"It's just…" she began, lips pressed tight. "Wilbert—that's my husband—and I have known the Kincaids since they moved here nearly two years ago. They're our nearest neighbors on that side," she explained, cocking her head in the opposite direction. "And, well, Wyatt never spoke to us about hiring a housekeeper. Had I known they needed one, I would've applied for the job." She sniffed loudly, then went back to casting a line into the water.

Emma took Cassie's comment as a dismissal, then moved about thirty feet downriver, watching her new neighbor from a distance. She seemed friendly; however, her remark about the housekeeping job gave Emma the impression Cassie and her husband needed money. Showing up in nineteenth-century Whisper Creek hadn't been Emma's idea. It certainly took her by surprise. And most likely, Wyatt took pity on her, which is why he offered her the job.

Guilt settled in. What right did she have to take away someone else's job when she didn't plan to stay?

****

Emma wrinkled her nose at the sudden smell of manly sweat and horses. She turned around. Josh stood there, grinning.

"Aren't you just fresh as a daisy?" she commented, then continued setting the table.

He poked her in response, which elicited a burst of laughter from her, then plucked a potato slice from the platter and popped it into his mouth. "Smells mighty fine, Mrs. Cole," he told her.

"Please, call me Emma." *Mr*. Cole didn't exist, so

why be reminded of her lie by being called *Mrs.*? "Dinner's ready, so as soon as your brother…" her voice trailed off.

Wyatt walked into the kitchen, tugging down his sleeves. She found it mesmerizing to watch the muscles in his forearms flex with each twist and turn as he slowly pulled the fabric of his shirt over sun-kissed flesh. Her mind wandered, wondering what the rest of his flesh looked like—minus the shirt, that is. Was it all yummy and bronzed by the sun? Hard and lean from days of working in carpentry?

Oh, hell, do not go there, girl.

Too late. Memories swirled in her mind. Yes, she had seen him naked before—somewhere in time. *When*? *Where*?

She cleared her throat, then said to Wyatt in a somewhat breathy voice, "I was just about to call you in. Dinner's ready."

Wyatt gave her a smile. "Thank you," he said, taking a seat at the head of the table while Josh sat at the other end. He tore off a chunk of bread from the loaf in the basket, glanced at her, then smeared a pat of butter across the top. "Aren't you going to eat?"

"Yeah, we might worry you're trying to poison us if we don't see you eating, too," Josh teased with a wink.

What nineteenth-century employer expected the hired help to dine at the same table? She didn't want to overstep any boundaries, so she hadn't set a place for herself. "Well, I—"

"Sit down," Wyatt urged her, kicking out the chair with his foot. "You dine with us. To hell with propriety," he added.

I'll just add reading minds to the list of things that make you irresistible.

She mentally chided herself and pressed her hands down the front of her apron. "Thank you," she said, then grabbed a setting for herself and took the seat between the two men. Millions of butterflies fluttered in her stomach. Her face flushed, and it wasn't from standing over the hot grill, either.

"How was your first day?" Josh inquired, spearing a potato with his fork. For whatever reason, he grinned like a kid with a big secret he couldn't wait to tell. What's up with him?

Emma methodically cut up the trout and vegetables on her plate. "Short, so I didn't accomplish much, with the exception of dinner."

"Tomorrow's another day," Wyatt commented with a waggle of his eyebrows.

Half listening to the men blabber on about the weather, carpentry, and a few other boring topics, she pushed the fish around on the plate, taking a few bites here and there. No doubt, traveling through a time portal wreaked havoc on her system—as did sitting this close to Wyatt. If she extended her arm just a few more inches, she could touch him.

What's wrong with me? This isn't the first time I've had the hots for a guy. Geez. Her flesh warmed to a steady simmer. She fanned herself and caught Wyatt watching her.

He smiled, got to his feet, walked into the pantry, and returned with a bottle of wine and three Mason jars.

"Hope you don't mind," he said, pouring a healthy serving of the red liquid into each jar. He handed one to her, then Josh. "It's just been me and my brother, so you'll have to excuse our informality. I'm sure being from New York City, you're accustomed to finer things."

They clinked glasses; she took a sip. It tasted strong but flavorsome. "I'm just happy to be here." If she had to be stuck in the past, may as well be under the same roof as the most handsome man she'd ever laid eyes on.

Josh swirled the liquid around, eyeing both her and Wyatt over the glass rim. He opened his mouth to say something, but his brother spoke first.

"Speaking of you being here," Wyatt began, "just *how* did you end up in Montana?" His gaze went from her to Josh then back again. "You said something to Mrs. Heughan about your coach being attacked by outlaws."

Shit. Shit. Shit. She took another long sip of the wine. The liquid helped her relax, but it also created an unsettled flurry in the pit of her stomach. *Think fast.*

"Yes," she stated, gathering her thoughts—or rather, more *lies*. "As I told Mrs. Heughan, my, um, husband passed away a few months ago. I decided to purchase a ticket on the railroad and head west. Little did I expect my coach would be…attacked by outlaws." She paused for a moment, reflecting on the letter she received from her nineteenth-century self and the newspaper clippings found in the study before traveling back in time. "Rumor has it the Boyd gang is responsible."

Wyatt and Josh exchanged a glance. *Uh-oh, what did I say?* Judging by the look on their faces, she'd said something wrong. A lead weight dropped in her stomach. *Crap.*

Josh leaned forward, his gaze steady. "How do you know it was the Boyds?"

"Oh," she stammered with a shrug. "Well, I don't for certain. It's just that afterward, I thought I overheard one of the lawmen mention the name. I didn't stick around too long before getting on another coach to…Whisper Creek."

Wyatt drained half the wine in his glass, then looked directly at her. "Lucky you escaped, then. The Boyd gang aren't the type to let their victims live." He paused, as if waiting for her to say something. She didn't.

"I'm curious," Josh chimed in. "Where did you board the stage initially?"

"Oh, it was in…Helena." It sounded more like a question because she had no idea where the railroad lines connected in 1882. Butte? Helena? She pushed her plate away, drank the wine, then stood up. "May I get you gentlemen anything else to eat or drink?"

Wyatt leaned back in the chair, studying her. Josh drummed his fingers on the table, eyes on his brother. How long could she keep up this charade?

Long enough to find a way back to the twenty-first century—and until she could unearth more details on the fire. She had no idea how *that* was going to happen either.

Josh wiped the corners of his mouth with a napkin. "Thank you for dinner, Emma. Best I've had in ages." He stood up, stretched, and announced, "I'll be tinkering with the plumbing if you need me. 'Scuse me." He winked at her, cast a quick glance toward his brother, then walked out the back door.

Wyatt handed her his plate. "I agree. Dinner was

delicious. Thanks."

Emma nodded, then moved to the sink and washed the dishes. Being in close proximity with Wyatt proved to be hazardous to her senses. Blood raced in her veins. She felt warm, too—her lady bits simmered. She liked Wyatt. *Really* liked him. But they came from different worlds, different times. It didn't seem right to pursue anything with him.

It's the nineteenth century, for crying out loud. If I made the first move, I would most likely be branded a whore. Then again, maybe I'm supposed to make the first move. I mean, I remember him from…somewhere. Maybe this is the husband I wrote about in my letter!

Wyatt clasped his hand over hers. Emma emitted a gasp. She turned quickly, and dishwater water sluiced down her wrists, dripping onto the floor. Their eyes met. Her heart raced a little—correction, a lot!

"How about an after-dinner drink?" he proposed, rubbing his thumb across her soapy knuckles. "Something tells me you could use one."

Warm swirls wreaked havoc on her. Their eyes locked. Her heart thumped in a wild rhythm. "Indeed, I could," she managed.

She pulled her hands away, wiped them on the dish towel, then followed him into the parlor, where he poured them each a whiskey. They toasted. She sipped. Slowly. The amber liquid seared a path down her throat, quickly making its way to her head to calm her senses.

This entire time travel journey—or whatever it could be called—shook her to the core, beginning with the letter from her nineteenth-century self to meeting a man she would love to do naughty things with. Just the idea of it made the blood rush to her face.

"A penny for your thoughts." Wyatt closed the distance between them. His tall frame towered over her. He rested an elbow on the mantel, and with his other hand, swirled the liquid around the glass. His eyes, compelling and magnetic, remained on her.

Emma swallowed. What could she say? *Hey, I've got it bad for you. Why don't we see where this goes? Or how about I'm from the twenty-first century, and I came back here to prevent a string of fires, save my husband—probably you—and find my way back to the future.* Yeah, neither one of those sounded like a solid option.

"I was just thinking…how quickly one's life could change," she admitted truthfully.

Dipping his head slightly, he said, "You're referring to your trip here?"

She nodded, taking another sip. "For starters."

Wyatt gestured to the chair on one side of the hearth, while he took the other. He watched her from under hooded brows. "Do you want to talk about it?"

She shook her head. "Not really. I kind of want to forget what happened, even though I know I can't."

"Sometimes, it's good to talk about things. It helps clear the mind; helps to heal."

She met his gaze. "You sound like a therapist."

"Pardon?"

She waved a hand. "Nothing."

"What does, er, did your husband do for a living?"

Her eyebrows shot up in surprise. "Why do you ask?"

He shrugged. "You're an educated and privileged woman, even though you know your way around a kitchen," he explained. "However, I've got a feeling your husband was on the wealthy side." He paused. "Am I close?"

She took another sip. That fuzzy effects associated with alcohol tickled her senses. *Educated, yes. Wealthy, not so much.* "Yes," she lied.

His left eyebrow rose a notch, indicating for her to continue. She didn't. "Perhaps, in time, you'll share with me?"

She lifted her gaze to his. "In time," she allowed.

Time. Which time would that be?

****

Traveling to 1882 should have allowed her the luxury of sleeping late the first morning in the nineteenth century. Not happening, thanks to some loud hammering, banging, and who knows what else coming from the rear of the house.

Emma tossed the quilt aside and marched barefoot into the kitchen. She stood inside the doorway. Wyatt had his back to her, but Josh spotted her, grinned, then nudged his brother. He gave her a wink, then crawled under the counter and continued to whack the pipes with some kind of iron tool resembling a wrench, whistling as he did so.

Wyatt, on the other hand, turned to her; a slow grin tugged the corners of his lips. His gaze swept over her from head to toe, lingering on her bare thighs. A shimmer of desire in his blue eyes caused her heart to jolt. *He's checking me out*!

She clutched the fabric of his loaned linen shirt against her chest, feeling a surge of heat from her core all the way up to her face.

"Sorry," she mumbled at last. "I heard all this

noise. I thought…"

Wyatt's face split into a wide grin; he walked toward her. "Nice shirt," he said, stroking her gently on the sleeve. "Looks better on you than me."

Wait. Are you flirting with me?

Her face burned. "Excuse me," she said, backing up toward the door. "I'll just go, um, get dressed."

Wyatt moved to block her only escape. He raised his right arm and leaned against the doorjamb. His eyes lingered on hers for a moment. He seemed to be in a playful mood. Had she not been wearing his shirt, maybe she wouldn't feel so flustered. And vulnerable.

"We'll leave for town in an hour," he told her, his eyes shimmering. "Will that give you enough time to get ready?"

"Town? Oh, right. Yes, I'll just hop in the show—" *Oh, crap.* No showers in the nineteenth century. "I mean, I'll…" What *did* she mean? According to Wyatt, he built a bathroom in the house, but the pipes hadn't been connected yet. Judging by the mess in the kitchen, it looked like they were trying to rectify that.

"Come with me," he said, as if reading her mind. "We're not as primitive as you might think."

He walked down the hall. She padded along behind him, clutching the shirt fabric tighter. Wyatt opened the nearest wardrobe, pulled out a towel, and handed it to her.

"Outside behind the privy, there's a shower stall. Don't worry, it's got a wooden enclosure, so I can't peek, even if I wanted to." He smiled at her, then walked away.

Holding the towel against her protectively, as if that would help tamp down the heat she felt at his nearness, she watched him walk down the hall, then turned and went outside. It would be a warm day, judging by the heat of the sun. And it was still morning.

She climbed into the shower and stood under the freezing water gently flowing from the makeshift spout. It did nothing to squelch the rush of desire pulsing through her body.

Day two. How would she ever survive her attraction to him?

****

Every moment spent with Wyatt made her insides sizzle. She liked him. And he liked her. Who cared that she came from another time? There would be no harm in enjoying each other. They were both consenting adults, right?

She closed her eyes and drew in a deep breath, envisioning their union in her mind. How his strong, powerful hands would gently touch her skin, running his hands up and down her body. How his lips would mold perfectly to hers, while she tasted his breath, whiskey sweet and...

Wyatt pulled the wagon to a halt, jolting her out of such delicious thoughts. In the next instant, his hands circled her waist to help her down. When her feet touched the ground, her legs wobbled like gelatin. His hands tightened around her waist, preventing her from falling and embarrassing herself.

"You all right?"

She nodded. "Yes, thanks."

He removed his hands. "I need to take care of a few things in here." He tilted his chin toward his shop on Main Street. "Take your time at the store. I'll meet you there in about an hour."

She smiled. "Sounds good."

He winked at her, tipped his hat, then unlocked the shop and stepped inside. She sucked in a deep breath, hoping it would steady her nerves—no such luck—and walked away.

She tilted her face up to the sun; the warmth felt good. A gentle breeze kissed her skin. Checking first to make sure she wouldn't get run over by a speeding carriage, she crossed the street. Someone called her name; she turned around.

Mrs. Heughan picked up her skirts and hurried down the boarded sidewalk toward her. "I thought that was you!" the other woman said when she reached Emma. "It's lovely to see you again."

"You as well," Emma returned, shading her eyes from the bright sun.

"I so enjoyed your company yesterday," Mrs. Heughan told her, reaching for Emma's hand. "I do wish you would stop in for a cup of *tea*."

Emma smiled. "I'd love to."

"Wonderful! Let's be on our way, then, shall we?"

What. Now?

She followed Mrs. Heughan into the shop and sat in the same seat from the other day. Her hostess poured whiskey into two teacups, handed one to Emma, then sat down.

"If you prefer tea or coffee, I do have some made," Mrs. Heughan offered.

Considering the hour, she thought it best to go slow. She drank enough yesterday to last a while. "Tea would be lovely, thank you."

"You'll have to forgive me," Mrs. Heughan said, removing the tea cozy. She poured Emma a cup and handed it to her. "It's so rare I meet a young woman, such as yourself, with whom I feel a strong kinship. You and I are a lot alike. Both from different worlds. Different cities."

Emma cocked her head and smiled. "I thought I detected an accent. But you're not from the states."

Mrs. Heughan nodded. "Chicago." She giggled and covered her mouth. "I had a schoolteacher who came from England. And because we all learned vocabulary from her at a young age, we all imitated her accent." She threw her hands up. "It doesn't hurt my business. The men all think I'm this cultured woman from across an ocean, while the ladies around here, well—" She lowered her voice, as if afraid someone would overhear. "To be honest, they aren't too...friendly."

Emma frowned. "Really?"

The dressmaker leaned back against the chair, suppressing a sigh. The sheen from the burgundy velvet cushion gave her brunette tresses additional warmth.

"Perhaps, because I'm a widow, I notice it more," she stated simply. "I no longer have a husband; therefore, the women here see me as a threat. As someone who would dally with their husbands privately. A liaison, if you will."

Emma's eyebrows shot up. "Seriously? I mean, are you sure?"

The other woman nodded. "Quite." She waved a hand dismissively. "And before you even think of asking, no, I haven't. But that's what the women in this town *think*. And you can't just come right out and say anything. It's a very sensitive—not to mention, scandalous—subject."

"Yes," Emma agreed. "Tell me, Mrs. Heughan—"

"Please, call me Anne," she said with an infectious smile. "I do hope you would consider me your friend."

"Anne it is." She smiled in return and raised her teacup. "To friendship."

They clinked cups, sipped, then Anne spoke mostly of town-related goings-on, giving Emma a sense of her temporary home. She didn't want to think of nineteenth-century Whisper Creek as her permanent home. The twenty-first century still waited for her. She just didn't know how or when she'd get back there.

Noting the time on the clock, Emma changed the subject. She still had to do shopping at the mercantile before Wyatt picked her up. "What do you know of the Boyd gang?"

Anne's eyebrows shot up, surprised. "They're bad news. They've robbed countless banks and stages over the last dozen or so years." She sipped. "Why do you ask?"

Emma hated telling more lies, but it needed to be done to find out the truth. "I think they're responsible for my...stagecoach robbery. At least, that's what I overhead," she said, gazing down into the cup. "Word has it that they're also known for arson."

Anne shook her head vehemently. "If the Boyds torched something to the ground, what would be in it for them?" She paused, tapping her forefinger on the edge of her cup. "However, I do recall hearing, upon occasion, they burned stables to lure out the horses to steal and sell." She shrugged. "If you want to know more, I suggest you stop in and see the marshal. I'm sure he'd be able to tell you a thing or two."

Chapter Four

Wyatt ran his hands over the smooth wood finish of the bureau. He blew off the extra dust, causing a swirling cloud to slowly sprinkle its way onto the floor. He whacked the sandpaper against his pants, then wiped his hands on a damp rag. His love for woodworking started as a kid. Carving small items for his parents here and there—benches, book ends, crates, and whatnot—eventually led to the art of carpentry he would never tire of. He loved the smell of fresh-cut lumber, the feel of wood just after a good sanding, and the pungent smell of an oil finish. Though things had changed over the years, especially since he arrived in Whisper Creek, his love for his art had not.

His shop consisted of furniture for paying customers; however, several items he crafted for his own pleasure—the bureau being one of them. Indulging in his craft took his mind off his present circumstances, not to mention the events of the last two years since ending up in Whisper Creek. He had no intention of ever making the journey. But once he arrived, he had no choice other than to stay. So, he decided to make the best of it.

The bell above the door chimed. Sam Hutcheson—Wyatt's first friend in Whisper Creek—ambled into the shop. They happened to be the same age and enjoyed discussing numerous topics, which always kept conversation interesting. And, truth be told, if it hadn't been for Sam, Wyatt didn't know what he would've done those first few months, alone in a new town.

Sam doffed his hat, closed the door. "How's business, my friend?"

"Busy," Wyatt replied, spreading his arms toward the furniture.

Sam eyed the bureau appreciatively and ran a hand across the surface. "Smooth as silk. For you?"

"Yep," Wyatt admitted. "I'll make another two like it for customers before whipping up something for my parlor."

Sam chuckled. "I sure do like the phrases you come out with," he said with a shake of his head. "Maybe when you're done with that, you could give me a hand at my place?" Sam asked, rubbing his eyes. "I'm trying to get the new well pump working and not doing such a good job. I may know plenty about breeding horses, but my plumbing and carpentry skills need a lot of work. You help me, and you got yourself a horse for your troubles."

Wyatt waved a hand. "Not necessary."

"But I insist."

Wyatt smiled. "All right then. How about one of those new fillies in your paddock?"

"All yours."

Sam extended his hand. And with a handshake, the deal was sealed. A man's word still meant something in parts of the world.

"Why don't you come over tonight?" Wyatt suggested. "You could meet our new housekeeper. She's—"

"Mighty pretty," Sam supplied, grinning.

Wyatt's eyebrows took a southward dive. "How would you know?"

Sam cocked his head in the direction of the door. "Saw her with Doc Wilson a bit ago. Heading to the marshal's office. Then I ran into your brother, and he set me straight." His grin widened. "You're sweet on her."

Wyatt frowned. "She's a widow."

"Don't mean you can't be sweet on the lady," he reasoned. "And, well, not that I ever thought I'd want to court another woman after Millie..." He looked down at his dusty boots. "Hell, and tarnation, why does it still hurt so much, Wyatt? Been five years."

Wyatt squeezed Sam's shoulder. Only once before had Sam spoken of Millie and their unborn daughter's death. "The deeper the love, the deeper the grief," he told him. "You take your time, my friend. Grief knows no time limits."

Sam's blue eyes clouded over. He sniffed and cleared his throat. Wyatt noticed a few strands of grey in his friend's russet hair.

"I'd best be going. Thanks, Wyatt."

Wyatt clapped him on the back. "See you tonight?"

Sam donned his hat, nodded, then walked out.

Wyatt peered out the window. Main Street bustled with normal late morning activity. Shopkeepers swept floorboards in front of their establishments. A stray dog darted across the road, dodging horses and wagons. His gaze went in the direction of the marshal's office even though he couldn't see it from his shop, wondering what Emma wanted with the lawman.

He pushed out a deep breath and returned to the bureau, gliding his hands back and forth across the smooth surface. It had been sanded down so much it almost felt like smooth silk, not a rough spot anywhere. His thoughts immediately drifted to Emma, wondering if her creamy skin would feel as silky under his hands. Damn woman. Ever since she stumbled out of his barn, confused and unsteady on her feet, his insides got turned upside down and inside out. He couldn't recall a time when his heart had beat as fast as it did when he initially saw her.

He couldn't explain it, the pull he felt. Recognition hit him over the head like a bat. And after she fainted and he carried her into the parlor, déjà vu flooded his senses. Memories swirled around him, gripping tight. He couldn't recall anything specific, but he knew she *belonged* in his arms. Crazy, right?

Leaning against the bureau, he raked both hands through his hair, then looked up at the ceiling, searching for answers. He liked Emma. A lot. Hell, more than a lot. But he hired her to be his housekeeper. And he promised not to take advantage of her.

If he made his intentions known and asked to court her, then it would be different. Right? She liked him. He could tell by the way she watched him, how her delicate cheeks flushed when their eyes met, and how she got all jumpy around him.

Hell, yes, he liked the idea of wooing Emma, getting to know her inside and out, developing a close, physical intimacy they both *wanted*—one he found himself fantasizing about since she dropped into his life unexpectedly. He thought only teenage boys woke up in a sweat and fully aroused. Wrong.

The clock on the wall chimed. He cursed. He hated being late. Quickly, he locked up the shop, hopped in the wagon, then headed for the mercantile, but making a pitstop along the way.

****

"My apologies for being late." Wyatt smiled as he handed Emma a small wooden box with a thin brown ribbon wrapped around it. "Forgive me?"

She eyed him suspiciously before pulling off the ribbon. After she removed the top, she peered inside. The sugary sweets were a cross between gumdrops and some kind of chewy taffy that he selected at the confectioner's shop down the street. He hoped she had good teeth. He tried some once. And, once, was enough.

"Bribery works every time." She laughed, then waved a hand. "Kidding. But thank you. And don't worry about being late. I got caught up, myself."

"Shopping?" he queried, arching an eyebrow.

Her gaze returned to the box of sweets. She fidgeted, then gave a small shrug. "No, chatting with the marshal, actually. What a lovely man," she added, popping a candy into her mouth and chewing heartily.

He stared at her pointedly. "You in some sort of trouble, darlin'?"

She shook her head, swallowed, and made a face as if the candy had been too sweet—or maybe too sticky. "Just getting acquainted with him and the people around here. Geez, I think I lost a filling." She worked her jaw, chewing until she made a face. "I wanted to know if there are any outlaws nearby causing trouble. That's all."

He tugged his hat lower to shade his eyes from the warm sun. "You could've asked me, darlin'. Don't forget, I've lived here longer than you."

"How could I forget?" she said with a roll of her eyes. And something about the way she batted those beautiful chocolate eyes made him want to haul her up against him and kiss her senseless. Her lips, full and enticing, had his complete attention, especially when she ran her tongue across her bottom lip. Like now.

He groaned, then glanced at the store. "Did you get everything on the list?"

"Yep. You can pull up around back. I'll let Mr. Majors know you're here—at *last*," she added, and stuck out her tongue playfully, before entering the store.

What I'd love to do with that tongue. Better not go there. He still had to ride home with her. Not a far ride. But far enough that riding with a bulge in his pants for any length of time, while their thighs touched sitting side by side, wouldn't be comfortable. His trousers already grew tight. Damn it.

He hopped into the wagon and steered it around back. The shop owner greeted him with everything all packed up and ready to go.

"Appreciate the business, as always," Ben Majors said, extending a hand to Wyatt. "And might I say, your new housekeeper is such a delight. Quite the negotiator, too," he grumbled.

Wyatt arched an eyebrow in Emma's direction. "Negotiator?"

"Hmm, she thought some of our goods are priced too high and somehow convinced me to charge you less," the shopkeeper supplied, before Emma could reply.

"Well, then, Mr. Majors, I can see my decision to hire Mrs. Cole is already paying off." He winked at Emma, then stocked the wagon with the purchased supplies of canned goods, sacks of flour and sugar, and other household staples.

Once he paid the bill, they headed toward home. Wyatt watched her out of the side of his eye. His thoughts drifted to what her creamy, silky limbs would feel like writhing beneath him. Christ, he wanted to just forget about propriety and kiss her until they lay naked in each other's arms, tangled in the sheets.

He shifted, trying to relieve the pressure of his trousers against his hardness. One thought of her, and he felt like a sixteen-year-old again.

"Penny for your thoughts," she said softly.

He turned his gaze toward her. His eyes swept over her body, thinking of every sensuous warm inch of her flesh beneath her dress. "You might not want to go there...*yet*."

It had only been two days, but already Wyatt felt like he'd known her his entire life...and wanted her even longer than that.

****

The way Wyatt looked at her when he said "yet" made Emma's insides sizzle. Her entire body quivered with pleasure. Thoughts of what she wanted to do to him—touch him, taste him, tease him—raced through her mind. The look in his eyes revealed he wanted the same.

The wagon rolled to a bumpy stop at the rear of the house. Emma jumped out. She needed to put distance between them. Her nerve endings still tingled.

As she rounded the wagon to release its gate, Josh walked toward them, wearing what could only be described as a shit-eating grin. His gaze swiveled from her to Wyatt, then back again. He shook his head, laughing to himself.

Wyatt hopped out and took notice as he rounded the wagon. "What?" he barked.

"I've got great news!" Josh caught up to them, still grinning. "You and the lovely Mrs. Cole can both enjoy a *long* hot bath indoors tonight."

Heat shot through her veins at the suggestion, rattling her to her core. "*What*?" she cried.

Wyatt glared at him. "Josh—"

Josh laughed, amused. "Not *together*, of course. Although, that might not be such a bad idea for you two. I fixed the pipes," he explained. "All water now leads out to the extra well we built way out back."

While history hadn't been her area of study back in her college days, over the years, she did like to watch cable shows and read books on how modern conveniences and technology came about. From what she recalled, indoor plumbing was more common in larger metropolitan areas. Out in the rural lands, such as where she was in Whisper Creek now, it didn't seem commonplace until nearly the turn of the century. Maybe Wyatt was one of those jacks of all trades type of guy who was ahead of his time? He certainly knew a thing or two about more modern conveniences and contraptions.

Wyatt tossed a heavy sack of flour at Josh, who caught it before it could burst on the ground in a heap of white, then disappeared into the house.

Josh held up his hand and said, "Wait for it."

A few seconds later, they heard Wyatt's excited shouts of *woohoo* and a few choice expletives.

Josh heaved the sack of flour onto his shoulder, then grabbed the sugar sack under his other arm. He leaned forward in a conspiratorial whisper, "Just for the record, the tub *can* fit two. In case you were wondering." He winked at her, then went inside.

Emma's temperature shot up a good ten degrees at the delicious thought of sharing a steaming hot bath with Wyatt. She fanned herself. The muslin dress clung to her heated flesh, making her uncomfortable in more ways than one. She clenched her eyes shut, willing the image of their naked bodies entwined, pleasuring each other as water sloshed over the sides of the tub, to go away. No such luck.

Thanks, Josh.

"You okay?"

Her eyes popped open. Wyatt watched her with amusement. "Um, yeah," she stammered, then grabbed the small crate filled with lighter items. "Just peachy."

Once inside the house, she put the foodstuffs away and tidied up the kitchen and pantry, trying to ignore the heated blaze burning her lady bits. It could only be compared to trying to douse a campfire with a single drop of rain. Day two under Wyatt's roof, and her body burned like an inferno, thinking things she shouldn't, knowing she wouldn't be there long enough to act on.

Someone said her name. Startled, she whirled around. How long had he been standing there?

Wyatt smiled apologetically. "Didn't mean to startle you. I just thought you might like to see the tub."

Yes, with you in it, all naked and—Stop that!

Biting the inside of her lip did absolutely zero to redirect *that* train of thought. In another moment, blood would be dribbling out of her mouth, judging by how hard she bit down.

"Sure," she managed at last, wiping her hands on

her apron.

He led her down the hall to the opposite side of the house. She frowned. Had there been a bathroom in the bedroom wing, she would've noticed it before.

He stopped abruptly and grinned, rubbing his hands together. "It's my secret hiding place," he explained. With his forefinger, he plucked a small gold ring out of the wall panel and gave it a gentle tug. The panel opened.

"Huh," she muttered, impressed.

"After you," he said, with a sweep of his arm.

She cast him a wide glance, then stepped into the room. The dark mahogany floor made a stark contrast to the oversized boat-shaped bathtub with a makeshift pipe leading from the tub and disappearing into a floorboard. There was a wide sink and an old-fashioned toilet with a pull cord hanging from the tank above. A linen cabinet, white wainscoting, and a summery floral wallpaper with dusty pink roses and yellow morning glories completed the room.

"I plan to christen this baby tonight." Wyatt ran a hand along the edge of the tub before turning his gaze to her. "You're welcome to do the same."

With you in it?

She swallowed, looked away, and mumbled a quiet, "Thank you."

Wyatt closed the distance between them in one long stride. She tilted her head back to meet his piercing blue gaze. A slow grin turned up the corners of his mouth, sending her blood racing again.

He raised a hand, and she thought he just might touch her. *Please, please, please.* She closed her eyes. Her heart pounded in anticipation; however, the touch never came.

When she opened her eyes, he stood by the door.

"Before I forget," he said, all business-like, "my neighbor Sam Hutcheson is joining us for dinner tonight. I take it you'll be able to accommodate another mouth to feed?"

Breathe.

"Of course," she managed.

He made no attempt to leave, yet there was an inquisitive cock to his head. "Emma," he began.

She waited. Her heart thudded. "Yes?"

He opened his mouth to say more but stopped. Tapping the doorframe, he pushed out a deep breath, then shook his head. "I'll be in the barn until dinner." He walked out.

Emma's heart banged against her chest in an excited rhythm long after he left. *All this teasing and flirting, enough already. I want you, damn it*! But as much as she liked Wyatt, it would be pointless to start something with him when she didn't plan to stay in Whisper Creek—more specifically, the nineteenth century.

Once she found out how to stop the fires and how to get back to her time, she would be out of there.

Or would she?

****

While daydreaming about one particular man from the nineteenth century could easily fill *all* her waking hours, Emma thought it best to spend her time trying to figure out a way back to the future—and how to dig up more information on the Boyd gang. She didn't have much to go on except their name. And didn't know for certain if they were even responsible for the fires. But it was the only name from the newspapers she found on the desk in the future.

Usually, felons, thieves, outlaws, whatever their names, had a weakness. Something in particular to *lure* them to take action. If she could just figure out what could bait the Boyds, maybe she could help prevent the fires.

Right. And when the marshal or Wyatt asks me, "How do you know all this?" What am I going to say, "Oh, I'm from the future, and I received a letter from my nineteenth-century self, telling me to return to the past and stop the fires?" Sure. That'll go over like a lead balloon.

This particular line of thinking only got her more frustrated. Instead, she had to keep her mind busy, so she opted to plan the rest of the week's meals, sorting out a variety of proteins, carbs, and grains.

Next on her to-do list: get the good wine, as Josh called it, from the pantry. The storeroom sat at the rear of the kitchen, accessible through a single door. Inside felt much cooler than the rest of the house. The small room reminded her of an air-conditioned room on a hot summer day in the future.

Against the back wall stood a handcrafted wine rack stacked with more than two dozen bottles of homemade wine, judging by the bottling. Before she could reach it, she spotted an envelope on the floor. She didn't recall seeing it earlier when stocking and arranging the purchases. Curiosity got the best of her, so she picked it up and opened it.

The envelope contained a variety of newspaper clippings, all yellowed with age. Unfortunately, none of the meticulously cut-out excerpts had dates on them.

But all the clippings mentioned the Boyd gang/brothers/whatever and a banker named Griffin Grey.

Where did they come from, she wondered? They were as delicate and dated as the letter she wrote in 1882. Where these from here—the nineteenth century?

She pulled one out. It read:

...Mr. Griffin Grey told reporters, "It's unfortunate these people lost their homes, their life savings, and valuables caused by the fires. Tragic loss, indeed. However, my bank has its doors open, ready and waiting to assist the residents of Whisper Creek in rebuilding all they've lost. As for the Boyd brothers, well, I expect the law will catch up with them sooner than later."

While the Boyd gang has been implicated in the fires, there has been no direct evidence to connect them or enough to indict them...

How odd. Who was Grifin Grey, anyway? Not wanting to get caught snooping, she stuffed the clippings into the envelope and placed it back where she found it, sticking out from underneath the shelving unit.

Now, for the wine. All the bottles looked the same. Not a single label to differentiate any of them. Did it matter which one she chose?

"The best wine is on the bottom row," a familiar voice said from behind her.

Emma spun around. "You have to stop doing *that*! You startled me."

Wyatt stood at the bottom of the four-step staircase, making the room feel smaller with his large frame. A smile tugged the corners of his mouth. "I apologize," he said, closing the distance between them.

Her pulse raced at the soothing sound of his voice. He had a determined look in his eyes. The scent of him, outdoorsy with fresh-strewn hay, tickled her nose. Her eyes couldn't stop themselves from sweeping over his body from head to toe. He wore a white linen shirt tucked into snug-fitting doeskin-colored breeches, outlining sinewy legs. His rolled-up sleeves exposed perfectly corded forearms. Strong hands rested on tapered hips. And, oh, how she wanted to wrap her legs around those hips.

Stop that!

"I thought you might have heard me call you."

Focus!

She shook her head, gaze averted. He stood inches from her. Heat radiated from his body, surrounding her, wrapping around her senses. The room no longer felt chilly; it felt like a sauna. How could this man have such an effect on her?

Time to leave, so she could breathe again.

Grabbing a bottle of wine from the bottom shelf, she mumbled, "Excuse me." She ran up the steps and into the kitchen. Once there, she sucked in a few deep breaths of air.

Get a grip. He's not the first man I've been attracted to. Stop acting like it!

Wyatt emerged from the pantry, closed the door, then leaned back against it. His eyes held hers. Could it be possible he read her thoughts? Did he feel the same?

"I'd appreciate you making extra food tonight so Sam can take home the leftovers," he said. Not what she expected. "He doesn't really look after himself."

"Of course," she said, relieved for a distraction.

But he made no move to leave. Her heartbeat pounded in her ears. A moment passed before she prodded, "Is there something else you wanted?"

"Plenty." He took a step toward her, then stopped. An easy smile played at the corners of his mouth for a brief second, then vanished. "Actually, that's all for now."

Emma waited until he left, then wiped her sweaty hands down the front of her apron. Being in the same room with Wyatt rattled her senses. She'd only been in 1882 for a couple days, and already she *wanted* her employer in the worst way.

Maybe I'm supposed to. Maybe he's part of the "family" mentioned in my letter.

If that's true…then she'd never return to the future.

****

"Mighty fine meal, Mrs. Cole," Sam said, raising his glass. "Very glad the Kincaids here hired you. You saved them from starving to death," he added with a smile.

Emma laughed and waved a hand. "Oh, these two managed just fine without me."

He chuckled. "I haven't had such a nice evening since before…Millie passed."

She reached across the table and squeezed his hand, knowing full well what loss like that could do to a person. "I'm so sorry for your unfathomable loss."

He nodded and sat back in the chair. "She'd have liked you. My Millie. I could see you two being friends."

She smiled. "I would've liked that. Maybe when you're ready, you could tell me about her?" Those who lost loved ones always wanted to talk. It keeps their person alive.

He nodded, sorrow lingering in his eyes. "Well, you just let me know if you ever get tired of working for these two. My house could use someone like you. I got Mrs. Burns doin' small chores here and there, but her cooking doesn't even come close to yours." He leaned closer to whisper in a conspiratorial tone, "Just don't tell her I said that."

"Cassie, you mean?" When Sam nodded, she went on, "I met her yesterday by the lake. It'll be our little secret, but I'll be sure to swap recipes with her."

The conversation turned to construction, woodworking, and problems with the well over at Sam's house.

Then Sam looked at Emma and said, "Did you know that Wyatt here is a genius?" He pointed a thumb at his friend. "And he's got some *wiiiild* imagination, too. I told him he should become an inventor, what with all the ideas he's drumming up."

She cast a quick glance in Wyatt's direction. "Oh? Do tell."

Wyatt shrugged, shifting in his seat. "It's nothing, really."

"You call *flying* machines nothin'?" Sam looked at Emma again, suddenly animated by the topic. He leaned in. "Wyatt here said someday there's goin' to be these—what did you call them?—air-ee-planes? And their wheels are goin' to be made of some kind of flexible tar or some other material. He said it's like a flying train. Imagine that—a train that *flies*!"

Emma's ears perked up. Air-ee-planes—as in *airplanes*? Airplanes wouldn't come into existence for, at least, another, what, twenty-something years. How could Wyatt know anything about them? Granted, many people in history predicted the future—Nostradamus and Verne, among others. Wyatt happened to be a smart guy. No doubt about it. After all, not everyone in the nineteenth century knew how to install indoor plumbing and rig up a shower system.

"I'd like to hear more about those," Emma said to Wyatt. "The air-ee-planes, I mean."

Wyatt waved a hand, keeping his gaze averted. "Just something I read in a book. Nothing special."

"Nothin' special?" Sam yammered on. "You even drew me a picture. Nothin' like anything I'd ever seen before. I wouldn't be surprised if you're the inventor, and we'll be hearing about it in the newspapers someday."

Wyatt fidgeted, quickly changing the subject to plumbing. And that ended the discussion.

Later, after Sam departed with a basket full of leftovers and Josh retired for the evening, Emma put the last of the dishes away. She stretched, emitting a loud yawn. What she wouldn't give for a nice hot shower and to slip into freshly laundered sheets. It's the little things she missed.

"You sound tired," Wyatt commented, leaning against the kitchen doorframe.

"I could sleep for a month of Sundays," she admitted, stifling another yawn. "I'm ready to crash—I mean, ready for bed."

He shoved his hands into his pockets and tilted his head sideways as he spoke. "I, uh, was going to try the new tub tonight, but I'm too tired for a lengthy bath. Why don't you have a go at it? It'll do you good."

A long, hot bath sounded even better than a hot

shower! "I will," she replied without hesitation. "Thank you."

"I'll show you how to fill the tub." He crooked his finger. "Come with me."

She followed him into the bathroom. He pointed to different items as he spoke. "Step on this lever—" He tapped it with his foot. "—to let in water. But don't step on it too much, otherwise, you'll flood the place. And this—"

She held up a hand. "Whoa, flood the place? That doesn't sound like you know what you're doing."

He grinned. "I do, but I'm having to deal with…antiquated materials. Indoor plumbing and sewage have yet to make their way out here to back of beyond. We're not in Chicago, so, I'm doing the best I can with what I have to create our indoor living more comfortable. It's better than running outside, don't you think?" He gave the pipe in the floor a solid shake. It didn't budge.

"Expecting it to bust open?" she teased.

He chuckled. "Never can tell. It wouldn't be the first time."

"What?"

He waved a hand. "Think you can manage?"

"Yep."

He rubbed his eyes wearily, mumbled a curse. "I forgot to add bath soap to the shopping list, so you'll have to make do with what I have." He pointed to the bar of clear soap on the counter.

"Lucky you hired me then," she told him, smugly. "I'll be right back." She ran to the pantry, then returned a moment later with a variety of bath soaps in different shapes, sizes, and textures, plus a small brown bottle filled with oil, and a pair of large cotton gloves.

His eyebrows furrowed. "You're taking a bath with gloves on?"

"No, silly." She put the items on the counter. "The soap is for bathing, and the oil and gloves are for you. Well, for your calluses. The oil will help soften them." She grabbed the bottle. "Here, let me show you. Sit down."

Emma put the toilet lid down and pointed to it. Wyatt sat, rubbed his hands on his pants, and waited. She perched herself on the edge of the tub with its thin rim, close enough their knees touched. She opened the bottle of oil and said, "Put your hands out. Palms up."

He did, eyeing her warily while she tilted the bottle, filling the concavity in each of his palms with a small pool of oil. She put the bottle aside, then took his left hand in hers and massaged the oil into his hand, kneading his fingers, rubbing the calluses…smoothing, and rubbing, again and again.

"This concoction contains several different types of oils, plus chamomile. It'll help loosen the dead skin," she explained, concentrating on his hand, warm with the friction from hers. "Every night before bed, you should wash your hands—or better yet, soak them in warm water first, then massage this oil into them."

He sat with eyes closed, head tilted back. "Um-hmm."

She smoothed the oil into his flesh and closed her eyes, losing herself in the thought of what those hands would feel like sliding across her body, smoothing the same oil into her skin, one limb at a time. Massaging, kneading…*teasing*.

Her temperature skyrocketed. She swallowed hard.

How much of this teasing could she take? *Teasing*? Oh, to hell with teasing. She *wanted* him. Wanted him more than she'd wanted anyone. *Ever*. Wanted to be under him. On top of him. Touching him. Kissing him...

"Emma," he whispered.

"Mmm," she responded, engulfed in the sensation of his hands in hers, while delicious thoughts of what she wanted to do with him—and *to* him skipped through her mind. She massaged, smoothed, and rubbed. A heady sensation, making her more than just warm and fuzzy, washed over her. She burned. For him. To her core. She wondered what he would do if she were to—

"Emma!"

She opened her eyes. Her heart hammered wildly, causing her breath to come in short bursts. Was that his body heat—or hers?—blanketing her, filling the small room? His eyes, heavy-lidded with desire, gazed back at her. She licked her lips. And waited.

They stared at each other. Without words. For several moments.

Wyatt finally pushed out a deep breath, then shifted. "As much as I'd love to have you continue working your magic on my...*hands*," he said in a low, gravelly voice, "I think it'd be safer for us both if I left you to your bath now."

Their hands remained joined.

She hadn't moved.

Neither had Wyatt.

After a moment, she finally nodded and attempted to get up. Instead, Wyatt pulled her closer. The blood pulsing through her veins vibrated in her ears. He leaned in and pressed his lips to hers. A gentle, soft kiss making her senses tingle. His tongue traced the outline of her lips, tasting and teasing until she opened her mouth to let him in.

He groaned and clasped his arm around her back, pulling her closer. She slipped her arms around his neck and suddenly found herself in his lap, on top of the hardness she caused.

He whispered her name over and over as he trailed kisses from her lips, down her neck to the collar of her dress. *Damn that collar.*

She slid a hand into thick tufts of his dark blond hair. The kiss deepened. His tongue delved into the depths of her mouth; his arms wrapped around her, pulling him against her. Oh, how she wanted this!

"Emma," he whispered against her mouth.

"Mmm," she managed. She clung to him, to the promise of what his kiss meant or could mean…if only she would just stay in the nineteenth century.

No, she couldn't think about that. She had to *be* in this moment. His lips. On hers. Clutching her arms around his neck, she tried to get closer. But it would never be close enough.

"Emma." Wyatt gripped her shoulders and set her back from him. She gazed into those orbs of endless blue. Her chest heaved. He closed his eyes and inhaled deeply. "As much as I'd love to go on kissing you…"

He didn't finish that thought. Instead, gently picked her up and set her on her feet, gazing down at her. She swayed a little.

He whispered her name again. "Emma."

She licked her lips. And waited.

Without another word, he walked out of the bathroom and closed the door behind him.

Emma pushed out a breath, pumped the foot lever, and ran a cold bath.

She needed it.

Chapter Five

"You look like shit," Josh remarked. He poured milk into a coffee mug before taking a gulp, eyeing Wyatt with that all-knowing smirk.

Wyatt glanced at the clock on the wall. Barely seven and way too early for Josh's humor. Had it been any other morning, he wouldn't care. Yeah, he could just imagine how he looked. He'd spent the entire night wide awake, thanks to a major hard-on, thinking about Emma—and that sweet taste of a kiss they shared. He knew what would've happened had he *not* walked out of the room when he did. So why did he?

He yawned, rubbed his face wearily, then spooned sugar into a mug and stirred. "Thanks," he retorted.

Josh laughed, raised his mug. "Think nothing of it." He took a sip, then set the mug down. "Let me guess. Your surly attitude has to do with a sleepless night filled with thoughts of the lovely Mrs. Cole. Am I right?"

He glared at his brother. "We both know there's no *Mr.* Cole, so cut it out."

"Yeah, but she doesn't know *we* know." Josh pulled apart a muffin and took a bite. "When are you going to talk to her?" Wyatt gave him a blank stare, so Josh rolled his eyes. "About how she *really* got here."

Wyatt held up a hand. "I don't want to force anything out of her. I want her to trust me enough to tell me the truth. It's only been a few days. Let's give her some time."

Josh poured more coffee and consumed another chunk of muffin. He chewed thoroughly. "Time is one thing when it's on your side, little brother. But you know the gossips are going to have a field day with this."

Wyatt's gaze snapped to his. "Because we hired a housekeeper?"

"Not just *any* housekeeper—a young, gorgeous, widowed housekeeper living *alone* with two bachelors," he clarified. "People in this town will eat that shit up. If one of us had a wife, it wouldn't make a bit of difference. But you know how it is here."

Wyatt finished his coffee and put the mug in the sink. "Nothing we can do about that now. Tough shit if the townsfolk don't like it."

He walked out of the kitchen and down the hall to the bathroom, stewing because he knew Josh was right. But he'd worry about that later. Right now, with it still early and quiet, a steaming hot bath beckoned his aching muscles. Having spent the night fighting the damn hard-on that Emma left him with, he needed something to soothe him. And a cold shower outside wouldn't cut it. Only her soft body would do the trick.

He groaned, pumped the water lever with his foot, and yawned. The water wouldn't be hot, but it would do. He was too lazy to heat it. Stripping out of his clothes, he climbed in, rolled up a towel and tucked it behind his head. Eyes closed, he leaned back, and allowed his thoughts to once again drift back to the previous night. Had it been up to him, he would have carried her into his bedroom, stripped her of her clothes, and slid right inside her warmth. They wouldn't have stopped until dawn.

"Oh, pardon me!"

Emma stood inside the door, her hand still on the knob, gaze averted. She wore her hair loose around her shoulders, and the yellow cotton dress fit her like a glove.

He pushed himself up to hide his arousal. "Looking for something?"

Quickly, she turned and said over her shoulder, "I left these in here last night." She reached for her hairpins but dropped them on the floor. She scrambled to collect the scattered mess, doing her best not to look in his direction when they kept slipping out of her grasp. "Pardon me. I'll just leave you—"

"Emma," he said, cutting her off.

She stiffened. "Yes?"

"I forgot to get a towel. Would you mind setting one out for me?"

Without looking at him, she reached into the wood cabinet and pulled out a folded towel. He laughed at her attempt to not let her eyes wander anywhere near him. She placed the towel on the toilet seat. "Anything else?"

He paused, just to see her squirm. "That's all. Thank you."

She nodded, then bolted out of the room.

Wyatt chuckled then sank back into the water. But his smile quickly vanished. Seeing her did nothing except increase his desire.

He reached over the rim of the tub for the nearby bucket and poured cold water on himself, hoping it would help cool him down. It didn't.

****

Emma spent the better part of last night trying to get Wyatt out of her head. Damn him for being so yummy in all the right ways. It didn't help when she walked into the bathroom to find him in the tub—fully naked and aroused. She had been tempted to strip out of her dress and join him.

I should've. Yeah, coulda, shoulda, woulda. Stop being such a coward.

Shaking her head, she placed a tray of muffins in the oven and checked the time. As she returned to the counter to mix a batch of cookies, the sound of an approaching wagon caught her attention. She wiped her hands on a towel, then went to the front door.

"Hello-ooo!" Anne sing-songed, setting the brake lever on the buckboard. She gathered her skirts and climbed down.

As the town's only dressmaker, Anne certainly outfitted herself in the best fashions—a walking testament to her talents. The color of her dress reminded Emma of a dark chocolate cappuccino. The skirt draped in the back and hung perfectly over a matching underskirt. Her mahogany hair had been swept up in an elegant knot. With that dress, Emma thought her friend belonged in Paris rather than the Western frontier.

"Lovely to see you again, my dear," Anne said, pulling her into a quick embrace when she reached the top of the steps.

"I'm so glad you came by." On Emma's first day at Wyatt's, it became evident how isolating life out on a ranch or farm could be, especially for nineteenth-century women in charge of households, husbands, children, and chores. Only a few days, and she longed for female companionship. Anne's visit was just what she needed today.

She led Anne inside to the parlor where her friend removed her bonnet and circled the room, assessing every detail, especially the woodwork.

"Charming. Did Mr. Kincaid do all this?" she asked, spreading her hands.

"The entire house too." Emma nodded. "If you'll give me just a moment," she continued, heading for the kitchen, "I'll put out some tea."

"That would be lovely," Anne called out. "Except for the tea. I like my *special* tea, as you know."

Emma laughed. "I haven't forgotten."

Within moments, she returned with a plate of biscuits and a tea setting. She whisked the decanter off the bar and poured whiskey into two teacups neatly perched on matching saucers, keeping the one less filled for herself.

Anne raised her cup in a toast, then sipped gracefully. "This house suits you," she told Emma. "It's very inviting. And it already feels like you're the lady of the house and not the housekeeper."

Emma said nothing; instead, she glanced around at the dark wood moldings and burgundy and gold Victorian wall coverings. It did feel like home. Her home. *Their* home—with Wyatt, that is.

Anne smiled and took another small sip, then briefly closed her eyes in contentment. "How are you adjusting to life out here in Montana? I know it's only been a few days, but you appear serene and settled."

Oddly enough, Anne was right. While she still needed to figure out *how* she arrived in the past, not to mention how to get home, she liked the rhythm of the household. Housekeeping wouldn't be a line of work she would've chosen for herself in the future, but considering she now lived nearly a century and a half into the past, it suited her circumstances.

"Well, I do enjoy working for the Kincaid brothers," she admitted, hiding a smile. Her thoughts immediately filled with images of Wyatt. *In. The. Tub.* "Never a dull moment. That's for sure."

"I shouldn't think so." Anne placed the cup on its saucer. "I hope you don't mind me dropping in like this, but there's a reason for my visit." She paused. "I wanted to see if you'd be interested in participating in the quilting bee. With me."

Emma had a biscuit halfway to her mouth. "Quilting bee?"

Anne nodded, almost sheepishly. "Ever since I came to this town, the women here…well, they haven't exactly accepted me, as I mentioned to you. And, well, I thought, since you and I are both widows, if we were to join the quilting bee together and they get to know us, perhaps, they wouldn't think such things…about me," she added quietly.

"Do you really care what small-minded women think or say?" she scoffed. "Anne, you're a brilliant woman. You own a business. You're beautiful and intelligent and kind."

Anne wiped at the corner of her eyes. "You're a dear for saying so."

"Well, it's true. Who cares what they think? I, for one, don't think you need to join a quilting bee to stop their tongues from wagging. This is a small town. People will talk, no matter what you say or do. The solution is to not let it bother you. Easier said than done at times, I know. But it's true."

Anne sat back, gazing at Emma. "You're a strong woman," she said. "I am, too, but you're strong in a different way. In a good way, of course." She shrugged. "I wish I could be more like you."

"You're stronger than you think." Emma reached out and squeezed her hand. "I would love to join you in the quilting bee, but not for that reason. I think it would be fun. But there would be no point, seeing as I can't sew."

"Can't sew?" Anne's eyebrows shot up in utter disbelief. "My goodness, how can that be possible?"

She shrugged. "I'm sorry."

Emma wanted to make new friends while she remained in the past—for however long that would be. But in the twenty-first century, she didn't need to know how to sew. If her clothes required taking up a hem or new buttons, she took them to a local tailor. Maybe she should've paid more attention to her mother, who tried to teach her those things as a child.

"Quite all right," Anne sighed with a wave of her hand. "Oh, before I forget, when you and Mr. Kincaid come to pick up your wardrobe Friday, you must see the new collection of jewelry from Paris. I've put aside several pieces to match your new dresses." An elegant eyebrow arched in question. "Perhaps, you can persuade him to buy you something?"

Emma thought for a moment. "Do you order a lot of jewelry from Paris?"

Anne shook her head. "Not too much. It's quite costly. Only a handful of women in Whisper Creek are married to railroad barons and wealthy enough to afford precious gems. I just wish I could find someone in town who knows how to make jewelry, so I could sell it in my shop. Then, the women of Whisper Creek could look as fashionable as they do in Paris for a fraction of the price," she added.

"There is someone in town." When Anne looked at her questioningly, Emma explained, "I'm a jewelry designer. I mean, I used to be when I lived in New York."

Anne's mouth dropped open. "Why, my dear, you certainly are full of surprises. Do tell!"

"I started designing jewelry when—before my husband died," she explained, eyes averted. How long could she keep up this widow charade? "I thought it would be a good way for me to make some extra money. I managed to sell some pieces to local jewelers before I, er, traveled out here. I can do the same for you if you want. It would help me, too. I need to make some money, but mainly have independence."

Anne clapped both of her hands together. "This is wonderful! I know where you can get gems and metals. When you come to the shop on Friday, we'll discuss all the details."

Emma smiled and raised her teacup. "To new beginnings."

****

After Anne's wagon rolled out of sight, Emma decided to pay a visit to the barn—formerly known as the garage in the twenty-first century. She stared up at the tall wooden structure, hoping to find some clues within on how to return to her own time. Her palms sweated. She shook her hands.

"Okay, here goes," she muttered.

Mustering up the courage and sucking in a deep breath, she stepped out of the bright sunshine and into the cool darkness beyond the double doors. She hadn't been in the barn since her "arrival" in the nineteenth century the other day and half expected something to happen.

The barn contained four immaculate stalls, hay stacked into neat bales, a wood ladder leading to the loft above, and Wyatt's workshop in the corner featuring a few pieces of furniture. A center beam ran the length of the ceiling with a rope hanging from it. Something about the organizational pattern of the barn sent a chill down her spine. An image flashed in her mind but too muddled to fully visualize.

Because her trip to the nineteenth century happened without warning, she couldn't recall exactly *where* she stood in the moment her world turned upside down.

Closing her eyes, she tried to recollect every little detail from the moment she stepped into the building…

The garage was spotless. The cement floor shined, as if recently painted. Two vehicles parked inside: an SUV and a pick-up truck. Neatly stacked crates on a shelving unit lined the back wall of the garage. Yes, she remembered!

What else?

Clenching her eyes tighter, she grasped at memories buried in her mind. She found one and clung to it.

A loud noise. Yes, a crash just outside the walls of the garage. It sounded identical to two cars colliding. Tremors shook the ground beneath her feet. And when she stepped outside…nothing of the twenty-first century remained. The future, as she knew it, had vanished. The garage had been replaced with a nineteenth-century barn. And Wyatt, the most handsome man she'd ever laid eyes on, stood before her.

Emma opened her eyes. Her breath caught, surprised to find Wyatt now standing inside the doorway, watching her. The man had a knack for showing up when she least expected it.

"Hi," he said with a lazy smile.

She swallowed and croaked out a meek, "Hi."

He hung his hat on a peg on the wall, casting her a worried look. "Are you all right? You look a little pale."

She shrugged. "Just…homesick, I guess."

He nodded, walking toward her. "Anything I can do to help?"

Yes, help me find the time portal or doorway, so I can go home.

She bit her bottom lip and said, "I don't think there's anything you can do. It'll just take some time. To get used to…all this, I mean."

He reached out and laid a hand on her shoulder, then with his other, tilted her face up. She breathed in the smell of his skin, outdoorsy and masculine. They stood so close; his warm breath fanned her face when he spoke.

"If there *is* anything I can do, you'll let me know?"

She licked her lips, focusing her eyes on his neck. If she met his gaze, it'd all be over. Already, she felt herself turning to mush. *Don't make a fool of yourself. Pull it together.*

"I will," she said at last. "Thank you." She had to

get out of there, but his hand remained on her shoulder. "I, um, didn't know you were back. You must be hungry." She had to change the subject. "I can make you and Josh—"

He shook his head, studying her face, tracing each feature with his eyes as if inspecting a rare jewel for authenticity. The look he gave her…sent a wave of recognition through her system. Their eyes locked.

"We had a bite earlier," he said, distracted. "Josh's still at Sam's, but he'll be back in time for supper. I came back to…" His voice trailed off. He looked at her in the most peculiar way. Eyebrows knitted together in confusion, he took a step back, shaking his head.

It was her turn to ask, "Is something wrong?"

"Yes—no." Wyatt closed his eyes and rubbed his forehead. He then shoved both hands through his hair, sweeping it off his forehead. When he opened his eyes again, he said, "This may sound weird, but I just had an intense feeling of déjà vu. It means this feels familiar. Like we've done this before."

"I know what it means," she told him. Her heart thudded. "But like we've done *what* before exactly?"

"*This*." He threw his hands up. "I can't explain it. It's all…fuzzy. But I get the feeling I've known you. Before now, I mean. The day we first met, I felt it very strongly." He paused. "But that doesn't make any sense, does it?"

Something tingled at the base of her spine, rising all the way up to the nape of her neck. She'd had that feeling, too. Perhaps it had something to do with how she *initially* got there, meaning her *nineteenth-century self* who wrote the letter.

But then, wouldn't her letter have said something

about Wyatt?

Wait. It did!

She closed her eyes, trying to recall the exact wording: *Get your ass back here to 1882 before the fires start. The lives of your husband, children, and neighbors depend on it.*

"You're looking pale again," Wyatt told her, concern etched into his features. "Here. Sit down." He led her to a bale of hay, stepped outside, then returned a moment later with a ladle filled with water. "Drink this."

Emma sipped; small drops of water dribbled down her chin. She handed the ladle back to Wyatt. He reached out and wiped her chin with his thumb. And, just like that, her skin burned under his gentle touch.

She should tell him about her letter and how she *really* got there. It might help explain that feeling of déjà vu they both experienced.

Then again, if she didn't recall being here to write the letter in the first place, how would he remember her?

Maybe she should keep it to herself for now. After all, a man from the nineteenth century would certainly laugh his head off at her story about traveling over one hundred and forty years back in time—or another dimension. That, or he would commit her to an insane asylum. Definitely not the way to go in locating the key to returning to the future.

"Would you like me to take you into town?" he asked at last. "To see Doc Wilson, I mean. You look a little woozy. I think your trip here is starting to take its toll on you."

Emma shook her head. "I'm fine. Just…homesick,

like I said. I'll be all right." She focused on pressing an imaginary line out of her skirt with her hands.

Wyatt sat next to her, pushed out a breath, then turned toward her. Their knees touched. "It doesn't matter how you came to be here, Emma," he began. "This is your home now. And I want you to settle in, make friends, and enjoy your new life here."

With you?

She touched his hand, then quickly pulled away. But he wouldn't let her. He reached for her hand, raised it to his lips, and pressed a soft kiss to the center of her palm, making her heart melt.

"If you change your mind about seeing the doctor," he said, "you'll let me know?" He stood up and waited for her response.

She could only nod. Once he left, she went outside to the shower stall, stripped herself of her dress, and stood under the cold spray of water until her heart rate returned to normal.

****

"The dress is absolutely gorgeous," Emma declared, twirling around in front of the full-length mirror. The yellow and lilac cream silk with coordinating underskirts would be perfect for the upcoming town fair in a few weeks. All feminine and summery, it made her feel like she truly fit in this place and time. "Anne, you're amazing with fabric and thread. I love it!"

"I've been doing this for so long, it's second nature," Anne commented, tugging the bustle and picking off a tiny piece of thread. "Plus, it's good to have some help with the larger orders." She inclined her head toward Mattie, the young waiflike seamstress she'd hired, who, now, smoothed down Emma's skirts to make sure they fell just so.

Emma didn't like anyone making such a fuss over her. She nodded her thanks to the young girl before turning to Anne. "All the outfits are beyond lovely. Thank you."

"Don't thank me," Anne said with a wave of her hand. "Thank your employer. He's most generous."

"That he is," she agreed, checking her reflection one more time in the mirror. She hardly recognized herself garbed in nineteenth-century fashion. If someone told her months ago, she would be transported back in time, she never would've believed it. Who would?

"That's it, then, as I think you've tried on everything we made for you," Anne continued, searching through the assortment of garments stretching across the counter. "Mr. Kincaid will be happy to know your wardrobe consists of undergarments, blouses, skirts, and several day dresses, as well as a few for the more important gatherings." As she spoke, she collected the clothes and neatly piled them into Mattie's arms, who then scampered off to fold and pack them up appropriately. "I'm also adding in, at no charge, a few nightgowns I think will be most appropriate for…late-night *tête-à-têtes*," she said, with a mischievous glint in her eye.

Emma's mouth gaped open, but Anne ignored her and instead poured whiskey into two teacups and handed her one.

"I couldn't help but notice he's sweet on you," Anne whispered from her perch on the settee so as not to be overheard by her assistant in the back room.

Emma sat down and took a longer than normal sip, letting the liquid burn its way to her stomach. After just a few visits, she had grown accustomed to Anne's daytime "tea." A sip here and there never hurt.

"I'm his *housekeeper*, Anne," she reminded her new friend. "That's all."

"Mmm." Anne placed the cup on its saucer, leaned back, and braced an arm against the back of the settee, studying Emma. "Don't mind me if I don't believe you, my dear." She waved a hand. "Of course, you're his housekeeper—*now*. But in a very short time, I think, you'll be *Mrs*. Kincaid, the lady of the house."

Emma flushed, completely taken by surprise. "W-what?"

"Emma, dear, we're friends now. It's all right to admit your feelings for him." Anne smiled and squeezed her hand. "Besides, I knew it the first moment I saw you two together. Those longing looks. The way his eyes never left you. Oh, yes, he's smitten. And you?" She cocked her head, assessing her. "You are, too. But you're afraid. Why?"

In the short time they had known each other, Emma found her new friend to be very astute. She genuinely liked Anne and her honesty. Could it be fate or just fortuitous they established this friendship? Whatever the reason, Emma felt gratitude for having another woman to talk to. One wise beyond her thirty-six years.

"I won't deny Wyatt and I have feelings for each other," Emma said at last. "But it can never be, for reasons I can't get into." She couldn't very well tell her new friend she'd traveled back in time and had no intention of staying. "Yet, despite the short time we've known each other, he and I have both had a sense of...déjà vu." When Anne frowned, she explained. "It means it feels like the two of us have previously experienced something being encountered for the first time," she explained. "Like, we knew each other before. That sort of thing. Does that make any sense?"

"I think I understand." Anne nodded slowly. She paused, cocking her head. "Do you believe in fate, then?"

Did fate have anything to do with time travel? Maybe it did. Who knew? Still, she couldn't tell Anne about how she ended up in 1882—or that she received a letter from her nineteenth-century self. The woman would think she'd gone mad.

"I guess I do," she allowed.

Anne nodded, smoothing out a wrinkle in her skirt. "I've been in this town longer than you, and I value our blossoming friendship, so I'm going to get straight to the matter." She paused. "The ladies in this town *love* to gossip, and their tongues are going to be wagging when they discover you are living with the Kincaid brothers."

"I *work* for them," she stated simply. "As their housekeeper. Of course, I'm living with them."

"You forget, dear, that both brothers are *unmarried*—and every man in this town with an unmarried daughter under the age of twenty is eyeing each of them as a potential suitor," she explained patiently. "Wyatt is a hard worker with his own business; Josh has been assisting the marshal, acting as some kind of unofficial expert, from what I hear. They are, indeed, most suitable marriage material."

"But—" She tried to interject.

Anne held up a hand and continued. "Now, mind

you, neither of the Kincaids want anything to do with matchmaking schemes," she said matter-of-factly. "Of that, I'm sure. Therefore, when the ladies of Whisper Creek discover that you—in all your flawless beauty and petite frame—are living in the Kincaid household, well, let's just say, you'll be the envy of every woman from here to Helena."

"But—but I'm a widow!" she argued as if it were true. "Surely, that must account for *something*."

Anne squeezed her hand. "My intent in telling you isn't to upset you, my dear. Coming from a big city like New York, you're probably not used to petty gossips and the like. I just wanted you to know how things are out here in Whisper Creek, so you're better prepared to handle whatever comes your way."

Emma tried to smile. "I appreciate your insight."

Anne picked up her teacup and took another sip. "Now, how about we discuss our partnership?"

****

Emma left Anne's shop with a spring in her step. The excitement of a business venture and partnership with her new friend sang of promise for her immediate future. Under their agreed-upon terms, Anne would loan her an advance to procure the needed gems and metals to start designing jewelry, and Emma would pay Anne back within six months.

When they brainstormed names, Anne suggested, "It should be something French—or at least something *sounding* French." She snapped her fingers. "Déjà vu," she announced. And that was that.

Their partnership would be her and Anne's secret. Wyatt and Josh need not know about it just yet. It didn't matter the century; it would be good to make a living for herself again. And while she appreciated a roof over her head and the housekeeping job with Wyatt and Josh, she had to do something creative—something that gave her purpose, not to mention money. She still didn't know how long she would be in the nineteenth century, so she had to make the best of it.

"Pardon me, ma'am."

Emma had been so deep in thought she wasn't paying attention to her surroundings and collided with someone. "My apologies," she said, regaining her balance.

The gentleman smiled. His silvery-peppered hair sparkled as a gentle breeze fanned it. He released her and stepped back. His dark gray suit looked new and quite costly. The color complemented his hair and ice-blue eyes.

He bent down to retrieve his hat off the ground. "There's nothing to forgive, ma'am." He inclined his head, then said, "Griffin Grey at your service."

Her eyebrows shot up. She knew that name. "Em—Mrs. Cole."

He took her hand, holding it a few more seconds than what would be deemed appropriate. "Mrs. Cole, it's my pleasure."

Two men accompanied him, both garbed in suits just as expensive. They looked much younger than Mr. Grey, and maybe even a handful of years younger than her thirty-year-old self.

"Tell me." He went on, as his eyes took an appreciative glance over her, "how is it your husband would allow you out of his sight?" The two men accompanying him took a few steps back before he continued in a lower tone. "Why, if I had a beautiful wife, such as yourself, I'd never allow you to leave my side," he admitted.

No matter the century, men could be ridiculously flirtatious when attracted to a woman. Case in point. "Thank you for the compliment."

He smiled and glanced around. "Where's Mr. Cole?"

She wanted to roll her eyes but refrained. Thankfully, before she could reply, Wyatt appeared at her side.

"There you are," he said, moving protectively in front of her.

Grey assessed Wyatt, then Emma. "Would this be your Mr. Cole?"

"I'm her employer," Wyatt supplied. "Wyatt Kincaid. And you are…?"

Grey stiffened. "Late for an appointment," he retorted, without shaking hands. He reached for Emma's hand once more, then said, "Until next time, Mrs. Cole."

Emma watched him leave. The two men with him followed at his heels, like two little lost puppies, until they reached the bank at the end of the street and went inside. Griffin Grey. That name rang a bell.

She tapped her chin with her forefinger. "Do you know him?"

Wyatt's jaw clenched. "Heard of him."

Chapter Six

Even though Emma hadn't stopped searching for a way back to her time, she enjoyed living in the Kincaid household and settling into her new life. But each day during the past month, she'd return to the barn and retrace her steps as best she could, hoping each step would be the step to take her back to the future. No such luck. Accepting defeat would not be an option. She would never give up her quest to return home.

Home. She sighed. She missed her life. Her work. Her routine. Sharing important things with her best friend. *Shit, what would Amber think of all this, of her disappearance*? Knowing Amber, her friend probably called the police, the FBI, and every other law enforcement agency on the planet to report her as a missing person. Great. She'd have a lot of explaining to do when she returned.

While she missed Amber terribly, Anne's friendship provided the female companionship she'd been lacking since she left the twenty-first century. Living with the Kincaid men made her yearn to sometimes just sit and gab with another woman. Her talks with Anne were mainly about the goings-on in town, news in the territory, and, of course, their partnership. Never about how she *really* arrived in town.

During her third week in Whisper Creek, the young

woman whom she'd met by the river on her first day showed up at the back door with two little children in tow, needing to borrow some sugar and flour.

Emma enjoyed Cassie's company. Their conversations were entertaining and fun. And usually interrupted by Cassie's two adorable children, Willie and Clara.

"I can't tell you how happy I am you're workin' for the Kincaids," Cassie confessed, smearing another spoonful of jam on one of the homemade scones Emma served. "And that you're my neighbor. It's such a bother to pack up the kids and ride into town. You're a hop, skip, and jump beyond our property." She bit off a large chunk of the scone and wiped up the jam that dribbled down her chin with a swoop of her forefinger.

The children played quietly on the floor; two-year-old Clara with her doll and four-year-old Willie with jacks.

"Yes, it's nice having another woman nearby," Emma agreed. "By the way, I made you some biscuits and bread to take home. It's one less thing you have to bake." She pointed to the small basket on the counter.

Cassie wiped the corners of her mouth with a checkered napkin, then took a sip of tea. "You're too kind. I'd love to have you join us for dinner—"

Emma held up a hand. "You don't need to be worrying about another mouth to feed," she interjected, glancing at the children. The young woman certainly had her hands full. "I'm happy to have you come here when you can manage. Otherwise, I can make us lunch and bring it to you."

"You're a gem," she declared. Catching Willie out of the corner of her eye, she said firmly, "Wilbert

Burns, you put that down. Right *this* minute."

Willie thought better about shoving one of the jacks into his mouth. He stopped when he heard the death threat in his mother's voice. His frown quickly turned into a dazzling smile.

"Yes, Mama," he said, then put the toy on the floor, looking quite proud of himself.

Cassie sat back in the chair, shaking her head. "Good Lord, he's a handful. Just like his father." Her eyes briefly clouded over with a different emotion, then she gave a little grunt of dissatisfaction.

Emma prodded, "What is it?"

Cassie folded her hands, staring down into her lap. "Wilbert," she admitted. "I just wish he was more...*attentive*. It seems he'd rather be in town every night than be with his plump wife." She sat up a little. "Not that I blame him. I haven't been able to lose weight since Clara was born. It's just...I hate those whores."

Whores? Emma's eyebrows shot up. "Pardon?"

The younger woman glanced at her children, then whispered, "It's been going on for quite some time. He visits the whores in the Copper Pan. One of them, anyway. I'm not sure which, but I know she's one of Madame Veronique's girls."

Eew. Emma's stomach rolled. "You know this for certain?"

Cassie nodded. "I smelled her cheap perfume on him again one night a few weeks ago. He came to bed but wouldn't touch me. The next morning, I found a lace ribbon in his pocket." She sniffed and wiped her eyes. "It wasn't mine."

"Maybe he purchased it for you?" she tried to

reason.

Cassie shook her head, then looked at her pointedly. "A wife knows when her man has taken up with a whore."

Emma had heard about men in earlier centuries frequenting brothels. The thought repulsed her, for more reasons than she wanted to think of. Aside from contraceptives not coming into use for another fifty or so years, what about sexually transmitted diseases? If Cassie's husband cheated, he could infect her with something. And from what she could remember, penicillin or antibiotics wouldn't be discovered until the 1920s. How then did people treat sexually transmitted diseases in the nineteenth century?

"Have you talked to him about it?" Emma asked.

Cassie looked at her like she had six heads. "*Talk* to him? And say what exactly?"

"Demand he stop seeing her," Emma charged. "He took vows, didn't he? He swore to love, honor, and cherish you, not lie, cheat, and betray. Correct?"

Cassie squeezed Emma's hand. "Lordy, Emma, you must've had a real nice marriage, so much nicer than mine. Unfortunately, not all husbands can be like yours. You're so beautiful and kind. I'm sure Mr. Cole would've never strayed," she said quietly.

Emma had to remind herself prostitution was legal in this century, allowing men the freedom to frequent houses of ill-repute to satiate their desires. Best tread carefully, so as not to upset her new friend. Women in the nineteenth century may have to put up with their philandering husbands, but it didn't mean they liked it.

"Sometimes a man—if spoken to in the right tone and at the right time—can be receptive to what you have to say." So said the woman from the twenty-first century.

Cassie didn't respond. Emma took that as a sign to end the conversation. She poured them each one more cup of tea before clearing the table.

"You're more sophisticated than the women 'round here," Cassie observed, watching Emma with her head cocked to one side. "Tell me, what do you think of this"—she lowered her voice—"suffrage movement? Are you one of them? I mean, do you think women should have the right to vote and own property and earn a wage?"

"Absolutely."

Cassie beamed. "Me, too. Only I would *never* tell Wilbert, of course. Stubborn man won't give up his whores. You think he'll ever support a woman's right to vote?"

She had a point there. And it wouldn't do them any good to discuss it further. It seemed Cassie liked the *idea* of women having rights but remained unwilling to stand up for herself, beginning with her husband. Baby steps.

Cassie stood up and straightened her skirts. "We best be going now," she announced. "Thank you for a lovely afternoon, Emma. Willie, Clara, collect your toys. We'll be on our way now."

Both children groaned.

Willie stomped a foot. "But I don't want to go yet."

Cassie glared at him. "You get yourself out that door, young man. We are leaving. *Now*."

He hung his head. "Yes, Mama. Bye, Mrs. Cole." He waved, then took his sister by the hand and waited outside.

"He's a good boy, but stubborn sometimes," Cassie admitted with a roll of her eyes.

"Wonder where he gets it."

Cassie laughed at that.

They said their farewells. Emma watched the wagon venture over the hill and out of sight. She hugged her arms around herself and shivered, knowing if she had been born in this century, she would be just like Cassie.

****

Wyatt ran his hands across the cabinet's smooth surface, checking for rough spots, blowing off residue left behind by sandpaper. He had finished the cabinets for himself, but this, like the other two he had yet to stain, was for new clients. Always grateful for customers keeping him in business, he now preferred to spend more time working in his barn than his shop in town. It would give him the opportunity to see Emma. But today, he had to finish a piece of furniture in his main shop.

The bell over the front door jangled, alerting him to an incoming visitor. Wyatt wiped his hands on a rag and zigzagged his way through completed and works-in-progress cabinets, bureaus, and the like, before winding his way to the front of the shop.

"Good day, sir."

A young man in a dark blue suit doffed his hat and gave a curt nod. The tight fit of his hat left an indent across his forehead. He clutched a leather-bound ledger under his other arm. He wiped a sleeve across his sweaty face.

"Would you be Mr. Kincaid, sir?" he queried, all businesslike.

Wyatt tossed the rag aside and glanced over the kid's shoulder to see if he brought anyone else with him. He looked familiar but couldn't quite recall where he had seen him before.

"Which one are you looking for?"

"Which one…?" The young man's eyebrows shot up in a sudden panic. "Oh, er, would you be Mr. *Wyatt* Kincaid?"

"In the flesh."

He nodded, relief settling over his youthful features. "Excellent, excellent. I hear you're the local carpenter with an extensive talent for the craft. And I can see firsthand that's true," he said in what sounded like a rehearsed speech, considering the kid didn't even look at anything in the shop. "Might you be interested in expanding your craft to making, or rather, building larger items?"

Wyatt sat on the edge of a table and folded his arms across his chest. A faint smell of sweat radiated from the kid's neatly pressed suit, though he wouldn't meet Wyatt's gaze. He was sure that if he yelled boo, the kid would shit his pants.

He leaned forward, towering over the kid. "Who are you?"

"Terribly sorry. I thought I introduced myself. Percy Rosler, sir. Nice to make your acquaintance." He extended his hand. "I work for the new Savings and Loan office in town."

Wyatt shook his sweaty hand. No doubt it came from nerves. He wiped his hand off on his pants. "Okay, Rosler, what do you want?"

"Not me, sir. My employer," he stated. "He would like to hire you."

"I gathered that," Wyatt said, rubbing his jaw. "Hire me for what?"

"My employer plans to contribute a substantial amount of financial support to further the development of Whisper Creek," he explained in a rush. "He believes this town could grow to be as vast as cities such as Helena or even Chicago. He's making several investments in the town, beginning with the construction and renovation of two buildings—details of which I cannot share at this time. But know that you would be handsomely paid for your services."

"Just get to the point, kid. Who's your employer?"

"Mr. Griffin Grey of Grey's Savings and Loan."

Now he remembered the kid. About a month ago on Main Street, he spotted Rosler and some other young sap trailing behind Griffin Grey, hanging onto his every word. That same day, he had to whisk Emma away from the man's prying eyes. Wyatt didn't know Grey personally, but he knew enough about his background in finance. None of it good.

"I see," he muttered, pondering why Grey wanted to hire *him* specifically. "Tell me, what does a New York City financier want with a small town like Whisper Creek?"

Rosler didn't answer. Instead, flipped open the ledger, rummaged through some papers, then handed one of them to Wyatt.

"Here's a letter from Mr. Grey outlining the details of his requests. It should answer all of your questions." He snapped his ledger shut. "Mr. Grey is staying at the hotel until his house can be renovated, which is only part of what he'd like to hire you for.

Wyatt glanced at the paper and scanned the

contents. From what he could see without reading it word for word, it looked legit. Grey wanted to hire Wyatt to renovate one house, as Rosler mentioned, as well as oversee a team of men to erect a building in town. He would be paid handsomely for his efforts. Why wouldn't Grey just hire a local architect, or at least, one from Helena? Why would he want to hire Wyatt?

He looked at Rosler pointedly. "What's the catch?"

Rosler's brows knitted together in confusion. "The catch, sir?"

He waved his hand. "What does Grey hope to gain from all this?"

"Why, I've already said he wants to contribute to the development—"

"—of Whisper Creek," Wyatt finished. "Yeah, I got that." But there had to be more to it. What rich guy travels across the country to set up shop in an unknown town? Why come all this way just to erect a few buildings when he could easily do that in New York with all his money?

"Tell your boss I'll have to think about it."

"Of course. Mr. Grey will be expecting your response. As I said, he's staying at—"

"The hotel. Yeah, I got that, too. Thanks."

After Rosler left, Wyatt grabbed his hat off the peg by the door and marched over to Marshal Reed's office. If anyone had been talking about the new man in town, the marshal and Josh would've gotten wind of it by now.

He walked inside the office. The marshal and his brother were in mid-conversation with none other than Griffin Grey. The three men stood in a circle and turned toward him as he closed the door behind him.

"Marshal," Wyatt said with a tip of his hat. He spared his brother a glance, then tapped eyes with Grey. "Hope I'm not interrupting anything."

"Not at all." The marshal waved him in closer, his expression unreadable. "We were just getting acquainted with Whisper Creek's newest banker." Reed turned to Grey. "Griffin Grey, this is Wyatt Kincaid."

Grey met his gaze, then a dark gray eyebrow rose as he glanced from Josh to Wyatt. "Ah. Brothers."

Wyatt gave a curt nod. Neither man extended a hand. "Just saw your man Rosler," he told Grey. "Very interesting proposition."

Grey eyed him up and down surreptitiously, while his smile remained in place. "I do hope you'll consider the offer."

Josh piped in with, "What offer?"

Before Wyatt could respond, Grey explained, "Your brother's an excellent builder—or so I'm told. I'm planning to have new buildings erected, and so, I offered him a job based on his reputation." He clasped his hands behind his back and turned to Wyatt. "Give it some thought. I'll expect your answer tomorrow."

He nodded at Wyatt, then to the marshal and Josh. "Gentlemen, I bid you good day." He shook hands with each man, including Wyatt this time, then left.

Once the door closed, Josh walked to the window. He looked back at Wyatt and the marshal and said what Wyatt had been thinking all along. "I don't know about this guy." He shook his head.

"What do you mean?" Marshal Reed asked, frowning. "You don't know what?"

Josh scratched the back of his neck, glancing at his

brother. "There's something about him I don't like—or trust."

"You don't even know him."

"That's the problem," Wyatt added.

The marshal chuckled as he poured himself a hot cup of coffee from the pot on the small stove in the corner. "You know, I could've said the same thing about you two when you blew into town a couple years ago," he said pointedly.

"But don't you think it's a bit strange," Wyatt pressed, "that a rich guy from New York comes all the way across the country to spend money in developing *this* particular town?"

"Maybe that's how it's done," Josh said, lowering his voice. "Maybe towns like Whisper Creek need wealthy bankers to set up shop and help with commerce."

The marshal shook his head. "You two say the darndest things." He took a sip of the hot liquid then made a face. It was obviously too hot. "Listen, fellas, I've lived in many small towns in my fifty-two years, and I can tell you that every town needs a few men like Grey to get it up and runnin'. For years, wealthy and pompous men like him would come from the east to lend money to help towns develop into small cities, if they hadn't struck rich in gold, that is. It's his money. I say, let him spend it."

"But he's not going to *spend* it, is he?" Wyatt tilted his head. "He's going to *loan* it. And my guess is it will probably be at some crazy-high interest rate."

"Let's give him the benefit of the doubt, shall we?" the marshal suggested. "After all, if I had believed the rumors about you when you first showed up, you'd have been hanged already."

Wyatt's eyebrows shot up. "What the hell for?"

Marshal Reed waved a hand then took a seat behind his desk. "You show up out of nowhere with no one to vouch for you. Either of you. You looked like something out of—I don't even know where, what with the way you were dressed and all. Townsfolk were saying you were an outlaw and murderer and—"

"All right, you made your point," Wyatt said, holding up a hand. "Just keep an eye on him."

"I'm the marshal," he reminded him. "I've got eyes on everyone in this town."

Chapter Seven

The lush navy velvet under the necklaces, cameos, and rings highlighted the unique colors of each gem. Emma smiled, proud of herself. In just one short month, she earned enough from her sales to pay Anne back on the small loan. She loved creating new pieces. Designing jewelry gave her a sense of creativity once again, something she feared she lost when she ended up in the past. Thankfully, it was like riding a bike. And it helped save her sanity

Of course, her new business didn't take away from searching for a way back to the twenty-first century. She would never give up on *that*. But instead of fretting constantly about circumstances she couldn't control, she took pencil to paper and created sketches before turning the gems and metals into something fashionable.

She had just finished the setting on an opal ring when she heard horses ride in. Quickly, she covered the jewelry and tools, then went to the back door just as Wyatt slid out of the saddle. He tossed the reins over the horse's neck and marched into the house with a determined stride. Without saying a word or acknowledging her in any way, he headed straight into the pantry.

Josh dismounted and followed at a quick pace. He spotted Emma and gave her a big smile. "Having a pleasant day, I hope?"

"Yes," she replied, as he breezed by her. "And you?"

"Peachy," he said with a wink. He followed Wyatt into the pantry, then closed the door behind him.

During her time in the Kincaid household, she had learned not to question the brothers when they did bizarre things. With a shrug, she turned her attention back to the jewelry and carefully wrapped each of the pieces in their respective velvet pouches before placing them in a small wood chest for safe keeping.

She debated telling Wyatt about her partnership with Anne. It shouldn't really matter because it wasn't any of his business. On the other hand, she didn't want him to get upset if he found out from someone else. It might make him feel as if he couldn't trust her. But he was her employer, not her husband. Besides, she had no clue as to just how long she would be in Whisper Creek—or Wyatt's employ. With any luck, the money from her jewelry business would be enough for her to— what?

It would be pointless to buy a place when she didn't intend to stay. She had everything she needed at the Kincaid household. Why leave? Plus, she liked being under the same roof with Wyatt. Being in such close proximity gave them a chance to get to know each other and flirt like crazy. Though, that too, was a dead end. Why start something that would only go unfinished?

The brothers' voices from the pantry grew louder. She couldn't help but overhear their conversation.

"What's your point?" she overheard Josh say.

"What's my—?" Wyatt barked, then stopped.

115

"Josh, that clipping isn't from the *Whisper Creek Gazette.*"

Were they talking about the newspaper clippings she discovered in there earlier? Had there been others not from the *Gazette*? She shook her head, clutching the jewelry chest under her arm, then went to her room and slid it under the bed.

When she returned to the kitchen a few minutes later, both Wyatt and Josh sat at the table, deep in thought. Wyatt drummed his fingers. Josh clasped his hands behind his head and rocked on the back legs of the chair. Neither one of them seemed to notice her.

She pulled the basket of potatoes closer and started peeling one. "Is everything all right?"

Wyatt turned in her direction and replied casually, "Fine."

"Did you find anything interesting in the pantry?" she teased, peeling a potato with a small knife. What she wouldn't give for a real potato peeler. Sometimes she missed the small things, like kitchen utensils and hairdryers and—

"We're low on beans," Josh replied. When she turned to look at him, he waggled his eyebrows. "Just needed to discuss something. You know, in private."

"You mean, the great outdoors isn't private enough? You two brawny men had to squish yourselves into a teeny, tiny, dark pantry?" She rolled her eyes. "And they say women are crazy. Hah!"

That got a dishtowel thrown at her. She whirled around and caught Wyatt grinning. "Oh yeah?" She grabbed a handful of string beans off the counter and tossed them in his direction.

He jumped up from the chair and caught a few of

them. He grabbed one of the checkered napkins on the sideboard and playfully tossed it at her. They both laughed.

Josh pushed back his chair and headed for the door. "I can see where this is going," he said with a chuckle. "And I can't be held responsible for delaying the inevitable. Have fun, kids."

"Wait!" Emma cried. "You can't leave. He outnumbers me—in size and strength alone."

Josh laughed. "I think you can handle him…in more ways than one." He nudged her, then bolted out of the house.

Wyatt snuck up behind her. He grabbed her arms, pinning them around her middle, trapping her against his chest.

"Let me go," she cried, playfully, over her shoulder.

Wyatt nuzzled her neck and whispered against her ear, "Never."

Emma felt the heavy *thud* of his heart bang erratically against her back, his uneven breath on her cheek. Warmth engulfed her senses, surging through her veins to her pulsing core. He rocked her side to side as if swaying to a song of their own. Her skin sizzled where his hands clasped her bare forearms.

She clenched her eyes, relaxing in his arms. A sigh escaped her. She leaned back, her soft curves molding to the contours of his body, all hard and lean and…Her eyes opened. The bulge in his pants pressing against her couldn't be ignored.

"Emma…" he whispered; his stubbly cheek rested against hers.

Everything about this embrace felt comfortable,

natural. As if she belonged in his arms. As if they had done *this* before…a thousand times over.

Her heartbeat thundered in her ears. His arms slipped around her waist, holding her tighter. He leaned his head against hers, whispered her name, then pressed a soft kiss to the back of her head. A second later, he swung her around in the circle of his arms.

Her gaze went no further than the pulse beating rapidly at his neck. *Ohhhh, that neck.* She would so love to kiss the little hollow below his Adam's apple, then kiss her way up to his slightly parted lips, run her tongue…

Stop it! *I'm not staying in the nineteenth century, so why start something I can't finish?*

Wyatt lifted her chin and gazed down into her eyes. His blue orbs hooded with desire. "I'd really like to kiss you."

Say yes.

She breathed raggedly between parted lips and nodded.

His warm breath fanned her face before his mouth touched down upon hers; his arms encircled her. His lips, deliciously soft, yet firm, gently caressed hers, tasting and teasing, driving her wild and making her insides flame with desire.

His tongue delved into her mouth, dancing and colliding with her own, exploring the depths. Her hands slid up the soft material of his shirt covering the sculpted muscles of his chest until they clasped around his neck. He grabbed her around her waist, pressing her against his hardness.

Wyatt groaned, then pulled his lips away to press soft kisses down the side of her neck. With a soft whisper into her ear, he sent shivers of delight to all areas of her body. Emma squirmed with the delicious sensation, warmth spreading from her belly to her lady bits. Her heart pounded. She clutched her hands in his hair, pulling him closer.

"Wyatt," she whispered, letting him kiss his way down her neck. He managed to undo a few buttons on the back of her blouse, which gave him access to her collarbone and the swell above her breasts.

His breath came in hot bursts against her skin. He gave little groans of pleasure as his mouth moved lower and lower still with that searing wet tongue. Then...

Dammit, he stopped.

Confused, she tilted her head back, slowly lifting her gaze. A sensuous light passed between them. To hell with the twenty-first century. She *wanted* Wyatt Kincaid. Right now. Right this minute. She hadn't expected to fall hard for him, but it happened. Why should she deny her feelings just because she would be leaving...?

Someday.

"Christ, Emma, I want you," he admitted, his voice like rough gravel. His left hand remained in the small of her back, while the other on her bare shoulder, scarcely holding up the front of her blouse. "I'd like nothing more than to lay you in my bed right this minute and do things to you that I've been thinking about since the moment you showed up on my property."

Then, why don't you?

"And I will," he assured her, planting a gentle kiss on her lips as if reading her mind. "But not yet."

Flustered, she tried to pull her clothes together to cover up her embarrassment of such blatant desire. But he wouldn't let her go.

It took a moment before he spoke. "Things are done…differently here than what I'm sure you're used to, living in a big city, and all." He paused. "That being said, I would very much like it if you would give me the honor of courting you."

Huh? Seriously? Court?

Yes, court. Like they did—or *do*—in the nineteenth century.

As much as she didn't care about propriety now, Wyatt did. He was a good man. Honorable. And men like him were hard to come by—in *any* century.

While she understood his intent, she didn't agree. Never the type to sleep around or have one-night stands, she wanted to throw caution to the wind because she had never felt like *this* for anyone else before. The heady sensation of falling in love completely thrilled and excited her yet remained terrifying at the same time. And she refused to let this be a one-night stand. She wanted more.

But how much more could it be when I'm planning to go back to the future?

"Yes," was all she could manage.

Wyatt lifted her hand, kissed it, then gently pressed his lips to hers before he spun her around to button the back of her shirt. That done, he turned her to face him again.

"Since we live under the same roof, it might be difficult to keep the fires to a minimum," he admitted. "Yet, given the proximity, it'll certainly help us get better acquainted." He gave her a devilish grin. "If we lived in another time and place, I wouldn't hesitate to take you into my bedroom, lay you down, and…" His face reddened. "Well, forgive me for being so bold."

She raised a hand and pressed it against his cheek. "I sometimes wish we lived in another *time* and place," she admitted, "where it was acceptable for you to be *so bold*."

****

Since they locked lips last night, Emma lived on Cloud Nine. It didn't matter that she got only five minutes of sleep. Wyatt filled her every thought. From the way his mouth touched hers to the burn her body experienced when he ran his hands over her breasts. If those feelings were any indication, she knew sex with him would be *a-maz-ing*. And what she wanted right now was to be wrapped in his arms again—and in his sheets, sharing his bed.

She chided herself for *wanting* to be so reckless with her body and her emotions. But seriously, who cared what *century* they were in? They were obviously attracted to each other. No one would know, other than the two of them, if they acted on their feelings. Right? What would be the big deal? Couples did this all the time in the twenty-first century.

Yeah, but this is the nineteenth century, girl. Most women don't toss up their skirts, no matter how much flirting and foreplay.

Since Wyatt still didn't know she arrived from the future, she'd best take it down a notch. She leaned her head back against the wooden rocker and sighed. Who could concentrate on *Twenty Thousand Leagues Under the Sea* when thoughts of lying naked, writhing, and bucking beneath Wyatt danced through her head?

Damn you, Wyatt, for being a gentleman.

The clattering sound of a wagon and the clip-clop

of horse's hooves caught her attention. She put her book aside as a horse-drawn Phaeton bumped its way over the dirt road toward the house. When the buggy came to a halt in front of the porch steps, she recognized one of the occupants as none other than Griffin Grey. Something unpleasant sank in her stomach.

He hopped out, waving off assistance from his companion, then doffed his hat as he climbed the front steps. "Good morning to you, Mrs. Cole," he said with a slight incline of his head.

"Mr. Grey."

"Lovely to see you enjoying such fine weather." He spread his arms wide, assessing the property before turning back to her. "Would it be too hopeful of me to think that Mr. Kincaid left you all alone today?"

For the first time since she arrived, Emma realized if a stranger came to the house and harassed her, she would be helpless to defend herself. While she had taken a few self-defense classes over the years, a five-foot-three woman against a man who had a hundred pounds on her wouldn't be a fair fight.

She folded her arms protectively across her chest. "Is there something I can help you with, Mr. Grey?"

He took a step closer. "I wish I could say I'm here to call on you—and I *promise* I will do so in the future—but at this time, I'm here to see Kincaid." He looked around again, this time purposefully. "Wyatt, that is. Is he here?"

Just last night, the Kincaid men locked themselves in the pantry discussing newspaper clippings about Griffin Grey, and today the man stood on their porch. Connection or coincidence?

"Mr. Kincaid is here," she replied haltingly. "May I ask what this is regarding?"

"You may indeed," he replied politely. "But, alas, it's between myself and Mr. Kincaid. Would you be so kind…?" He gestured with his hand toward the house.

Something about Grey didn't strike her as genuine. That he flat out refused to tell her his business, and politely so, didn't bother her. The way he looked at her made her feel uncomfortable. Not only that, his body language said he had ulterior motives.

"If you'll just wait here, I'll let him know you wish to see him."

Emma walked through the house, then out the back door and into the barn. When she got there, she found Wyatt sanding a large table.

He looked up and smiled. "Miss me already?" He winked then brushed off the dusty residue.

Always.

She smiled. "You've got a visitor." One perfectly dark blond eyebrow arched upward as he waited for her to tell him who. "Grey."

He brushed his hands on his trousers then walked toward her. "Did he say anything?"

She shrugged "Just that he wants to see you. He wouldn't tell me more than that." She waited for him to offer up some information.

Instead, he nodded. "Would you put on some coffee, please? We'll be in the parlor." And just like that, he headed toward the house.

"Men!" She returned to the kitchen to make coffee. It had been a week since she had burned a pot. What she wouldn't give to have her coffee maker. She loved that appliance. All she had to do was insert a cartridge, press a button, and *voilà*, coffee was served. Hot and delicious.

"It's the little things," she mumbled.

There were leftover muffins from breakfast, so she arranged them on a platter with a small bowl of homemade blueberry jam. When the coffee perked, she placed everything on a tray and carried it into the other room.

The men fell silent when she walked in. Grey and his companion sat on the sofa while Wyatt claimed a wing chair. She glanced at Wyatt questioningly, then at his guest. Grey smiled in return before his gaze tapped on Wyatt, then hers once again. She placed the tray on the table and began to pour.

"You have yourself one very fine housekeeper, Mr. Kincaid. Doesn't he, Percy?" Grey asked, addressing his companion.

Percy mopped the sweat from his brow with a handkerchief, nodding eagerly. "Yes, Mr. Grey." He didn't strike her as the type to argue. If anything, Percy would always agree with his employer if he wanted to keep his job.

"And quite a lovely one, at that," Grey added. He accepted the cup and raised it in thanks before turning to Wyatt. "I can see why you want to keep her out here. All to yourself. Alone. Nice little arrangement you both have."

Emma wanted to punch this guy—physically or verbally, it didn't matter—but refrained. It would be unladylike to cause a scene.

Without looking at her, Wyatt said, "Thank you, Mrs. Cole. That'll be all." Then he leaned forward and placed his elbows on his knees, glaring at Grey.

It took a few seconds to realize Wyatt dismissed her. She was infuriated that he hadn't addressed Grey for making sexist remarks. She bit her lower lip. *This isn't the twenty-first century. Things are different here.*

However, as she left the room, she overheard Wyatt growl, "Let's get something straight. My housekeeper is off-limits to you…"

She didn't hear what came after that.

****

"How did your meeting with Grey go?" It took great patience for Emma not to beg for details during dinner, but now that they decided to take their dessert outside, curiosity got the best of her. Or maybe it was the wine.

She took a slow sip and watched his profile in the amber glow of the fire. That chiseled face with high cheekbones and full mouth. The way his hair tickled his forehead in the soft breeze. She sighed, wishing he would kiss her again…for starters.

Wyatt reached for the bottle and refilled her glass, then his own. The night still held enough warmth to keep the chill away. She found it romantic, reclining on a picnic blanket with Wyatt in front of a firepit, sipping wine.

"He wants to hire me," he said at last. "Renovations on a house and oversee the company he engaged to construct a building in town. Grey feels he may be taken advantage of if he doesn't have someone local working with the builder."

Her eyebrows scrunched. "Griffin Grey doesn't strike me as someone who would ever be taken advantage of. There's another reason," she added.

He tilted his head, considering her words. "You

don't like him." It was a statement, not a question.

"It's not just that," she replied. "I mean, I hardly know the man, so I can't really say. But he does come off as pretty cocky, if you ask me. And since he's some fancy-shmancy financier from New York City, it's doubtful he's the type who could ever be swindled."

Wyatt looked like he would add something to that but refrained. She sipped the wine and stared into the deep flames of the fire, feeling contented in its warmth—or maybe it was Wyatt's nearness.

"Too bad we don't have any marshmallows," she mumbled. *Wait. Were marshmallows even a thing in 1882?*

"You like toasted marshmallows?" he asked, surprised.

She looked at him. "Do you even know what they are?"

He nodded. "Hard to come by out here, unless you get some special confections from Helena." He tossed back the rest of the wine then poured more. "Speaking of Helena, I need to go there to pick up and order supplies. Once the railroad arrives next year, it'll make life easier out here. But until then…" He shrugged. "I'll be gone a few days." He grinned. "Will you miss me?"

She rolled her eyes, hiding a smile. "Possibly."

He laughed. "That's better than a no."

"When do you leave?"

He paused. "Tomorrow morning."

Disappointment sank in her stomach like a lead weight. With him gone for a few days, life around the house would be quite different—and boring.

"Would you like to come with me?" His voice was low and gravelly, and he kept his gaze downward. "I can show you around the city. The ride is quiet, with beautiful scenery to hold your attention. And the city itself is something." He lifted his gaze to meet hers. "I'd like to show it to you. If you'd like, that is."

Heat surged to her face, hearing an unspoken promise in his offer. At least, she hoped that's what she heard. "That would be lovely."

Since she had moved in, they had been spending plenty of time together. But this would be different. It would be just the two of them. Alone. For several days. Away from the prying eyes of Whisper Creek. Heat coursed through her, just imagining what they could be doing in those days.

"I suppose I should prepare some food and a travel bag for the trip," she announced, forcing herself to think of something else.

He nodded and rose to his feet, then helped her up. They folded the blanket, banked the fire, then went inside. The aroma of leftover dinner smelled inviting as they entered the kitchen.

Wyatt went to the pantry and came out with a loaf of bread. "How about sandwiches? I'll have the leftover chicken and—" He looked at her. "What can you put in a sandwich if you don't eat meat?"

"I'll manage. Don't worry." She took the bread and placed it in a small basket along with some other items including muffins, biscuits, fruit, and napkins. Keeping her mind on the task at hand was better than the alternative, while Wyatt was so near. Her blood pressure was probably through the roof at this point.

"Emma," he groaned out her name.

She spun around. The look in his eyes made her insides pulse with a rhythm only he could compose. He rocked on his heels, glanced at the floor, then at her.

"Emma, I…" His voice trailed off.

Propriety be damned. She wanted him to kiss her. *Now*. All this flirting and teasing—*enough already*!

Did he read her mind? He must've, because in the next instant, he closed the distance between them and gathered her in his arms. Her hands slid around his neck, pulling him closer. His mouth caressed hers, gentle at first, then more demanding. Strong hands slid down her back to her gently cup her buttocks, pressing her against his hardness. She whimpered softly; he groaned in response.

"Emma, I need to tell you something," he whispered against her lips while they teased and tasted.

"I'm listening," she managed between kisses.

"I'm crazy about you."

Her heart knocked in her chest. "Glad to hear it, cowboy." She wrapped her arms tighter around him. "I'm crazy about you, too."

Is this really how they speak in the nineteenth century? Apparently so.

Their eyes locked. She expected him to pick her up and carry her into his bedroom, so they could get all this teasing out of the way once and for all. She wanted him. *Bad.* And she knew he wanted her, too.

He cradled her face between his hands. "Ah, Christ, Emma, the things I want to do to you." He whispered in a ragged breath. "I can't control myself when you're near. I don't know how much longer I can wait to be inside you."

Her legs officially turned into mush. His gaze traveled over her face and searched her eyes. All this foreplay drove her crazy—what a short trip! She wanted him. Naked. Inside her. No more waiting. She opened her mouth to tell him so, but he spoke first.

"I tell you what," he said, glancing at the ceiling then her. "If we—you still feel this way about me when we get back from Helena, let's not wait another second. All right?" He paused. "There are things I need to tell you first, and then you can decide if you still want me."

Still want you?

She dropped her lashes quickly to hide the disappointment. "What is it that could be so bad?"

He tilted her chin up. "Not bad, just…not something you're expecting."

She searched his eyes. "And you think it'll make me not want you, is that it?"

"I want you to *trust* me," he told her firmly. "If I gain your trust, everything else will fall into place."

She squinted her eyes. "Are you implying I can't or shouldn't trust you now?"

He rolled his eyes. "No. Look, it's nothing. Just some stupid stuff about my life before Whisper Creek. I want you to know the *real* me, Emma. Not the man you think you know me as here. Is that too much to ask?"

She swallowed, shook her head. "Then you should know the real me, too," she replied. "There are things about me—about where I came from you should know, as well."

"Okay, then. I look forward to having those discussions upon our return. In the meantime, I'll see you in the morning." He turned to go, then faced her again. "Make sure you lock your door tonight. Otherwise, I might be too tempted to sneak in." With a wink, he was gone.

She laughed and when she retired for the night,

closed her bedroom door but left it unlocked.

Chapter Eight

What have I done? Emma cringed. How on earth would she explain to Wyatt where she really came from? Thanks to an entire sleepless night—not to mention the bulk of the ride to Helena in the most uncomfortable wagon ever invented—running different scenarios through her mind—she came up with the same conclusion. If she told Wyatt she arrived from the future, he would think she's *nuts*. Crazy. Insane. Twenty-four cents short of a quarter. Who *wouldn't* think that?

The nineteenth-century population hadn't even *seen* a television, let alone an automobile or airplane. It would be impossible for them—Wyatt, in particular—to wrap their mind around her story about traveling back in time. Even in her own head, it sounded ridiculous.

She could just picture it: "*Newsflash, Wyatt. I'm from the twenty-first century and have no idea how I got here or how to go back. One minute I'm in a three-car garage, the next—wham! I'm in the nineteenth century. By the way, can you build me a time machine to take me back*?" Yeah, that'll fly.

"Why're you shaking your head?"

Emma turned to Wyatt. His hat sat low, shading his face from the warm midday sun. His rolled-up sleeves exposed tanned muscular forearms, giving her the

131

slightest hint of light blond hair. The reins fit comfortably in the grasp of his hands.

"I'm sorry, what?"

"You were shaking your head," he told her.

She shrugged. "Just wondering how long until we get there."

He leaned in closer, searching her eyes, before returning his gaze to the road ahead. "That's not what you were thinking," he said, knowingly. "But since you mentioned it, we should be there in about an hour."

"Good, because I need the bathroom. I mean, toilet."

"I can pull over, and you can—"

"No thanks," she interrupted, holding up a hand. "I'll wait."

He laughed. "You won't pee in the bushes, you don't eat meat, and you prefer to bathe indoors. Something tells me you were too sheltered in your big city life."

Yes, she enjoyed a pescatarian lifestyle for health reasons. Sure, she preferred a nice, hot shower. And no, she didn't want to take the chance of peeing in a bush with poison ivy. That happened to her once as a kid. And once was enough for *that*, thank you very much.

"My lifestyle was...different." She didn't want to talk too much about the past in case she revealed something she would later have to cover up.

"I'm curious," he said, reins taut, resting his elbows on his knees. "You and Grey are both from New York City. Ever hear of him?"

She shook her head. "No."

His gaze remained on hers for a long, silent moment. "I guess you can't know everyone in a big city."

She shrugged. "It would be impossible, don't you think?"

"I guess so." He looked down at the basket between their feet. "Got any food left in there? I'm hungry."

Thankful for the change of subject, she picked up the basket and rummaged through. "There are two biscuits left. One for each of us." She handed him one and took the other.

"Thanks," he said, biting off a chunk. "When we get to Helena, we'll check in at the hotel. I'll drop the wagon off at the livery, and then we can go have a proper meal."

Her stomach rumbled in response to that. "Sounds great."

"So," he said between bites, "tell me about your life before Whisper Creek."

A chunk of biscuit wedged in her throat, she nearly choked. She hadn't expected that. *Think fast.* "There's not much to tell," she said with a shrug. "I was, um, married for a short time. My husband died. I wanted a change. And here I am." *Liar, liar, pants on fire.*

He leaned in close, eyeing her intently. "What was he like? Your husband."

She may not have actually had an ex- or late *husband*, but she did have an ex-fiance she could talk about instead. *Stick to the truth as much as possible.*

"At first, he was very...charming. Handsome. Smart. Sophisticated. He could work a room like I've never seen before." She gazed off into the distance, remembering when she first met Brandon. "He was a hedge fund—I mean, he was um, a banker. A successful one, too. We met at a party—I mean, a social. We dated—courted for a while, then got engaged."

"What happened?"

Without thinking, she rambled on. "He cheated on me with his surgically-altered liposuctioned-nipped-and-tucked colleague who looked like she walked out of a fashion magazine. He broke off our engagement so he could marry her a few months later," she said quietly, recalling the last moments with Brandon in her mind. "He said I wasn't *rich* enough for him. He wanted a *powerful* woman, someone who made a ton of money. Can you believe him?"

Wyatt stared at her. "I thought you said your husband was *dead*?"

Her throat tightened. *Shit.*

"It's all right," he continued before she could tell further lies. "I didn't buy your story about a dead husband, anyway." He ignored her look of surprise. "I don't blame you for the lie. Montana is a tough place to live. Man or woman, you really need to have your wits about you out here. Just make sure you keep your story straight for those you do tell. Your secret is safe with me," he added.

Pushing out a deep breath, she mumbled, "Thanks for understanding."

There was a brief silence before he asked, "What are *lie-po-suction* and nipped-tucked or whatever it was you said?"

She waved a hand. "Just stupid expressions from where I come from." He stared her down until she explained, "It basically means the woman looked and sounded too perfect to be real."

After a moment, he prodded, "Is there anything

else you want to tell me?"

"Nothing that I can think of." His intense gaze on her made her squirm as she stared at the road ahead. "At least, not until we get back from Helena."

"Fair enough," he said with a nod. "When you're ready to talk, I'll listen."

An hour later, they rode into downtown Helena. Emma wished she had her much-missed smartphone so she could take photos and videos of her trip to a time gone by. A thrill of excitement coursed through her, knowing no one else had *ever*—to her knowledge, anyway—traveled back in time.

That made her think. What precisely brought her *here* to this particular year? Okay, so she got a letter from her nineteenth-century self, but why did fate or the Universe—or whatever caused this—bring her here to *this* place in time? Just to rescue a husband and children she didn't have—or didn't see herself having in the next six months? Emma knew how to tug on her own heartstrings, and the idea of a husband and children would certainly do that.

But what if my letter is wrong? Could that even be possible? What, then?

"Emma?"

"Hmm?"

Wyatt watched her intently, then cocked his head toward the large brick structure on their right, the one with the sign that read in big lettering *Cosmopolitan Hotel*.

"We'll stay here," he told her. "I have to get the wagon settled first. If you want to wait here, I'll only be—"

She shook her head. "I'll come with you, if that's

135

all right."

"Of course." Wyatt steered the wagon down South Main and then toward the nearest livery stable where he left a deposit for two days' boarding. Since they only had one carpetbag each, they could easily carry those back to the hotel.

Emma marveled at the sights, the smells, and the sounds of this bourgeoning city, so different than a bustling metropolis of the twenty-first century. While no other city on the planet could ever compare to New York City, in her mind at least, Helena fascinated her in many ways.

The majority of buildings were made of cement and stood at least three or four stories high. Smaller buildings, sandwiched in between the larger ones, were similar to the ones in Whisper Creek with their false-fronts and wood sidewalks and second-story verandas.

It smelled earthy, like dirt, horses, and chimney smoke. The city, devoid of all futuristic noises such as car horns, trucks, and buses, rang instead with the clip-clop of horses and the clickety-clack of wagons jostling over the roads toward their destinations.

Men were dressed in either three-piece tailored suits, fashionable of the day, or the more casual shirt, vest, and pants with high leather boots. The women were garbed in lovely dresses with tight bodices and overskirts accentuating hourglass figures. Such a stark contrast to the twenty-first-century fashion of anything-goes.

After Wyatt checked them in, they went upstairs to the second floor, and he opened the door to their room. The mahogany bureau, dressing table, two upholstered wing chairs banking the fireplace, and one stiff-looking sofa didn't grab her attention. The huge oak bed with its burgundy bedding and pillows screamed of all the naughty things she and Wyatt could do in that bed.

"I hope you don't mind the white lie to the clerk," Wyatt said, closing the door. "I had to tell him we were married. He'd have a stroke if he thought you and I were shacking up—I mean, if we were sleeping in the same room and not married."

The idea of spending the next few days within arm's length of Wyatt sent delightful little shivers to all parts of her body. If they had been in the future, by now, they would be sharing the same bed and having amazing sex. Well, she hoped they'd be.

"You're overthinking this," Wyatt's voice interrupted her thoughts.

She turned to him. "What?"

"Look, if this is too much, I can sleep on the floor. It's okay."

She shook her head. "No, it's not that." She touched his arm, then withdrew, and changed the subject. "I'm hungry. Can we go eat, please?"

****

Both famished from the long ride, Emma and Wyatt enjoyed a hearty meal at a quaint café just north of the hotel. Afterward, they strolled arm-in-arm down Main Street, experiencing the sights. The thoroughfare itself bustled. But the dust rising from the street in the wake of horses and wagons kept them on the boarded sidewalks whenever possible.

"Wyatt, look!"

The little shop across the street with a large, striped canopy above the square window had the word *Chocolatier* painted in gold on the glass. It had been months since she'd had chocolate. Before heading to Montana, she and Amber used to venture to their favorite chocolatier in SoHo to get their weekly fix. It seemed like an eternity ago.

They crossed the street to the shop. As soon as the door opened, the inviting aroma of cocoa mixed with sugar greeted them; a fragrance sure to tempt any chocolate addict to eat everything in sight.

"Mmm." Emma inhaled deeply and smiled. "My happy place."

"I can see that."

Wyatt ordered a box of the best chocolates and a small bag of assorted sweets. The server gave one chocolate to Emma to sample, then boxed up the rest. She took a bite and savored the rich, smooth creaminess as it melted on her tongue. It tasted *almost* as good as her favorite chocolate back home.

"Better than the ones in Whisper Creek?" he whispered.

She nodded. "No comparison."

After a few minutes of chatting with the shopkeeper about chocolate, they took their purchases and left. Outside, Wyatt held out the box and lifted the lid. "Go on," he urged her." I know you're dying for another piece."

"Are you kidding? I could eat this entire box in a millisecond," she assured him, eyeing the different shapes of assorted chocolate.

"What's your favorite?"

"All of them," she said, finding it difficult to choose.

He laughed. "I'm sure you must have a favorite." He paused. "Would the lady mind if I selected her one?"

Emma glanced up and into his dancing, playful eyes. "The lady wouldn't mind at all."

He picked a dark chocolate and held it inches from her lips. *Hello, butterflies*! *Welcome back.* Her heart raced. Playfulness-turned-desire flickered in his eyes.

"Open your mouth," he told her in a hypnotic and velvety voice. He held the chocolate in front of her lips. Her heart gave a thud, thinking of another scenario when she wanted him to say that to her. *Don't go there*!

Slowly, she raised her head and opened her mouth, accepting the decadent morsel, letting it melt on her tongue. His fingers grazed her lips, but he didn't move away.

"Later, instead of this chocolate, it'll be my tongue in your mouth," he told her, his eyes shimmering with desire.

Dy-ing. She groaned inwardly. What if she just grabbed him and kissed him right there on the spot? She didn't know anyone in Helena. Neither did Wyatt. And so, what if they did kiss on the street? It's not like they were going to rip each other's clothes off and have sex in public.

She swallowed the last bite of chocolate and wiped the corners of her mouth in true ladylike fashion, then blurted out, "Kiss me."

Wyatt looked around then at her, his eyes incredulous. "What—*here*?"

She nodded, a seductive smile turning up the corners of her mouth. "Yes, *heeeere.*"

One eyebrow arched upward. "Now?"

Her chest heaved; her body burned. "Wyatt Kincaid, if you don't kiss me soon, I'm going to—"

Wyatt wrapped an arm around her waist and crushed her body to his. He pressed his lips to hers, tasting and teasing, before thrusting his tongue inside her mouth. Her arms slid up and around his neck. Despite the layers of material in her skirt, his hardness pressed against her, sending heat in her direction. He was every bit as delicious as she wanted him to be.

"Is that you, Wyatt?"

Their kiss ended abruptly.

Wyatt spun around, standing protectively in front of Emma. "Wilbert," he said, then cleared his throat.

Crap. Cassie's husband. Emma patted her hair and gently wiped the remains of Wyatt's kiss and the chocolate off her lips.

"What're you doing in Helena?" Wyatt asked, trying to sound casual. But his voice caught, and he had to clear his throat again.

Wilbert took a step to his right to see who was behind Wyatt. He doffed his hat. "Hello, Mrs. Cole. I thought that was you." He looked at Wyatt, a grin spread across his face. "I sure see why you hired her."

Emma bristled. This was the second time she'd heard a comment like *that*. Did all these men think Wyatt hired her just to satisfy his sexual desires?

Yes, because this is the nineteenth century. Better get used to it.

Wyatt linked his arm through hers while addressing Wilbert. "We're courting," he explained simply.

Wilbert's gaze traveled back and forth between them. "Congratulations! I can't wait to tell my Cassie. She's going to be thrilled to bits. She adores the two of you."

Emma didn't care what Cassie thought, just as long

as his wife didn't blab it to the entire town. Both she and Wyatt happened to be unmarried and living under the same roof. It would be cause for speculation and gossip. Something the two of them could do without.

"Considering our living arrangements, it's a bit awkward," Wyatt went on. "We'd appreciate it if you keep a lid on it—I mean, keep it quiet for a while."

Wilbert's gaze went from Wyatt to her then back again. "I can see why you'd want to keep this a secret." He elbowed Wyatt in the ribs with a tilt of his head toward Emma. "Best of both worlds, eh?"

"Now, you listen to me—" Emma began, but Wyatt pushed her back a few steps.

"Let me handle this. Go back to the hotel," he said quietly. "I'll meet you there."

"But—"

"Emma," he said in a stern voice. "Whisper Creek is backward compared to where you came from. I've got this."

Reluctantly, she nodded, then turned on her heel and marched back to the hotel, fuming the entire way. *Backward, indeed.*

****

The small clock on the mantelpiece chimed for the eighth time before Wyatt finally returned. Emma bounded out of the chair, rushing over to him.

"What happened?" She must've sounded like an anxious housewife, so she amended, "I mean, you were gone for so long. Is everything all right?"

He closed the door, removed his hat, and tossed it on the bed, then sat in the chair. The light from a nearby lantern gave Wyatt's skin a warm glow. He shoved a hand through his hair and pushed out a deep sigh before casting his eyes on her, extending a hand. "Come here."

Without hesitating, she took his hand, allowing him to pull her into his lap. He wrapped his arms around her, holding her close. She held him around his shoulders and kissed the side of his head.

She made a scrunchy face. "You smell like a distillery."

He chuckled. "I thought if I bought Wilbert's silence with the best booze in Helena, it'd help shut him up."

"Will it?" she prodded when he didn't continue.

He shrugged. "I guess we'll see when we get back to Whisper Creek. One thing's for certain, he *will* tell Cassie." His fingers made an invisible line from her jaw down to her neck. "They're married. There are no secrets in the marriage bed. It'll be up to her, whether she keeps quiet or not."

She'd had some time to ponder the situation while she waited for him to return. "I'm sure there have to be other couples who met under similar circumstances, right? Would it really be so terrible if people found out we're courting?"

He tilted his head back and smiled. "Darlin', it's not the courting that would be so terrible. It's that we're living under the same roof. You're *unmarried*. Widowed but unmarried. I'm unmarried, as is my brother. That's a whole different ballgame." He slid his hand up her back to rest on her neck, massaging it gently. "Things are complicated here. Old-fashioned, to say the least. I won't be responsible for emptying my gun into some self-righteous son of a bitch for starting gossip that'll sully your reputation."

She rolled her eyes but had to acknowledge this is

how things were done in the nineteenth century—a man standing up to protect a woman, *his* woman, and her reputation. It was gentlemanly. Chivalrous. Sweet.

But would she really be here long enough to care what others in town said or thought? Once she returned to her time, the chatter would stop. Wouldn't it? That is, *if* she returned. So far, she hadn't been able to figure out how.

"Where I come from, this wouldn't even be an issue," she told him.

"I understand," he allowed, squeezing her. "But for now, let's just try to keep your reputation from getting tainted. We don't need to create a scandal, all right?"

"Works for me," she said with a sigh. "Does Wilbert know where we're staying?"

"Nope," he replied. "I made sure of that. I took the long way back to the hotel, so even if he followed, he'd have lost me across town."

She wrapped her arms tighter around his neck and lowered her head. "Then, we have nothing to worry about, do we?" she said in a throaty whisper, her lips inches from his.

A smile tugged at his mouth. "I do like the way you think, my sweet," he said, then pressed a gentle kiss against her lips. "But we had a deal. We agreed to wait until we returned from Helena," he reminded her pointedly.

"Seriously?" she scoffed. She waved an arm toward the *huge* bed that beckoned them to take advantage of it. "I don't want to wait," she confessed.

His eyes swept over her seductively. "Emma," he groaned, caressing her cheek. "Believe me, I want you, like no one I've ever wanted before. And I know you want me, too, but—"

Shivers spread in all directions, not to mention a simmering flame that would soon ignite into an inferno. "Yes, I do want you. *Now*."

"Christ." He groaned again, wrapped his hand in her hair, and pulled her head down to his. Smothering her lips with demanding mastery, he urged them open with his tongue. The kiss sent shivers of endless bliss fluttering in her chest. She buried her hands in his thick hair. Had she not been sitting in his lap, her knees would've buckled by now. Her arms tightened; the kiss deepened.

Wyatt slipped a hand under her knees and carried her to the bed. She swallowed. Her grip around his neck tightened, reluctant to be separated from him; because right now, a few inches would be too far. She needed to be close, needed his arms around her.

"Emma," he whispered; his breathing was as ragged as hers.

Her heart hammered in her ears. *Don't you dare stop now, Wyatt Kincaid.*

"I've wanted you from the moment I first saw you," he told her in a hoarse whisper. He gently eased her onto the bed, covering her body with his own.

Her arms pulled him closer. "Why couldn't I have met you sooner?" she whispered, raggedly. *Like, in another century. Preferably the one I'm from.*

He smiled. "I'm here now."

"Mmm." She pulled him toward her for another toe-curling kiss. Her heart pounded. And her lady bits ignited like someone put a match to gasoline.

Just as she was about to unbutton his shirt to run her hands over the smooth, broad expanse of his chest, there came a pounding on the door. Startled—but even more frustrated—at the interruption, she snapped, "Are you kidding me?"

Wyatt emitted a groan, dropped his head on her chest, and shook his head. "Rotten timing, whoever it is." Then, he barked in the direction of the door, "Go away."

The pounding continued. Wyatt cursed under his breath. He helped Emma up. She straightened her clothes, then looked in the mirror. Her disheveled hair gave the impression she had just risen from bed—or the arms of her lover. And her lips looked like they'd had a thorough kissing.

Wyatt winked at her, then went to the door and demanded, "Who is it?"

"Kincaid?" came the question in response.

Wyatt's hand hovered over the hilt of the gun on his hip as he cracked the door open to peek at the intruder. She had forgotten about his revolver.

"What do you want?" he demanded.

"Are you Kincaid?" the male voice asked in a quieter tone.

"State your business before I blow your head off."

Emma's eyebrows shot up, having never heard Wyatt be so harsh before. The man mumbled something in response. Reluctantly, Wyatt stepped out into the hallway and closed the door behind him. She waited a moment, then crossed the room and pressed her ear to the door.

She listened closely, heard nothing, then paced barefoot across the carpet. Why did Wyatt have to leave? Did the two men know each other? No, Wyatt growled he'd shoot the man's head off if he didn't state his business. That didn't sound like Wyatt.

Then again, how well did she *know* Wyatt? Not that well. He said they should wait because there were *things* he wanted to tell her about his past. It never occurred to her before, but what *if* Wyatt wasn't who she thought? What if he turned out to be an outlaw or a criminal?

Get a grip, girl. That's not Wyatt.

The sound of a key in the door startled her. She grabbed a nearby lamp, ready to hurl it at the intruder.

"Wyatt!" she cried, relieved when he walked in. He closed the door, noticed her stance, and arched an eyebrow in question. She put the lamp down and ran over to him. "What happened? Who was that?"

"Nothing to be worried about, sweet." He waved a hand. "Someone thought I was Josh and yammered on too much," he told her simply.

She put her hands on her hips. "That's it?"

"That's it," was all he said.

She watched him for a moment, but he said nothing further. Instead, he wrapped his hands around her waist and gazed into her eyes.

"I'd like nothing more than to have my way with you tonight," he admitted. "But after that little interruption, I realize we need to be back at the house—where no one can interrupt us. And we can take it as *slow* or fast as we want."

Her pulse raced at the thought. "I like your way of thinking, cowboy."

Chapter Nine

Since they returned from Helena two days ago, Wyatt hadn't said a word. The topic of their lives prior to when they met hadn't even come up—nor had he kept his promise about having his way with her and taking it as slow or fast as they wanted. Not that Emma expected him to pounce on her the minute they walked through the door, but still. She had expected *something* by now. A kiss. A caress. Some fooling around. But nothing. Zip. Zero. Zilch.

She *wanted* Wyatt. And not just sexually either. He was *the* guy—her guy. Everything she wanted: charming, funny, handsome, brave. And based on their mutual attraction, it wouldn't be much longer before they ended up naked in each other's arms.

But the guilt of delaying the truth ate at her. What would he do when he found out she came from the future? Or worse…what if she didn't tell him the truth and she found a way back without getting the chance?

He'll think I just left, skipped town, or maybe left him for someone else.

She swallowed down the burn at the back of her throat. Wyatt didn't deserve that. She had two options. One: tell him the truth and risk having him think she lost her mind. Or two: not tell him anything and return to the future once she figured out how. That is, *if* she found the way. Neither option sat well with her.

Still, there had to be a reason she came to be in 1882. As much as she held off admitting it or doing anything about it, her main focus should be finding out *why*. And from there, maybe she could figure everything else out.

But what if I can't find a way back?

She shook her head. "I can't go there yet," she muttered.

"Ma'am."

A gentleman passerby gave her an odd smile, then tipped his hat as he continued down the street. Same with the next man who passed her. She gave a mental shrug, then continued her walk until she reached Anne's shop. The bell above the door clanged when she stepped inside.

"Good morning, Mrs. Cole," Mattie said with a bright smile, taking Emma's hat for safekeeping. "I'll let Mrs. Heughan know you're here."

The young girl disappeared into the back room. A moment later, Anne appeared and embraced Emma in a sisterly hug.

"I want *all* the details, my dear!" she whispered, clasping Emma's hands in hers and dragging her to the sofa in the back room. "Mattie?" she called out to the young assistant. "Please bring us *tea*—it's already set on the tray."

"Right away," came the response from the other side of the portiere.

Emma settled on the sofa and arranged her skirts. "Details of what?"

Anne leaned close and waved a hand. "Don't be obtuse. It's all over town how you and Wyatt are courting. Normally, I wouldn't believe such drivel, but

I've seen the two of you together," she added, knowingly.

"But how…?" She shook her head and concluded, "Wilbert."

Anne nodded. "Afraid so. Apparently, his wife has a flair for the dramatic and decided that it was *her* business to inform everyone in town you're courting your *employer*." Mattie appeared with the tray of tea and placed it on the table. "Thank you, Mattie," Anne said, handing her assistant a piece of paper with scribbling on it. "Would you please go to the post office to see if the new delivery of fabrics has arrived and then stop at the general store? Mr. Majors should have today's items ready for you."

"Yes, ma'am."

"Thank you, dear." Anne waited until Mattie left the shop before she continued, "I thought it best to talk while she's not here."

Emma shook her head. "Well, that would explain the odd glances I got walking over here," she stated, tilting her chin toward the front windows. It didn't matter what century she lived in; she hated gossips. People like that were just a bunch of busybodies who didn't have anything better to do than wag their tongues when they should be minding their own business.

Anne poured the pot of special *tea* and handed a cup to Emma, who took a much larger sip than what was considered ladylike. The amber liquid burned a trail from her throat to her empty stomach.

"It's not easy living in this town," Anne admitted, lifting the dainty cup to her lips. "Take it from one who knows."

"How long will something like this take to blow

over?" When Anne frowned at her expression, she clarified, "I mean, how long do you think it'll take before everyone forgets this?"

Anne took a sip. "Small towns have small minds, my dear. But they'll find something else to talk about soon enough, especially when a wedding is involved."

Emma's eyebrows shot up. "Whose?"

"Mine." She put the cup back on its saucer and placed it on the tray. "While you and your dashing employer were off in Helena for a few days, which I still want to hear *all* about, Jonas—Doc Wilson—asked me to marry him," she announced and extended her hand revealing the engagement ring, like any newly engaged woman would do.

"Oh, Anne, that's wonderful!" Emma beamed, admiring the beautiful ring. "Congratulations! I wish you both so much happiness." She embraced her friend in a hug. "When's the wedding?"

"Soon. We're just waiting for Jonas's brother to join us. He's been detained in Boston." She waved a hand. "Being a doctor runs in the family, and he's caring for his daughter at the moment who is having a terrible childbirth."

They talked for an hour uninterrupted before Mattie returned, carrying items from the general store. With her was a young boy holding the parcels of new fabrics. Anne checked the fabrics and gave instructions to Mattie on where to place them and what to make as a sample to show in the window.

That done, Emma and Anne decided to have a light lunch at the outdoor garden café where they could enjoy the warm sunny weather.

"They don't serve *tea* like I do," Anne whispered

with a roll of her eyes once they were seated. "But the food is very good."

Emma shook her head and laughed. Anne and her whiskey-tea. "I didn't even know this place was here," she admitted. Perhaps, because it sat off the main street at the end of Second Avenue.

The café had a colorful garden filled with tables and chairs for outdoor dining, weather permitting. Inside, the café itself looked cozy and very Victorian with its mahogany furnishings and papered walls. It would be nice if she could just wave a magic wand and take some of the nineteenth century back with her to the future.

"I have some news for you." Anne wiped the corners of her mouth with the napkin. "The other day, a customer came in from Butte. Lovely woman. Her husband is someone important at the railroad." She rubbed her temples, as if that would help her recall. "The name escapes me. However, the husband bought nearly your *entire* collection for her, and still, she wanted something more."

Emma's eyebrows shot up. "Really? That's incredible. I'm flattered."

Anne took a sip of tea. "If you ask me, I think you'll need to hire help soon; what with the new wealthy railroad men spending money to adorn their wives with gems and baubles." She paused. "What did Wyatt say when you told him about our partnership?"

She shook her head. "I, um, haven't told him yet."

Anne looked surprised. "Why on earth not?"

"I'm not quite sure." Emma traced an invisible circle on the tablecloth, contemplating her real reasoning. This happened to be secret number two she kept from Wyatt. And she was not the type of person who kept secrets from those she cared about.

"Are you afraid he won't approve?" Anne asked directly.

Emma looked at her squarely. "I don't care whether he approves or not, Anne. He's not my—" When she saw Anne's eyebrows lift, she amended, "I just mean since we aren't married, he really has no say in what I do. Besides, I came here…alone, I need to do this for *me*." She took a sip of the tea. "What does the good doctor say about *your* dress shop? Does he approve?"

Anne's face lit up. "Believe it or not, he does. Before Jonas even proposed, I made it clear I would never give up my business for anyone but myself, so I do understand you not telling Wyatt." She shrugged. "The thing is, I've been considering it. Giving up my shop, once we marry, that is."

Anne had an entrepreneurial spirit, like herself, so it came as a surprise to Emma. Not many respectable women owned a business in the nineteenth century, but Anne certainly paved the way for others.

"Really?"

Anne nodded. "I've been working since I was a child. My parents never had enough money, so they put me to work at an early age. Over the years, I saved up some extra money by tutoring and opened a small dress shop in Chicago. Once Ronnie—my first husband—and I married, he didn't force me to sell it. He said, 'If it makes you happy, why would I take away your happiness?' " She paused, and a sadness clouded her eyes. "We had no children to dote on, so I think, perhaps, he had regrets. Then once he died, I decided to move out here. Too many painful memories there."

Emma squeezed her hand. "Yet, you were able to find love again. The doc is a good man, from what little I know of him. And for him to steal your heart, he must be a gem."

Anne gushed. "Jonas has such a kind heart. He enjoys helping people very much. Apparently, the sight of blood and the like don't bother him." She made a face. "I, on the other hand, nearly swoon if I see an open wound."

"Good afternoon, ladies."

Griffin Grey doffed his hat as he approached their table. He looked handsome in a dark grey suit and polished shoes.

"Pleasure to see you again, Mrs. Cole." Then to Anne, "Ma'am. I don't believe I've had the pleasure of making your acquaintance."

Emma smiled politely. "Allow me. Mr. Griffin Grey, may I present Mrs. Anne Heughan, owner of the women's dress shop."

"Widowed and soon to be Mrs. Jonas Wilson," Anne added.

Griffin took Anne's hand. "A pleasure, ma'am." Then he turned to Emma. "You look as lovely as ever, if I may say."

Emma lowered her gaze. "That's very kind of you, Mr. Grey—"

"Griffin," he insisted.

Emma inclined her head and caught Anne out of the side of her eye, whose eyebrow shot up in question. "Is there something we can help you with?"

He looked around then back at Emma. "I hear there's an Independence Day town fair next week."

Anne glanced up at the clear blue sky. "This time, I do hope the weather holds out. Last year it rained for days. We had to postpone the celebration for nearly a week!"

"Well, with you two ladies present, your beauty will shine bright enough to keep the darkest storm clouds away."

Oh, puleeze. Emma wanted to gag.

"You're quite a charmer," she mumbled, rolling her eyes that only Anne could see.

Griffin smiled. "I look forward to seeing you at the fair, Mrs. Cole, where I shall ask you to dance," he told her. "Rain or shine. Ladies." He donned his hat, then left.

Anne watched him over her shoulder until he was out of sight. "I wonder what Wyatt will say to *that*. This Mr. Grey fancies you, my dear."

Emma shook her head and made a face. "I'm not interested."

"I should say not. Your every heartbeat is for Wyatt. One just has to look at you to know how you feel." She leaned close and whispered. "If you and Wyatt are going to court, I don't need to tell you you'll have to find a new place to live. And the sooner, the better, as the gossips' tongues are already wagging."

Emma frowned. "A new place to live?"

Anne thought for a moment, tapped Emma's hand. "You'll stay with me. There's plenty of room above the shop. Once Jonas and I are married, you'll have the place all to yourself. This will give you two the time to court properly without the gossips having a field day, not to mention time to tell Wyatt about our partnership if you so choose."

Emma bit her lower lip. "You've got a point there."

"Then it's settled."

****

Settled, my ass. Why did everyone in the nineteenth century have to be soooo stuffy? Emma couldn't care less what these people thought. But she reminded herself society had a different set of norms *in the nineteenth century* than those of the future.

She pushed out a deep breath. Anne was right, of course. Maybe she would talk to Wyatt about it tonight at dinner.

A sudden rap on the kitchen screen door grabbed her attention. She wiped her hands on the towel, glanced at the clock, then answered the door. "Sam," Emma said, pushing open the screen door.

"I'm lookin' for Wyatt," Sam said, doffing his hat. Dark stains and dirt covered his clothes in a messy pattern. A sign of a project in progress. "I'm a bit stuck with something in the house, and I was hoping he could lend a hand."

She stepped outside and cocked her head. "You'll find him in the barn workshop."

His brows furrowed. "I just came from there. Didn't see him." Sam shrugged. "Of course, maybe he just went to take a lea—pardon me. To, um, use the outhouse."

"Feel free to check. In the meantime, I'll see if he snuck by me while I was in the pantry." While Sam went outside, she searched the house. No sign of Wyatt. She went back outside to meet up with Sam.

"He's not here," he told her, nodding toward the privy.

"Well, wherever he is, he couldn't have gone far.

Maximus is here," she said, inclining her head. The horse grazed in the paddock, and alongside the barn sat the wagon.

"I'll check 'round the property," Sam said, calling after her.

"I'll look in the barn."

She spotted a leaf of sandpaper sitting on top of the new desk for Doc Wilson. Wyatt couldn't be far.

Sam shouted her name. She followed the sound of his voice until she found him around the far side of the barn, kneeling beside an unconscious Wyatt. A wave of panic filled her senses at the sight of him. Unmoving.

"What happened?" She dropped to the ground beside Wyatt and touched his face. He was warm.

"Found him just like that," Sam said with a nod, rubbing his face.

Emma grabbed Wyatt's wrist, searching for a pulse. Thankfully, he had one. And it was strong. *He'll be all right. He has to be*!

Sam was already running toward his horse. "I'll go fetch Doc Wilson and be right back."

"Wait!" she called after him. "Don't you think we should take him into town, so Doc can tend to him there?"

"We'd have to hitch up the wagon and, depending on what happened, the ride could further injure Wyatt. I ain't goin' to chance it." Sam hopped in the saddle, yanking the reins. "I'll get a wiggle on and be back with the doc, lickety split." Then he rode off at a breakneck pace, leaving her alone with an unconscious Wyatt.

Over the years, she had watched enough medical shows to think something—or someone—knocked Wyatt out. It could be either an internal medical issue or an external force that rendered him this way. He had a strong pulse—that was good. But he wasn't stirring—that was bad. He was breathing—that was good. But he wasn't conscious—that was bad.

"C'mon, Wyatt," she urged him, stroking both sides of his face. He still had some color in his cheeks, but he needed to regain consciousness. "Dammit, wake up. Don't you dare die on me. I still haven't told you about the future. *Wake up!*"

It took another minute, but finally he stirred. He groaned, and as if in slow motion, rolled over to his side, clutching his hands to his head. She rubbed his back and said soothingly, "You're going to be all right."

"Keep doing that, and I'll puke," he rasped out. Then a second later, he tossed the contents of his stomach onto the dirt, just missing her skirts by a few inches. She had a handkerchief stuffed up her sleeve and used it to wipe his forehead and mouth. He lay back with his head in her lap, eyes clenched shut.

"Do you remember what happened?" she asked softly.

He winced and touched his head. "Yeah. I blacked out."

Men. It's like pulling teeth. "Do you remember what happened *before* you blacked out?" she pressed gently. "Did you fall? Were you sick? Maybe it was your stomach—"

"No," he said, touching the side of his head and wincing again. "But whatever it was, I now have a lump the size of a baseball."

"Let me see." Very gingerly, she touched her fingers to the side of his head. He winced. "Sorry. Doc

Wilson should be here shortly."

He tried to sit up but couldn't. "Doc?"

She nodded. "Sam found you," she explained. "He rode into town to get him. They should be back in a few minutes. How bad does it hurt?"

"Like I got whacked in the head with a bat."

She cringed. "Sorry, dumb question."

He tried to smile. "It's okay. I just want the pain to stop."

"I'm sure the doc will have something to help with that."

"Christ, I hope so."

She watched him for a moment. "Do you want to try sitting up?"

He opened his eyes and glanced up at her, trying to smile. "I like this view right now. No need to change it."

Gently, she stroked his forehead, grazing her fingers over the top of his head, hoping the delicate touch would soothe him and not make him nauseous again. He hadn't asked her to stop yet, so that was good.

"Close your eyes," she said softly. "And try to remember what happened."

He inhaled deeply, closed his eyes, and blew out a slow, deep breath; then repeated the deep inhale and exhale a few times before speaking.

"I was in the barn working on Doc's new desk when I heard *you* call my name. At least, I thought it was you. When I came outside, you weren't there." He rubbed his eyes then touched the bump on his head. "Next thing I know, I'm lying here in your lap."

"Just rest." She continued to stroke his forehead in

what she hoped was a soothing manner, until Sam and Doc Wilson rode in fifteen minutes later.

Medical bag in hand, Doc jumped off his horse and rushed to Wyatt's side. He checked Wyatt's pulse, heartbeat, and the dilation of his eyes. "What's your name?"

Wyatt gave him an odd look through one half-opened eye. "Doc, I know who I am."

Doc nodded, but he was all business. "Then you won't mind humoring me, so I can be assured of that. What's your name, where do you live, and what's your birthday?"

Wyatt sighed, then replied slowly, "Wyatt Kincaid. Whisper Creek. May fourth. 1988."

Doc's eyebrows shot up. "Nineteen-eighty—what?"

Wyatt coughed. "I mean, 1850. My head's a bit muddled, to say the least."

Doc looked at Emma. "Did he say anything to you when he came to?"

She shook her head. "Judging by the size of the lump on his head, I'm guessing he has a concussion."

Doc Wilson transferred his gaze from Wyatt to her. "How is it that a housekeeper can diagnose a concussion?" He wasn't expecting a response as he checked Wyatt's head and eyes again. "All right, my friend, on your feet. Sam, give me a hand."

The two men stood on either side of Wyatt and took him by the arms to help him stand. When he got to his feet, he wobbled.

"Sam, get behind him just in case." Then to Wyatt, "I'm going to make you do a few things here, so I can see how badly you're injured. It might seem silly to you, but again, humor me." He paused. "Stand up straight, arms out to the side, and follow my movements. Do the same thing as I do."

Wyatt waved a hand. "Doc, I'm fine. It's just a bump."

"You've got a concussion," he concluded, glancing back at Emma. "I want to make sure it's nothing more. Now hush up and do as I say."

Wyatt copied the doc's movements: placing his fingertip to his nose, balancing on one foot, then the other, then visually following a series of hand movements Doc made close to Wyatt's face.

Once Doc Wilson affirmed Wyatt had nothing more than a concussion, the men helped Wyatt into the house and deposited him on his bed. They removed his clothes and tucked him in before Emma returned with a few extra pillows from Josh's room.

"You'll need plenty of rest now," Doc Wilson told him. "But I'm going to ask Mrs. Cole here to wake you every couple of hours to check on you. Make sure you're still alive." He glanced at Emma, who nodded. "And I don't want you giving her a hard time about it. Understand?"

"I'll do as the doctor ordered," he replied, his voice fading. "Scout's honor."

Doc looked confused at that last comment. However, he was satisfied with Wyatt's answer. He turned to Emma. "Mrs. Cole, may I speak with you privately?"

"Of course." She glanced at Wyatt then followed the doctor into the hallway, worried something else was wrong.

"Nothing to be alarmed about, my dear," he told

her, reading her mind. "I just want you to give him plenty of fluids and wake him up every two hours or so. It's a nasty bump, but he should be fine. After about twenty-four hours, let him sleep as long as he wants. But not until then."

"Who do you think did this?" she blurted out. Doc's eyebrows shot up. "A bump like that doesn't just happen from a fall. Someone struck him."

He folded his arms across his chest and rocked on his heels, thinking. "You'd make a fine investigator." He shrugged. "I don't know, but I'm going back to town to speak to the marshal." He squeezed her hand. "I'll come by in the morning to check on him."

She thanked both the doc and Sam for their assistance. Once they departed, Emma poured water into a pitcher and placed it beside the bed. She brought a glass to her patient.

Wyatt took a sip, then patted the mattress. "If you really want to help me, come lay down beside me. I'd rest much better if you were in my arms."

Considering his current state, not much would be happening between them in the bedroom tonight. But still, to be *sooooo* close to him…Just the idea sent her heart pounding and her core pulsing.

She tried to hide her smile as she said, "I'd be happy to."

Chapter Ten

People-watching happened to be an amusing pastime. And in Whisper Creek, it also happened to be quite entertaining. While the scantily clad ladies adorning the saloons didn't normally dress for work when out for a midday stroll, from time to time, Josh would see one of Madame Veronique's girls hustling her bustle back to the Copper Pan. Now, instead, he found amusement in the sight of a little toddler trying to get his mother's attention by grabbing her skirts with his candy-coated fingers.

He glanced over his shoulder at the deputy currently buried behind a stack of paperwork. Anything he said, even if entertaining, wouldn't be a welcome interruption, judging by the look of consternation on Allen's face.

Since arriving in Whisper Creek, Josh spent a lot of time with both the marshal and the deputy. They were wary of him at first, wondering why he wanted to assist in their unsolved cases. However, considering Josh's background as a lawyer with experience in the courtroom, they soon welcomed him into their inner circle. He had become their go-to man for legal advice and such.

After a few months and a few valuable recommendations, the marshal offered to make Josh a deputy. Josh assured him he would prefer to keep things the way they were unless it became absolutely necessary to be deputized. He didn't want to upset Deputy Allen by being the newcomer stepping on his toes. The marshal understood. And so, Josh became their confidant and advisor.

Steam from the coffee warmed his face as he swallowed the hot liquid. It tasted too bitter and nothing like the real coffee he made every morning back home. *Home.* He pushed out a deep breath. It would be a long time before he or Wyatt could go back there. If ever.

Outside the window, life went on as it should in a lively town holding the promise of soon becoming a city as big as Butte or Helena. With the railroad scheduled to arrive next year, that alone would make a tremendous impact on commerce. If he hadn't followed Wyatt all the way out here, he would've missed it. Not exactly the smartest thing he ever did, but he really had no choice. He needed to make sure his little brother was all right.

"Where's the marshal?"

Josh turned toward the door as Doc Wilson and Sam barged into the office.

Deputy Allen looked up from his mound of paperwork and cocked his head toward the direction of the street. "Makin' his rounds," he replied as he got up and rounded his desk. "What can I do for you, Doc?"

Doc looked directly at Josh. "It's your brother."

Josh's heart gave a hard thud against his chest.

Doc raised his hands. "He's all right. Took a spill, is all. He's got a nasty lump. Mrs. Cole is tending to him now."

"I came over to get Wyatt's help," Sam explained. "Found him lying there 'round the side of the barn. Out

163

cold."

"He's got a concussion," Doc explained. "But he'll be all right."

Josh rubbed his temples. "What the hell happened?"

"Wyatt doesn't recall," he went on. "But judging by the location of the lump, I'd say someone clocked him over the head."

"You just said he took a spill." He had a bad feeling. It had been gnawing at him since Grey appeared in town. But maybe even before that. "Did he hear anything? See anything?"

Both Sam and Doc shook their heads.

"He doesn't remember nothin', 'cept walkin' outside the barn," Sam explained.

Josh glanced at Doc. "You sure someone did this, and he didn't just—" He waved a hand, looking for the right words. "—fall or knock himself out by running into something?" Not that Wyatt had ever been that clumsy in his life, but anything was possible.

Doc shook his head. "I'm quite sure."

Josh bit down on the inside of his cheek. He couldn't go into it now with either the marshal or Sam. But there could possibly be one explanation as to who did this. He had to talk to Wyatt. But that could wait. Since Doc assured his brother wasn't dying and Emma tended him, he had time to do some digging.

"Thanks, Doc," Josh said, shaking the man's hand. "Appreciate you taking care of my little brother." He left the office and walked to the Copper Pan Saloon.

He stepped through the swinging oak doors, and a cloud of smoke greeted him. His eyes took a snapshot of the room. Nothing out of the ordinary for a Monday.

Most of the men seated at tables played cards; some perched at the bar, sipping either whiskey or beer. Over in the corner, he spotted two of Grey's men, Rosler and…what was the other guy's name? It would come to him. He mentally snapped his fingers. Daniels! He watched Rosler look around, then wipe the sweat off his forehead with a handkerchief before drinking his beer. Daniels leaned in to speak with him, and, judging by the animated way his hands moved, he tried explaining something.

Josh went to the bar and ordered a beer. The huge mirror hanging over the bar allowed him to watch everyone covertly. His gaze went from Grey's boys to men at the other tables, then back again.

"Rotgut," someone next to him ordered from the bartender wiping a glass with a clean dishrag.

Josh recognized the voice and turned to greet his neighbor. "Hey, Wilbert."

Once the bartender served the drink, Wilbert raised it in a silent salute, then tossed it back. He made a face then slammed the glass back onto the counter.

Josh shook his head. "How can you drink that stuff? It tastes like turpentine."

Wilbert nodded. "Sure does," he rasped out. It sounded like it burned his vocal cords out, too. He pounded his chest twice. "But a little nip now and then won't hurt."

"How's your missus?" Josh asked, making idle conversation. His gaze casually drifted back up to the mirror, focusing on Grey's lackeys.

"Makin' supper, I hope."

Josh took a long swig of beer. "Lots going on in town these days, eh?" he said, motioning to the

165

bartender for another beer. "New buildings, new people."

Wilbert looked at him with a shrug. "Guess you could say so."

"Lots of changes coming," he went on. "With the railroad arriving here next year, I mean."

Wilbert nodded. "My Cassie wants me to work for the railroad, but...well, I'd rather work at the mine. I don't know nothin' about railroadin' work. She says there's more money in it, though."

Josh nodded. "She's right. Once the railroad comes, commerce will take a new direction, opening up numerous jobs in trades you'd never dreamed existed."

Wilbert stared at him, skeptical. "You sound so sure."

Josh glanced up at the mirror again. Rosler and Daniels got up to leave.

"Be right back," he said to Wilbert, then made his way toward the back of the saloon. He reached the men just as Rosler turned around and plowed right into Josh.

The younger man tilted his head up to see Josh's face. "Terribly sorry." Rosler's face turned red and beaded with sweat. "Oh, it's you, Mr. Kincaid. Good afternoon."

"Afternoon," Josh said, then gave a nod to Daniels. "Plans for the new building coming along all right?"

Daniels nodded. "Right as the mail."

"Speaking of that." Rosler glanced at his pocket watch. "We must be on our way. We can't be late. Mr. Grey hates to be kept waiting."

Josh nodded and caught a glimpse of the large clock on the opposite wall. Almost four o'clock.

"Please tell your brother, we look forward to seeing

him tomorrow," Rosler added, backing away quickly.

"Yeah. About that," Josh said, reaching for his arm. "It might be a few days before you see Wyatt again."

Daniels looked from Josh to Rosler then back again. "He's contracted to—"

Josh waved a hand. "Yes, I know what he's contracted for. But he had a…minor accident."

Rosler's brows furrowed. "What happened?"

Josh glanced from Rosler to Daniels. He didn't want to alert anyone to his suspicions, so he kept it vague. "He slipped in the barn and hit his head when he fell." Off their surprised looks, he continued, "Don't worry, he'll be all right. Doc Wilson says he just needs some rest. In the meantime, I'll be taking his place until he's back on his feet. That way, business will continue."

Both men exchanged a glance. "We'll let Mr. Grey know," Rosler said. "Please tell your brother we wish him a speedy recovery. Excuse us."

Josh had been a lawyer for several years. He knew body language and how to detect lies. It didn't look like either of those men knew about Wyatt's whack to the head.

****

Emma returned to the kitchen to clean the pots and pans used to prepare broth for her patient. She checked the clock on the wall. Hopefully, Wyatt would be sleeping until she poked him in another hour. Without her smartphone to set a timer or an alarm clock at her fingertips, it would be a long night. She wouldn't allow herself to sleep. It was necessary to wake Wyatt up every two hours as the doctor ordered. Wyatt had

167

several clocks in the house, but none of them had an alarm. Did they even have alarm clocks in 1882?

Two cups of strong tea were more than enough. She switched to wine. One glass would do. Sitting back, she closed her eyes and sipped the burgundy liquid, welcoming its warmth and heady feeling. The night had grown chilly, so she made a small fire in the parlor. Between the heat and the wine, she wanted to stay curled up on the sofa all night. But she had a patient to tend to.

She was glad Josh hadn't returned. His absence gave her more alone time with Wyatt. And there was no telling how much longer that would last. Once she found a way back to her own time...

It's been weeks now, and if I'm being honest, I really haven't bothered to look. Maybe part of me wants to stay here.

Stay here?

Wanting and doing are two different things. She didn't belong in the nineteenth century. Yes, it would be an experience of a lifetime—no one else had ever gone back in time.

But leave the future for good? Never return? She had a hard time wrapping her head around the possibility.

Then again, what if she gave up her quest of returning to the future so she could live out her days with Wyatt in Whisper Creek?

The clock on the mantel struck eight. Time to check on Wyatt. She banked the fire in the hearth before padding down the hallway to his room. Except for the lingering light of the sunset filtering in through the window, his room was dark.

She approached the bed and, for a moment, watched him sleep. He looked peaceful; she didn't want to wake him. She touched his forehead, then the side of his face. Thankfully, he didn't have a fever. Gently, she shook his shoulder. "Wyatt, wake up."

Slowly, his eyes fluttered open. He blinked a few times, looked at her, then closed his eyes again. "What is it?" he grunted.

"Are you all right?" she asked softly, touching his cheek again.

"I would be if you stop waking me," he grumbled, rubbing his eyes. "What time is it?"

"Two hours since the last time you asked." She watched him for a minute. "Do you remember where you are?"

He made a snorting noise. "Of course. I'm home."

"And where is home?"

"You're not the doc," he said testily. "But if it makes you happy, I'm in Whisper Creek. My name is Wyatt Earp, and I was born in—"

"You're Wyatt Earp now?" Emma dipped a washcloth into the small basin by his bed and squeezed out the cold water before gently pressing it against his forehead. "You better stop messing with me, cowboy."

Wyatt opened his eyes and gave her a wide grin. "Just kidding. Wyatt Matheson Kincaid at your service, my lady." He touched the bump on his head, then closed his eyes and took a long, deep breath. His features softened as he relaxed against the pillows. "Thank you, darlin'. I don't know what I would've done if you hadn't been here."

She frowned. Something he'd said struck her. "Did you say Matheson?"

He nodded. "Yep. Josh, James, and I all have the same middle name."

It had to be a coincidence, right? After all, the James Matheson she met lived in the twenty-first century. They couldn't possibly be related.

"Since I know Josh, tell me about James."

"Not much to tell," he mumbled through a loud yawn. "He's the oldest. Thirty-six. And a lawyer. Like Josh. A damn good one, too."

"Lawyer?" Goosebumps appeared on her flesh. The James Mattheson she knew in the future had the same profession as Wyatt's brother. *Okay, this is too weird.* But easily explainable. The James Matheson of *MATHESON & KINCAID* could definitely be a *descendent* of theirs.

"I'm the only one who didn't go into the family business," he continued, stifling a yawn. "In case you were wondering, I'm the black sheep," he added with a grin, then quickly drifted off to sleep.

She remained perched on the edge of the bed, her hand on Wyatt's leg, watching him sleep. A mild breeze blew in through the oversized windows, making the drapes dance in a soothing rhythm, lulling her senses. Having the same name could be just a coincidence, right? After all, they were centuries apart, so what did it matter? Maybe because there would be a tie to Wyatt in the future once—*if*—she returned.

His legs twitched suddenly, and his arms flailed, bringing her back to the present moment. He mumbled, but she couldn't quite make out the words. She bent over him and shook his shoulders. "Wyatt, wake up. *Wake up!*"

His face was bathed in a sheen of sweat. He sat up

quickly and winced. "What the—" He rubbed his eyes, looked around the dimly lit room, then focused on Emma. "Water, please," he rasped out.

She poured water from the pitcher into a small glass and pushed him back down on the bed, before pressing it to his lips. He took a few sips then lay back and closed his eyes. The small clock next to the bed ticked away in the silence.

"What's bothering you?" she asked.

"Just a weird dream."

"Want to tell me about it?"

He pushed out a deep breath, then a slow grin touched his lips. "I dreamed I went back in time, like, *centuries* back, and met the most beautiful woman I've ever seen in my life." His blue eyes impaled her.

The hair on the back of her neck stood up. Déjà vu? "You mean back to the…eighteenth or seventeenth century?"

"Something like that."

Odd that he would have a dream about traveling through time when she lived it firsthand. "How did you manage to go back in time?"

He shrugged. "I don't know. I was just…there."

Her eyes narrowed. "You were thrashing about. Can you recall what disturbed you?"

He frowned. "Someone was trying to…hurt you. Actually, they were trying to set the place on fire with you in it."

A flicker of apprehension spread through her. The letter she received from her nineteenth-century self specifically mentioned a fire. She swallowed with difficulty but found her voice. "Tell me about the fire—I mean, the dream."

171

He lifted a shoulder in a shrug. "It's only a dream, sweetheart. There's no need to worry." He reached for her hand and raised it to his lips for a warm kiss. "Come to bed. You promised me earlier you would. Or was I just imaging *that*?" One blond eyebrow arched in question.

"No, but you need your rest," she said firmly, trying to hide her smile and the warm flood flowing through her like lava. "Doctor's orders."

"I'd get more rest if you'd lay next to me."

She sighed, knowing he wouldn't give up on this. "All right. I will, but first, I need to do a few things around the house. I'll be back in time to wake you—" She glanced at the clock. "—at ten o'clock."

Satisfied with her answer, he closed his eyes, clasped his hands over his chest, and quickly drifted off to sleep.

With her patient off to dreamland for the next while, Emma gave herself permission to luxuriate in a lavender-infused bath. She marveled at how ingenious Wyatt could be. He had built his own house, with Josh's help, and installed a nineteenth-century bathroom with tub, toilet, and makeshift pipe system. She had no idea how all the mechanisms worked—or how he even came up with the idea. He would do well in any century, she thought.

After her bath, she slipped into a nightgown and matching robe, then grabbed a lamp and padded back into Wyatt's room, surprised to find him awake.

"It's about time," he grumbled, leaning up on one elbow and glancing from her to the clock. A playfulness shimmered in his eyes.

"It's not even ten," she argued, placing the lamp on

the table next to the bed. "I'm early."

He chuckled. "Felt like an eternity waiting for you to return." Then he held out his hand. His gaze slid downward from her eyes all the way to the tips of her toes, then back up to her face. "Come to bed."

Emma's stomach did all sorts of flips and whirls. She clutched the fabric of the robe closer, but the silky material did nothing to douse the simmering fire within. Licking her lips, she asked, "Are you hungry?"

A grin spread across his lips. "Indeed, my sweet. But not for food," he clarified.

Her insides rattled. The thought of them devouring each other with their hungry mouths danced through her mind. Body to body. Flesh on flesh. Skin on skin. She drew in a deep breath, trying to tamp down her bourgeoning desire. Wyatt had a concussion, she reminded herself, which meant, they couldn't let things get crazy. Not until Doc Wilson gave him the all-clear.

"Stop overthinking things and just come to bed." He lifted the blanket and scooted over, making room for her. "Nice robe. Take it off," he told her, wriggling his eyebrows.

Slowly, she untied the robe and let the soft material slip off her shoulders and down her body. Desire shimmered in Wyatt's eyes. He watched her every move. She placed the robe over the back of a nearby chair, then crawled in beside him. He tucked the blanket around her with one hand and pulled her close with his other. She listened to the strong thud of his heartbeat as she rested her head on his smooth bare chest.

"Isn't this much better?" he asked, stroking her arm in a soothing manner.

Better? Oh, hell yes. "Yes, but you need your rest."

"You smell incredible," he whispered, burying his nose into her hair, and rubbing his face against her.

Heat surged to her lady bits. She bit her lip. *This is torture—deliciously sweet torture. But you've got a concussion!*

Instead, she asked, "How's your head?"

He gently squeezed her. "Throbbing."

She tried to sit up, but he clasped her tight to him. "Do you want aspirin—I mean, laudanum or something?"

He gave her a throaty chuckle. "I wasn't talking about *that* head."

"What—oh, you rascal!" she said, and swatted him playfully.

"You asked," he teased.

Her hand slid up the front of his chest to rest on his shoulder. His smooth skin felt warm. Instinctively, she draped her right leg over his and was instantly aware of his nakedness. No pajama bottoms. No boxers—*did men wear boxers in the nineteenth century?* Nothing. Just bare flesh. All naked and yummy. She sucked in a deep breath. How would she remain this close without touching him…*there?*

Wyatt kicked the blanket aside and within an instant, covered her body with his own. He rested on his elbows, taking the weight off her, cradling her face between his hands.

Her heart pounded in her ears. She licked her lips and reminded him lamely, "You've got a concussion." As if *that* meant anything at this moment.

"I know."

"We shouldn't—"

"Emma," he whispered, gazing her into eyes. "No more waiting."

She swallowed, knowing it would be pointless to argue, especially when her body ached for his touch.

She wanted him.

He wanted her.

"No more waiting," she agreed.

He lowered his head to claim her mouth in a hot, hungry kiss, scorching her insides and sending new spirals of ecstasy through her. She slid her arms around him, clutching him closer. Through the thin gauzy material of her nightgown, every hard inch of his throbbing desire and perfectly sculpted muscles taunted her.

He groaned against her lips. His hand seared a path down her abdomen and onto her thigh, resting there only temporarily. A rhythmic pulse throbbed between her legs, causing her breath to come in short bursts. Impatiently, he hiked her nightgown up to her waist and pressed himself even closer to where she burned the hottest. He tore his lips from hers to trail kisses down her neck, her shoulders. His masterful tongue elicited shivers to every fiber of her being.

Wyatt kicked back the covers, then pulled her gown off so she lay completely naked beneath his gaze.

Emma bit her bottom lip, watching his eyes travel up and down the length of her, his hands following the trail his gaze left. Everything inside her screamed his name. How she wanted him inside her. *Now*.

"Patience," he whispered.

He reclaimed her lips, crushing his body on top of hers. Flesh on flesh. Their skin, slick with desire. Totally aroused now, she clasped his head tighter to deepen the kiss. Shivers of delight tingled everywhere in her body. His hand roamed intimately over her breasts, teasing the buds to form hard, little peaks between his fingers. Their tongues meshed and melded, taking and giving, demanding and passionate. She wanted the kiss to last forever.

His mouth left hers to watch his fingers gently outline the circle of her breasts. His tongue followed, caressing her sensitive swollen nipples. She arched her back, curling into the curve of his solid body. As he nipped and teased, attending one nipple then the other, her fingers bit into his shoulders.

"Wyatt," she pleaded, tossing her head back and forth.

"Mmmm." He suckled hungrily on one breast while caressing and molding the other with a skilled hand. Her fingers tugged his hair. He lifted his head briefly, only to have his tongue lick its way down to her ribs to her stomach. His hands searched for pleasure points and quickly found them. She gripped his shoulders, digging her nails into his flesh.

Wyatt kissed her lower and lower still, teasing her—gently, slowly. In her impatience to have him inside of her, she pushed his hands away, but he remained steady in pleasuring her. His expert touch sent her to even higher levels of bliss. He worked his magic with his tongue, exploring and probing into her warmth until a searing white heat, like the brightest lightning, spread throughout her veins, racking her body with tremors of delight. She called out his name and clutched his massive shoulders, finding her sweet but violent release that left her breathless.

He ran his fingers gently over the hollow of her

belly, then planted a gentle kiss on her lips. "Liked that, did you?" His voice was dark, husky velvet.

"Mmm-hmm," was all she could moan in response. Her mind and limbs turned into complete mush. She gazed into those blue orbs, cradling his face between her hands. "I want to do that to you." Then she pulled his lips into a deep kiss, raking her teeth over his bottom lip, and wrapped her legs around his middle, pulling him closer.

"Next time," he told her, then without notice, slid his hardness inside her in one swift motion.

She hadn't been expecting *that* and eagerly welcomed him into her body. How she had fantasized about this moment, this night since she met him...Every kiss, every taste, every emotion was better than she could imagine.

He lifted her thigh, giving him fuller access, driving into the depth of her. She wrapped her arms and legs around him and met each and every one of his fervent thrusts. Together, they found the tempo that bound their bodies together, soaring higher until the peak of delight was reached, exploding in a downpour of fiery sensations.

Chapter Eleven

Emma would've preferred to stay in bed with Wyatt. She couldn't get enough of him. And for someone with a concussion, he operated in marathon mode. During the wee hours, as they lay entwined, fully sated for the umpteenth time, his fingers caressing her body, it hit her—she had fallen in love with Wyatt Kincaid. The notion gripped her heart, squeezing tight. Now she would never be able to let him go…

Or return to the future without him.

The idea of leaving Wyatt behind in the nineteenth century while she returned to her life in the future didn't sit well with her. She debated what to do. Should she ask him to go? Given the choice, would he even *want* to?

There's only one way to find out. He needs to know what he's getting himself into. I have to tell him the truth.

It didn't matter if he ended up thinking she lost her mind; he deserved the truth. Maybe not this minute, but sometime today.

She stretched and sighed contentedly, then opened her eyes to check on her patient. What she found instead made her shriek and clutch the blankets under her chin.

Josh leaned against the doorframe with his arms folded across his chest, feet crossed at the ankles. He tilted his head, his gaze intently on Emma. "So, this is how you nurse my brother back to health," he teased.

An unwelcome blush crept into her cheeks. Her face burned. Josh was only teasing, but still. "I, um…" she trailed off.

Wyatt stirred at last. He rubbed his eyes, then focused one squinty eye on Josh. "What are you doing here at this ungodly hour?" he demanded, his voice rough and sleepy.

Josh's eyebrows shot up. "Ungodly—Bro, it's nearly *ten*."

Wyatt glanced at the small clock near the bed, squinting slightly. "So, it is."

Emma wanted to get up and dressed, but she and Wyatt were completely naked. She sank even further back against the solid safety of Wyatt's body. He pressed a kiss to her head and poked her ribs, making her squirm and giggle.

"Judging by the looks of things," Josh went on, "I'd say you're feeling *much* better, little brother."

Wyatt grinned. "Like a new man."

Josh chuckled and shook his head. "You may want to get dressed," he told Emma. "I figured I'd do you the favor of seeing me first instead of having Doc Wilson barge in on you two. He's here to check on Wyatt."

"Very kind of you," she allowed, suddenly feeling like a teenager caught hiding her boyfriend in her bedroom. *Wait*? How did Josh know they would be sleeping in the *same* bed?

Josh gave her that all-knowing grin, then turned and left the room.

She glared at Wyatt. Amusement flickered in his eyes. "You're just relishing this, aren't you?" she demanded.

"Yep." He reached out and clasped a hand behind her head to pull her in close for a soft morning kiss. "Get dressed, and then send the doc in. Don't worry, Josh won't say anything to him about how you took advantage of a sick man," he teased.

"If you didn't already have one lump on your head, I'd clobber you myself." She gave him a playful swat, then slipped into her nightgown and robe. "I'll make breakfast." She bent over to press a kiss to his lips before heading for the door.

"Emma?"

She turned around and waited for him to say something. Instead, he shook his head. "Never mind. It can wait."

What couldn't wait any longer was telling him she came from the twenty-first century. Just the thought caused a whirl of anxiety. What would he say to that? What would he *think*?

She nodded, then said, "When you're feeling better, there's something I'd like to share with you."

He gave her a curious look but nodded. "Sure."

She pushed out a deep breath, then padded down the hallway. Josh had already put on a pot of coffee; the aroma greeted her as she stepped into the kitchen. He and Doc Wilson were seated at the table, laughing about something.

"Good morning, gentlemen," she said politely.

"Mornin'," Doc said, rising from his chair, keeping his gaze averted. His face suddenly went to a deep shade of red. "Pardon me while I go check on my patient," he announced, then left the room. Quickly.

Emma watched him go, then looked at Josh.

"What's with him?"

"Your, um, *dishabille*," Josh indicated with a wave of his hand.

"Riiiight." Because in any century, housekeepers didn't greet morning houseguests in their robes. "Sorry. I forgot. I'll be right back."

Emma ran to her room. She quickly changed into a skirt and blouse and tied her hair back in a low ponytail before stopping in the bathroom to brush her teeth. Within moments, she returned to the kitchen to find Josh pouring coffee.

"I've never seen my brother like this before," he told her, handing her a mug.

She nodded, glancing back in the direction of Wyatt's room. "I know how worried you must be. I am, too, but Doc says—"

He waved a hand. "Not about his injury." He paused, his eyes on her. "He's crazy about you."

Her stomach did lots of swirly whirls. She didn't think men spoke to each other about their feelings for women—in *any* century, so this was warming to hear. But she had to play it cool. "Oh?"

He rolled his eyes, then sat down. "Don't give me *oh*. You were both in the same bed, not to mention naked, and in each other's arms this morning," he said pointedly.

A slow burn crept into her cheeks. "Well, the feeling is quite mutual, I assure you."

"I sure as hell hope so." He leaned back in the chair, assessing her as he sipped his coffee, then asked, "So, what are you going to do?"

She looked at him, confused. "About what?"

"Now that you and Wyatt are an item, are you

going to stay in Whisper Creek or go back…to New York?" he asked.

The look he gave her, not to mention the tone of his voice, implied he somehow *knew* the truth—*her* truth. About the future. But how could he know *where* she really came from? She hadn't even told Wyatt. Maybe it was just her imagination.

"If Wyatt ever kicks me out of the house," she began, "I guess, then maybe I'd go back."

"That's not likely to ever happen, and you know it." He leaned on the table, cupping the mug in his hands, his gaze steady. "Just do me one favor. As my friend. If there's the slightest chance you won't be…*staying* here, you'll tell Wyatt sooner than later."

She swallowed. "Of course."

"Thank you."

"Am I interrupting anything?" Wyatt strode into the kitchen wearing a pair of snug-fitting fawn-colored breeches and a twill shirt he hadn't bothered to tuck in.

Doc pulled out a chair from the table and helped Wyatt ease into it. For someone recovering from a concussion—not to mention an endless night of mattress dancing—he looked exceptionally healthy. Even his color had returned.

"Not at all," Josh replied. He glanced at Doc Wilson. "What's the verdict, Doc? Is my little brother going to live?"

"For a very long time, I assure you," Doc replied, squeezing Wyatt's shoulder. "One more day of rest, and then he can be about his business." He looked at Emma. "Make sure he doesn't overdo it. No heavy lifting or manual labor until he can stand without swaying."

"Swaying?" Wyatt grumbled with a wave of his

hand. "You don't know what you're talking about."

"Doctor's orders," Doc told his stubborn patient.

"I promise to keep an eye on him," Emma assured him, giving Wyatt a subtle glare. "And I promise to give you a full report."

"That could be scandalous," Wyatt murmured. Then he poked Emma. "I thought you said you were making breakfast?"

She whirled around to the stove then back again. "Who's hungry?"

"Already ate," Doc said, holding up a hand. "Thank you, though. Besides, I best be getting back to the office," he added, grabbing his hat off the peg by the door.

Josh tossed down the rest of the coffee then placed the mug on the counter. "I'll be on my way, too." He turned to Wyatt. "I promised Sam I'd help him since you're still milking all the attention," he taunted.

Wyatt shook his head. "Hell, since when do I ever take a sick day? You could at least let me enjoy it."

Emma and Josh both rolled their eyes. She waited until he and the doc left then started breakfast, which consisted of eggs, sautéed vegetables, and toast. Before she could plate them, Wyatt's strong arms slipped around her waist. He nuzzled her neck, rubbing his whiskered face against her skin, making her squirm.

"Good morning, beautiful," he whispered. Just that little bit of hot breath on her ear sent shivers of delight all through her body. Heat pulsated in her core. He spun her around to face him.

"Good morning," she replied, locking her hands around his neck. "Feeling better?"

"I'd like to show you just how much better." Then

he claimed her lips in a fervent kiss that curled her toes and left her heart pounding.

"Wow," she said, licking her lips. "Judging by *that* kiss, I'd say you're on the road to a full recovery, Mr. Kincaid. But maybe you better kiss me again. Just so I can make a thorough evaluation."

"Oh, I'll kiss you all right." He scooped her up in his arms and walked out of the kitchen and down the hall. "In fact, I'll do more than kiss you."

Tingles and delicious tremors erupted. "Doc said no heavy lifting!" she reminded him. "Put me down."

"Right. Like *you're* heavy."

When they reached his room, he put her down in front of the bed. She reached up to gently check the bump on his head. The swelling had gone down considerably.

"How's your head?"

"Just a mild headache now," he assured her, deftly unbuttoning her blouse. "Nothing for you to worry about, I assure you." He pushed it off her shoulders, letting it fall to the floor, so she stood there in only her bra.

In her haste to dress, she had slipped into her bra— not the usual undergarments of this century—since it was the only thing she could find in a hurry. He looked at it but didn't question her, then smirked and reached around to unclasp it, slowly sliding it down her arms. That, too, got tossed aside. She unbuttoned her skirt and shimmied out of it, letting her clothes pool around her feet. Her skin tingled now that she stood completely naked.

She reached out to help him remove his shirt and pants, but he shoved her hands away, swiftly removing them himself until he stood equally as naked. Warmth engulfed her. Everything inside her burned. Damn, he was incredibly handsome. Corded muscles on every inch of him. Muscular thighs. Six-pack abs. Well-defined arms. Full lips that gave her the sweetest kisses. And the bluest eyes she'd ever seen. Inside, she melted a little every time she looked at him.

"What are you thinking?" he asked, running his hands up and down her arms. The soft breeze from the window caressed her skin, sending goosebumps everywhere. One of his hands slid up her side to cup her breast, gently tweaking her nipple until it hardened. She took a step closer and slid her hands up the broad expanse of his chest.

"I was thinking…how much I want you…inside me." She licked her lips, then pulled him closer and pressed her mouth up to his.

His arms tightened, clutching her against his solid body. "What a coincidence," he whispered between kisses. "I'm thinking the very same thing."

He collected her in his arms and laid her gently on the bed. She wrapped her arms around his middle and grasped his buttocks. Within seconds, he was deep inside her.

****

How difficult could it possibly be to find one tiny portal through time? Apparently, next to impossible. Emma pushed out a deep breath and traced her steps around the barn for the hundredth time. A part of her *needed* to find the time portal to prove to Wyatt she wasn't crazy. That, or…

Find it only to walk through it and go back to the twenty-first century *without* him.

A chill swept over her. No, she wouldn't leave without telling Wyatt the truth. She owed it to him, especially now.

Unfortunately, telling him might be something outside the realm of her control. After all, when she found the portal the first time, it transported her instantaneously. Who's to say that wouldn't happen again? If it did, she'd never get to tell Wyatt the truth.

Ironic. The one time in her life she manages to find *the guy,* and the only thing that could keep them apart would be time. *Not fair.*

Emma pushed out a deep breath and leaned against the doorway, kicking the stray pieces of hay at her feet. The longer she delayed telling Wyatt the truth, the harder it would be for her to leave when the time came. She had to be completely honest with him. How else could a strong foundation be built in a relationship if honesty wasn't part of it?

Seriously, what sort of relationship do I plan to have with him if I go back to the future and leave him trailing in nineteenth-century dust?

Okay. So, she still had to work out all the details. If—*when*—she found a way back, maybe he would go with her. *If* they could travel together at the same time, why not? But she had no way of knowing if that was even possible.

Yet.

She sighed. *No, Wyatt belongs here, in the nineteenth century with his brother and the life he built for himself.* He wouldn't survive in the twenty-first century. People from his time hadn't even *seen* an automobile. She couldn't imagine having to explain airplanes, rockets, and space stations—not to mention everyday technology like cell phones, computers, and TVs. The world Wyatt knew would be gone, except in history books. It would be next to impossible for someone to adapt to moving forward in time by *two* centuries. Going backward was much easier, or so she thought.

Wyatt came up behind her and wrapped his arms around her waist, resting his chin on her shoulder. "Penny for your thoughts." He turned her around to face him, then kissed her gently on the lips. "You've got something on your mind. What is it?"

It's now or never.

She moved out of his arms to pace, wracking her brain for the right words and wringing her hands.

"What I'm about to tell you is probably going to sound completely and utterly bonkers. I mean, irrational, to you," she began, waving her hands to accentuate her words, "not to mention the most bizarre thing you've ever heard in your life, so please bear with me."

"Take all the time you need," he said.

"Okay, here goes." She pushed out a deep breath, tears threatening to sting the backs of her eyes. She blinked several times, hoping she could get the words out without changing her mind. "It has to do with…how I got here. To Whisper Creek. I mean, on your property. That day."

He waved a hand. "Go on."

She sucked in a deep breath. "I'm not sure how it happened or *why*, for that matter. But when I entered the barn"—*shit, this is going to sound crazy*—"I was in the *twenty-first* century, and the barn wasn't a barn. It was a different type of building altogether," she explained, waving both hands for emphasis. "I then heard what sounded like a car crash—I mean, an accident, a collision, with two large vehicles—do you even know what a vehicle is? Two large tractors, let's say. Oh, geez, if you don't have engines, then you don't have tractors. Anyway, the next thing I know, I'm standing in front of your *barn* in the *nineteenth* century." She shook her head and threw up her hands. "There must be some kind of time portal or doorway to the past on your property, it's the only explanation I can think of."

She faced him, waiting for the barrage of questions or a look of utter disbelief. Neither came.

"It sounds ridiculous, Wyatt, I know," she rambled on. "But it's the truth. One minute, I was in my own time, the twenty-first century; then the next, I'm here. In 1882!"

Still, he said nothing.

"You saw how I was dressed when I got here. Surely, you must've thought *something* wasn't right." No response. "Wyatt! *I'm from the future*," she stressed, stomping a foot with each word for emphasis.

Silence.

"C'mon, doesn't all this sound *ridiculous*? For chrissake, we're talking time travel here!" Still silence on his part. "Damn it, you thick-headed cowboy, do you understand what I'm telling you?" She waited. But he sat there, looking as calm as ever. "Say *something*!" she demanded.

He shoved a hand through his hair then rubbed his face, pushing away from the doorframe. For a moment, he paced, then stood in front of her.

She clenched her eyes. *Here it comes. Please just*

don't tell me you think I'm insane.

"Let me ask you something, Emma." He paused. "Do you want to stay here?"

She threw her hands up in the air, frustrated. "Didn't you hear what I just said?"

"Loud and clear," he assured her. "Now, answer me. Do you want to stay *here*? And I don't just mean in Whisper Creek. I mean, the nineteenth century."

"Wyatt—" She stopped, confused suddenly.

In two steps, he walked over to her and took her hands in his, kissing each one. "I have listened and heard every word you said, Emma. And, believe me, I do understand what you're telling me." He paused. "And the reason I understand is because there are...*others* who arrived here just as you, somehow falling through time, unsure of how they got here."

She stared wordlessly at him, her mouth gaping open.

"It's true," he said with a nod.

This unforeseen yet stirring news caused the words to catch in her throat. "H-how can that be?"

He shrugged. "I don't know how, just as I don't know how you got here, either. But I do know there's a part of you wanting to find the fastest way home, to get back to your life there." His voice softened. "But there's also part of you that wants to *stay* here and experience history firsthand, to see if you could be happy and live out the rest of your days here. Am I right?"

She nodded. "How—?"

He shrugged. "Like I said, others arrived here just as you. Mind you, it's not a known fact around town. Most people would think it's some kind of magic or witchcraft—or who knows what else. Only a select few know of this, so we need to keep their—and your—secret under wraps."

Something finally clicked in her mind. "Then you believe me?"

His lips spread into a slow smile as he squeezed her hands. "Yes, I do." He touched her cheek. "So, what do you plan to do? Do you want to stay here or…go back?"

Her heart said, *Stay here. With you. Forever.*

Instead, she said…

Nothing.

Wyatt grabbed her arm. "Emma," he said firmly, pulling her up against the length of him. "Do you want to stay here? In the past. With *me*."

Damn him. Of course, she wanted to stay with him. But she didn't belong in the past, in centuries gone by—just as he didn't belong in the future with her.

"Do you want *me*?"

She gazed into his eyes and nodded. "Of course, I want you."

"Then choose me. Stay with me."

Chapter Twelve

Early morning and Main Street already hummed with excitement while community members set up their goods around the square in a choreographed process for the annual Independence Day celebration. Considering there wasn't a cloud in the sky, festivities would most likely continue well into the night, unlike the previous year when it rained for nearly a week straight. People who lived miles away pitched tents on the outskirts of town just to partake of the merriments. Only once a year did Whisper Creek put on a grand bash like this one, complete with parade and fireworks. No one wanted to miss it.

Wyatt stood in front of Town Hall, shoved his hands in his pockets, and kicked a few pebbles at his feet. He pushed out a deep breath recalling the conversation he'd had a week ago about Emma arriving from the future. More pointedly, the part about her choosing him and staying put in Whisper Creek. But the subject hadn't come up again. Mainly because he hadn't broached it. He feared she would choose going back to her own time over him.

Thankfully, she wanted him as much as he wanted her. He could feel it in her touch, see it in her eyes when she gazed at him. Theirs being a budding new relationship, he couldn't be certain if what they felt for each other would be strong enough to stop her from returning to her future life.

And, damn, he wanted to know all the details about that life of hers—how she grew up, and when, and where she went to school, her first crush, that sort of thing. But how could he ask the questions when he feared bringing it up? He couldn't be sure, but maybe she planned to leave as soon as she found out how. And getting close to him would only get in the way of that.

Shit. He hadn't thought of that until just now. He definitely didn't want her to leave. He wanted her to stay with him. She had only been in his life a few months, but if she decided to go, it would be unbearable.

Maybe if they could figure out *how* the portal worked, they'd have all the time in the world. They would be able to come and go as they pleased, traveling from one century to another, having the best of both worlds.

Somehow, he doubted the gods of fate would be *that* generous. No one could be so lucky. He'd been around long enough to know someone would have to make a sacrifice.

"Wyatt, good to see you." Wilbert cuffed him on the sleeve.

Wyatt had been so deep in thought; he hardly heard his name. He shook Wilbert's hand and glanced up at the sky. "Good day for a fair, isn't it?"

Wilbert nodded. "My Cassie and the little ones are thrilled to bits that the sun is shinin' this time 'round. Although, the heat's a bit much." He doffed his hat, fanned himself, then nodded in the opposite direction toward one of the merchant tables where Cassie spotted them and waved. "Cassie's goin' to sell some of her pies. She won the Blue Ribbon last time, remember?"

Before Wyatt could say anything, Wilbert donned his hat and yammered on, "Heard you had an accident last week. Yet, here you are, lookin' right as the mail."

"Nothing more than a clumsy fall." He excused it with a wave of his hand. "How're things at the mine?"

Wilbert shrugged. "Grimy." He looked around, scouting the crowds. "Will Mrs. Cole be joining you today? Cassie's cotton to her. She's happy to have another woman livin' close by."

Wyatt removed his hat briefly to wipe his brow. The day would turn out to be a scorcher. "I'll be sure to tell her to stop by Cassie's table."

Wilbert smiled and shook Wyatt's hand again. "Much obliged."

After Wilbert left, Wyatt's thoughts drifted back to Emma. He'd be damned if he'd lose her to the twenty-first century without a fight.

With a determined stride, he walked to the marshal's office to find his brother. The only person he trusted to help him come up with a plan.

****

Emma spent most of the morning with Anne in the town square, helping her friend sell some merchandise. Since starting her own business back in the future, Emma knew a few tactics that could help Anne's business. She had recommended having a small selection of goods for sale, such as ready-made dresses, scarves, purses, and of course, jewelry.

By lunchtime, her stomach grumbled, and she decided to take a walk before sitting down for a light meal at the cafe. The exercise would do her some good, too.

There were times, like now, when she longed for twenty-first century fashion. Because on a ridiculously hot day like this one, she'd be wearing a short sundress with spaghetti straps, a sunhat, and flip-flops instead of a long-sleeved gingham dress with a fitted bodice that made her skin stick to the fabric. She contemplated having Anne make her a lighter summer dress similar to what she wore in the future, so she could stop sweating profusely, but that would only cause an uproar by the conservative men and women of this town. She had no doubt future fashion would be frowned upon in this century. Instead, she'd have to settle for something cool to drink in a shady spot.

Before she could reach her destination, someone called out to her, "Ma'am."

Emma turned, shielding her eyes from the blinding sun. Thanks to the lack of sunblock in this century, she already felt her face burn. *When was sunblock invented, anyway?* Not soon enough.

The man appeared to be about her age, give or take a year or two, if she had to guess, and a good head taller. His light brown suit looked much too fine a material for Whisper Creek. When he mopped his face with a handkerchief, she spotted what looked like a hint of a tattoo on his right wrist. Did tattoos exist in 1882?

"I apologize, ma'am," he said, stuffing the cloth into his pocket. "You look like someone I know." He paused, his smile fading. "I'm sorry to have bothered you."

Emma smiled. "No bother."

He nodded in response but didn't take his leave. "You'd think I'd lost my manners," he admitted, shuffling his feet. "I'm Carl Brody."

"Hello." She inclined her head. "Emma Cole."

His eyes widened for a flash of a second. And though she didn't extend her hand, he reached for it. "Pleasure, Miss Cole."

Pulling her hand away, she corrected him, "It's *Mrs*. Cole." She couldn't put her finger on it, but something about him didn't seem right.

Brody smiled, and after a quick glance around, turned back to her. "You live in Whisper Creek, I take it?" Before she could respond, he rambled on, "I'm in town to conduct a little business. Oh, and, for the festivities, of course." He looked down at his feet then back at her. "I don't know my way around. Would you happen to know where I could find Grey's Banking and Loan office?"

She pointed. "Right behind you."

He glanced at the building then back at her before mopping his face again. "Dang, it's hotter than the blazes."

"Understatement of the year," she mumbled. What she wouldn't give for five minutes of air-conditioning.

Brody dabbed away the sweat. The clothes didn't seem to match him. And something else, too. He didn't seem to fit the scene—of Whisper Creek, that is.

"By any chance, have you seen Mr. Grey?" he asked, then amended, "Perhaps I should first ask if you know Mr. Grey."

She knew Wyatt had a meeting with Grey that morning, though she couldn't be sure where. "Not personally, but I know of him, yes. I haven't seen him around today, though. If you don't catch him at the office, you're bound to run into him at the fair."

"Much obliged," he said with a nod.

"Good day," she said, then continued on her way until she reached the café.

She found a table under the cool canopy of a fragrant cherry tree, sat down, then pulled a small fan out of her reticule. Closing her eyes, she leaned back, enjoying the cool breeze. What a difference a little shade and fan made.

"Mind if I join you?" asked a familiar voice.

She opened her eyes and smiled. Her heart raced. "Of course."

Wyatt sat down across the table just as the waitress came to take their order. Within moments, water and wine arrived. Emma poured a glass of each, quickly drinking the water and poured another.

"Does it always get this hot here in the summer?" she asked, fanning herself again.

"Thirsty?" he asked when she emptied her second glass.

"Parched."

He smiled. "Not always," he said, back to her question. "Don't forget, we're in the mountains and the heat can be intense at times. And I doubt you're used to wearing layers of clothes in such heat."

"Got that right." She nodded, picked up her fan again. "How's Josh? I haven't seen him since your accident."

Wyatt waved a hand. "Fine. He's been helping Sam with a few things around his house."

"Why doesn't he come home—er, back to the house?"

He looked at her pointedly. "Because he wants us to have time to ourselves...*without* interruption."

Heat surged to her face; she worked the fan faster.

Why did she suddenly feel like a teenager? *Because I'm in love with him, duh.* "Oh."

No wonder her insides fluttered, her cheeks flushed, and fire spread between her legs whenever he was near. They were both attracted to each other, yes. But Emma knew their attraction went so much deeper. Since she landed in 1882, she had the distinct feeling as if she had been here before—*with* him. In his arms. In his bed. Living out her days in the nineteenth century. She loved Wyatt for his inner strength and character long before she ever tapped eyes on him.

"What are you thinking about?" he asked, breaking into her thoughts.

She put the fan on the table and stared at him. "It's been a week, Wyatt. You haven't asked me *anything* about—" She looked over her shoulders to make sure no one could eavesdrop. "—the future, how I got here, or anything else about it, for that matter. Don't you care?"

"Of course, I care." He leaned forward and lowered his voice. "It took you two months to tell me. You were probably afraid I'd laugh at you or think you were a witch or something." He paused. "I know you have other things you want to talk to me about and ask me. And when you're ready, I'll listen and answer. No pressure."

Why did he always say the right thing? The man had the patience of a saint, too. Damn it, how come life couldn't be fair? Here, she found the man of her dreams, only to have to lose him to the past when she'd return to the future.

If she returned.

Wyatt reached across the table for her hand, gently

tracing little circles in her palm. His eyes never left hers. The simple little motion sent her body into overdrive.

"There's something I want to share with you," he told her.

She squinted her eyes, analyzing his face. "I can't tell if that's good or bad."

"It's good," he said. "Tonight. All right?"

You suck for making me wait, she wanted to say, but refrained. Instead, she retorted, "What, so, you're just going to keep me in suspense until then?"

A slow smile curled his lips. "It'll be worth the wait. At least, I hope so."

"Ohhh," she said, feeling more warmth spread southward. "I see. It has to do with *that*." Heat tinged her cheeks.

He chuckled. "You have a one-track mind, Miss Cole," he teased.

She tossed her napkin at him. "You're the one that suggested it, Mr. Kincaid."

His left eyebrow arched questioningly. "I did no such thing. But I'll tell you what I'm going to do." He pulled her hand to his lips and placed a kiss in her palm. "I'm going to escort you around the fair today," he told her, then lowered his voice. "Have you in my arms at the dance later and then naked in my bed tonight. No suggestion about it. Consider it a promise."

"You're a rascal," she said with a shake of her head.

"And you love it."

She laughed. "Yes, I do. And I—"

I love you, she almost said, but bit her tongue.

****

Emma and Wyatt spent the rest of the day laughing, eating, and drinking their way through the fair. During the afternoon, a gentle breeze helped take the edge off the heat, but Emma still longed for a summer dress like the one hanging in her closet in the twenty-first century. Sometimes she felt stifled here—by clothes and culture. Even so, she wouldn't trade this experience for anything. Wyatt was here, after all.

After her second serving of punch, she excused herself and went to Anne's dress shop where she changed into a more appropriate dress for the dance to come that evening. It had been a scorcher of a day, and it felt nice to slip into something clean and light.

She walked out of the shop. The young gentleman she'd met earlier in the day stopped half-way up the steps to the boarded sidewalk, dangling his hat between his hands.

"Why, Mrs. Cole," Brody said. "You're looking mighty pretty."

She smiled, turning to leave. "Thank you, Mr. Brody."

He offered his elbow. "May I escort you to your destination?"

The men in the nineteenth century were chivalrous if nothing else.

"I'm not going far, just back to the square," she told him. "For the dance, you know."

"I'd be honored to walk you there."

After a moment of hesitation, she accepted, and they walked toward the square. "Were you able to conduct your business today?" she asked, making idle conversation.

"Yes, ma'am," he said. After a moment, he asked,

"Might I ask, where's Mr. Cole?"

Before she could respond, she spotted Anne and Doc Wilson walking arm in arm toward them, heads bowed together, laughing.

"Thank you for the escort, Mr. Brody," she told him. "But I must be going." Then she picked up her skirts and scurried toward her friend, leaving him on the sidewalk.

"You look stunning, my dear," Anne declared, taking in a sweeping gaze of the lilac and yellow dress she made for the occasion, then turned to her beloved. "Doesn't she, Jonas?"

Doc Wilson beamed. "Indeed, she does, sweetheart."

"I love it," Emma told her, patting her skirts. "Thank you."

Anne waved a hand. "No need to thank me, dear. The minute I saw you, I imagined the dress in my mind and knew it had to be yours." She pulled her into a quick hug, then looped her arm through the doc's as he led her away.

"Wait. Where're you two going? The dance is this way," Emma said, cocking her head toward the square.

"Oh, we'll be along in just a bit," Anne assured her with a wink, then turned to go.

On the other side of the square, she spotted Wyatt in a heated conversation with Marshal Reed and Deputy Allen. It didn't take a rocket scientist to decipher body language. She could clearly see both lawmen were upset about something. Wyatt shoved a hand through his hair, then yanked his hat back on.

"It's about time," Cassie said, rounding the table to give Emma a brief hug. Then she pulled out a fan from the pocket in her skirt and waved it frantically in front of her face. "My, it's hot today. But don't you just look fresh as a daisy," she remarked, going from one topic to another. "I've nearly run out of cakes and biscuits with all the customers. Wish I'd baked some more."

"Had I known you were going to sell baked goods, I certainly would've helped you," Emma told her, counting the handful of items that remained on the table. "I can't believe you baked as much as you did."

"That's sweet of you to offer." She reached for a small wooden box and tucked it beneath the chair. "The money is good; otherwise, I wouldn't bother." She gazed up at the sky. "Just glad the weather held out. Last year, my goods got rained on, and I lost a pretty penny, unlike the previous year."

"Hopefully, this year will more than make up for it."

Cassie nodded. "Say, how's Wyatt?" She leaned closer and said, "I heard he had a horrible accident last week."

Emma's brows furrowed, forgetting how quickly news traveled. "He slipped and hit his head. But he's fine now."

"Slipped, you say?" She pursed her lips, then waved a hand. "Thankfully, that's all it was. My Wilbert took a nasty spill at the mines one day. Thought he was a goner." She paused, perhaps to replay the memory in her mind. She shook her head. "Some men need to be more careful."

Emma's gaze drifted across the square to Wyatt, still engaged in deep conversation with the marshal and deputy. She opened her mouth to ask Cassie something when she spotted Josh walk up behind Wyatt, clapping him on the back. He whispered something, then the two brothers took their leave.

She shook her head and looked at Cassie. "Sorry?"

Cassie rolled her eyes. "I'm going to pack up here, so I can enjoy the rest of the night. Wilbert's been watching the kids all day and is probably ready to strangle the two of them. Besides, I don't want to miss the dance." She collected the last of the items and placed them in a basket before patting down her hair and smoothing her skirts. "Will I see you and Wyatt there?"

Emma nodded. "Yes, of course."

"Until then," she said, then walked away with the money box under one arm.

Emma watched her go, then turned her gaze toward the square in search of Wyatt. No sign of either Wyatt or Josh.

"My God, you look beautiful."

At the sound of the velvety voice, she spun around and into Wyatt's arms. He smiled down at her and clasped his arms around her back, pulling her scandalously close.

His lips pressed a gentle kiss to her forehead. "Mmm, you even smell delicious, too."

"Thank you," she said, feeling her insides turn to simmered mush.

He stepped back slightly to admire her dress. "I haven't seen you wear this one before."

"Anne made it special for me. Do you like it?" She raised her hands as she turned, modeling the dress for him, tilting her head, and sashaying her hips in a seductive manner.

Desire twinkled in his eyes. "It's perfect. And it'll

look even better pooled on the floor beside my bed later," he promised her quietly.

She glanced around to make sure no one else stood in hearing distance, then swatted him playfully on the arm. "Keep your voice down."

He pulled her close. "There's no one around." Contrary to his statement, fairgoers were everywhere waiting for the dance to begin. "How about a drink and then we can hit the dance floor?"

"Perfect."

They ventured over to what could only be described as the bar area, but instead of ordering punch, Wyatt asked for champagne. He took the two glasses, handed one to Emma.

She raised an eyebrow. "What's the occasion?"

He grinned as if he knew something she didn't. "Does there need to be an occasion to toast *my* beautiful woman?"

She smiled at that and clinked her glass with his. "To us."

Chapter Thirteen

After their fourth dance, Wyatt led Emma to a nearby table, where they relished some light refreshments. She watched other couples sashay around the dance floor in a waltz—and other dances she didn't recognize. How nice it would be if she could pick up this entire fair and plop it into the twenty-first century. Everything seemed sooooo romantic here.

"Well?" he prompted, resting his beer on the table with a light thud. "What do you think?" When she gave him a confused look, he added as he leaned closer, "About your first nineteenth-century festival."

Emma smiled. "It's fun. This reminds me of the town fairs where I grew up. Lots of people and food. Laughing. Good times. The only difference is we have rides."

He fidgeted. "Rides?"

"You know, mini Ferris wheels, tilt-a-whirls, and—" She stopped. "Sorry. I forgot you're not from there."

"It's all right." He smiled, but kept his gaze averted. "I've been to carnivals before that had some zany apparatuses. Please, go on."

"Some of them are hard to describe when you haven't seen them. Basically, they're big"—she waved her hands, searching for the right words—"contraptions or mechanical devices that people go on to create enjoyment." She threw her hands up. "When we get home, I'll draw you a few pictures, so you get an idea. You may understand better when you see the drawings."

He tilted his head, gazing at her. There was a spark of some indefinable emotion in his eyes. "I have something for you." He reached into his pocket, pulled out a small blue velvet pouch, and handed it to her.

Emma recognized the pouch immediately. Her heart thudded.

"Open it."

She stroked the plush fabric, glanced at him questioningly, then slowly opened the pouch. The beautiful necklace slid into her palm. A knot formed in her throat. Gold, pearls, and amethysts. Out of all her designs, this one happened to be her absolute favorite. She almost didn't part with it. But Anne assured her it would bring in a pretty penny.

"Wyatt—"

"Do you like it?"

"Wyatt—"

He took the necklace from her palm and clasped it around her neck. Her dress had a low neckline, and the beautiful amethyst gems matched perfectly.

When he sat down again, she reached for his hand. "Wyatt, there's something I have to tell you."

He squeezed her hand. "I already know." When her eyebrows shot up, he went on. "You think I haven't seen you making jewelry for the past two months? Emma, there's not much that goes in my house I don't know about."

She bit her lower lip. "Are you mad?"

"Because you didn't tell me?" He waved a hand. "I

figured when you're ready, you would. Besides, if designing jewelry makes you happy, who am I to deny you happiness? I'm sure your work also gives you a bit of independence, which is what you're used to, being from a more advanced century, right?"

She nodded. *Why are you so perfect? Why did it take me traveling back in time to find you?*

He reached out and caressed her neck, tracing the necklace that fit so well. "Anne told me she had a hard time convincing you to part with it." He shrugged. "I just wanted you to have something that brings you a little joy."

She swallowed back the lump of tears. Why couldn't men like him exist in the twenty-first century? And, dammit, why did he have to make it impossible for her to want to leave 1882?

"Don't you two look smashing," Josh stated, arriving at their table. He took Emma's hand and kissed it, wriggling his eyebrows at Wyatt, before saying, "You better save a dance for me later or else."

Emma laughed. "If I must, I must."

"I hate to interrupt you two from making googly eyes at each other all night," Josh said to Emma, "but I need to speak with Wyatt privately."

"Now?" Wyatt growled.

"It'll just take a few minutes."

Wyatt scowled at his brother and pushed out a deep breath. "The marshal is a bit short-staffed, so a bunch of us law-abiding citizens offered up our services to help keep the peace during the festivities," he explained as he got up, kissing Emma's cheek. "I'll be back shortly."

She shook her head as they walked away. Both brothers had the same gait, the same swagger to their hips, the same gestures. They were a lot alike in many ways, yet uniquely different. Wyatt was her every heartbeat; Josh, the brother she never had. Returning to her time would change all that.

With a deep breath, she returned to the square to watch the dancing from the sidelines. Anne and Doc Wilson joined her as another tune began, and couples glided around the dance floor.

Across the square, she recognized one of the men who worked for Griffin Grey. Percy Rosler spotted her and waved, albeit awkwardly.

Anne followed her gaze. "A friend of yours or Wyatt's?"

She shook her head. "He works with Griffin Grey."

Anne nodded, then took notice of her necklace. She clasped her hands together and smiled. "I knew it would look perfect with the dress."

Emma traced the gems at her neck and smiled. "He *knew*."

"Of course, he knew." Anne nodded. "When he stopped in the shop the other day, he asked me if you had a favorite," she explained. "What was I to do? I couldn't very well let him leave empty-handed." She touched the necklace, then Emma's shoulder. "Judging by the way he looks at you, my dear, I'd say you two will be at the altar before Jonas and me."

Emma's eyes widened. Her heart did some crazy fluttering. "The *altar*? Anne, there's no way—"

Anne waved a hand. "From what I can see, you're his every breath. It's only a matter of time, dear."

If Emma remained in the nineteenth century, there *could* be a chance for her and Wyatt. She could easily see herself married to him for the rest of her days.

The thought of going back to the future didn't sit so well with her anymore. When she told Wyatt where she came from, he said, *Choose me. Stay with me.* She hadn't given him a concrete response. What the hell was wrong with her? In fact, she hadn't given him *any* response. She couldn't. Just the thought of it tore her up inside—the struggle of wanting the best of both worlds.

How could she remain in the past when she wanted to find a way back to the future? In this case, she definitely could *not* have her cake and eat it, too.

"Mrs. Cole."

Both Emma and Anne turned around at the same time. Griffin Grey looked rather dashing in a dark charcoal suit. The crisp shirt appeared a bit too starchy, but the vest and silk tie complemented him well.

"You are as bright and beautiful as the rising sun," he told Emma. "I hope you don't mind me saying so?"

She mentally rolled her eyes but gave him a stiff, "Thank you."

"Mr. Grey," Anne said, extending a hand and diverting his attention. "I'm not sure if you've already met my fiancé, Doctor Jonas Wilson," she said by way of introduction.

Both men shook hands; the doc wrapped his arm around Anne's waist. "I'm sure our Independence Day fair is quite different from what you're used to in a big city," Doc said.

Grey gave a tight smile. "Very different, but definitely entertaining. However, I must admit, I'd enjoy it much more if a certain lady would honor me with a dance," he said, turning his attention back to Emma. "Mrs. Cole?" he prodded, offering his arm.

How bad would it look if she refused? Were

nineteenth-century women obligated to accept a dance even if they didn't want to? Did women only dance with their husbands? She glanced at Anne for some indication, but her friend gave her a look that said she didn't want to get involved.

Absently, Emma gave a curt nod and allowed Grey to lead her to the dance floor and into a waltz. Oblivious to the music or the man in whose arms she danced, her thoughts went back to what Anne said about Emma beating her to the altar.

If she *were* to stay here and marry Wyatt, could she eventually forget what waited for her in the twenty-first century?

Which is what, exactly?

She had no family to speak of. She lived alone. Her best friend Amber was probably worried sick about her by now. And she had her jewelry business. Other than that, what did she really have in the future that she couldn't have *here*?

"I see your mind is elsewhere," Grey said, breaking into her thoughts. She tripped clumsily on his feet and apologized. "May I ask what has you so distracted?"

Squaring her shoulders, she tried to remember the steps of the waltz...*one, two, three, one, two, three...*"I apologize. It's been a very hot day, and I'm actually quite tired."

"And yet you look radiant," he told her.

Dude, stop with the syrupy compliments.

She spotted Anne and the doc on the dance floor, hoping they would come rescue her. As in, *right now.* Where the hell did Wyatt go to? He should be interrupting this dance.

"Thank you," she responded at last.

"Of course, it's none of my business, but a beautiful woman such as yourself, living under the roof of an *unmarried* man is highly inappropriate."

She stopped dancing. "You're right, Mr. Grey; it's really none of your business."

"I'm sorry if I offended you," he amended quickly. "It's just, I would rather not see your reputation needlessly sullied."

"As if it could be," she scoffed. "I'm a married woman."

He ignored her response. "I have a solution, you see."

Of course, you do, pompous ass. The smug smile on his face indicated he would tell her his solution whether she wanted to hear it or not.

"Come work for me. I need a housekeeper."

Perish the thought.

"Thank you, Mr. Grey, but I'm really not interested."

"The men and women in my employ in this godforsaken town," he went on as if she hadn't spoken, "all currently reside at the hotel. Expenses paid by my company, of course."

"That's very generous of you, Mr. Gr—"

"Griffin," he corrected her.

"*Mr*. Grey," she said firmly. "Again, while I appreciate your offer, I'm not looking to leave my current position."

His grip tightened around her waist. She tried to put some distance between them.

"You should reconsider," he told her.

"The lady said she's not interested," Wyatt barked over the music.

Several nearby couples turned to stare, but as they didn't sense a brawl, continued their sashays around the dance floor.

Griffin's nostrils flared. He released Emma, who then quickly stepped next to Wyatt, accepting his proffered arm. "Can't blame me for trying," he admitted, trying to hide a tinge of hostility in his eyes.

"We discussed this," Wyatt growled. "Or need I remind you?"

Griffin raised his chin a notch. Turning to Emma, he said, "It was a pleasure dancing with you, Mrs. Cole." He cast a quick glare at Wyatt before walking away.

Wyatt didn't say another word. Instead, he swept Emma into his arms, whisking her effortlessly around the dance floor, two bodies moving as one as if they had been dancing together for years.

Her belly fluttered at the strength of his strong arm embracing her, his firm hand clasped around hers. She gazed up, meeting those blue eyes. He winked then pulled her closer than what was considered appropriate. At that moment, she didn't care what anyone else thought. There was no other place she'd rather be than in his arms.

"Did everything go all right with the marshal?" she asked as they circled the dance floor.

"Hmm? Not exactly." He shrugged. "A brawl started in the saloon, so Josh and I accompanied the deputy to see what the fuss was about. Turns out, some out-of-town loudmouth Easterner got caught cheating at cards."

"Sounds like fun. Did you throw him in jail?" she asked, not sure what they did in this century for someone cheating at cards when money was involved.

He shook his head. "Deputy decided the man should give back the winnings versus spending a night in jail, which didn't go over well. The troublemaker stormed off." He gazed into her eyes. "Now, do you want to tell me what all that with Grey was about, or do I have to keep wracking my brain?"

She frowned. "I thought you overheard him?" When Wyatt shook his head, she explained, "He wants me to work for him. Apparently, he pays all expenses for his employees in this 'godforsaken town,' as he put it."

Wyatt stopped dancing. His eyes sparked with anger. "Why, that no-good son of a bitch."

"What are you getting so riled up about? I've no intention of leaving you—er, quitting my job."

His scowl quickly turned into a smile. "Glad to hear it, darling, but with Grey, it's more than offering you a job." He lowered his voice. "Emma, the bastard wants to *bed* you."

She laughed and waved a hand. "Even if he were the last man on this earth, it wouldn't happen, I assure you."

Wyatt pushed out a breath. "You know, I have to admit. I really despise guys like him. Entitled. Wealthy. Arrogant. Thinks he can have whatever he wants."

She touched his cheek, then slid her hand around his neck, about to pull his head down for a kiss, then remembered where they were. "Can we stop talking about Grey, please? It's a very boring subject."

A mischievous grin tilted his lips. "I've got a better subject." He swept her around the dance floor once more. "Much more interesting, I assure you."

"Well, don't keep me in suspense."

"It's about what I'm going to do to you tonight when I get you into my bed," he whispered, his breath hot against her ear.

Delicious warm shivers darted up and down her body with anticipation. Her feet stopped moving to the music. She gazed up into his eyes, daring to ask, "And what do you have in mind?"

His smile widened. He lowered his head and claimed her lips in a kiss that nearly made her legs buckle beneath her. She clung to him and melted in his arms, drinking in his passionate wet kiss. Her heart pounded, and her body ignited. He clasped her against him, tight enough she could feel the heat from his throbbing desire pressing against her through the material of her skirts. She met his demanding lips eagerly. Hungrily. Heedless of the cacophony of gasps and murmurs that quickly surrounded them.

Lifting his mouth from hers, Wyatt gazed into her eyes. Her heart pounded against her chest as she struggled to catch her breath. A slow, sensual grin tugged at his lips.

Finally, whatever was going on around them registered in her brain. No one danced. The music stopped. Couples on the dance floor either stared at them in absolute horror or turned away to snigger behind cupped hands.

"After *that* kiss, the townsfolk won't look favorably on us living together under the same roof," he told her. Then, he took her hands in his and lowered himself to one knee. "I love you, Emma. Marry me. Be my wife. Stay *here* with me."

A collective gasp surrounded them as the fairgoers

waited for her response. Without taking any time to think about her answer—or the *consequences*, should she return to her own time—she blurted out, "Yes!"

Quickly, Wyatt slipped a ring on her finger before he swept her into his arms and kissed her thoroughly. She clung to him—and the promise of what he offered.

Setting her back on her feet, Wyatt pressed a soft kiss to her forehead. "I promise you won't regret it," he told her.

Cheers went up, and within seconds, they were separated as a group of men swarmed Wyatt and clapped him on the back, offering cigars—why was that a thing?—while Emma passed from one embrace to another. Despite their earlier sneers, the women all offered their congratulations until, at the end of the group, she found herself in Anne's arms.

"What did I tell you?" Anne said, knowingly, pulling her into a hug. "The way that man looks at you." She shook her head. "I wish you both all the happiness—"

Gunshots rang out in rapid succession, ricocheting off a nearby building. Pieces of brick went flying. People screamed, and the crowd dispersed in all directions. The tables and chairs, which seconds ago were neatly arranged around the square, were overturned like a tornado swept through town. The entire square evacuated to resemble a ghost town, minus the rolling stray tumbleweeds.

Wyatt grabbed Emma by the wrist, shoved her behind him for protection, while deftly moving her to safety. Doc did the same with Anne, and the four of them took shelter in a nearby alley, Wyatt at the front and Doc bringing up the rear.

He peered around the corner of the building. A crowd gathered at the end of the street. Black smoke billowed out of the front windows to the Copper Pan Saloon. About thirty feet away, the marshal gave orders to a dozen men, including Josh.

"What is it?" Doc asked, unable to see.

He turned to the doctor. "You got a gun?"

Doc Wilson nodded. He removed the pistol from the holster hidden beneath his jacket. "Always."

"Good. Stay here with the women. I'll be right back."

"Wait!" Emma grabbed his arm. "Where are you going?"

"Don't worry. You'll be all right." Wyatt looked at the doc. "Just stay out of sight. I'll be right back." He gave her a quick kiss then hurried off.

Wyatt dashed to the end of the street and through the crowd. And in time, too. The smoke quickly turned into a blazing fire, unexpectedly blowing out all the windows. Everyone ducked for cover, fleeing into alleys, hiding under wagons, and crouching behind troughs to protect themselves from the glass and debris raining down and blanketing the street.

His ears rang from the blast. He spotted Josh and ran over to him, pulling his brother away from the throng, while dusting himself off in the process. "What the hell happened?"

Josh coughed and pounded his chest, then brushed off the dust from his sleeves and trousers. "Cooney started shouting he smelled smoke," he said between deep breaths. "A few minutes later, everyone came running out, shooting off rounds. By the time we got here, the place was on fire."

"Anyone inside?"

Josh shook his head. "I think everyone got out in time."

For years, the Copper Pan Saloon had been the busiest watering hole in Whisper Creek. Pretty soon, it would be reduced to a mound of rubble, judging by the intensity of the fire. Wyatt had seen worse fires in his time. And even with a few small horse-drawn steamer fire trucks and dozens of firemen doing their best, sometimes, buildings couldn't be salvaged. This would most likely be another one of those times.

"Where's the deputy?"

Josh scanned the crowd. "Probably went to round up more help—" Before Josh could finish that sentence, a second explosion went off.

Wyatt shut his eyes, covered his head, and ducked just as the wreckage poured down on them.

"I gotta get back and help," Josh told him, shoving a hand through his hair, shaking out glass and small fragments of wood. "Where's Emma?"

Wyatt cocked his head, brushing off his jacket. "Back there with Doc Wilson."

Josh clapped him on the back. "It's going to be a long night. Get her out of here."

Wyatt ran back to the alley. Emma immediately jumped into his arms. He hugged her reassuringly, rubbing her arms. "The saloon caught fire," he explained.

"Is anyone hurt?" Anne asked, worry creasing her brow.

He shrugged. "Josh thinks everyone got out in time."

"I better go see if anyone needs medical

assistance," Doc Wilson said, holstering his gun. "Ladies, might I ask for your help tonight? I may have some patients who will most likely need bandaging and a gentle hand. I can't be at both places."

"Of course," Anne said, taking his arm. "Why don't Emma and I get everything ready for you?" The doc was about to argue, so she told him, "I've seen you set up your exam room enough times, dear. I think I can manage." She pressed a kiss to his cheek. "We'll be all right."

Wyatt took Emma's hand and gave it a reassuring squeeze. "Go, and don't leave Doc's office until I come for you." He glanced over her head at the doc and Anne. "Understood?"

Emma nodded. He kissed her then watched her leave, looking back as Anne nearly had to drag her away. Once she reached the doc's office, he went back to the scene of the fire.

Several men had burns and lacerations on their arms and faces. Firemen remained busy trying to put out the fire. Those fighting the fire had a long night ahead of them. He wished there was more they could do to douse it. But times being what they were, well, they didn't really have the means.

"Wyatt!" Sam's clothes were covered in streaks of soot and bits of wood. He brushed himself off, then whacked his hat against his leg a few times. Nothing helped to get rid of the fragments. His face was streaked with grime. "Glad you're all right."

"You, too, my friend." Wyatt clapped him on the back.

"Dang shame."

"Did you see what happened?"

Sam nodded. "I stopped in to have a drink before heading home. Cooney was mumbling something about smellin' smoke, though I couldn't smell nothin'. Within seconds, he was yelling at everyone to get out. We hightailed it out of there, and a minute later, the place exploded like hell arrived."

Wyatt looked his friend over from head to toe. "Are you hurt anywhere?"

Sam shook his head. "Nah. Just smoky, is all." He waved a hand. "Besides, I think there may be those more injured than I am. And I'd feel more useful if I could help get them to the doc."

"I'm with you," Wyatt said. "Let's go."

Chapter Fourteen

Wyatt hated the devastation fires caused. He'd seen too many of them over the years—house fires, building fires, forest fires. Some begun by a fluke of nature, others intentional, but all leaving a trail of destruction and heartache in their wake. This fire was no different. But thankfully, the owner was still alive and kicking due to his good sense of smell that saved him and his patrons.

He removed a handkerchief from his pocket and mopped his face, still full of soot. The handkerchief turned black, but he couldn't get all the grime off. He spotted a bucket of drinking water for the workers and dipped the ladle, then took a long drink before wiping his mouth on his sleeve.

Fighting the fire all night left him with no time to think about Emma. Until now. He pushed out a deep breath and dropped his head back to stare up at the predawn sky. When Emma said yes to his marriage proposal, she probably didn't give much thought to how her life would be here in the *nineteenth* century. Hell, he knew she didn't have time to think about it. That's why he asked her the way he did. She couldn't very well say no in front of the entire town. They were crazy about each other—loved each other. But would that be enough to keep her here—in the past—and happy? With him?

He just hoped they never come across the damn portal that would lead them back to the future.

"Wyatt?" Covered in soot from head to toe, Josh's blond hair looked dark and stringy. All Wyatt could see were his green eyes and the white creases around them caused by squinting.

"Are you all right?" Wyatt asked.

Josh nodded. "Yeah, you?"

Wyatt waved a hand. "What's the latest?"

Josh shook his head, glanced back at the saloon. "Now that the fire's just about out, the chief's going in to investigate." He paused. "Listen, I've got some news. Marshal Reed deputized me a few hours ago."

Wyatt stared at him. He ran a hand through his hair and mumbled something under his breath. "Josh—"

Josh held up a hand. "Not now. All right? I know it's not how we thought this would go. Neither one of us expected to end up in Whisper Creek—or for this long."

"Yet, here we are," Wyatt quipped. "Hey, listen, before you head back in there, I have some news, too."

Josh's face broke into a huge grin. "She said yes, right? Can't say I didn't see it coming. Congratulations, little brother!"

Wyatt shook his head. "I can't tell if it's the smartest move I ever made, or the dumbest." He rubbed his temples. "I love her more than life. But she doesn't want to stay here."

Josh clamped a hand down on his shoulder. "I've never seen two people crazier about each other than you and Emma," he told him. "*Now* is not the time to worry about the future. Bro, she came here for a reason." He paused. "Besides, you know as well as I do, no one has been able to find a way back. Not yet anyway."

His jaw clenched. "What if she finds it first? The time portal."

Josh thought for a moment. He lowered his voice. "*If* that does happen, and it just might, are you prepared to follow her back to the twenty-first century?"

"Wyatt! Josh! Come, quick!"

Ben Majors waved at them frantically. Wyatt bolted toward the saloon and ran up the steps, Josh at his heels. He stopped abruptly just inside what would've been the entrance with its swinging half doors. Firefighters carefully picked through the charred rubble. Everything had been burned to an unrecognizable pile of ashes. The ceiling had disintegrated. And the long bar that once lined the entire wall was reduced to cinder.

His gaze stopped at the sight of a badly burned corpse. He glanced toward the fire chief then the marshal. No one spoke. He moved closer to inspect the remains, but couldn't determine whose body it was. All that was left were bones and some patches of skin.

Marshal Reed sighed heavily, then tossed Wyatt a badge. They stared at the remains of what was once the lively body of one of Whisper Creek's finest deputies.

"Let's get him over to the doc's," Josh said quietly.

Someone brought in a tablecloth. They placed it over Deputy Allen's body and carefully carried him to Doc Wilson's office down the street.

Wyatt and Josh kicked in the door when they arrived. "Incoming," Wyatt shouted as they barged into the office. The door banged against wall, then slammed closed as they rushed inside. They lay the body on the examination table, then moved back.

Emma brushed by them to turn up the lanterns. Wyatt noticed the blood-soaked apron tied around her waist.

"Let me get Doc Wilson," she said groggily. Before she could turn around, the doctor hurried into the exam room.

"What's all the…" His words trailed off when he saw the form on the table. He glanced questioningly at Wyatt and Josh.

"Deputy Allen," Josh supplied grimly.

Emma gasped, covering her mouth.

Doc Wilson pushed out a breath, hung his head, then rubbed his eyes. He turned to Emma and suggested pointedly, "Why don't you go get some rest now, Emma?"

"Listen to Doc," Wyatt chimed in.

She nodded.

Doc ushered her toward the staircase in the rear. "It's been a long night. For all of us. You've been a tremendous help, and I thank you. There's another bed in the guest room where you can lie down."

Emma nodded silently, took a quick glance at Wyatt, then climbed up the stairs.

Doc glanced at both brothers. "You two really need to get some sleep."

Wyatt rubbed his eyes. "I'll sleep when I'm dead," he remarked with a loud yawn. "We just wanted to bring you the deputy."

"Fires are unfortunate." Doc Wilson pulled back the cloth, shook his head, and spoke softly to the corpse. "Sorry, it had to be you, my young friend."

"I promise, we'll get to the bottom of this," Josh vowed, heading toward the door.

Doc glanced up at him. "Was it arson?"

Josh paused. "That'd be my guess." He touched his soot-smeared forehead in parting, then walked out the door.

"I'll come back for Emma in a few hours," Wyatt added, closing the door behind him. He hauled his tired ass down the dawn-lit street. The sun was rising, brightening the sky with golden colors, casting a warm glow over the town. Based on the picturesque view, this should be just another regular day and not the morning after a fatal fire.

Hours ago, the townsfolk had been celebrating an annual joyous event alive with music, dancing, and merriment. Now, it looked more like a ghost town. Businesses closed and shuttered. Traces of the celebration drifted by, due to an easy breeze that snatched up papers and decorations, making them skip across the ground in rhythmic fashion. The only people up and about now were the ones working on the cause of the fire.

Wyatt sat on a wood bench facing the square, dropped his elbows on his knees, and hung his head. Exhaustion crept into his bones. While the night started out just how he planned, it certainly didn't end that way. All he wanted was to propose to Emma, get her into bed, and find them a preacher come the dawn. In that order. If he didn't give her too much time to think about their engagement—or her predicament, he could get her to the altar without any obstacles.

He debated with himself on whether he was right or wrong in wanting her stay in the past. In wanting her to give up her dream of returning home to the future. Couldn't Whisper Creek become her *home*? It became his.

Hell, when he arrived in town, he didn't think it would be for long, either. Now it'd been nearly two years, and he made a home for himself here. Why couldn't she?

From the first moment she walked out of his barn, he'd known exactly where she came from—and *how*. He should've told her right then there were others who slipped through time just as she did.

Only, he was afraid if he did, she wouldn't stop searching until she found the time portal—or whatever it was called.

He couldn't risk losing her. There was no way to explain the pull he experienced in their initial meeting. Something inside him screamed he knew she would come. That they belonged together.

And now…*now* that he had fallen in love with her, he would never be able to let her go. He would do whatever he had to do to keep her here. In Whisper Creek. In the past.

****

Emma had only met the deputy a few times, but it didn't stop her from tearing up during the funeral service. She hated death and all that followed for the ones who were left behind to pick up the pieces. According to the marshal, the deputy had no family. His parents died a few years ago with influenza, and he had no siblings. But he was courting a young woman, Abigail Landry, who now clutched the marshal's arm, wiping away tears on her cheeks, barely able to control herself.

The small graveyard behind the church filled with local shopkeepers, friends, and neighbors of the deputy—basically everyone in town. Even Griffin Grey and his colleagues attended the funeral. Due to the nature of the deputy's death, there would be no open casket for people to pay their respects. The marshal wanted the deputy buried quickly, so he could get back to the investigation. His death wouldn't be in vain.

When Reverend James closed the sermon, he gestured to the marshal, who left the bereaved Abigail standing next to the preacher.

Marshal Reed, visibly distraught, needed a moment before addressing the mourners. "Bobby Allen was the finest deputy I've had the pleasure to work with," he managed in a gravelly voice. He removed his hat and cleared his throat. "Everyone in this town loved and respected him. It's unfortunate he died in that fire. But I promise all of you: Justice will be served." He paused, gazing at all the mourners' faces. "This fire was no accident. It was intentional. And we will find out *who* started it—and make the culprits pay."

A collective gasp echoed around her. *Arson*?

Something pierced Emma on the inside. Could this be connected to the fires mentioned in her letter? *Get your ass back here to 1882* before *the fires start*. Her letter said *fires*—plural. Could this be what she wrote about?

Her legs trembled, threatening to give out from under her. Wyatt noticed and wrapped his arm around her waist and led her away from the graveyard to a nearby bench under a tree.

"Are you all right?" he asked, rubbing her arms.

She closed her eyes and nodded. "Just a little…lightheaded."

"Well, if you swoon, I'm sure someone around

here has smelling salts."

After a few deep breaths, she glanced back at the graveyard. Each of the mourners paid their last respects by throwing a flower on the casket before leaving.

"Wyatt, there's something I...have to tell you." She stammered. "It's about—well, this may sound a bit crazy—"

A thick blond brow arched. "You mean, crazier than you're from the future?"

She smiled. "No, I guess that kind of takes the cake, doesn't it?"

He took her hand in his. "Go on."

It took her long enough to figure how to tell him she came from the future—and she'd had plenty of time to think about *that*. And still, she hadn't been that articulate.

Here goes...

"It has to do with what I found, or rather, learned, before I arrived here." She sucked in a deep breath. "The long story short is I received a letter written to *me* from...*myself*, dated December of *this* year. The letter said I was to find a way back to 1882 before the fires start, so I could help prevent them." She looked at Wyatt. "According to my letter, people will die."

The lives of your husband, children, and neighbors depend on it.

Wyatt held his breath. He stood up and paced, shoved his hands in his pockets. His shoulders tense.

She waited for him to say something. "Do you believe me?"

"Of course, I do," he told her, his eyes focused on the ground.

"Then...what is it?"

He shoved a hand through his hair and cursed under his breath. "I've been holding out on you, Emma." When she looked at him questioningly, he went on, "I know more about the future—and the past, than I've let on. Much more. And I'm ashamed I haven't said anything up to this point."

She frowned. "What do you mean?"

"I—I don't know how to explain this." He dropped his head back and stared up at the sky, as if searching for the right words. "I discovered there was a fire here in Whisper Creek. I wrote to Josh about it. Him, being a lawyer and all, he did some digging." He paused. "The short of it is—well, Josh couldn't find any solid *evidence* anyone was behind the fire or fires. It's all circumstantial."

"Wait." Her brows furrowed. "Which fires are you talking about? When did they occur?"

"Mr. Kincaid?"

They both turned toward the reverend, the Bible clasped tenderly in hand. The older man cast a kind smile at Emma, then walked directly to Wyatt.

"We can proceed now," he told them. "Mrs. Heughan and Doc Wilson are waiting for you both inside the church, along with your brother."

"Thank you, Reverend." Wyatt reached for Emma's hand. "Ready?"

She took his hand and stood up. "Ready for what?"

A smile touched his lips. "To be my wife."

Knock me over with a feather, why don't you? Her belly did major flip-flops. "Wait. What?"

He kissed her hand. "Considering our very public engagement last night, I asked the reverend if he wouldn't mind marrying us today."

She glanced at the reverend who smiled warmly at her. "But…isn't it in poor taste to marry moments after a funeral? The deputy hasn't even been buried yet."

"Not at all, my dear," the reverend replied. "While you may be a widow, it's still highly improper now that you're engaged to remain in the same dwelling as your betrothed. Besides, this is a small wedding. No harm in celebrating life while you're living it."

"Of course," she mumbled.

"Splendid," said the reverend, waving the Bible in the air. "I'll see you both at the altar."

Emma watched him walk up the steps and into the church. Wyatt looped her arm through his. For a long moment, she gazed at him.

She stopped, forcing him to turn around at the bottom of the church steps. "Neither of us knows how long I'll be here for." She threw her hands up in the air. "What if—what if I find the time portal or whatever it's called and go back tomorrow? What, then?"

He placed his hands on her waist and lowered his head to press a gentle kiss on her lips. "Then we'll make one amazing night to remember," he told her, before his lips came crashing down on hers.

Her arms slid around his neck, pulling him in tighter. She met his kiss, delicious and demanding. Her knees went weak, and her heart pounded.

He lifted his head away from hers, panting. "Or you could just stay here…forever," he added.

If he kissed her like *that* again, she just might.

Instead, she said nothing.

When they entered the church moments later, her breathing returned to normal. Anne embraced her, then pressed a small posy of wildflowers into her hands. A colorful collection of Montana's most beautiful wildflowers, all yellows, blues, and purples with a touch of white.

"I picked these when Wyatt told me this morning," she said.

"They're beautiful," Emma said. "Thank you."

Josh came over and shook Wyatt's hand, then pulled Emma into a hug. "Welcome to the family, sis," he said, smashing a kiss to her cheek. "By the way, I'm the one giving you away." He winked at her, then turned to Wyatt. "Go on. Get!"

Wyatt and Anne walked to the altar to stand before the reverend, waiting for Josh to escort her down the aisle. Even without music or other guests, this would be a day Emma would remember forever. The day she married an amazing man from a time and place she never dreamed she'd ever experience. A day she would look back on, decades from now—whether she remained here, or returned home…

Home.

Forcing that thought from her head, she pressed the posy to her nose and inhaled the floral fragrance. It smelled like the flowers in the field just outside Wyatt's house—soon to be *their* house. Some wedding this turned out to be. She was still in the same dress from yesterday! With all that transpired, there was no time to return home to change clothes.

When they reached the altar, everything became a blur. One minute, Josh stood beside her; the next, she held hands with Wyatt, repeating their sacred vows after the reverend. It all happened so quickly she didn't even cringe when the reverend said, "…to love, honor, cherish and *obey*…"

"I now pronounce you man and wife…" Whatever came after got drowned out by Anne, Doc Wilson, and Josh applauding—and the scorching kiss Wyatt bestowed on her, making her go deaf to anything else in the church.

Wyatt lifted her off the ground and swung her around. "There wasn't time to buy you a wedding ring," he whispered. "But I promise to fix that first chance I get." He set her down and kissed her softly this time.

"Hey, I gave the bride away," Josh interrupted, shoving Wyatt aside. "I should at least get a kiss for that." He embraced Emma, hugged her, then placed a brotherly kiss on her lips. "He can be a cocky son of a bitch," he whispered, "but he loves you more than life."

She glanced at Wyatt, currently being congratulated by Anne and Doc Wilson. He met her gaze, smiling.

In just a few short months her life had been entirely turned upside down.

And it would be again when she found a way back home.

****

The late afternoon setting sun cast a golden glow on everything from the wild grass and trees to the vibrant array of wildflowers blanketing the property like a bright summer quilt. The perfect setting for two people about to experience a new beginning.

Wyatt helped Emma out of the wagon then gathered her into his arms and carried her through the back door, accidentally bonking her head on the doorframe.

"Ouch!" she cried, rubbing her head.

"Sorry."

She laughed at his clumsiness until he set her down just inside his bedroom—correction, *their* bedroom.

"I'll move all your things in here while you take a bath," he told her and pressed a soft kiss to her forehead. He tucked a loose curl behind her ear, tickling the side of her neck.

She covered his hand with her own. "Very kind of you, but I think you should go first," she teased, eyeing his soot-stained clothing up and down. "You need one way more than I do."

He quirked an eyebrow at her. "Implying I'm filthy?"

"Implying? No." She shook her head and pinched her nose. "You smell like a—" She almost said barbecue but that wouldn't be appropriate, considering they'd lost the deputy in the fire. "—like a chimney."

"I do, huh? We'll see who smells like a chimney, just you wait." He pulled her to him and nuzzled her neck, raking his stubbly chin against her sensitive skin.

She giggled, screamed, and squirmed against his bristly stubble. "Stop! Come on, you know what I mean."

He stopped and tweaked her under the chin. "You go on and I'll have a shower outside. But when you're done, you're mine," he added, his lips brushed against hers as he spoke.

Waves of ecstasy flooded through her veins and everywhere else at the suggestion of what would come later. "I have a better idea," she whispered, slowly sliding her hands up his chest to clasp around his neck. "Why don't I join you?"

An arched eyebrow indicated his pleasant surprise. "Oh?"

She nodded. "Mmm, you'll be saying a lot more than *oh* when I'm done with you, Mr. Kincaid."

"Then allow me to escort you, *Mrs*. Kincaid," he said, offering his arm. "Time is of the essence."

They raced to the outdoor shower, laughing and swatting each other along the way. Wyatt quickly stripped out of his clothes. Considering the many layers Emma wore, she couldn't be as swift. Thankfully, though, she skipped the corset when she initially dressed. Had she worn it, she probably would've swooned in such extreme heat.

Wyatt grew impatient with all her slow fussing. He reached out and ripped her chemise in half, exposing her breasts. "I'll buy you another."

Kicking off her knickers, she jumped into his arms and wrapped her legs tightly around his middle. He clasped her buttocks in his grip, squeezing them in a massaging way. His demanding lips captured hers and she returned his kiss with reckless abandon. He tasted like the buttery berry scone they shared on the ride home. He turned on the faucet and stepped inside the shower.

Emma let out a scream. Cold water dribbled down her back. Instantly, her nipples puckered, and goosebumps appeared everywhere else.

"Give me a minute," he said, reaching for the soap. "I'll have you warmed up in no time."

He lathered up his hands, handed her the bar of soap, then ran his hands up and down her arms, legs, torso, gently massaging the soap into her tired limbs then…tenderly caressing her lady bits, teasing her before delving inside her warmth.

The stroking of his fingers sent pleasant jolts

through her. The soap slipped out of her hands and landed who cares where. Moaning, she leaned back against the wall and let him have full access to do with her as he pleased. She spread her legs wider and gripped his shoulders as his mouth soon followed the trail of his fingers, beginning a lust-arousing exploration of her most delicate area.

Within minutes, he had her crying out his name, clutching her fingers in his hair as her body rocked with delicious spasms of ecstasy. When the waves subsided, he pressed his face to her heated skin and kissed his way up her belly, then chest until his lips met hers. It was all she could do to stand. Her legs were so wobbly, they felt like melted butter.

"Oh my god. *That* was...delicious," she admitted, almost in a love-drunken slur. He wrapped his arms around her waist; she slid her hands up the broad expanse of his chest and around his nape. She tilted her head way back to gaze into his blue eyes. "It's only fair our marriage be a two-way street, don't you agree?"

"Wouldn't have it any other way," he said, and his breath fanned her face as he spoke.

"Good," she said with a nod, then announced, "My turn."

She shoved him back against the wall, then kissed her way down to his hardness she couldn't wait to have inside her, before taking him fully in her mouth. His fingers tangled tightly into her hair as she teased and caressed and tortured him in the same sensual way he did with her just moments before.

It wasn't long before he hauled her to her feet, grabbed her by the buttocks and impaled her. He pushed her against the wall for support, thrusting into her, deeper and deeper still, until they both found the release they craved.

After a few moments trying to regain their breath, not to mention strength, Wyatt reached for a towel to dry her off before carrying her into the bedroom—now, *their* bedroom, so they could continue exploring each other in comfort.

Chapter Fifteen

The saying, "life could turn on a dime" probably didn't take time travel or time portals into consideration. In an instant, Emma had gone from being a single-lost-in-time-twenty-first-century time traveler aching to return home...to a married woman living in the nineteenth century. All because she received a letter from her nineteenth-century self. Who'd have thought? She had a hard time wrapping her mind around all of it.

Guilt clenched her heart. A part of her still wanted to return to the future. But now that she and Wyatt were married it would be much harder to leave when the time came.

If the time came.

Her heart raced. What if she *never* found the damn portal—or whatever? What if she ended up living out the rest of her life here in the *nineteenth* century?

Would it really be so terrible, staying here?

Things could be worse. She could've ended up in the mediaeval times with absolutely no running water or electricity of any kind, not to mention zero modern medical inventions. But there were many things she liked about life in the nineteenth century, mainly no annoying distractions, like constantly buzzing cell phones. Televisions and noisy modes of transportation, such as cars, buses, or planes were nonexistent. People relied on games, cards, and just enjoying each other's company as every-day entertainment. Music could be experienced by all, whether at the town square or in the theater.

So, what if she *didn't* make it back to the future? At least, here she had a man who loved her, the hope of children to come, and a small group of delightful new friends. But with no family ties in the future, maybe staying here wouldn't be the *worst* thing in the world to happen to her.

Maybe going back would be.

By the time she reached town twenty minutes later and opened the door to Anne's dress shop, her mind reeled.

Over the last several months, Anne had become a close friend and confidant. Would she be as understanding as Wyatt when Emma revealed she came from the future? She hoped so, because right now, she needed some female advice.

The bell jangled a second time when Emma closed the door behind her. She was surprised to find Anne glaring at her, hands on hips, eyebrows raised in question.

"Correct me if I'm wrong, dear, but didn't you just get married yesterday?" When Emma nodded, she went on. "Then, what on earth are you doing here? Shouldn't you be in bed with your husband?"

Emma flopped down and removed her hat. She kicked out her feet, dropped her head back on the chair, and pushed out a deep breath. The clanking of china meant Anne prepared to serve her favorite indulgence.

Her friend came over and squeezed Emma's hand. "Is everything all right, dear?"

Emma sat up, accepted Anne's special *tea*, and

took a slow sip. Who cared it wasn't even lunchtime yet? She needed something to take the edge off. And a shot of whiskey would do the trick.

Anne waited for her to say something. But what could she say? Blurting out she came from the future probably wouldn't be the best idea. Unfortunately, she couldn't quite figure out how to tell her friend the truth without vomiting out an info dump.

She waved a hand. "Yes, everything's fine."

Instead, they spoke about the events of the last few days: the deputy's death, Emma's wedding, and Anne's upcoming nuptials. Then the bell over the front door rang.

"Ladies, sorry for the interruption." Josh greeted them, doffed his hat, and walked over to Emma. "I just saw your husband. I hope you know he would much rather be at home with you than at work."

She smiled. "I know."

Anne stood. "I doubt this is a social call, Deputy. Is there something I can do for you?"

"There is, actually." Josh nodded. "I hate to be a bother, but—" He unrolled a thick sheet of paper and handed it to Anne. "—have you ever seen this man before?"

Anne studied the broadsheet. "Who is he?"

"Marshal Reed thinks he may have something to do with the fire," he explained. "Someone in town saw him leave the saloon just before the fire started. It could be nothing. Or it could be something. We need to look into all the leads."

She gestured to Emma. "You might want to see this, dear."

Emma took the sheet. The image could only be

described as a crude sketch of almost any twenty-five-year-old man in Whisper Creek. A photograph would've been more helpful. She studied the rendering. There was something familiar about the slant of the man's eyes. Had she seen him before? Possibly. Hard to tell based on the outline.

"Come to think of it," Anne said, rubbed her chin, "I saw him at the fair. He stopped at Mrs. Burns's table. Purchasing some muffins, I believe."

"I'll be sure to speak with Cassie, then." Josh turned to Emma. When she didn't say anything, he pressed, "What about you, sis? Have you seen this guy?"

Emma shrugged. "I'm not sure. I mean, it's a bit hard to tell. I wish you had a pictu—er, photograph, or a better sketch."

Anne tapped Emma's arm. "You did see him," she stated with a nod. "Just before you joined me and Jonas, remember?"

Emma studied the sketch. Yes, yes! She remembered thinking at the time the young man's clothes didn't suit him. He seemed out of place in a way. And didn't he have a tattoo—or something resembling one?

She handed the sketch back to Josh and nodded. "Yeah, I remember him now, though the sketch is way off. But if it's who I think, Anne's right. He was at the fair looking for Grey's office. He asked me where to find it."

"Was that the only time you saw him?"

She thought for a moment. "No, I saw him a few times throughout the day." She shrugged. "Just in passing. But that's it. Nothing eventful to report, I'm afraid."

"He spoke with you. Did he happen to tell you his name?" Josh pressed.

She snapped her fingers repeatedly, as if that would provide the answers. "Brady? No. Bently? No, that's not it." She held up a hand. "Wait, Brody. Yes, Carl Brody."

Josh ran a hand over his face, muttering curses under his breath.

"What? You don't look happy," she observed. "What's wrong?"

He rolled up the sketch and tapped his thigh with it. "We were hoping it was a member of the Boyd gang."

Hearing the name sent a surge of anxiety through her veins. The Boyd gang headlined the newspaper clippings she found in the Kincaid pantry—quoting Griffin Grey—as well as the ones she found on the desk in the future house. They had to be one and the same.

Emma did a mental facepalm. *The newspaper clippings! Why didn't I think of this before? Duh.* She could be on to something now.

"What?" he demanded when she didn't say anything further.

"Nothing," she replied with a shake of her head. "Just…that name."

"We both know the Boyds had zero to do with your alleged stagecoach robbery," he said pointedly. "What else you got?"

Josh knows how she arrived in Whisper Creek?

Before she could ask how, he explained. "Wyatt told me."

"Wyatt knows something about the robbery?" Anne pressed, frowning. Her gaze volleyed between the two of them.

"Not exactly," Josh replied, waiting for Emma to answer.

Please don't tell Anne, she pleaded with her eyes. Emma wanted to be the one to tell her friend the truth. But the timing had to be right.

Josh pushed out a breath then nodded. "We'll talk," he assured her, then turned on his heel and left the shop.

Anne watched him leave. "What did he mean?"

Emma picked up her hat. "I just remembered there's something I have to do," she blurted out, pinning her hat on and heading for the door. "I'm sorry. I'll see you later."

Before Anne could protest, Emma walked out of the shop and went directly to the *Whisper Creek Gazette* office. Surely, something would turn up in the newspapers.

****

The bell above the door clanged. Even with the fresh breeze blowing through the large open windows, Emma detected the smell of ink and paper, among some other odors she couldn't quite place. The front office looked tight, but considering the length of the building, she assumed there had to be more printing space beyond the back counter with its partial flip-up door that allowed entry into the back.

The wall-to-wall counter doubled as a desk. The young clerk behind it looked up from the newspaper to greet her. "May I help you, ma'am?"

"I hope so," she replied with a smile. "I noticed Whisper Creek doesn't have a records office yet, so I'm hoping you keep copies of old newspapers."

His smile widened. "Indeed, we do. We have

newspapers dating back at least a decade from the *Gazette*'s first days of printing." He nodded. "What specifically are you looking for?"

"Information on fires in the area," she told him. "Not just in Whisper Creek, but maybe nearby towns and even Helena." He looked at her questioningly, scratching his jaw, so she explained, "Fires—as in arson, or fires where no cause was found. Homes, businesses, that sort of thing."

He pushed away from the desk, pulled out a typed list from a drawer, and scanned the contents. He searched through a dozen or so neatly organized stacks of newspapers on the back counter and a few drawers in a nearby cabinet, referring to the list.

"Oh, and anything you have on the Boyd gang would be helpful as well," she added.

"That we have plenty of," the clerk commented over his shoulder.

After several minutes, he divided the newspapers into two piles, then plopped both down in front of her. The taller pile had to be at least eighteen inches high. *Lovely. Where was the internet when you needed it?*

"Anything related to arson will be in this pile," he explained, tapping the smaller pile. "And anything on the Boyd gang will be in this one." He drummed his fingers on the taller one. "I'm afraid you'll have to read through quite a lot to find exactly what you're looking for."

"That's all right," she said. "I appreciate your help. Thank you."

He smiled. "Name's Willie Harper, ma'am. Just let me know if you need anything else."

"Thank you, Mr. Harper." She shoved both piles to

one side of the large counter, doubling as Willie's desk. In case someone else came in looking for information or to conduct business, she didn't want to be in the way.

The newspapers were less than a decade old and made of strong paper, so she wasn't worried about accidentally ripping the pages. She just didn't want to flip through them too quickly, lest she miss some important information. Judging by the number of papers, she would be there all night.

Unfortunately, after researching half the stack related to the Boyd gang, she couldn't find anything more than the usual bank robberies or assaults. Nothing out of the ordinary for typical nineteenth-century outlaws.

Just as she was about to close the last newspaper, a familiar name caught her attention. She glanced at the publication date, October 12, 1881. Last year. It read in part:

...Griffin Grey, one of the East Coast's wealthiest financiers, lost his fiancée in a deadly house fire just yesterday that also took the lives of some members of his housekeeping staff. The couple was set to wed next week. Their union would've made them the third wealthiest couple in New York City. Unfortunately, this isn't the first tragedy for Grey. Ironically, his first wife also perished in a fire some years ago...

Two women in Grey's life *died* in a fire had to be more than coincidence. That would be like getting hit by lightning twice. What are the chances?

Eyes on Willie, she pulled out that newspaper from the pile, folded it, and discreetly slipped it in her skirt pocket. "Mr. Harper?"

He looked up, and his face turned a shade of red

when she smiled at him. "Ma'am?"

"I'm finished with these," she told him. "But would it be possible to take some of them home with me?" It looked like he was about to protest, so she added, "Just to borrow. I promise to return them in a few days. As you said, there's a lot to read through."

His eyebrows knitted together. "Well, I don't rightly know. No one's ever asked to do that before, and the editor isn't here to give the say-so. He's off interviewing the marshal and deputy about the saloon fire." Off her crestfallen look, he added, "I tell you what. I'll speak with Mr. Dwyer when he returns. Can you come back tomorrow?"

Emma nodded. "Why, yes, I can. Thank you."

As she reached the door, he called out, "Ma'am?" She turned around. "May I have your name, please?"

"Mrs. Kincaid."

His eyebrows shot up. "You're the new deputy's wife?"

She smiled and shook her head. "No, his brother Wyatt is my husband."

"Apologies." He blushed at his mistake, then said, "Nice makin' your acquaintance, Mrs. Kincaid."

It was the first time someone called her *Mrs.* Kincaid—other than Wyatt. The sound of it coming from others warmed her to hear it. But it also...cemented her life here in the nineteenth century.

It wasn't just her anymore. Now, she was part of two. Part of an "us"—*till death do us part*.

And the other part would never want to venture with her to the future.

****

After brushing down Maximus and leading him to

243

his stall for the night, Wyatt went into the house through the kitchen. Whatever Emma cooked for dinner smelled delicious, but he needed a bath first, based on the amount of sweat that poured out of him. That and a tall whiskey.

"Good evening."

He turned around at the sound of the sultry voice to find Emma standing in the kitchen doorway, dressed in nothing but a blush-colored gauzy silk robe. The gossamer material rested against her taut nipples. His body reacted instantly. Everything inside him ignited.

Silently, she glided toward him and took his hand, led him out of the kitchen, down the dimly lit hallway, and into the bathroom where a steaming hot bath awaited.

He looked at her, arched an eyebrow. "What's this?"

She rolled her eyes, then helped him unbutton his shirt. "It's called a bath, silly." She pulled the shirt off him, tossed it on the floor, then reached for his pants.

He grabbed her hand. "If you touch me now, I won't be able to wait, and I…need a bath first."

She wrinkled her nose. "Indeed, you do. Get in."

"Thanks a lot."

She shrugged. "Just sayin'."

He removed his boots and socks, then tossed his pants on top of the growing pile before climbing into the tub. The water was hot and inviting. He leaned back and closed his eyes, inhaling the musky fragrance of wet soap. He opened his eyes and held out a hand. "Thank you."

Emma perched herself on the edge of the tub then pressed a kiss to his cheek. "Mmm, salty," she commented. "I figured you'd had a long, hard day and could use a bath. Oh and—" She reached back to the counter and handed him a whiskey. "—this."

"I swear, you must have ESP—I mean, you read my mind." He took a long swallow, tilted his head back, and gazed into his wife's eyes. He couldn't explain why, but ever since she showed up on his property a few months ago, he knew there was something special about her. It had nothing to do with her being from the future; it was something innate. A recognition. He couldn't quite explain it—or how he *knew* they were meant to be together.

He watched her lather up the sponge, drop the soap into the water, then gently caress his aching muscles, beginning at his feet. He couldn't remember the last time he'd had a foot rub. Probably never now that he thought about it.

Slowly, she kneaded his muscles, working her way up his calves then his thighs. Hell, she took her sweet time—and he didn't mind. Between the soothing stroke of the sponge and the skillful touch of her hands, she would soon send him over the edge.

And, Christ, that edge rapidly neared, especially when her hands reached his hardness, gently stroking him. He felt the electricity of her gentle caress spread to every inch of his being, burning him to the core.

When he opened his eyes, she watched him, chest heaving, and eyes heavy-lidded. There was only so much more he could take of this. But he let her continue the slow, sweet torture. He waited while she washed his chest and neck, then massaged his arms, one at a time, from fingertips to shoulders.

She leaned over, and her robe slipped open,

exposing one of her breasts. He reached up a wet hand to hold the silken globe in his hand, running his thumb across her nipple. She sucked in her breath. He wrapped his arms around her waist and pulled her on top of him, water splashing *everywhere*.

"Wyatt!" she shrieked. "I'm soaked."

"Well, what did you expect, my lovely little temptress?" He nuzzled her neck, causing her to squeal. "You get me all hot and bothered, and you just sit there like you're not feeling it, too? I don't think so," he told her, pushing the wet material off her shoulders.

He shifted her body until she straddled him. Grabbing her hips, he lifted her and slid into her silky warmth. She threw her head back and gripped his shoulders, meeting his every thrust, while creating a rhythm of waves splashing over the rim of the tub, splattering onto the floor. He grabbed her buttocks and pulled her down on him. Hard. She cried out then dipped her head for a demanding, heated kiss.

"We need to move this party to the bedroom," he announced in a ragged breath.

In the next instant, they were out of the tub, dripping a stream of water from the bathroom to the bedroom.

He laid her wet body on top of the bed and covered her with his own. Immediately, she wrapped her legs around his middle as he entered her. His body vibrated with liquid fire as she met his every thrust, deeper and deeper still. Their bodies sang in exquisite harmony as they soared to a blissful shuddering ecstasy.

****

The next morning after Wyatt left for work, Emma walked to the *Gazette* office to return the borrowed newspaper. Thanks to the ominous cumulus clouds blanketing the sky, the air had a damp chill. She just hoped to make it to town before the rain started. Considering the century, she didn't have the luxury of those mini pocket umbrellas, nor did she bother to bring the large black one Wyatt kept in the pantry.

About a half-mile into her walk, a wagon sped by her at a breakneck pace. If she hadn't heard the rickety wheels and thunderous hooves bearing down on her, she probably would've been run over. She jumped off the road just as the wagon sped by her. Oddly enough, the driver resembled Cassie. Why was her friend riding at such a fast pace? Was something wrong with the children?

When she reached town, she went directly to Doc Wilson's office, thinking it might have been an emergency. But she didn't see Cassie's wagon in front of the office or anywhere else down the street. Perhaps, she had been mistaken.

A clap of thunder rumbled in the distance. Emma looked up at the dark, gray sky and groaned. The smell of rain teased the air. It wouldn't be long now until the downpour, which prompted her to hurry to the newspaper office.

The same young clerk who had been there the day before greeted her. "Mornin', Mrs. Kincaid," he said, smiling broadly. "You certainly brighten up this dreary day."

"Kind of you to say so, Mr. Harper." She smiled in return and approached the counter. "Would you mind if I took another look through those newspapers you showed me yesterday?"

"I kept them aside just for you." He grabbed the

two piles and placed them on the main counter.

She smiled her thanks. Once he turned away, she removed the newspaper that she took yesterday from her pocket and slipped it into the pile. "By any chance, were you able to speak with your editor?"

"Yes, ma'am." He went to the other counter once more, picked up a small stack of newspapers, and slid them across the counter. "Mr. Dwyer said you could borrow these. I'm afraid he won't part with the rest of them. Though, you could stay and look through them if you still need to."

"That won't be necessary. This is most helpful." She grabbed the makeshift string handle wrapped around the stack and headed for the door. "Thank you."

She stepped outside, and the sound of heavy raindrops plunking on the pile of newspapers cradled in her arms, smearing the inky text, indicated the heavens would open up momentarily. She clasped the pile closer to her chest and walked briskly toward Anne's dress shop, hoping to make it before it poured. No such luck. By the time she got inside, she was soaked.

"Mrs. Kincaid!" Mattie hurried toward her with a small towel she exchanged for Emma's wet bundle. "Mrs. Heughan's in the office," she said, nodding.

When Emma stepped through the portiere, Anne looked up and snapped the ledger closed. "You picked a fine day to shop," her friend said, then greeted Emma with a hug.

Anne gestured to the sofa and poured a cup of her special tea for each of them.

"It wasn't raining when I left." Emma dried off her arms and smoothed her hair as best as she could. She sat down, set the towel aside, and took the cup from

Anne.

"I'm glad you stopped in," Anne said, smiling behind her teacup. "I've got news." She paused. "Jonas's brother will be here next week. We're *finally* getting married on Wednesday."

Emma reached out and squeezed her friend's hand. "That's wonderful! Though, I'm surprised you didn't wed sooner."

Anne waved a hand. "I didn't mind waiting. It's important to Jonas that his brother be here to witness the nuptials. He's the only sibling Jonas has. Besides, what's a few weeks when we're spending the rest of our lives together?"

"He's very lucky to have you," she told her sincerely.

Anne smiled, then added with emphasis, "And you'll be happy to know, I've decided to keep my dress shop and hire another seamstress."

"Wonderful!" She clapped her hands. "What made you change your mind?"

"Well, I gave it some thought. After all, why should I have to do everything when I can afford to hire someone else to sew my designs? Furthermore, it'll get me out of the house for a little bit each day while Jonas is at work. I would be too bored at home by myself."

Emma raised her cup. "A toast. To modern women."

They clinked cups and sipped.

"And how is married life treating you since I last saw you yesterday?"

"Great. Of course, it's only day three." She laughed, then gazed down into the teacup, swirling the amber liquid around. Day three...of how many? Those days would dwindle if—*when* she figured out a way back to the future. How long would her happily-ever-after last then?

Anne reached out and touched her hand. "What's bothering you?"

She shook her head and shrugged. "It's nothing. Just some unresolved things from…before I arrived in Whisper Creek."

An eyebrow arched in question. "Another man?"

"What? No. Nothing like that. Just that I might have to go back. To New York, that is. And I'm not sure it's something Wyatt would want to do or could do. He…has a life here. His brother's here. He loves Whisper Creek."

"Whether he loves Whisper Creek or not, he loves you more, and he would want you two to be together. Of that, I'm sure," she said pointedly.

"I guess so," she commented lamely. "But what if it's something he can't control? We never know what's going to happen tomorrow. It's not like we have a manual explaining this is how many days each of us gets to live or be married or—" She stopped abruptly, realizing she said all that out loud. "I'm rambling. I apologize."

Anne tilted her head. "I've seen the way your husband looks at you, Emma. He would give you anything you wanted. Anything within his power." She paused. "And if that means going back to New York, he will go, especially if it makes you happy."

"What if he *can't*?"

What if he can't find a way back, but I can? What then?

How could she leave him here in the nineteenth

century while she went on to live out her days in the future? She clenched her eyes shut, wishing the thoughts to go away. But they kept racing through her mind.

"I just mean…" Emma waved a hand. "Never mind. I'm being silly. Wedding jitters, I guess," she said, hoping it would be a plausible excuse.

The bell above the front door rang. Within seconds, Mattie appeared in the portiere, followed by a young boy with a cap on his head, dressed in shirt, vest, and breeches, all rain-soaked. He clutched a small brown envelope streaked with water stains.

"Well, hello, Michael." Anne turned to Emma and explained, "Michael is the postmaster's grandson." She turned back to Michael. "A bit wet for you to be outdoors now, isn't it?"

"Yes, ma'am." He looked down at the soggy envelope, then Emma. "Are you Mrs. Kincaid?"

Emma glanced from Anne to the young boy. "I am, yes."

"For you, ma'am." He handed her the envelope then tugged his hat on. "Good day." He scampered out the door, the bell above the door jangling in his wake.

Emma eyed the envelope. Something akin to anxiety tingled down her spine. The envelope happened to be the same size and texture of the one she had received from her nineteenth-century self. She turned it over and read the writing on it:

Please deliver on July 7, 1882
Mrs. Wyatt Kincaid
at Designs by A

"Aren't you going to open it?" Anne prompted her.

A wave of nausea overcame her. She didn't

recognize the handwriting, but the envelope looked familiar. Slowly, she opened it and pulled out a folded sheet of paper. It read:

Expect the unexpected.

That's it? Nothing else? No other words? The color drained from her face, and her heart thumped at what this could possibly mean.

"Emma, are you all right?" Anne asked. "Is it bad news? Speak to me, dear," she pressed when Emma didn't respond.

"I'm fine." She handed the note to her friend.

Anne read it and looked at her. "I don't understand. What does this mean?"

"I have no idea."

****

The sun had already begun to set, gradually descending the orange-violet sky. The scent of wildflowers filled the air, combined with a fragrant kiss of hemlock from the towering trees continuing to draw a steady but gentle breeze. Montana sunsets never disappointed, Emma mused.

She headed to the barn to tell Wyatt dinner would be ready soon. The dirt crunched under her shoes, reminding her to make a pair of summer flip-flops. Her everyday shoes remained uncomfortably too hot and snug for this time of year. Unfortunately, she would only be able to wear the flip-flops around the house. If anyone else saw them, it would be difficult to explain her unusual-looking footwear. Then again, maybe she'd start a new trend with the local housewives. *Or how about a new reality show—Housewives of Whisper Creek.* She laughed.

An odd sound, one she hadn't heard in quite some

time, hailed from the barn. The sound of it was almost like…a party of some sort? She listened closely to several voices, but none belonging to anyone she knew. No, the tinny sounds appeared to be coming from…*Could it be?*

She stepped inside. Wyatt sat on a bale of hay, elbows resting on his knees, holding something in his hands. She watched him laugh and wipe his eyes, oblivious to her presence. The sounds of voices and laughter came from the gadget in his hands. It filled the barn. Her heart pounded.

What the—

She froze just a few feet away from him, staring at the cell phone cradled in his hands as he watched a video. A *video?*

"Wyatt…?"

For a split second, he must've forgotten his surroundings. The look he gave her was unrecognizable. He stood up and quickly shoved the phone inside his pocket.

"You found my phone." From the moment she arrived in the nineteenth century, she'd been unable to locate it. And she had looked everywhere. She assumed she'd left it in the twenty-first century because she didn't remember bringing it to the garage-turned-barn.

His brows drew together. "W-what?"

She motioned to his pocket. "My phone. Where'd you find it? I thought I lost it in the—" She waved a hand, trying to come up with the right word. "—time portal, gateway thingy. Whatever it's called."

Wyatt rubbed his face then shoved a hand through his hair. He clasped both hands behind his head, stared up at the beamed ceiling. A muscle quivered at his jaw.

He stood like that for a few moments, before dropping his hands and turned toward her. Something was wrong. She sensed it.

"Emma…"

The way he said her name made her skin tingle. And not in a good way, either. She licked her dry lips, then swallowed nervously. A lead weight dropped into her stomach. "What is it?"

"This phone—" He removed it from his pocket and waved it. "—isn't yours."

Her brows scrunched together. "It's not? Then whose is it?"

He searched her eyes. His jaw tightened. "Mine."

It took a moment for his words to sink in.

"*Yours*?" Her eyes widened. "But h-how is that e-even…poss-i-ble?"

He held it up. Yes, it looked like her cell phone, but the cover was different. Hers was purple; this one, gray. He pressed the home button on it, and a photo appeared on the screen. She recognized Wyatt and Josh and—*is that James Matheson*?

Her heart thundered in her ears. The shock of what he said hit her full force, siphoning the blood from her face. Her fingers froze like icicles. Her body went numb from the inside out. All this time! How had she not known? Not guessed? How could she have possibly missed the clues?

He took a step toward her. "I'm so sorry, Emma. I should've told you sooner. I wanted to but…" He paused. "Forgive me?"

A million thoughts collided in her mind, overwhelming her senses. She had never expected this. Wyatt was from the future? "Forgive you?" she rasped out, shaking her head.

He stepped closer. "Yes, forgive me for not telling you when you first got here that you weren't the only one," he said quietly. "I wanted to but…I can't explain it. I knew you were coming. I knew you would be from the future." He shrugged. "I guess I wanted you to settle in and see if you liked the nineteenth century before you discovered the truth."

"What difference would that have made?" she managed, staring off into the distance. How could she wrap her mind around all this? "I don't *belong* here."

His jaw clenched. "I guess, maybe, I was also trying to soften the blow for when I told you about…the time portal."

She lifted her gaze to him. "What about it?"

He drew in a deep breath. "We think it only works one way."

She frowned. "*We*?"

He nodded. "Josh. Me. I came from the future, just as you did. Nearly two years ago. Quite by accident. Just like you. A few months later, Josh arrived. Also, by accident." He sighed. "We've been trying to figure out how the portal works but…" He shrugged.

"But…?" she prodded.

"We've been through every scenario we could think of." He counted out on his fingers as he explained. "Alignments of the planets. Winter solstice. Summer equinox. Solar flares. Tides. Moon phases. You name it, we thought of it. We tried to figure out how anything could tie into the time portal, or whatever it's called. But every time we tried to find the exact spot we stood in when we arrived to test our theory…it was unsuccessful. Neither one of us has been able to make it back, no matter what we tried."

"Then maybe you're not trying hard enough," she scoffed, then swiveled quickly, turning her back to him.

He came up behind her and put his hands on her shoulders. She shrugged them off. "We're all stranded in the nineteenth century, Emma," he said quietly, and his breath tickled the back of her neck. "Josh, me, and you, too."

Pulsing anger seeped its way through her veins. She couldn't determine which was worse—being lied to by Wyatt or being forever stranded in the past. She chose one and went with it.

"How could you?" She spun on her heel and charged, "You lied to me."

He held up a hand. "No, I didn't lie. I just didn't tell you a secret. I withheld information. There's a big difference."

She smacked her forehead. "I can't believe you're saying something as asinine as that in your defense."

"Had you ever asked me if I personally came through the portal, I would've told you everything."

"What?" she shrieked. "So, because of some technicality of how I worded a question, this is somehow *my* fault?"

He shook his head and threw his arms up. "Not at all. I'm just saying…" He pushed out a deep breath. "Think about it. Is me not telling you any different than you not telling me you're from the future? They're both secrets. They're both the same."

Well, he had a point there. But at the time, she didn't *know* he was from the future and worried he would consider her insane and throw her in an asylum. Still, if Wyatt had told her he came from the future right away, maybe she wouldn't have felt so alone.

He reached for her. She pulled away. "Before you arrived, I had this weird feeling of déjà vu. I knew my soulmate would be coming, but I didn't know how or when. I can't put it into words. Then when you arrived on my property, it was like a flash of memories swarmed my mind. I *knew* you from somewhere, knew we shared a life together. It's hard to explain. I wanted to say something, but I didn't want to scare you away. I didn't know what you would think. And then if I told you about the portal…" He shrugged and turned away.

Some of her anger deflated. She sat on the bale of hay and rubbed her temples. *It's one thing to want to go home—to the future. But it's another to be told I can't.*

"Maybe there's another way," she said quietly. "I mean, if Josh, you, and I *somehow* all made it here, then there must be a way to return to the future."

He kicked at the pieces of straw on the barn floor, shoved his hands into his pockets, and mumbled. "Good luck finding it, then."

Her gaze snapped to him. "Don't tell me you've given up looking?"

He scratched the length of his jaw and walked in a circle before returning. "Emma, I…"

She shot to her feet and advanced on him. "The Wyatt Kincaid I know wouldn't give up looking for a way home. He would exhaust every scenario he could think of. Unless…" Her voice trailed off. *Unless you didn't want to find it.*

He took her hands and led her back to the bale of hay, urging her to sit beside him. Reluctantly, she did. He reached into his pocket then handed over his phone.

"When you came in before, I was watching this

video." He pressed the screen, and the video came on. "It was taken at my parents' fortieth wedding anniversary. We—Josh, James, and I—threw them a surprise party. It was just six months before they died in an avalanche. They went skiing and…" He cleared his throat. "The phone only has ten percent battery left, so I don't put it on much. It's difficult to rig up a charge for it. But I wanted to see them—to tell them about you, our wedding. I wish they could've met you," he added quietly.

She squeezed his hand. "I'm sorry, Wyatt. I didn't know."

He squeezed back. "I'm sorry I didn't tell you about me or the portal. I was afraid if you figured out a way to go back, you'd leave here. Leave *me*. And, well, the truth is, I love you too much to live without you. I loved you even before you arrived. I know it sounds silly, but it's true."

Reality hit her full force. Tears slid down her cheeks. "I love you, too, Wyatt. More than anything."

He gazed into her eyes. "More than returning to the future?"

She ignored his question by pressing her lips to his, unsure if she tasted her salty tears or his.

Chapter Sixteen

"I'm amazed I didn't pick up on all your little twenty-first century idioms." Emma leaned back, tracing an invisible line from Wyatt's jaw to his lips. A gentle breeze danced over her naked skin. She draped a leg over his waist, anchoring her husband to the blanket in front of the firepit. "Talk about being blind as a bat. I should've figured it out."

Wyatt touched her cheek. "I'd hoped you would. You have no idea how I agonized over how and what to say."

"Oh, I can imagine," she averred, reflecting on the inner turmoil she experienced before telling him she came from the future.

He kissed the tip of her nose. "But *you* seem to have adapted your vocabulary. You sound like a born-and-raised Whisper Creek citizen of the nineteenth century."

"As do you." She kissed his lips. "Mainly when you're around others, that is," she amended.

"Method to the madness. Like I said, I was hoping you would've picked up on it—or at least my plumbing skills."

She laughed. "Yeah, that alone should've been a dead giveaway."

He wrapped his arms tightly around her. "And speaking of plumbing skills, I would very much like to have my way with you tonight, Mrs. Kincaid."

A smile tilted the corners of her lips. "That would be fine with me, Mr. Kincaid."

Their lips hungrily found each other. She straddled his hips. The blanket slid down her body, puckering her nipples when the cool night air caressed them. His hands moved magically over her breasts, then seared a path down her body. He touched her silky warmth, teasing and caressing her until she begged him to be inside her. He gripped her hips and entered her in one hard thrust.

"Wyatt," she moaned, meeting each and every thrust.

She tossed her head back, enjoying the incredible sensation of having him inside her. It was hard to concentrate on anything else, but something in the distance caught her eye. And glanced in that direction.

"Wyatt?" She drummed on his chest. "Stop."

His grip on her waist tightened, his body bucking beneath her. "Never."

"I'm serious. *Stop*!"

He stopped. His gaze followed hers toward the west. Fire exploded into the night sky, flames and smoke climbing higher toward the moon.

"Shit." Wyatt jumped up, yanked on his breeches, then tugged his shirt over his head. "It's coming from Wilbert and Cassie's place."

Emma dressed hastily. Wyatt ran into the barn, then moments later, emerged on Maximus, riding bareback.

"I'm going over there," he told her, kicking Max's sides, and jarring him into motion. "Head into town as fast as you can and get help," he shouted over his shoulder.

With no horse at her disposal now, the quickest way Emma would make it to town was on foot—and in sneakers.

She ran into the house and rummaged through the mahogany wardrobe until she found her twenty-first-century clothing which had its own special place buried beneath all her new belongings. She slipped into her button-down shirt, skinny jeans, and sneakers. The familiar feel of her own clothing against her skin felt good. But there was no time to dwell on that.

Without wasting any more time, she hightailed it into town as fast as her legs would move. Her stamina for endurance activity remained at a high, making the one-mile run in under ten minutes without collapsing on the way, thanks to years of yoga, Pilates, and gym workouts.

"Help!" She ran down Main Street, kicking up a swirl of dust behind her. The town appeared eerily quiet, except for the saloons. "Somebody, help! Marshal Reed!"

The marshal and Josh simultaneously burst out of the office. She doubled over to catch her breath, then inhaled and exhaled slowly, deeply.

"What is it?" the marshal demanded.

"Fire…There's a fire," she gasped out between breaths.

Josh put his hands on her shoulders. "Wyatt?"

She shook her head. "Wilbert and Cassie."

Josh took off, most likely to tell the fire chief. Marshal Reed let her catch her breath. He took her inside his office, then poured her some room-temperature coffee. She hated black coffee, but she needed something to drink after that run. And judging by the sparse furnishings and lack of refreshments, it was probably all he had.

"Just breathe," he told her. "And when you can, tell me what happened."

She took one more sip then placed the metal cup on the desk, but not before making a face. "Wyatt and I were…outside. That's when we saw the smoke…coming from the Burns's place." She waved a hand. "He rode over there, and I came here for help."

The marshal folded his arms, rubbed his jaw. He was about to say something, but his eyes focused on her attire. Eyebrows scrunched, he eyed her up and down. "That's some getup you got on there," he commented, nodding toward her sneakers.

She flexed her feet. "Special shoes from…back east," she explained. "The outfit, too. I, um, sometimes wear this around the house. Easier to clean in." Then she tucked her feet beneath the chair, so her footwear would be out of his skeptical view.

"Never seen a woman in breeches that *tight* before neither," he muttered, rounding the desk. He sat down in the old wooden chair, folded his hands across his chest, and kept his gaze on her. "Hardly appropriate. But seein' this is an emergency…"

Thankfully, Josh returned, to save her from further scrutiny. From the doorway, he announced, "The fire department is on the way." Then to Emma, "Are you coming?"

She jumped up, waved to the marshal, then headed for the door. When she got outside, Josh was already in the saddle. No other horse in sight.

"You can just ride with me," he said, reading her

thoughts. Without giving her a chance to argue, he leaned down, extended an arm, then swung her up behind him. She wrapped her arms around his waist. He steered the horse toward Wilbert and Cassie's place.

The plumes of smoke and the acrid smell of burning timber became noticeable half a mile away. When they finally arrived on the property, her heart lurched at the frightful scene.

Dozens of firefighters—mostly uniformed but a good number of nearby neighbors-turned-volunteers, including Sam Hutcheson—did their best to extinguish a blaze that didn't look like it would ever get under control. And with the only horse-drawn steam fire truck Whisper Creek had to douse the fire, it was doubtful the fire would be extinguished in time to salvage the house. Back in the future, the hoses would be hooked up to nearby fire hydrants. Here, they had to rely on the one hose being cranked off a reel with two large wheels nearly as tall as Emma, one tank, and whatever water could be pulled from the nearest well, lake, or river. Thankfully, there was a well and the lake sat nearby.

Josh reined the horse in. Emma slid off and ran toward the blazing structure. But Josh was faster. He grabbed her by the arm and yanked her back so forcefully she crashed into his chest.

"Are you crazy, woman?" he shouted over the roar of the fire. "It's way too dangerous to go over there."

"Then why did you bring me back here?"

"Just stay put," he ordered her, then marched off toward the fire to speak with one of the firefighters.

Emma remained far enough away so as not to be in the way of the men who courageously battled the blaze—or close enough to get herself burned should the embers burst into the dry night air. Her gaze searched frantically for a sign of Cassie, Wilbert, and their children, silently praying none of them had been trapped inside the house.

She and Wyatt spotted each other at the same time. Without waiting another second, he ran to her, then pulled her into his arms. He was covered in soot, but his own scent of masculinity and sweat made her feel safe, even though her nerves were on edge.

She pushed away from him and searched his face for good news. "Did you find them?"

He shook his head and squeezed her tight. "Their horses and wagon were gone when I arrived. I don't think they were home."

She should have been relieved. However, the absence of two horses and the wagon didn't necessarily mean they were safe.

Someone shouted a warning. Everyone immediately scrambled away from the burning structure. Wyatt grabbed her around the waist to steer her away, though they were still close enough to feel the heat from the blaze. Within seconds, the frame collapsed to the ground, sending flames everywhere, along with a whoosh of heat.

A few minutes later, Josh came running over, his face grimy with soot and sweat. "Fire chief says no one was inside," he assured them.

"Thank god," Emma muttered.

"One of the firefighters—" Josh cocked his head toward the group of men trying to contain what was left of the fire. "—saw Wilbert at the saloon earlier."

"What about Cassie?" Wyatt asked.

He shrugged. "Wilbert made no mention of Cassie.

He was, er, occupied."

Emma recalled what Cassie said about Wilbert—how he took up with one of Madame Veronique's girls. Was he referring to that?

Josh removed his hat to wipe away the sweat with a handkerchief that he then stuffed back into his pocket. "I'm going back to town to see if I can find Wilbert."

Wyatt nodded. "If you find him, let him know he and Cassie can stay with us."

An eerie feeling crept into her bones. Something about the way the night played out made her uneasy. Like what she wrote in the letter from her nineteenth-century self was coming true.

Of course, it's coming true. You're the one who wrote it.

But how could it possibly be she slipped through time, lived here for who knew how long, then managed to get a letter to her future self? None of it made any sense.

But it's happening. Just as my letter stated.

She pushed out a deep, unsteady breath and stared at the remains of the house. The one-story home was destroyed, burning away into a pile of cinder and smoke. Hopefully, Cassie and Wilbert were somewhere safe.

****

"I don't like this one bit." Marshal Reed removed his hat to smooth back his thinning hair. He scowled at the fire chief. "Wilbert's a fine citizen of Whisper Creek. You can't just go around accusing him of starting fires willy-nilly."

"Not accusing," Chief Harris stated, still in his gear from fighting the fire just hours before. The smell of smoke emanated from his entire body. "We just want to question him, is all."

Wyatt looked at his brother. Since when was Wilbert Burns the suspect? The man's house burned to the ground, charred to cinder. How could they even think it was him?

"Seems to me that you're rushing to judgement," Wyatt commented. For that, he received a glare from all three men. He threw up his hands. "Just because the man was in a brothel the night of the fire—and his wife is nowhere to be found *yet*—doesn't make him guilty."

"Maybe not," Harris agreed. "But it does seem awfully coincidental, if you ask me."

"Maybe it's just that," Wyatt stated. "Coincidental."

"Meaning no disrespect here, especially to your brother wearin' the badge." He cocked his head toward Josh. "You're a carpenter, not a lawman. What business is it of yours?"

Wyatt glanced at his brother then back to the fire chief. "Wilbert's my neighbor. And my friend. I just don't want to see an innocent man get accused of something he didn't do."

"You don't know he's innocent for sure," Harris pressed. He gripped his hat so hard, his knuckles turned white.

"If you knew Wilbert the way I do, you wouldn't be saying this."

"This isn't your business," he charged, advancing on Wyatt. "Stand down. Or I will make you—"

The marshal stepped between them, shoving Harris back a step. "I won't have any unnecessary fighting or accusations in my office. You hear me?" It was a question not meant to be answered, although his gaze remained on the fire chief.

"I hear you," Harris ground out, glaring at Wyatt. "I still think you're hidin' somethin' about Burns."

"Questioning Wilbert won't do you any good," Josh explained, which got him a lethal glare from the marshal. "We've got another lead."

Harris's eyes volleyed between the two lawmen. "Who?"

"Can't say at the moment, but I can tell you the charges involve more than just a fire."

"Fire is *my* jurisdiction in this town," Harris barked, wiping a sleeve across his weary and soot-stained face, erasing some of the grime. "You two may be the law in this town, but when it comes to fires, it's me and my men riskin' our lives. And *we* are going to do the investigating. So, I would appreciate you lettin' me in on what's going on. Otherwise, Wilbert Burns is goin' to be arrested for arson."

Josh and the marshal exchanged a glance. "You try arresting him, and I'll throw your ass in jail so fast your head'll spin," the marshal growled. "Now get out of here and go do your job."

"You got no right tellin' *me* what to do," Harris snapped. "I don't report to you."

"No, but you report to me," Mayor Clarence stated from the open doorway. Clad in a crisp gray suit, hair neatly combed back, he glared at the fire chief long enough to make him look down and fuss with the helmet in his hands. The mayor closed the door behind him, shutting out the mid-morning sun. His mustache twitched. "You've been shoutin' so loud, I could hear you down the street."

"Apologies," Harris grumbled. "It's just that the marshal and his deputy here aren't all that forthcomin' with information I need."

"I spoke with both the marshal and deputy earlier," he stated, gazing from both lawmen then back again.

Harris's eyebrows narrowed. "Is that so?"

"You and your men should be proud of the fine job you all did trying to extinguish that fire." The mayor shook his head. "Cryin' shame the house couldn't be salvaged. If you really think someone *deliberately* started that fire, I'd like to hear why." He waited. "*Now*, if you please."

Chief Harris's face turned red. He glared at Josh before turning back to the mayor. "Wilbert and his entire family were out of the house. My men found a lantern overturned. They believe it's what started the fire."

Mayor Clarence waited for more. "And?"

He shrugged. "How could a lantern turn over if no one was there to push it over or smash it?"

"You're the fire chief. For chrissake, act like it." The mayor shook his head. "I can't rightly see how you're going to accuse an innocent man of starting a fire when he was a mile away. In a brothel. Hell, you better come up with something more substantial before I find a replacement for your job."

Harris clenched his jaw. "Wilbert was at Madame Veronique's for the evening—*after* the fire started," he bit out. "It had to be him!"

"Why are you gunnin' for Burns?" Wyatt accused, folding his arms across his chest. "What did he ever do to you?" He paused, cocking his head. "Maybe you don't like it that he frequents the same girl at Madame

Veronique's as you do?"

The fire chief's face turned a deeper shade of crimson. Wyatt hit that nail on the head. But before Harris could say a word, the mayor held up his hands.

"Gentlemen, let's not forget we're all on the same side here. We all want to find out who—*if* anyone—caused the fire."

"For all we know, it could've been a freak accident," Wyatt added. "Those things do happen, you know."

"Not twice in one town," Harris snapped.

"Chief Harris," Josh began, "it might be in the best interest of the town—and yourself—if you wait a few days before arresting anyone."

Harris's eyebrows shot up. "Another one that thinks he can tell *me* what to do."

"I agree with the deputy," the mayor pronounced. "Let the marshal and his men continue their investigation. However, I do expect the marshal will share something with us all. Soon." He looked at Marshal Reed.

The marshal nodded. "Of course."

Harris yanked on his helmet then marched across the room. He swung open the door and stormed out of the office, leaving it to bang against the wall in his wake.

Wyatt leaned against the desk and watched the silent conversation between his brother and the marshal. The marshal gave a slight nod to Josh, who then turned to Wyatt. "Need your help, little brother. You up for it?"

He grinned. "I'm your huckleberry," he said from his favorite movie, *Tombstone*.

Josh rolled his eyes and chuckled. "You've just been dying to say that since we got here, haven't you?"

"You know it."

****

No matter how much Emma tried to keep herself busy, she couldn't stop thinking about her letter. The words played over and over in her mind: *Get your ass back here to 1882 before the fires start. The lives of your husband, children, and neighbors depend on it. Hurry!*

The second fire had already occurred. How many more would there be? It was hard to fathom more destruction could be on the way. Her letter was dated December 1. Five months away. What else could happen between now and then?

A loud thumping on the front door grabbed her attention. She put the *Gazette* down and walked through the house as the thumping persisted. "Who is it, please?"

"Willie," came the child's muffled voice from the other side of the door.

She pulled the door open, surprised—and relieved—to find Cassie's two children. Clara clutched her doll tightly to her chest with one hand, looking like she might make a mad dash any second; her other hand squeezed Willie's. Both children smiled, albeit timidly.

"Willie, Clara," Emma greeted. "I'm so glad you're all right."

Willie's brows scrunched. "Yes, ma'am."

Judging by the look on the little boy's face, he didn't know what she referred to. She wouldn't upset them by asking. She looked beyond the porch. But Cassie's wagon was nowhere to be seen. "Willie, where's your mommy?"

"Mama told us to give you this." Willie handed her a folded piece of paper. He draped his arm around Clara's shoulders and hugged her close.

She read the scribbled note. Her heart sank at the words:

Emma,

You're my only true friend.

Please care for Willie and Clara until I can send for them. I've made a grave mistake. I'll explain everything when I see you.

Your friend,

Cassie

"Come with me." Stuffing the note into her skirt pocket, she shepherded them into the house. Clara clung to Emma's leg with one arm while her other clutched her doll.

Emma kneeled in front of the little girl and pulled her into her arms. "It's all right, sweetie. Your mama is…she had to go away for a little while, but she'll be back soon." She caressed Clara's cheek. "In the meantime, you and Willie are going to stay with me and Mr. Kincaid. Would you like that?"

The little girl nodded, clutching her doll tighter, and leaned into her brother. Willie tried to be brave for his little sister, Emma could tell. But his face was filled with fear.

"Good," Emma said. "Because we are going to have *soooo* much fun together."

"Can we go fishin'?" Willie asked. "Mama said you would take us."

"Fishing it is, then," she said with a nod, then heard a belly rumbling. She had no idea how long it had been since they last ate. And a child's concept of time was different than that of an adult. "But first, why don't I get you two some lemonade and lunch?"

"Yes, please!"

In the kitchen, the children sat obediently at the table, waiting patiently while she poured lemonade and set out muffins for the three of them. Mentally, she planned the rest of the day's meals. Were kids in the nineteenth century just as picky eaters as they were in her time? Geez, she hoped not.

"Tank yooou," Clara said, biting into a blueberry muffin, crumbs bounced off her chin and onto the table.

"These are better'n Mama's," Willie said as he tore off a chunk too big to fit in his mouth. He stopped eating when he realized what he'd said.

"Don't worry, it'll be our little secret." Emma winked at him. "I'll make us all an early supper, all right?" The kids nodded in response and kept eating.

If only she and Wyatt had use of their cell phones, now would be the ideal time to let him know what was going on with Cassie and Wilbert's children. Unfortunately, she would have to wait for him to return.

In the meantime, she stewed. What kind of mother would just abandon her children the night after a fire consumed their home?

Chapter Seventeen

Wyatt perched himself comfortably at the long mahogany bar, his hand wrapped around a glass of the saloon's finest whiskey. It tasted a bit too medicinal for his palate, but it would do. He'd spent the last three hours nursing it. Only the bartender noticed. Sadly, he was not spending this Saturday night with his bride in the throes of passion. Instead, he was watching one man in particular seated at a Faro table. It gave him the chance to watch the man's reflection in the bar-length wall mirror without being noticed—or caught staring.

The stuffy odors of sweat, tobacco, and cheap perfume pervaded the air. He took a sip of whiskey and turned to lean his elbows back on the bar, shifting his gaze to survey the room.

Since the Copper Pan burned to the ground a few nights ago, most of its regulars crammed into the Silver Spurs, making it a bustling night for business. A piano player banged out catchy tunes on a slightly off-key upright piano as one of Madame Veronique's young ladies led the song in a pleasant soprano voice. He even found himself tapping his foot to a few of the melodies. Scantily clad dancing girls sashayed around the room, swinging their hips seductively, while some draped themselves provocatively across the laps of many an eager gentleman.

He spotted Madame Veronique at the rear of the

saloon, fanning herself while flirting with a man he didn't recognize. Her girls were raking in the dough. Over the course of the three hours he'd been there, he'd seen more men than he could count slip up the back steps, each led by one of Madame's girls to the rooms above the saloon, only to return a short while later with a sated smile and eager to blow more money on Faro or poker.

Since Josh had been deputized, he'd asked Wyatt to be his eyes and ears around town. It wouldn't look right for Josh to be mixing with the locals and eavesdropping on conversations. They would think they were being accused of something. Josh needed someone he could trust—and someone no one would be suspicious of. Wyatt, of course, would do anything for his brother. And if that meant undertaking a little reconnaissance mission, he had no problem with it. Especially if it meant helping find whoever started the fire at the Copper Pan, and perhaps, the one at Wilbert and Cassie's place, too.

He couldn't grasp the notion that Wilbert Burns had anything to do with the fires. Wilbert wasn't a pyromaniac, nor was he someone who would ever break the law. He'd known Wilbert and Cassie since he got to Whisper Creek, and neither of them seemed to be the type to start trouble. Unfortunately, after Wilbert was questioned by the fire chief last night, he took off. No one had been able to find him since. Needless to say, it wasn't looking good for Wilbert.

"You gonna drink that whiskey or nurse it all night?" came a familiar voice. Sam walked up to the bar and pushed his hat back so that it dangled from the string around his neck.

"I prefer to drink slowly," Wyatt told him, grinning. He signaled to the bartender. "Tastes better that way."

"If you say so." When Sam got his whiskey, he clinked glasses with Wyatt. "Here's to slow drinkin'." Then he tossed back the entire contents of the glass and signaled to the bartender for another.

Wyatt laughed. "I guess your definition of slow differs from mine."

"You just need to catch up, is all." He signaled for another, then leaned in to say, "Gets lonely at home. Feel like the walls are closing in." When his glass was filled, he let it sit without touching it. "Sometimes I just need to…feel something other than numb." He gestured to the booze.

Wyatt gently gripped him on the shoulder, knowing too well what grief did to a person. "You don't owe anyone any explanations. You'll get no judgements here."

Sam nodded. "I know. Thank you. I just thought by now…"

Wyatt squeezed his shoulder. "'Death leaves a heartache no one can heal; love leaves a memory no one can steal.' Grief never ends, my friend."

Sam nodded then looked him in the eye. "You a poet now, too?"

Wyatt laughed. "Not at all. It's something I heard once." He took a sip. "Why don't you come around tomorrow for dinner? Josh and I miss your company."

Sam smiled, bowed his head. "I'll do just that. Much obliged."

They spoke for some time about the goings-on in town and the latest fire over at the Burns' property.

Wyatt had gotten so wrapped up in the conversation he almost forgot to check on the Faro game.

By the time he looked back, one of the men he'd been watching earlier—the one who looked like a member of the Boyd gang, according to a recent *WANTED* poster the marshal showed him— disappeared. Damn it.

Luckily, he caught a quick glimpse of one of the Madame's girls leading him up the back steps.

Sam followed his gaze. "Lookin' for someone?"

He shrugged. "Thought I recognized the card player from another town."

Sam reached for the glass and took a slow sip before responding. "If you ask me, two fires in a week don't add up. I can't explain it, but there's no way in tarnation you could ever convince me Burns did it." He shook his head. "No, sirree."

Wyatt met his gaze. "I agree."

Sam waved a hand. "Pity he took off after they questioned him, though. Looks like he's runnin' when I know he ain't."

Wyatt sipped his whiskey, swallowed slowly, and let it burn its way down his throat to catch fire in his belly. This stuff was stronger than what he made at home and didn't taste half as good. "Notice anything suspicious in town?"

Sam's eyebrows furrowed as he shook his head. "Nothing I can put my finger on. My gut says this don't add up right, though. It's like someone's out to get us."

They talked some more, then Wyatt said farewell and ambled across the room to settle himself in the empty seat at one of the poker tables. The men either tipped their hats or gave him a nod of acknowledgment as they tossed money into the pot. He recognized all of them from town, knew them by name, but he wouldn't consider any of them friends. He tossed in a few coins and glanced around the room. From where he sat, he could keep an eye on the rear staircase and anyone who went up or down it.

Thanks to many years of playing poker every Thursday night with his brothers, he was damn good at it. He won the first round in minutes. He was just about to ante up at the second game when someone clapped him on the shoulder.

Living in the nineteenth century for nearly two years taught him many things. One of which was not to make a sudden movement if someone grabbed you. It could mean a bullet in the gut, as he'd seen quite a few times in the Copper Pan and out on Main Street.

"Got a minute?" came his brother's low voice above his ear.

Wyatt slowly turned and grinned. But his grin faded when he saw the look on his brother's face.

Josh cocked his head toward the bar. Wyatt collected his winnings, threw in a few coins for the dealer, then excused himself. He followed his brother to the end of the bar to speak privately.

Josh glanced around then back at Wyatt. "What do you got?"

"Not much," he admitted. "Though I think I spotted someone who may—or may not—be part of the Boyd gang. Can't exactly tell, considering those sketches aren't the most accurate." He shrugged. "I was waiting for him to come back downstairs."

Josh nodded. "If you saw him out on the street, do you think you'd recognize him?"

"Yeah, I think so."

"Good. Because I need you to come with me." He paused. "There's been a development."

Wyatt didn't know what to make of that but followed his brother out of the saloon, down the street, and into Doc Wilson's office. The front room was empty, but he could hear the doc talking with someone in the exam room behind the other door. He looked at his brother for clarification.

"You'll see," was all Josh said.

He glanced at the clock on the wall and pushed out a deep breath. The late hour reminded him he hadn't seen Emma since earlier that morning. He hoped she would be fast asleep by now. The idea of leaving her so soon after the fire at Cassie and Wilbert's didn't sit well with him. But thankfully, she understood and supported his decision to help Josh and the marshal. Still, he didn't like it. She was alone the day after their nearest neighbors' house went up in flames. He didn't want to admit someone in town had a penchant for arson, and their house could be next. Besides, they'd only been married for a few days, and the separation made his heart ache.

The door to the exam room swung open. Doc wiped his hands on a small towel, tossed it aside, then closed the distance between the three of them.

"He's got a nasty bump on his head," he said, cocking his head toward the room. Then he looked at Wyatt. "Reminds me of what happened to you. I didn't like it then, and I don't like it now."

Wyatt glanced from Doc Wilson to his brother and back again. "I'm sorry. What's going on? Who's got a nasty bump?"

Josh looked at Doc and explained, "I thought I'd bring Wyatt over to see for himself."

Doc nodded, shoved a hand through his hair. "Wilbert's on my examination table with a lump on his head bigger than the one you had," he told Wyatt. "I've given him laudanum to dull the pain."

"Someone tried to bash his head in," Josh explained.

"He was heading home from town when someone walloped him good," Doc said. "Threw him off his horse. Albert Dwyer found him and brought him here."

Wyatt rubbed his jaw. "So, he wasn't running," he said pointedly, glancing at his brother.

Doc's eyebrow shot up. "Running?"

Josh ignored that as he asked the doctor, "Is it all right if we speak to him?"

Doc nodded. "Just keep it brief."

Josh walked into the exam room. Wyatt stopped in the doorway. Doc Wilson did a good job of bandaging Wilbert up, but he could still see a tinge of blood seeping through the bandage on one side. He remembered when he got whacked on the head and touched the spot where he had the lump. To this day, he still couldn't remember the details.

"I hear you have one helluva headache," Wyatt said, walking to one side of the examination table.

Wilbert tried to smile but winced instead. "Hurts like hell." He closed his eyes and managed to sit up with Josh and Wyatt's help. "Josh said…house couldn't be saved." He looked at Wyatt. "Thanks for tryin'." He touched his head and winced again, battling the pain. "Anyone seen…Cassie and the little'uns?"

Wyatt and Josh exchanged a glance. "No," they

said in unison.

"Do you have relatives Cassie could've gone to stay with?" Josh asked.

Wilbert tried to shake his head. Obviously, the movement caused him pain, judging by the look of anguish on his face. "We had a quarrel," he admitted.

"About what?" Josh pressed when he didn't continue. Clearly, his deputy hat was on.

Wilbert rubbed his eyes and licked his lips. "She wanted to take the children and...leave me. Live in a big city. Live the life...I could never give her." He paused before turning his gaze back to Josh. "If you can't find her, my guess is she left."

"Any idea why she would do that?" Wyatt asked gently.

Wilbert shrugged, but based on his body language, he must've had an idea. "Ain't got a clue. Hell, I thought she—we were happy. Lord knows she can't afford to live in a big city," he muttered under his breath.

"We'll find her." He put his hand on Wilbert's shoulder. "But first, we need to get you home to rest."

"I ain't got a home," he muttered miserably. "In case you forgot, my house burned to ashes."

"You can stay with me."

"Before you go making plans," Doc Wilson cut in, "I'd like Wilbert to stay here for a few days for observation. Doctor's orders." He turned to Wilbert. "I've got a room upstairs with a comfortable bed. Once you're feeling better, you can go stay with the Kincaids." He paused. "Sound all right with you?"

A small smile tugged Wilbert's lip. "Much obliged, Doc."

"I'll see him upstairs." Wyatt wrapped his friend's arm around his shoulders and slowly helped him across the room and up the steps.

Once inside the spare room, Wyatt set him down on the bed, raised his legs to rest comfortably, and tucked the pillow beneath his head. "Don't you worry. We'll find Cassie and your children."

Wilbert closed his eyes, touched his head, then let his hand fall. "Bring my children back, Wyatt," he whispered. "But let their whorin' mother stay gone."

Wyatt wondered if it was the laudanum talking or was there more to their quarrel than Wilbert wanted anyone to know?

He knew sometimes Cassie would visit with Emma. He wondered if she had told his wife anything about the inner workings of their marriage. Perhaps, he could unearth a clue in whatever she discussed with Emma during their last visit. Then again, would Cassie open up to Emma? Nineteenth-century women might not be as open and forthcoming about intimate issues like they were in the twenty-first century. Women of the past were very private. Unlike the future when most women confided in their therapists, doctors, and best friends. Still, he hoped Emma could shed some light on what transpired between the two and what might cause Cassie to skip town lickety-split sans children.

When he went downstairs, Doc was busy cleaning up the exam room, wiping blood off the table. Josh paced. Neither of them noticed he had returned; they were both deep in thought.

"Something happened with those two," Wyatt announced. Josh stopped pacing. Doc Wilson glanced at him but continued to clean. "I don't know what, exactly, but it was a pretty heated argument. Based on what Wilbert said, I don't think he wants Cassie to come home."

Josh raised an eyebrow. "Lover's quarrel?"

"Maybe more than that." He paused. "If a man doesn't want his 'whoring wife' to come back..." He shrugged. "Maybe she's got someone on the side?"

Josh looked surprised. "Cassie? Can't picture that." He shook his head. "Then again, anything's possible." He folded his arms across his chest and looked at Doc Wilson. "When will he be up for questioning?"

Doc scratched his jaw. "He's got a nasty bump that's gonna hurt for quite a while. But I'd say he'll be more coherent in a day or two if you can wait that long. If you tell me when you're coming, I'll wait to give him laudanum until you've spoken with him."

Josh nodded, glancing at Wyatt. "Appreciate that."

Wyatt wasn't a lawman and was merely assisting his brother, but he knew when to bow out. He stepped outside, letting the cool summer night air wash over him. The smell of tobacco smoke, dirt, and horse dung hung in the air. He stepped off the sidewalk and onto the street. The town still bustled, mainly with half-drunk men as they searched for their horses or stumbled to the next watering hole.

Leaning against a nearby post, he folded his arms and glanced up at the star-filled sky. He once looked up at those same stars from another place in time. Would he look at them again from the future—or was he destined to stay in the past? He thought of that every so often, especially now that he and Emma were married. He couldn't bear to think what he would do if she ever returned to the twenty-first century, and he didn't—or vice versa. He swallowed down the lump rising in this throat.

His brother exited the doc's office and walked over to Wyatt.

"Everything all right?" Wyatt asked.

Josh rubbed the back of his neck and pushed out a deep breath. "I've gotta see the marshal. Why don't you head home and spend some time with that wife of yours before she divorces you for abandonment?"

Wyatt laughed. "I'll do just that."

****

The sudden sound of a horse thundering toward the house woke Emma. She stole a quick glance at the clock on the mantel. One o'clock. She slipped into her robe and stumbled through the house.

By the time she opened the back door, Wyatt had already dismounted and led Max into the barn. It would take him several minutes to unsaddle and brush down the horse, so instead of waiting inside for him, she padded across the yard to the barn.

She leaned against the doorframe, watching him smooth one hand across the lean muscles of the horse's shoulder, brushing him down with the other. The lingering scent of tobacco from his night at the saloon, along with the distinct odors of horse and hay, mixed with the fresh night air wafted in her direction. Beneath it all, though, she could still decipher Wyatt's own male scent. And the thought of tossing him down right there and having her way with him more than crossed her mind. She smiled to herself, listening as he sang quietly—but too quiet for her to make out the words—stopping only long enough to yawn. Loudly.

Pushing away from the door, she sashayed toward

him. "My, aren't you a handsome cowboy," she crooned. "You know, my husband is in town looking for bad guys. Whatdya say we go into the house and fool around before he gets back?"

Wyatt looked up but didn't stop brushing the horse. A smile curled his lips. "I like that idea, right fine, ma'am. But I wouldn't want to be the target of your husband's wrath. From what I've heard, he loves you more than life and would slay any man alive who dared touch you."

"Slay?" She giggled, shaking her head in amusement. Slowly, she closed the distance between them, reached up to touch his cheek, then pulled his head down to kiss him, all teasing aside. "I've missed you," she breathed against his lips. "You look exhausted."

"I am," he admitted. Yawning again, he stretched his arms upward then back. "I need a long, hot bath. But first, I need you." He wrapped his arms around her waist and kissed the side of her neck, just below the ear. It sent little shivers in all directions. "I don't like coming home this late, but it couldn't be helped. How was your day?"

"Interesting." She slid her arms around his neck. "While I've learned to live without a cell phone these last few months, today I could've used one to share some news."

He arched an eyebrow. "There's news? Out here, in the back of beyond?"

She nodded. "Cassie dumped her kids on our doorstep this morning. Apparently, she left town." She reached into her robe pocket and produced Cassie's note. "Willie gave me this."

He read it, then tucked it back into her pocket. "Well, at least we know they're all safe."

"*All?*"

He nodded. "Wilbert's at Doc's. Dwyer—the owner of the *Gazette*—found him on the side of the road unconscious," he explained. "Someone clocked him over the head. He's in bad shape, but he'll be all right."

Her brows furrowed. "Why would someone want to hurt Wilbert?"

He rubbed the back of his neck. "Maybe the same reason they wanted to hurt me." He gave her a long look. "C'mon, Emma. We both know I didn't get that lump on my head from a fall. I've been in construction all my life. I'm not *that* much of a klutz. Someone assaulted me." He shrugged. "But for what reason, I've no idea."

"None of this makes any sense."

He rubbed her arms and pressed a kiss to the tip of her nose before picking up the brush again. "It might not now, but it will."

Emma wanted to ask him what he meant by that, but clearly, he wasn't about to elaborate. His jaw was set. Whatever assistance he provided to the marshal and Josh, she assumed it included a confidentiality agreement. She had to respect that.

After tending to Max, they strolled into the house. Emma ran a bath for Wyatt. A minute later, he came into the bathroom behind her, stripped out of his clothes, and climbed into the tub.

"It's not hot enough!" she warned him, not wanting him to freeze his balls off.

He settled in the tub, then leaned back and closed

285

his eyes. "Doesn't matter. I just need to relax. Give me fifteen minutes and then come for me. Okay?"

She pressed a kiss to his forehead, set out a towel, then left him to check on the children. They were sleeping peacefully in Emma's old room, curled up in each other's arms. Clara's dolly was tucked in the crook of one arm while Willie slept with his arm draped protectively across his sister. As soon as Wilbert was up to it, she would make sure the children saw him. They were too young to understand why their mother would up and leave them at a neighbor's house then take off. Hopefully, when she gave them the news in the morning that their father was staying at Doc's for a few days, she could give them a little bit of happy.

After making a light snack for Wyatt, she returned to find him leaning back against the rim of the tub with his eyes closed, humming to himself.

She smiled and set down the plate of sliced tomatoes and boiled egg on the vanity. He heard her come in and opened his eyes, one at a time. "Fifteen minutes," she affirmed, handing him a mug of beer.

He took it and sipped it, then balanced it on his bent knee, watching her. "How are the kids?"

She put the lid down on the toilet and sat facing him. "So far, so good. Willie's trying to be brave and look after his sister. He thinks his mom will return for them. Clara believes she's just having a sleepover." She sighed. "Thankfully, they're sound asleep now."

He nodded. "They can stay as long as they need to. Once Doc gives Wilbert the all-clear, he'll come here, too, for a while."

She nodded. "The kids will love that."

He reached out and squeezed her hand, then pulled

it to his lips for a soft kiss. "Did you ever consider the children referred to in your letter are Willie and Clara?" She gazed off into the distance, and he tugged her hand, bringing her attention back to him. "I just mean, seeing as this is now July and your letter was written in December, there would be no way to give birth to multiple children in such a short timeframe."

"It's certainly possible." She looked at him, having thought the exact same thing when they showed up on her doorstep. "But...there's more."

One perfectly shaped eyebrow arched in question. "More...?"

She reached into her other pocket to pull out the letter she received while at Anne's shop, then handed it to Wyatt. He shook the water off his hands first, read it, then handed it back. "Do you know who it's from?"

She shrugged. "I don't recognize the handwriting." She put the letter back in her pocket. "In the meantime, let's get you into bed."

He grinned. "And just what will you do to me in bed, Mrs. Kincaid?"

Such a simple question sent heat coursing through her veins, spreading to her core. She took his wet hand in hers. "Come and find out."

Chapter Eighteen

Along with the aroma of freshly baked huckleberry scones and blueberry muffins wafting through the kitchen, Emma detected a hint of summer flowers in the air. Outside the window, the children chased each other in a game of tag. Poor Clara got tagged more than Willie. In the week since they had come to stay with them, Clara began calling her Auntie Em, which made Emma smile. Little did the children know there would be a famous *Auntie Em* from a book that hadn't been written yet.

Being called that reminded her of the book's premise. Throughout the entire story, Dorothy *wanted* to go home. And that's what Emma had wanted since the day she landed here because there was no place like home. Right?

But things were different now.

Now, *this* was her home. This time. This house. This town. How could she possibly leave?

"Penny for your thoughts," Wyatt said, planting a whiskery kiss on the side of her neck.

She squealed, then and wrapped her arms around his waist. He smelled of soap and his own masculine scent. "It'll cost you more than a penny."

"I think I can afford it." He lowered his head and gently kissed her, nudging her lips open with his tongue. His hands slid down her back, grabbing her buttocks to push her against his blatant desire. Her heart pounded. And the heat quickly spread from her mouth all the way down to her throbbing core. Whenever he kissed her, she was heated, simmering with passion. How could she ever tire of kissing him?

"Aw, hell," came a voice somewhere behind them. "I didn't mean to...I'll just be..."

Wyatt whirled around, pushing Emma behind him to collect herself. "It's all right, Wilbert," he said, waving him in. "How're you feeling this morning?"

He met Wilbert in the doorway and helped him over to the table where he pulled out a chair for him.

"Better," Wilbert said with a nod, taking the proffered seat. "I didn't mean to, er, interrupt you there. I just smelled them biscuits," he said to Emma. His face was tinged red. "My stomach started rumblin'."

"No worries." Emma waved a hand. She served him a plate with a scone and muffin on it, then poured him some coffee. "The children are outside," she said, nodding her head in the direction of their laughter.

"I can't thank you both enough for what you've done for me and the children," he told them, glancing from the window to the mug on the table. "Means a lot to me. Appreciate it."

Wyatt squeezed his shoulder. "What are friends for?"

Wilbert smeared a bit of jam on the scone then took a bite. "Mighty delicious."

"Glad you like it. I also made another pot of chicken soup for you. Doc Wilson said you're still to get plenty of liquids."

"Much obliged."

She glanced at Wyatt. The one question Wilbert

hadn't asked hung in the air. Did either of them hear from Cassie? They hadn't. But then, it had been a busy week. Anne and Doc Wilson were married the same day Doc gave the all-clear for Wilbert to move to her and Wyatt's place so he could recover, having nowhere else to go. They were more than happy to take him in. And Emma liked having the house hum with guests.

Since Wilbert joined the household, he'd spent most of his time either sitting on the porch, watching his children at play, or napping. Emma made sure to get him up and walking several times a day, doctor's orders. Wyatt spent most of his time in town helping the marshal and Josh while putting in a few hours here and there at his shop. She wondered how he managed not to collapse from exhaustion.

"I've got to head over to Sam's for a bit," Wyatt announced and wrapped his arm around Emma's waist. "I'll be back in a few hours." He planted a kiss on her lips, then breezed out the back door.

"You got yourself one fine man there," Wilbert told her, raising his mug in a salute.

Emma smiled, watching her husband disappear into the barn to saddle Max. "Don't I know it."

She filled Wilbert's mug with coffee, then went about tidying up the bowls and utensils before checking the second batch of biscuits in the oven. After pouring herself a hot cup of tea, she sat down across from Wilbert, studying him as he sipped coffee and gazed out the back door to the yard where his children frolicked. His face stiffened as he watched them. He looked away, rubbing his eyes.

"I'm a good listener," she told him softly.

His gaze snapped to hers, surprised. "You women

usually are," he surmised. "And good talkers, too. But we men never seem to want to talk. Do we?"

"Not usually." She paused, tilting her head as she watched him. "But I think *you* do."

He shrugged, staring down at the mug. "It's Cassie," he blurted out, fidgeting in his seat. "Damn woman's been…hell, Emma, she ain't been faithful to me these last seven months."

"That's the pot calling the kettle black, isn't it?" She was about to apologize for her harsh criticism, but Wilbert raised a hand.

"I've kept company with one of Madame Veronique's women, yes," he admitted. "I was with her the night my house burned, in fact." He rubbed his head, devoid of the bandages now. "But I wasn't the one who left first." He closed his eyes, inhaling deeply. "I don't understand what happened. It's like she forgot we have two children who need her—I need her. She's supposed to be home, taking care of them and me. Not gallivanting across the territory with some—" He waved a hand again but didn't continue.

"Do you know for certain there's…someone else?" she asked delicately. Cassie had never mentioned *that* to her. Then again, it wasn't like she and Cassie were besties where they felt the need to divulge all the juicy details. Still, her friend gave her no indication she strayed. Only that Wilbert had.

"Months back, I got injured at the mine." He rolled up his sleeve, exposing a six-inch scar on his forearm. "When I came home, a horse was tethered out front. But when I got inside, it was just Cassie. I demanded who was there. She got hoppin' mad. That's when I noticed she was hardly presentable." His face hardened.

"It was midday, and she was cavortin' with some—" He waved a hand angrily.

"Are you sure?"

He gave her a sour look. "If you saw the way she was dressed, you wouldn't be askin'. 'Sides, by the time I went back outside, the horse was gone."

"Did she say anything about it?"

"Just that I was crazy as a loon for thinkin' such things. At that point, she'd been sleepin' in the children's room for a couple months already." He shrugged. "Afterward, I saw the same horse 'round town a few times—and tethered outside my house every so often when I snuck home early."

"But you never saw who it was?"

He shook his head. "Nope."

She hesitated then admitted, "Cassie told me you were the one who strayed." The expression on his face turned from anger to sadness. She reached across the table and touched his hand. "I'm sorry. None of this is any of my business, Wilbert. You've been a good friend to Wyatt. And, if there's anything either of us can do, I hope you would just ask."

"Can you find the man she's cheatin' with, so I can kill him?"

****

Wyatt sat in the hard, brown leather chair, watching Griffin Grey puff away on a cigar. Smoke clouds engulfed him; the smell of tobacco sat heavy in the air. Grey slowly circled the room, his gaze fixed as he puffed away on the cigar. Wyatt didn't like him. Hadn't from the first. He couldn't quite put his finger on why, either. Maybe because the man had an eye for Emma—or because he just was a pompous ass, full of himself, narcissistic even. It didn't matter. His business with Grey would be ending next week. He would be finished with the renovations then and could wipe his hands clean of Grey once and for all.

Grey stopped in front of the window, glanced outside, then turned to Wyatt. "How's married life treating you?"

Wyatt tapped his hat against his leg in impatient irritation. He came to pick up the remainder of the money Grey owed him. Discussing his wife was not an option. "Let's cut the small talk. What is it you want?"

"To the point, I see," Grey remarked, nodding. After a long pause, he admitted, "I'd like you to come work for me." He held up a hand as Wyatt was about to launch into the many reasons why he wouldn't. "Now, I know what you're thinking. You already *do* work for me."

Wrong. There was one reason why Wyatt took the job. He wanted to see what Grey was up to, so he had ammunition to give to the marshal and Josh.

Grey paused and poured them each a whiskey. He handed one glass to Wyatt. "I have a large project I'd like you to oversee."

He accepted the whiskey, took a sip, stared at Grey, but didn't ask. He didn't care.

Grey moved away from the window and perched himself on the edge of the desk, flicking the cigar. Ashes drifted to the floor, catching on his pant leg, which he brushed off. "I've purchased a large plot of land," he continued. "And I'd like for you to work with the building and architecture company I engaged. You know the laws, codes, and such of the Territory. And while I have some faith in their skills and abilities, I don't want to be cheated."

Wyatt cocked his head. "Why would you think they would cheat you and I wouldn't?"

He puffed on the cigar. "Anything is possible. Needless to say, I want someone I've hired personally to work there."

"Where is *there*?"

"Butte."

Wyatt shook his head. "That's seventy-five miles away."

Grey nodded. "I'm aware of the distance. But believe me, I would make it worth your while." He paused. "In fact, I'm willing to *triple* your weekly rate."

Wyatt wasn't interested in working for Grey ever again—no matter how much the jerk wanted to pay him. Still, for a man like Grey to offer Wyatt that kind of money, there had to be a reason behind it. "What's the catch?"

Grey's eyebrows shot up, surprised. "Catch?"

Wyatt tugged the collar of his shirt. The room had suddenly grown warmer. "Yeah, you're going to *triple* my weekly rate. That's a lot of money. There must be a reason for it."

Grey moved away from the desk to return to the window, then clasped his hands behind back. It was a moment before he spoke. "I'd like this project completed in record time before my investors come from New York. Having your wife there would only be a…distraction. Therefore, I'm willing to pay you handsomely for your, er, separation—"

Wyatt bolted out of the chair, closed the distance between them. He grabbed Grey by the vest and shirtfront. "Let's get something straight." His tone was lethal. "I don't like you. I don't trust you. Never have. Never will."

Grey stiffened. "You're smarter than most of the local men around here," he went on, even though Wyatt's grip tightened. "I need someone smart to help me with my business. But you're certainly not a true local. Are you? What is it now, two years you've been in Whisper Creek? Perhaps, you're running from something...or someone?"

Wyatt's face was damp with sweat. *Why was it so damn hot?* "That's bullshit," he charged.

"Is it?" Grey paused, eyed him. "You look a little flushed. Feeling all right?"

No, he didn't. It felt like the room swayed. He caught a glimpse of Grey's untouched whiskey on the desk. "Why, you little piece of shit," Wyatt snarled, tightening his grip. "You poisoned me."

A slow grin curled his lip. "Is that any way to speak to your employer?"

"I'll never work for you again," he ground out.

"Oh, I think you will," he said, patting Wyatt's hand still bunched around his vest and shirt. "After all, you wouldn't want anything to ever happen to your lovely wife. Would you?"

Wyatt staggered as he pulled his arm back, so he could punch Grey in the face. But he didn't get a chance to hit the bastard. Everything around him faded to black.

****

Josh climbed the front steps of his brother's house two at a time. He pounded on the front door but didn't wait long enough for someone to answer. He barged inside and met up with Wilbert in the hallway.

Wilbert rubbed his head. "What's all the pounding for?"

"Where's Emma?" Josh demanded impatiently.

He shrugged. "In the barn, maybe? I must've dozed off. She was outside earlier playin' with the children."

Josh marched through the house and out the back door. He spotted Clara and Willie playing a game of catch under the shade of the hemlock trees. They saw him and waved. Clara took advantage of the distraction to toss the ball way out of Willie's reach.

"*Emma*," Josh shouted, rushing toward the barn. Thankfully, he found her sweeping the floor.

She stopped when she saw him, dropping the broom. "What's wrong?"

He closed the distance between them and put his hands on her arms. "I need to speak with you. It's important."

Her face went pale. "Josh, you're scaring me."

He gestured for her to sit on the nearby bale of hay while he paced. He removed his hat and shoved a hand through his hair before turning to her. "Wyatt didn't tell you *everything* about…" Christ, this was going to be more difficult than he thought. "Wyatt told me what you both spoke about regarding the future—including the time portal. But he left out one important detail." He paused. "You're not the only one who received a letter from yourself, telling you to go back." He paused. "Wyatt did, too."

"What?" she croaked out.

He nodded. "Just like you, Wyatt received a letter from his nineteenth-century self. He wanted to tell you. He should've. At least you now know about us being from the twenty-first century as well—and the portal."

He paused. "But I'm worried, though, because now…"

She shot to her feet. "Is he all right? Josh, what's going on?"

Josh squeezed her shoulders. "Someone overheard me and Wyatt talking about the future. About the time portal."

"When? Just now?"

He shook his head. "No. I don't know when exactly. I overheard two drunken idiots at the saloon laughing about it. They don't look familiar. But one of them said, 'No one can just drop in from the future. And who knows what a time portal is, anyway?' Without holding a gun to their heads, asking them to repeat it, there's little I could do. And since no one else besides the three of us knows about the time portal or the future, it's safe to say these clowns overheard us." He pushed out a deep breath. "I don't know *when* or how. Wyatt and I have always been so careful. We never discussed it in public. Ever."

Emma sucked in a deep breath. "Do you think someone could've been deliberately spying on me and Wyatt or you and Wyatt?"

He nodded. "It's possible."

Her brows furrowed. "But who?"

"That's what I need to find out. When will Wyatt be back?"

She glanced out the door to the light of day. "Soon, I'm sure. He went to Sam's to help fix a few things."

Josh nodded. "I don't want to leave you alone here with Wilbert. He's still not in the best of health to protect you should you need it."

"Do you think…someone is after him—or us?"

"I wish I could say no," he admitted. "Go pack a

bag. I'm sure Anne will let you stay with her and the doc until we get this sorted out." He gave her a quick but tight hug and then set her away from him. "I'm going to Sam's to get Wyatt. When we get back, we'll all head into town together."

Before she could nod, Josh was out of the barn. She wondered who could've overheard them. Josh said they were always careful when discussing the subject.

She paced then circled the inside of the barn, searching her brain for a clue. When she first told Wyatt she came from the future, they were *inside* the house. The next time they spoke about it, she found him out here in the barn, watching a video. He told her about his parents and how they died, and how much he missed them.

She stopped.

That had to be it! But who would be eavesdropping on them out here on their own property? It didn't make sense. None of it made sense—the letter she wrote to herself from this century (when did she travel back here the *first* time? She had no memory of it.), Wyatt and Josh arriving here from the future, and now this letter that Wyatt wrote to himself as well. A huge piece of the puzzle was missing, but if she found that piece, everything would fall into place.

Think.

Deep in thought, she circled the barn again but lost her balance when the ground suddenly trembled. Then she heard what sounded like a crash coming from somewhere outside. The barn shook like an earthquake—as if the plates beneath the earth's surface shifted. *Oh crap.* The last time she felt anything like *this*, she ended up in 1882!

Her head spun, and a swift whiplash of dizziness rattled her mind. She licked her lips repeatedly, hoping the taste would offer some detail on what was happening. Her hands were clammy; the thudding of her heart pounded against her chest. The smells of the barn quickly faded and changed into…something she hadn't smelled in a long time. Motor oil and paint.

How did it suddenly get so dark?

Blackness engulfed her. She was falling, slipping…through the cracks of time. Her senses spiraled out of control. She couldn't speak. She tried, but her voice was nothing more than a silent scream.

She kept falling…falling still. The heavy fog consumed her mind. It soon became too difficult to remember anything…

Then strong but soft arms surrounded her, pulled her toward safety, slowly lifting her out of the miasma.

She tried to speak, but her mouth was too dry. Somewhere in the distance, behind the fog and darkness of time, she heard someone crying.

Finally, when she found the energy to open her eyes, a familiar smiling face greeted her. And for a split second, relief engulfed her. She was safe!

Then…

"*What are you doing here*?" Emma demanded, blinking away the haze. She rubbed her temples, trying to sit up. Why was she laying on hard cement? *Cement*?

Her best friend wiped tears away from blue eyes. Amber looked insulted, though relieved at the same time. "*Me*? Is that any way to greet your best friend?" she snuffled. "I've been worried sick about you for months. *Months*! Do you hear me? Where the fuck have you been?"

Emma clenched her eyes shut and expelled a long, slow, agonizing breath. Her mouth was beyond dry. Licking her lips did nothing to help. "*Months*?" she repeated, feeling like she had cotton stuck on her tongue.

"Yes, months!" Amber shrieked, gently shaking her. "For chrissake, Emma, I thought you were dead!"

If Amber was *here*, that meant...

Oh no.

When she had the strength, she glanced back at the barn—correction, the *garage*—and swallowed back the sobs threatening to erupt. Icy fear twisted around her heart, making it nearly impossible to breathe. Dread blanketed her, making her shiver uncontrollably.

How could this happen? How could she have been catapulted back to the future while Wyatt remained in the past?

Her worst nightmare had come true—she returned to the twenty-first century. *Without* Wyatt. The reality of the situation hit her like a head-on collision.

With wobbly legs and Amber's help, Emma clumsily got to her feet. "I've got to go."

Amber's features scrunched. "Go where?"

"I've got to get to Helena," she said weakly, trying to stand without tipping over. "To see James."

Amber's brows rose. "James Mattheson?"

Emma glanced at her questioningly. "Yes. Do you know him?"

"He's the one who told me to meet you here. *Today*." She paused for a millisecond. "He said I'd find you here, but he didn't explain how he knew or where you'd been. I thought it was all some kind of joke."

"James," she mumbled.

Amber gripped her shoulders and gently shook her. "Now, would you mind telling me who the hell James Mattheson is and where the fuck have you've been for the last four months?"

****

Wyatt emerged from Grey's office and shielded his eyes from the bright sun. Whatever the bastard put in the whiskey did a number on him. Once he got his balance and could see straight, he mounted his horse and lit out for home.

By the time he got there, his headache was nearly gone, but he was so damn thirsty. He wondered what Grey slipped him. Laudanum, perhaps? Nah, had to be something more herbal as he didn't taste anything medicinal in the whiskey. Why did Grey have it in for him? It didn't make sense.

When he got to the house, he pulled Max around back and slid out of the saddle, then loosely tethered the reins around the post. The hair on the back of his neck stood up. Something was wrong. His eyes scanned the property. Nothing seemed out of the ordinary.

He ran into the house, shouting for Emma. He stopped just inside the back door and listened. It was quiet. Too quiet. Where the hell was everyone?

"Willie? Clara?" he barked.

He searched every room. Where the hell was everybody? He went back outside. The wagon was gone. He pushed out the breath he was holding. That would explain why Wilbert and the kids weren't there, but what about Emma? There was no sign of her in the barn either.

He paced and felt something judder beneath his feet. He stopped in mid-step to look down. It wasn't anything tangible, but it almost felt like…a tremor. Beneath the earth's surface. Like a small earthquake.

His heart lurched in his chest.

The last time he felt anything remotely like *that* was when Emma arrived from the future. His mind soundlessly screamed. His heart raced, nearly exploding in his chest. The taste of anguish filled him to the core. He shook his head at the realization she could be *gone…*

Forever.

Chapter Nineteen

"And there you have it," Emma said, waving a hand. She took another sip of iced tea, carefully avoiding the sudden splash of ice cubes sliding toward her mouth when she tilted the glass. By no means was it an easy conversation. Her story sounded ridiculous. She cringed, listening to herself explain the events that transpired. But Amber *knew* her. Surely, she would understand. And believe her.

But Amber stared at her like she had suddenly sprouted six heads. Her perfectly arched auburn eyebrows scrunched downward, and the way her lips pursed said she wasn't buying Emma's story.

"Riiight," Amber said, moving to the side bar to pour a large volume of bourbon into her iced tea. She drank it quickly, then poured more over the remaining ice, staring at Emma. "Soooo, let me get this straight. For the last, what, five months, you traveled to the year 1882, married a cowboy named Wyatt, made a new best friend, learned how to cook dead flesh, and you expect me to believe all *that*?"

"It sounds outrageous, I know." Emma held out her glass, waiting for a shot of bourbon. She could use it now to steady her nerves. "When I went back in time, I certainly didn't believe it myself. But it's true." She stared at her friend. "Have you ever known me to make up something like this?"

Amber shook her head. "No, but I have to admit this is the *biggest* crock of shit I've ever heard in my life," she scoffed, flailing her arms, and spilling her drink on the rug. "Time travel." She shook her head, then glowered at Emma. "How am I supposed to believe time travel? You're just bat-shit crazy, girl. Or maybe you need some serious drugs to fix whatever fantasies are clouding your judgement."

Amber had a heart of gold, the strength of an army, and the patience of a thousand saints. But she liked to curse. A lot. It never bothered Emma. Amber was always careful who she vented to. Only in times like these, when she was angry or surprised, her colorful patois erupted.

Emma leaned into the cozy chair and closed her eyes; her heart constricted with anguish. Within an instant, life as she knew it with Wyatt was over. When she first landed in the nineteenth century, all she wanted was to return home—to her time. And now that she had, she wanted nothing more than to return to the past. Live the rest of her days with her husband, raise a few children, and continue running her own business.

Thinking about it made her nauseous. Without taking a sip, she put the glass on the table and stood up. "I promise to explain more later. But first, I need a hot shower, then we're going to Helena to meet with James Mattheson. If he sent you to meet me here *today*, then you can guarantee he'll confirm what I'm telling you is the truth."

Amber stared at her long and hard. "All right then," she allowed reluctantly, her gaze sweeping over her nineteenth-century attire. "After you shower, I'll drive you there myself. But first, what's with the getup?"

Emma glanced down at her blouse and long skirt. "It's what I wore…there."

"Uh-huh." Amber nodded then tossed an overnight bag at Emma. "Change of clothes." She shrugged. "In case Matheson was right, I figured you'd need something else to wear."

"Thanks."

Emma knew the layout of the house and could find her way blindfolded. The layout was almost the same as the house she lived in with Wyatt. In the past. She found the bathroom, turned on the hot water, then stripped out of her clothes and climbed into the shower.

The modern-day shower with its powerful head jets felt wonderful. While Wyatt had made their outdoor shower as modern as possible with limited supplies of the nineteenth century, it felt good to use shower gel, shampoo, and a much-needed razor.

She stood there for a long time, letting the steaming hot water sluice down her body, hoping the sound of the running water would drown out her sobs. This journey was entirely unexpected. *It wasn't supposed to happen.* Not like this.

But I wanted to return to the future ever since I arrived in 1882. I finally, get my wish, and now I don't want it.

She wanted Wyatt.

She wanted Whisper Creek.

She wanted the nineteenth century.

Only now, she remained trapped in her own century. A place she no longer wanted to be—or felt she fit in. Why couldn't she have realized that before it was too late? Would it have made a difference to the time travel gods? She would never know now.

An hour later, when she emerged from the bathroom, showered, and wearing a clean set of borrowed clothes from her friend, she overheard Amber speaking to someone—or rather, screeching at someone in the other room.

Quickly, she padded into the living room and stopped abruptly in the doorway, accidentally stubbing her bare toe on the saddle. "Ouch."

"Emma!"

James smiled when she hobbled into the room, rubbing her toe. The first time she'd met him, she had no idea who he was. But having known and married Wyatt, she could see how all the brothers resembled each other. Both James and Wyatt were blessed with the same piercing blue eyes and light blond hair, though James's was a shade lighter. He stood as tall as Wyatt, but not as muscular, from what she could tell by the fit of his clothes.

"You know, you could've told me you were Wyatt's brother to begin with," she scolded, folding her arms across her chest.

"And ruin all the fun for you?" He waved a hand, then walked over to her and pulled her into a hug. Amber must've given him a crazy look because he explained, "Hey, she's family now. I'm allowed to hug my sister-in-law."

"*Sister-in*—?" She threw her hands up in the air. "Would one of you please tell me what the fu—hell is going on here?" Amber demanded. With strangers around, she tried to suppress her colorful vocabulary. "My best friend disappears for *months*," she rambled on, "only to return with a story about time travel. *Time travel*. Seriously? You," she said, poking a finger in the air toward James, "better come up with an explanation that doesn't include aliens, Star Wars, Stargate, or shit like that. Otherwise, I'm calling the cops."

"No need for that," James assured her calmly. "Sit down, and I'll tell you what I know."

Amber cast a glare in Emma's direction then reluctantly sat. She folded her arms stubbornly across her chest while James explained everything, beginning with Wyatt and Josh traveling back in time to the letter Emma received from her nineteenth-century self.

Every few sentences, though, Amber would continue her tirade of the incredulity of time travel. James would hold up a hand to silence her, so he could continue.

As James yammered on, Emma's thoughts went back to the last moments she saw Wyatt that morning—well, the morning in the nineteenth century—when he told her he was going to Sam's. He looked deliciously handsome. All she wanted was to lead him into the bedroom and have a quickie before he went off. But they didn't. What would he think once he discovered she was gone? Surely, he would *know* she didn't mean to go.

"Well?" Amber prodded, gently tapping Emma's toes with her own.

"Well, what?" Emma asked, then looked to James. He was about to say something, but then Amber cut him off.

"You disappear for over four months, then come back wearing some"—she waved her hand around—"crazy costume I know you would *never* be caught dead in. And I'm supposed to believe there's a time portal that transported you back to 1882. Is that it?"

Emma smiled. "Yep, that's it."

Amber stared at her, hands on her hips, jaw clenched. Her eyes narrowed. "I know I'll regret this," she began reluctantly, "but considering the way you appeared out of thin air, I'm going to go out on a limb here and say that I think there's *some* truth in what you're saying." She paused. "I just don't understand *how* it could be possible." She flopped down on the sofa. "How did you get back?"

Something tightened around Emma's heart. "Actually, I'm not quite sure. I don't know how it all works. All I know is I didn't plan to return. One minute, I was in the barn—in the nineteenth century—then the next, I was here. With you." She looked at James. "Do you have any ideas on this? After all, you were the one who gave me the letter in the first place."

James stood up, shoved both hands through his hair before facing her. "Do you remember that cryptic letter you received the other day? In the past, I mean."

"No," she said, then stopped and thought for a moment. "Wait. Do you mean the one that said to expect the unexpected?"

He nodded. "That was from me."

She took a quick breath of utter astonishment. "I don't understand. How could you send a letter from the future *to* the past? Doesn't it work the other way around?"

"Whoa. Whoa. *Whoa*," Amber shouted, jumping to her feet. "You mean that you," she said to James, "went back there, too?"

James shook his head. "Not exactly." Emma saw he was trying to choose his words wisely. "For nearly a century and a half now, there's been talk of Whisper

308

Creek being haunted. From time to time, people would go missing randomly. But, they weren't missing. They traveled back in time."

"*What*?" Amber exploded.

Emma touched her friend's arm. "Let him explain."

"I'm not sure how Wyatt found the portal—or how anyone else did, for that matter," James continued. "We thought there was only one way back—here in the garage. There could've been more. Who knows?" He shrugged. "In any case, Wyatt was able to send us— Josh and me, that is—a letter explaining what happened. In chronological detail. Then when Josh decided to try to go after Wyatt, we took precautions. Just in case he made it."

"What sort of precautions?"

"I sent Josh back with that letter for you, along with some other items," he explained. "We still weren't sure how the time portal worked—or if there was only one, seeing as how both my brothers went back from this property and nowhere else. But once Josh got there, I received more letters from him and Wyatt, explaining events transpiring in 1882. One of those letters was actually from you," he told Emma. "That's when I first contacted you."

"All right," Amber scoffed, throwing her hands up. "I've heard enough. You're no Neil deGrasse Tyson or Doc Brown, that's for sure, and she's no Marty McFly either. But c'mon, people. Now, you're talking crazy. Like loony-bin crazy. I may have to call the mental institution for the both of you."

"Amber," Emma warned. "I know it's a lot to digest. Believe me, I get it. I would have a hard time believing you if the tables were turned. But I know you.

And I know you wouldn't make up something like this. Besides, I need to know what happened."

After a moment, Amber pushed out a breath, then sat down. "Fine," was all she said.

Emma looked at James. "How did Wyatt initially go back?"

James didn't answer her because his attention was set on her left hand. He crossed the room and took her hand in his, admiring her ring. "Only an engagement ring," he said. "No wedding ring?"

She shook her head. "There wasn't time."

His brows knitted together. "Oh, but there was."

She gave him a quizzical look. "I don't understand."

"You're wearing our mother's engagement ring," he explained. "I sent Josh back with it. Wyatt had the wedding ring here in the twenty-first century he was supposed to give you on your wedding day."

Tears pooled in her eyes, thinking back to that day. "He said there wasn't time. Not with our quick engagement, then the fire and the deputy's funeral."

"Deputy Allen?" When she nodded, he asked, "How?"

Her brows furrowed. "You don't know? He died in the fire at the Copper Pan Saloon."

James shook his head. "Christ, you all may have changed history." He rubbed a hand over his face, the gravity hitting him. "The deputy wasn't supposed to die in that fire—the marshal was." He paused. "After Marshal Reed's death, Josh was elected marshal." He rubbed his jaw, contemplating. "This is starting to make sense."

"Really?" Amber retorted sarcastically. "Because

none of this shit makes any sense to me. And I'm a smart woman. College-educated, even. But this talk of time travel and now changing history?" She shook her head. "I've heard all I want to hear." She looked at Emma. "I'm sorry, hon. This is a shit ton to swallow. I've spent the better part of the last five months worrying my ass off about you, and this is the best you can come up with?"

Emma grabbed her friend's arm. "Amber, wait!"

Amber kissed Emma's cheek. "I love you, Emma. And I'm beyond relieved you're not dead or kidnapped like I originally thought. But I don't know if I have it in me to grasp what you guys are talking about. I need time to digest this"—she waved a hand—"this insanity."

"You should stick around, Amber," James told her pointedly. "This involves you, too."

Amber's face lost some color. "Say, what?"

"There's a lot more." James nodded, then held up a hand. "First, I need to make a call." He reached for the cell phone in his back pocket. "I received another letter from Wyatt," he explained, while searching for the number in his phone. "This one said not to open it until tomorrow. I should've brought it with me, but I wasn't expecting to see you *today*. I'll just have my intern bring it here."

****

Less than an hour later, the doorbell rang. The three of them were so engrossed in conversation no one heard a car drive up. James took the liberty of answering the door while Amber poured another round of iced tea, but Emma declined, filling a tumbler with ice water instead.

James returned to the living room with his intern. And when the young man stepped into the living room, the tumbler slipped out of Emma's hand, crashing to the hardwood floor. Water, ice cubes, and shattered glass splattered everywhere.

She gasped. The blood froze in her veins. "*You!*"

The intern seemed even more surprised to see her. The color in his face drained to white. He could pass for a corpse. While he was dressed in a twenty-first-century suit this time, his face was the exact same as she remembered from another century.

"I know you," Emma accused, trying to recall his name. He looked so familiar. She wracked her brain—what was his name? And where exactly had she seen him? *Think!*

James shot her a surprised look before gazing at his intern. "You do?"

She nodded, remembering. "We met during…the Fourth of July celebration. He asked me for directions to Grey's office."

"When was that?" James pressed.

She looked at him. "In *1882*."

"1882? He went back in time, too?" Amber cried. She said no more after that, but her gaze darted from the newcomer to James to Emma, then back again, while she sipped heavily on her bourbon-laden iced tea.

The young intern shook his head. "I'm afraid you have me mistaken for someone else," he told her. He glanced at James and shrugged.

"Your name's Brody," Emma charged. "And you've got a tattoo on your right wrist. A cross."

James grabbed Brody by the arm, shoved him further inside the living room. Brody winced, trying to get his arm free, but James wouldn't let go.

"I don't know what she's talking about, Mr. Matheson!" he cried. "Honestly."

"Really?" James yanked Brody's sleeve up. And sure enough, there was a tattoo. A small one, but a tattoo, nevertheless. A small cross on the underside of his wrist. "Then how do you explain that she knows *your* name and you have a tattoo on your right hand?"

He shrugged again. "Coincidence?"

James clenched his jaw in the same way Wyatt did. His eyes turned a stormy shade of blue. "You little shit," he ground out. "You've been spying on me all this time."

Brody shook his head vehemently. "No, not you. I swear!"

Emma stepped closer. Her gaze swept over him distastefully from head to toe. "No, it's Wyatt and Josh he's been spying on," she deduced.

James cursed more colorfully than Amber's angriest tirade, then grabbed Brody by the shoulders and shook him. "You have exactly five seconds to tell me the truth before I beat the shit out of you," he warned. "And when I do, there'll be nothing left in any century for anyone to find. You got that?"

Brody, half James's size, swallowed nervously and nodded. "Y-yes."

James released him but didn't move away. "First, where's the letter?"

The intern nervously fumbled with his suit jacket. He produced the letter in question, then handed it to James, who checked the seal. He glowered at Brody.

"Did you open this?" he demanded.

Brody shook his head. "No, I…figured I'd wait

313

until you opened it, so you wouldn't notice."

James pushed out a slow, deliberate breath. "All these months, you've been digging through my files." He paused. "For what purpose?"

Brody swallowed again. "Mr. Grey asked me if I wanted to experience the adventure of a lifetime," he began quietly, eyes averted.

"Grey?"

He nodded. "He said I'd make a ton of money. All I had to do was travel back and forth—between the twenty-first century and the nineteenth. I thought he was nuts at first. I mean, time travel? Anyway, he convinced me it'd be worth it."

"When did he first approach you?"

Brody's gaze lifted toward the ceiling. "Maybe two years ago," he said with a shrug. "Somewhere around there."

"That's around the time Wyatt went back," Emma said quietly.

James nodded. "How did Grey know about time travel?"

Brody licked his lips and shrugged. "I don't know. All I know is what he told me. That there would be a way for me to go back and forth between centuries. But I'd have to dig up dirt on Wyatt and Josh Kincaid."

"What sort of dirt?" Amber asked, chiming in.

"You know, just stuff. Like who they married, what they did for a living, when they *disappeared*," he said, using air quotes to emphasize. "That sort of thing."

Emma's blood boiled. "How did you find the portal?"

His gaze nervously shifted from her to James then

back again. "It's on your property," he said like they should've known. "He showed me where it is."

Emma and James exchanged a glance. While none of them could figure out how the portal worked, Grey knew. And Brody knew. "You will tell us how to use the portal," James threatened him. "Or else."

Brody nodded, visibly swallowing.

"How often does Grey go back and forth?" Emma asked.

"I don't know," he replied with a shrug. "Used to be a lot. Then he started sending me instead. Said he couldn't take all the blackouts and headaches it caused. I didn't mind it so much. I mean, who else could travel between centuries? It was cool, you know. Anyway, I was sworn to secrecy." He looked at Emma. "When I first saw you at the fair, I couldn't believe it. I saw your photo in Mr. Matheson's office, and well, to see you back *there*, actually scared the shit—sorry, scared the heck out of me."

"Does Grey know I'm from here—the twenty-first century?"

"I don't think so," he admitted. "I mean, it's possible. But I only saw your photo at Mr. Matheson's office. I never relayed information about you to Grey. Though, he did ask me if I'd heard of you."

"And what did you tell him?"

He shrugged. "That I hadn't. At least, I thought I hadn't. Then I saw you. But I never told him I knew you were from the future, um, here."

"What the hell does Grey want by using the portal?" James barked.

"Money," supplied Amber, finally joining the conversation. "I'll bet you dollars to donuts Sherlock is having Watson here bring him information on insurance policies and landowners from the nineteenth century. He's looking for a way to make his millions in the past, to carry forward to the future." She arched an eyebrow at Brody. "Am I right, Scoop?"

He nodded. "Yep."

There was only one thing to do now. Obtain the proof and get it back to the past to prove it—and have Grey arrested.

While Emma didn't know how she traveled back and forth, Brody did. James read her mind. A smile turned his mouth upward as he draped an arm around Brody's shoulders. "You and I are going to have a little chat about how you're going to right this wrong," James told the younger man.

Brody glanced nervously at Emma then back to James. "Are you going to have me arrested?"

James contemplated that for a long moment. "That depends."

"On what?"

"You."

"You can't just throw me in jail," Brody argued.

"I'm a lawyer. Wanna bet?" James challenged. "And my little brother is a lawyer in the nineteenth century. So, either way, buddy, you're screwed if you don't help us." He ushered Brody into the kitchen and sat him down at the table.

Reluctantly, the young man sat, but with his arms folded across his chest. James took out his cell phone, opened the voice memo app, and said, "Now, let's start from the beginning."

Chapter Twenty

In the days after Emma vanished, Wyatt spent hours upon hours every day in the barn, searching for a sign, a clue, anything from her. He thought if he stayed in there long enough, he just might find *something* to tell him she didn't intend to go back to the future. More specifically, her disappearance was all some kind of freak accident. The thought of living out his days without her did more than rip his heart out. He couldn't fathom a life without her. And as long as he and Josh remained in the nineteenth century, there was hope of her returning—or perhaps even him going back to the future.

Without Emma, there would be no life here—or anywhere—worth staying for, living for. He needed to find her. He *must* find her.

Since he didn't know *how* he had arrived in the nineteenth century, to begin with, he didn't know how he would ever figure out a way back. He and Josh had explored every avenue, thought of every scenario, and still, they couldn't find a way to return. So, how did Emma? It had to have been accidental. If she had known about it, she would've told him. Wouldn't she?

Wyatt shoved both hands through his hair, then tilted his head back. He stared up at the beamed ceiling and pushed out a deep breath. He needed a miracle. But those were in short supply.

"Maybe we overlooked something." Josh's voice jarred him out of his thoughts. They were back in the barn, searching once more for a trace of Emma.

"No shit," he scoffed.

Josh rubbed the back of his neck, thinking. "You said you found a wedding ring on the property in the future just before you were sent back here, to the past, right?"

Wyatt nodded.

"Well, what if you have to have something from the future in order to go back there? I mean, what if you need something in your hand from the time you want to visit?"

Wyatt thought about that. "Like a token?"

"Exactly."

He shoved a hand through his hair, thinking. "But what token?"

"Let me think." Josh paced. It was several moments before he spoke again. "Emma was wearing Mom's engagement ring, right?"

"Yeah, so?"

"So, what if those two things *together*—her wearing the engagement ring, and you holding the wedding ring—have some kind of, I don't know, transportational pull?" Wyatt gave him a dubious look, so he held up a hand and explained, "What if all you need is Emma? We assume she made it back there. If she did, *maybe* it had to do with her wearing Mom's ring. I don't know for certain, but if that *is* the case, then you're good to go, especially since you have the wedding ring."

Wyatt mulled that over. "But what if it's not that?"

"Then we're back to square one." He paused. "By

the way, why didn't you give Emma the wedding ring?"

Wyatt kicked the dirt around. "I told her I didn't have time to buy a ring. Truth is, I wanted to have it engraved first. I planned to surprise her with it the night she…went back."

Josh nodded, gripped him by the shoulder. "You'll be able to give her that ring soon," he assured him. "I know it."

This was the first time Wyatt felt tears burn his eyes since his parents died several years ago. He cleared his throat. "She's the best thing that ever happened to me, Josh. I don't care whether she wants to live in the future or here, but she's not going to live in either place without me."

Josh smiled. "Then we best figure out a way to get you back to the future."

Wyatt chuckled at the absurdity of it all. Shaking his head, he said, "You know, I could really use that flying DeLorean about now."

They both laughed then walked deeper into the barn. Slowly. Half expecting Wyatt to vanish instantly.

He didn't.

****

"Are you out of your effing mind!" Amber shouted, trying to keep a lid on her colorful rant. "You just returned. Now you want to go *back*?"

Emma had been in the twenty-first century for exactly three days. And that was three days too long. In that time, though, she and James came up with a plan to send her back.

Apparently, Brody *knew* how the portal worked, but he wasn't willing to give up the details, lest James have him arrested. They couldn't very well tell the

319

twenty-first century local authorities they'd found a way to travel through time. Or that Brody was bringing information on insurance policies and landowners back to his boss in the nineteenth century to use for his own advantage.

Instead, they decided to keep him under house arrest for a while. At least, until he explained how the portal worked. But he was tight-lipped about it, refusing to tell them anything. Right now, Brody was in the guest room with a bodyguard James hired—someone he'd known a long time that could be trusted.

Emma raised her hands in a plea of silence. "Amber, please. Don't make this any harder for me. You heard what's in Wyatt's letter—and what Brody said. I have to go back."

"Your life is *here,*" Amber pleaded. She took Emma's hands in her own, squeezed them tight. "Why would you want to give up everything and live in the nineteenth century? It's so…so nineteenth century. And old-fashioned. And the men smell," she teased. "They don't even have deodorant, for chrissake."

Emma smiled. "*You* are all I have here. My mom's gone. I have no other family. The only thing that would keep me here is you." She paused. "My husband is in the nineteenth century. And I love him very much. I married him, so I could have a life with him, not without him."

Amber pulled her into a tight hug. "I love you but hate you at this moment."

"I know." Emma returned the hug fiercely. "You've always been my best friend. And I will love you with all my heart forever. But going back to Wyatt…it's where I belong." She paused, pulling away.

"Someday, you'll meet someone, too, and you'll understand."

Amber rolled her eyes. "This sucks. You travel back in time and find Prince Charming. Yet I'm stuck here, and I get nowhere."

"Maybe you should come back with me?"

Amber laughed. "I don't know if I could ever do without a hot shower, hairdryer, or cell phone."

"I thought so, too, at first. But you'd be surprised how easily those things are to give up."

"Well," she hedged. "Maybe I'll drop in for a visit. After all, you came back. So, since it's not a one-way trip, I'd think about it."

James returned from the other room where he was busy making phone calls, having his team at the office do some research on Grey and Brody. He shoved his cell phone in his pocket and stopped abruptly when he saw the two of them. It was uncanny how much he looked like Wyatt and Josh. The same shape of face, the same build, the same height. Her heart ached a little more for Wyatt just then. He was so far, yet so close.

"Everything all right?" he asked, gazing from one to the other.

Amber wiped her eyes. Emma nodded. James sat down on the chair next to the sofa, facing Emma. A lock of blond hair fell onto his forehead, and he ran a hand through his hair, sweeping it off.

"Do you really want to do this?" he asked her.

She nodded. "Of course."

He smiled, reached for her hand, and enclosed it in his grasp. "Give my brothers a big hug from me. Tell them…" His voice caught. "Tell them I miss them. It's not the same without them."

"Maybe you should come with me?" she suggested softly.

He shook his head. "Nah, the nineteenth-century Old West is not for me," he told her with a wave of his hand. "Besides, I need to stay behind and make sure you get back there safely."

"Wait," Amber said. "You mean there's a chance something could happen to her when she goes through the portal, or whatever it's called?"

"Aside from feeling dizzy," Emma began, "I don't think so. Wyatt and Josh didn't suffer, nor were they harmed in any way when they went through either." She shrugged. "None of us knows how this portal really works, but it doesn't seem like it's harmful. If Brody could come back and forth as often as he does, I should be fine."

"Speaking of Brody," James began. "I've come up with a solution to keep him here."

"What?" Emma and Amber blurted out at the same time.

"Let me worry about that." He stood up and pulled Emma to her feet, taking her hands. "You better get going. Wyatt's waiting for you." Then he handed her a letter. "I'll brief you on what Grey's up to, but be sure to give this to Josh the minute you arrive. Brody came through on one thing. He said you'll need to hold this or keep it in your pocket when you go through."

Emma had already changed into the clothes she wore the day she arrived in to the future. She didn't want to return wearing twenty-first-century attire, lest anyone but Wyatt or Josh find her. It was still unclear how this whole time-travel thing worked, anyway. And she wasn't sure if only three days had passed in 1882, the same as it did here.

James must've read her mind. "It's relatively the same amount of time, give or take a few days. That is, if Brody's telling the truth. I'll get more information out of him. And if I can swing it, I'll stop in for a visit." He drew in a deep breath. "Ready?"

She nodded. "Ready."

Chapter Twenty-One

Wyatt perched himself on the edge of the marshal's desk, arms folded across his chest, one leg dangling. He and Josh exchanged a glance as they waited for the lawman to decide. Josh shrugged. Marshal Reed stared out the window overlooking a busy Main Street. He stroked his jaw, chewing over their discussion.

A witness had come forward earlier under strict anonymity regarding how Griffin Grey conducted business illegally. They had all wanted to nail Grey, but they couldn't quite figure out a way. Then this witness stated—in a letter to the marshal—he had evidence that Rossler was the one who commissioned the recent fires under Grey's orders. Fires, not just in Whisper Creek but also in other territories east of Montana.

Unfortunately, there was no evidence in writing between Grey and Rossler, but this letter revealed conversations that occurred between the source's contact, Rossler, and Grey. While it was all circumstantial, if they played their cards right, they just might be able to nail him.

If the witness turned out to be unreliable, well, then they had nothing to go on. Grey would get away scot-free, and they would be back to square one.

Wyatt removed his hat to wipe his forehead with the back of his hand. It was another hot day, but thanks to the ominous rain-threatening clouds, it wasn't as hot as it had been the day before. He grabbed a handkerchief out of his pocket, mopped his brow, then donned his hat.

The sound of the old clock on the wall ticked away the seconds, then minutes, before the marshal finally turned around.

With a curt nod, he looked at Josh and ordered, "Bring Rossler in for questioning." He rummaged through his desk until he found what he was looking for. To Wyatt, he said, "I'm deputizing you."

Wyatt's eyebrows shot up. "Wait, what? Me?"

Marshal Reed nodded. "Rossler will most likely shit his pants at seeing Josh. But if you're there too, and word gets back to Grey you're a lawman, maybe both men will think twice about lyin' to me. 'Sides, Josh, and I need all the help we can get if this is actually going to lead to his arrest. And right about now, you two are the only ones I trust."

Rossler would be an easy confession, no doubt. The young man was as skittery as a long-tailed cat in a room full of rocking chairs. But Grey? Wyatt knew Grey would not cave easily. He was arrogant and devious. It's why he had Rossler do his dirty work. No paper trails. Nothing in writing. Only one employee's word against that of a successful financier who owned several businesses across the country. Who would the jurors believe in a trial? Grey, hands down.

Once the marshal took care of the legalities of the deputizing, Wyatt signed a form before being bestowed with the infamous tin star of a deputy U.S. marshal. That done, he and Josh headed over to Grey's Banking & Loan office. The two brothers stood outside for a moment, surveying passersby, giving anyone who walked close to the building a look that told them to stay away.

Wyatt shook his head. "This is so…"

"Surreal?" Josh supplied.

"Yeah. I mean, one minute, I'm a carpenter. The next, a deputy U.S. marshal. Weird, huh?"

"Not as weird as traveling a hundred and forty years into the past."

"You got that right."

Josh nodded. "Let's do this."

Both men walked inside with purposeful strides but stopped upon entry. The temporary office looked more like a bank. On one side stood a long counter with three teller windows every few feet. On the other side of the office were two long mahogany desks with matching guest chairs. Toward the back, a door that most likely led to either Grey's personal office or a staircase to the second floor.

Daniels, one of the young men Wyatt had seen with Grey from time to time, sat behind one of the desks. He looked up; his face lost color.

Josh rested a hand on the hilt of his gun hanging low on his hip. "Where's Grey?" he demanded.

Daniels, no more than twenty-two or thereabouts, swallowed nervously. He glanced at the rear door. "I-I don't k-know. He was h-here earlier," he stammered.

"Keep an eye on this guy," Josh said to Wyatt while he went and searched what was through door number one.

An alarm broke through the silence. It sounded like it came from the other side of town. Both brothers exchanged a glance, then bolted out of the building and down Main Street. The bell atop the fire station rang urgently. They ran toward the marshal's office and caught sight of the fire wagons way ahead of them, speeding out of town.

"I don't like the looks of this," Josh said as they reached their horses and hopped in the saddles.

They rode about a half mile until they spotted the smoke billowing up toward the sky over the next hill.

Wyatt swallowed uneasily. The smoke came from the direction of his property. Shit! He nudged Max on faster, galloping over the hills. As he got closer, he realized the smoke originated at Sam's place, not his. They took a turn and headed for his friend's property instead.

Wyatt jumped out of the saddle before his horse even came to a halt. Sam stood outside the barn, watching it quickly go up in flames. He spotted Wyatt and Josh and ran toward them as the firefighters started pumping water onto the burning building.

"Are you all right?" Josh demanded.

Sam coughed, wiping away the streaks of smoke on his face. He leaned over, hands on his knees, sucking in deep breaths. "Right as rain," he assured them.

"What happened?" Wyatt demanded.

"I don't rightly know," Sam said, shaking his head. "I came outside because I heard someone yellin'. Sounded like a woman shriekin'. As I neared the barn door, the whole building just ignited." He straightened and cocked his head in the direction of the firefighters. "Thankfully, the fire department spotted the smoke from town and came as fast as possible. Otherwise…"

"Wait," said Wyatt. "You said you heard a woman?"

Sam shrugged. "Yeah, she was shoutin' my name. It's what made me come outside."

"In here!" the fire chief shouted, waved his men over. He was in the large doorway, flailing his arms. The men with the hose maneuvered in that direction, aiming the water through the doorway. One of the firefighters disappeared inside, followed by another.

"What's going on?" Wyatt asked, eyeing his brother.

"They must've found something," he replied.

"Or somebody," Sam added.

The first firefighter lumbered away from the burning barn, toward them, carrying someone in his arms. A woman. Her dress was streaked with grime. She lay unconscious in his arms.

As they came closer, Wyatt recognized the dress. It belonged to Emma. And it was the last thing he saw her wear before she went back to the future.

His heart lurched. As soon as his legs registered what his mind said, he ran toward the firefighter. Up close, he recognized the man under the mask as Joe Cadmus, who gave him a curt nod as he transferred the limp body into his arms.

Wyatt collapsed to his knees, laying Emma gently on the dirt. He checked her pulse. She had one. And it was strong. But she wasn't breathing. Thankfully, he knew CPR and began administering it, while Sam and Cadmus watched on, gaping in shock.

"Is he actually kissin' her while she's unconscious?" Sam gasped, watching as Wyatt pinched Emma's nose and placed his mouth over hers.

"It's way of getting air into her lungs," Josh explained. "It's a form of First-Aid from—um, from where we come from."

Cadmus's eyebrows shot up in disbelief, but he nodded, then reluctantly returned to his fellow firefighters to help extinguish the blaze that was nearly now under control.

Wyatt was oblivious to everything and everyone around him. All that mattered was Emma. "Breathe, dammit!" he shouted at her, between breaths.

Two more firefighters emerged from the burning structure, carrying yet another body. They laid the man on the ground. Josh rushed over to him to administer CPR, heedless of the firemen who shouted at him to get off the man, not kill him. It was Grey's man Rossler.

"Dammit, woman," Wyatt roared as he pumped her chest. "You traveled back in time to get to me, you better breathe!"

Emma coughed and gasped for air, then rolled to her side. She alternated between coughing and breathing slowly. While Wyatt patted her back, his tears of terror quickly turned into those of joy.

After a few moments, when she stopped coughing, he pulled her into his arms. She smiled up at him, and her cheeks had a healthy, rosy glow. He tucked a tress behind her ear, blinking back the tears. "You came back to me," his voice cracked.

"I never wanted to leave," she told him, then wrapped her arms around his neck for a tight embrace. Gently, he pulled her to her feet and held her against him. "It was by accident," she continued, cradling his face between her hands. "I never wanted to leave you. I hope you believe me."

"I believe you," he assured her. "But how did you get back?"

A smile curled one corner of her lips. "I have something of yours," she told him, with a saucy tone. "Apparently, I needed something from the time I want to return to."

His eyebrow quirked upward. "The engagement ring?"

She shook her head. "That was your mother's, and it's from the future. What I have was made in the past, traveled to the future, and is now back where he—or she—belongs."

It took a moment for him to realize she was pregnant. And when he did, Wyatt let out a loud whoop of delight. He picked Emma up and twirled her around and around before setting her down. He dug into his pocket, then slipped something on her finger.

She looked down and smiled. "James told me you had this."

"It's yours."

"I know." Without taking the ring off, she said, "It's inscribed. Wrapped around my heart."

"Indeed, you are, my love," he told her, lifting her off the ground again as he kissed her.

When Josh joined them, Wyatt was forced to set Emma down. His brother pulled her into his arms for a quick hug. "You have no idea how miserable this lug was without you," Josh told her. "Thank god you're back—and safe."

"And pregnant," Wyatt added with a grin.

"Holy shit." He looked at Wyatt. "*That* must be the token." When Emma looked at them questioningly, he explained, "We finally figured out you need a token from the time you want to travel to in order to get there. Long story. I guess you figured it out as well, huh?"

Emma smiled. "I have to admit, I wasn't the one who came to that conclusion. It was actually your big brother," she announced. "Who, by the way, asked me to give you boys this letter." She reached into the pocket sewn deep in her dress and pulled out the letter. "Evidence against Grey. You can use it to convict him."

Wyatt and Josh exchanged a glance. Josh tore open the letter and skimmed through several pages, then handed it to Wyatt.

"So how did you end up in the barn?" Josh asked.

"Never mind that," Wyatt said. "*Why* were you in the barn?"

"James knew Grey's next target was Sam," she explained. "If he succeeded in burning down his barn, then Sam would have to go to Grey for a loan to rebuild it—paying a very high-interest rate. Since we knew the date and time of the fire, all I had to do was think of that exact moment when I went through the portal. I took Rossler by surprise, that's for sure. He almost peed himself when he saw me. He kicked over the lantern, which is what started the fire."

Sam joined them just then and pulled Emma into a hug. "You're sure a sight for these sore eyes." He set her away from him, looking her over from head to toe. "Are you all right? What in tarnation were you doin' in my barn, woman?"

She took his hands and squeezed them. "I'm great, actually. And happy to be home." Then she wrapped her arm around Wyatt's waist and tilted her head back for a kiss, ignoring the second part of his question.

"Wyatt said you had to go back East for a bit," he went on. "Didn't think you could make it there and back this quickly. Must've been some train."

"Faster than a speeding bullet," Wyatt remarked.

****

Emma wrapped the shawl around her shoulders, resting her hands gently on her rounding belly, and watched the falling snow through the kitchen window. The snow-covered paddock looked so peaceful and quiet, a picture-perfect postcard. Several feet of snow accumulated over the last few weeks, but it never looked as beautiful as this back in the future. Once the snowplows and cars sloshed through it, turning it into a sandy, muddy mess, the snow lost its appeal. And shoveling was a bother.

But here, there were no snowplows or cars. Just wagons, horses, and people. While they were snowed in for a few days at a time here and there, she didn't mind it so much. It gave her and Wyatt more time to be alone. To get to know each other. And prepare for their new little bundle.

It didn't slip her notice that today was December 2—one day *after* she had first written the letter to her twenty-first-century self. Crazy how much her life changed in a handful of months. One stroll through a modern-day garage catapulted her back to another century where her life began. Everything she loved was here—Wyatt, Josh, her new friends, and soon, her new little baby. What was there to go back for? She just hoped Amber would someday forgive her. But now that they knew how to travel back, maybe Emma would return to visit her best friend someday.

Maybe, being the operative word. Truth be told, she had no desire to ever return to the future.

"Penny for your thoughts," Wyatt whispered as he came up behind her, wrapping his arms around her rounded belly.

She tilted her head back against his chest, placing her hands over his. "The baby's kicking," she said, moving his hand to the spot.

"So, I can feel," he told her, turning her around to face him. "But that's not what were you thinking about."

Her arms slid around his neck. "How is it that you always know what I'm thinking?"

"I didn't say I knew *what* you were thinking, just that the baby kicking wasn't exactly it. Not that you don't think about that." He kissed the tip of her nose. "But, well, you know what I mean."

She nodded. "I was thinking…how blessed I am to be here. In your arms."

"In the nineteenth century," he added. "And here, you thought you wanted to go back to the future," he teased. "What else?"

"It's December the second."

"That didn't escape my notice."

She nodded. "It's odd, but I don't know how I could've actually written that letter and sent it, but somehow I did. It's a day later, and the problem I initially wrote about no longer exists," she went on.

"Yep," he agreed. "Grey and his two minions are behind bars and will probably never see the light of day. Brody confessed to being the anonymous witness, so now we nothing to worry about."

She rolled her eyes. "Would you please stop talking and make love to me instead?"

He grinned, then swept her up into arms. "With pleasure, Mrs. Kincaid. With pleasure."

A word about the author…

Heather began writing as a child, inspired by her mom who loved to write fiction and poetry. Putting pen to paper—or rather fingers to keyboard—she began writing in the genres she loves—romance, time travel, and sci-fi. After writing several romance novels, *Wrapped Around My Heart* makes its debut with The Wild Rose Press. She is currently working on two follow-up books in the *Kincaid Brothers* series and a middle grade sci-fi adventure. When she's not writing, you can find Heather spending time with her beloved fur babies, Emma and Rascal.

http://booksbyha.com